Threads of La Serenìsima Book 1

FEATHERS SHARP AS KNIVES

Kristina Atkins

Purple Door Press

Cover Art by Carlos Quevedo.

Cover Design by Kharis Courtney.

Map by @mnash884

First edition 2023

Pronunciation Guide

Imelda Albizzi ee-MEHL-dah ahl-BEE-tzee

    Arturo ar-TOO-ro

    Primo PREE-mo

    Italo EE-tah-lo

    Anselmo Errari ahn-SEHL-mo ay-RRAH-ree *double rs are rolled*

    Betta BEHT-tah

    Venezia Dandolo veh-NEH-zee-ah DAHN-do-lo

    Lazaro LAH-zah-ro

    Ulisse Contarini OO-lee-say kon-tah-REE-nee

    Ceso CHAY-so

    Calixta Heraclius cah-LIHX-tah hehr-ah-KLEE-us

    Nikkoforos nee-ko-FO-ros

    Janus Komnenos JAH-nuhs KOM-neh-nos

    La Serenìsima Repùblica de Rialto LAH seh-reh-NEE-see-mah ray-POO-blee-kah DAY ree-AHL-to

    El Mar Muriseano EHL MAHR moo-ree-say-AH-no

    Ilios EE-lee-os

    Palàso Dogal pah-LAH-so DO-gahl

    Eraclea eh-rah-KLAY-ah

    Doxe DO-zay

    Corincanto ko-reen-CAHN-to

    Mè siora MAY see-OR-ah

    Mè sior MAY see-OR

For a more comprehensive pronunciation guide and a note on language, please turn to the back of the book, just after the epilogue.

For trigger warnings, please turn to the back of the book, just before the acknowledgments.

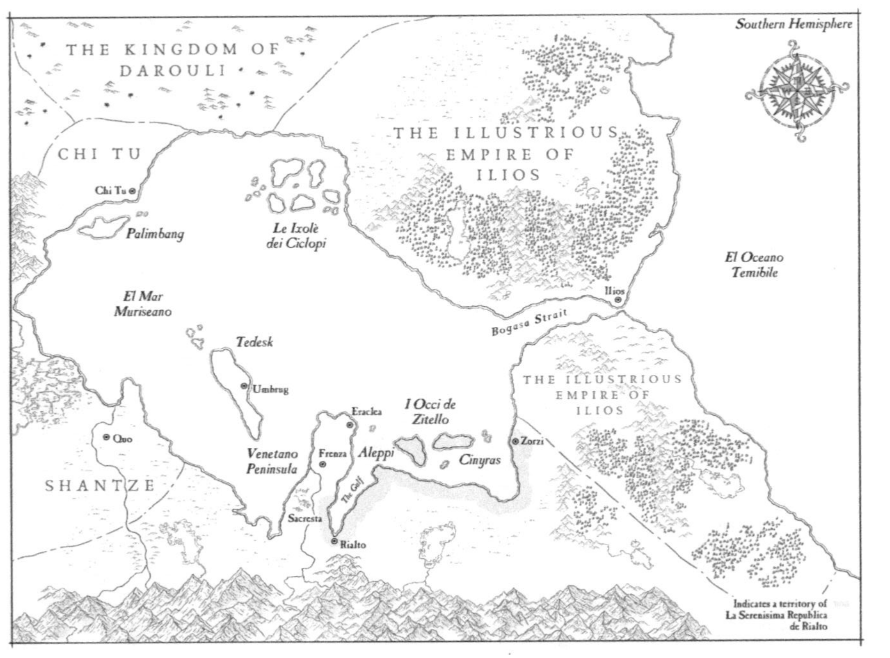

Southern Hemisphere
THE KINGDOM OF DAROULI
CHI TU
Chi Tu
Palimbang
Le Ixolè dei Ciclopi
THE ILLUSTRIOUS EMPIRE OF ILIOS
El Oceano Temibile
El Mar Muriseano
Tedesk
Umbrug
Ilios
Bogasa Strait
Eraclea
I Occi de Zitello
Quo
Venetano Peninsula
Frenza
Aleppi
Cinyras
Zorzi
THE ILLUSTRIOUS EMPIRE OF ILIOS
SHANTZE
The Gulf
Sacresta
Rialto
Indicates a territory of
La Serenisima Republica
de Rialto

PROLOGUE

Humid air hung thick in the canal as the góndola crept through the water. Betta rubbed her sleeve, checking for the reassuring bumps under the fabric. Six strings of corincanto wound and tied around her upper arm to ensure they'd stay clean all day as she worked her hands raw cooking food she wouldn't eat. Her joints didn't throb as they usually would—a small gift from the enchanted threads. They healed her physical pain, but they couldn't lift the burden of the life she'd lived. Neither could they ease her dread of tonight's errand.

A dark errand that would forever change her son's life.

Anselmo, her son, perched at the front of the boat. "I've never seen the tide this high." He watched the city glide by with eyes too wary for his thirteen young years.

"Highest Acqua Alta we've had in a decade," the gondolièr said. "The water will be past your mother's knees." He looked the boy over. Betta was no small woman, and Anselmo had already matched her height. "Yours as well."

Betta massaged her fingers and rocked with the gentle sway of the boat. It had been a long day of kneading dough, cooking meals, scrubbing dishes. A day made longer for the monotony. Most nights, she'd follow her duties by collapsing into a sunken sleep. Her exhausted mind craved the release. Even tonight. Especially tonight. But she'd been planning this appointment for thirteen years. She couldn't turn back now.

"You missed our turn," Anselmo said to the gondolièr. "We live on Giuffa."

"We're not going home," Betta said.

Anselmo didn't reply, but his relaxed posture straightened into a soldier's stiff pose. Good. Everything was a lesson.

The city streets were quiet as always during Acqua Alta. Everyone filled their doorways with sandbags and stayed in for the night. Only the richest ventured out. Their islands were too tall for even the highest tide to trespass onto their pristine cobblestone streets. Usually Betta and Anselmo hurried home when the water grew deep, but tonight they would break tradition.

The góndola wound through the canals. The summer air clung to her skin, and beads of sweat slipped down her neck. Voices echoed out from houses they passed. The boat reached the perimeter of the city, and the lagoon spilled into view. Moonlight reflected off the softly lapping waves, night birds called to one another, and a galley patrolled the deeper water. These outer-ring buildings, their paint faded and cracked, sagged against each other like a group of stumbling drunks. The Council maintained the retaining walls on Rialto's many islands, but the residents here were too poor to manage anything beyond pure survival.

Last time Betta had been to the island of Sordo, black lacquered gondole had lined the dock—nobles frequenting the city's only brothel. No rich man or woman's appetite was strong enough to wade through the dirty Acqua Alta. Tonight the dock sat empty and quiet save for the creak of wood. The gondolièr pulled up and tied the boat to a cleat.

"Will there be boats in the morning?" Betta asked.

The man shrugged, barely a movement, as if the question was irrelevant. "Most take the bridges. Too poor for gondole out here."

Betta hesitated, watching Anselmo step off the boat. His young face pulled tight in a grimace as water spilled into his boots.

"I can come back," the gondolièr said, "but it will cost extra."

"We'll meet you here at first light."

She paid the man, and he counted the coins. "You gave me too much."

"For your discretion."

He pursed his lips, his gaze passing back and forth from Betta to Anselmo. Then he pocketed the money. "Grassie, mojer."

Betta stepped onto the floating dock, then down onto the road. Normally, the dock sat at least a meter below the surface of the island. The water was as high as the gondolièr said, drenching her to her knees. As was frequent in the summer, it smelled of fish and human waste. The tides refreshed the canals every six hours, but eighty thousand people made their mark in the time between. At least it wasn't cold.

"Where are we?" Anselmo eyed the decaying buildings. The windows held no glass, most boarded up or covered from within by burlap. A child cried nearby. From the other direction came the shouts of a marital fight.

"The cruel world." Betta sloshed through the water. "Your friends Imelda and Arturo live in the glittering nest of luxury. Even you and I enjoy relative comfort. But this is what reality looks like. This is the suffering of the weak. This is the life of the poor. Remember that."

The boy shuddered. The rawness of the island made an impact, causing his hands to clench and his movements to stiffen. He needed to see the ugly side of life. He needed to know why she raised him as she did. If the tide weren't so high, she'd walk him past the brothel so he could see the painted faces of desperation, the women and men who saved everything they had for a scrap of silk corincanto to make them appear beautiful, hoping to attract more clients so they could afford food. The building stood in the center of Sordo. The lights were always blazing, yet it managed to feel as dark as the night of a new moon.

But Betta's dress was soaked through, weighing her down. The strands of corincanto around her arm helped, but they were temporary. Soon she'd remove them, and a lifetime of scars would resume their familiar ache.

They arrived at a building that looked as worn as the others. But when Betta knocked, the door was stronger than it seemed. A dotted line of corincanto had been stitched into the wood at the top, undetectable unless someone was looking for it. Most likely wool for strength.

The top half of the door cracked open. "Yes?" A man's voice stretched from the darkness.

"It's me."

The half closed, and the whole opened, revealing an ascending stone staircase. Water spilled over the sandbags on the threshold. An old man holding a candle gestured for them to enter. Anselmo instinctively put a hand in front of her.

Betta sharpened her voice, just enough, not a sword but a kitchen knife. "Do you want the life of a noble or a peasant? Do you want to be strong or weak?"

He looked at the street around them again. Peasant or noble, Sordo or Riga, and, Betta was willing to bet, the chance of marrying a common woman or Imelda Albizzi. Not that he'd ever confided such to her, but she saw the way her son watched the daughter of Betta's employer. Anselmo dropped his arm and started up the stairs.

The man closed the door behind them. "Go through the door at the top."

The room beyond was sparse. A pockmarked table sat in the center. The opposite wall held three shelves filled with instruments Betta had never seen. She was a cook. Before that, a mercenary. She'd stitched up her share of wounds, but that was it.

The old man entered. "Boy, take off your pants and lie on the table." His voice was commanding, far more than anyone would expect from someone his age. He was full of secrets, though Betta knew none of them. She could feel them though, as surely as she felt the squish in her soaked shoes.

Anselmo stared, frozen. Betta nodded, and he did as he was told. His eyes widened in fear, but he was obedient. His wet boots flopped onto the floor like a pair of pike.

"This is Ceso," Betta said. "He's going to help you."

Anselmo grunted, like a scared animal trying to fool a predator. "He's a maghiarzo, isn't he?"

"Some call me that." Ceso held out a hand to Betta. "You have the thread?"

She rolled up her sleeve, retrieved the strings of corincanto, and offered them to Ceso. Her normal pain and fatigue assaulted her. She sagged as she had the first time she'd strapped on a bronze cuirass.

Ceso ran the crimson threads through his fingers. "Wool for strength. Cotton for healing. Silk for structure."

"The quality is good?"

"It is. And such long strands. You've got yourself a small fortune with the silk alone."

Betta was keenly aware of how much the corincanto had cost. She'd saved since Anselmo was born. She wouldn't always be around to teach and defend him. She'd lived a hard life, and it was catching up with her. But these six strands—they would be his guardians. Her way of protecting him once she was gone.

Ceso retrieved a knife from the shelf.

"Mare. Tell me what's going on." Anselmo's voice broke as fear and puberty merged into one.

Ceso cocked his head. "The boy doesn't know?"

"You don't tell a lamb you're leading it to the slaughter."

The old man turned to Anselmo. "We're going to put this corincanto in your femoral arteries. That's the tube that carries blood from your heart into your legs." He spoke as he twisted one of each string together, so the three became one. Then he tied a small knot at one end of the strand. He repeated the process with the other three. "The threads will empower your body beyond mortal limits. You will be a god among men."

Anselmo sat up. "That's heresy." His voice was so small, so scared that Betta's heart ached. This would make him stronger. Not just the corincanto, but the experience. He would endure more than most even feared. She reminded herself in the most confident inner-voice she could muster.

The old man seemed amused. "According to the priests, I said goodbye to my soul a long time ago. I'm doing just fine."

"Aren't you afraid of Fógo?"

"It's hard to be afraid of something you don't believe in."

Anselmo gaped. This was his first time meeting a non-believer. He was still so young, so naive. Would she have time to teach him everything he needed?

Ceso fixed him with a serious look. "What kind of god is threatened by a mere mortal with corincanto in his body? Not one worthy of worship, if you ask me."

"What do you believe in?"

"Myself. Corincanto. A man's potential."

Anselmo looked around the room, doubt clearly written on his face in the frown on his lips and the knit in his brow. He appraised Ceso again. The man was old, but his clothes were nicer than seemed on first glance, and his posture was straight and strong. This man was not beaten by the cruel world—he was thriving in it. Betta watched her son take in this observation. She could almost hear his brain whirring through the thought process, noticing the crimson of corincanto sewn into Ceso's shirt. Her lessons, though harsh at times, were helping him, informing him, guiding him.

Saving him.

He gripped the sides of the table, and his voice found its strength. "Will I be stronger than the minotaurs in the labyrinth?"

"You want to be in the Lion guard, eh?" The old man smirked. "Getting these as young as you are, you'll be one of the greatest soldiers to ever live."

"Will it hurt?" Anselmo asked.

"Immensely. I suggest wine to ease the pain."

"I don't have extra money," Betta said.

Ceso chuckled. "This stuff isn't worth paying for. But it has plenty of alcohol."

"No," Anselmo said. The uncertainty had fled from his voice, though perspiration formed along his forehead. "The pain will make me stronger. Right, Mare?"

"Yes, my son."

"Impressive, but foolish." Ceso pulled a short, fat stick from the shelf. The bark had been scored by countless teeth. "This might help."

Anselmo put the stick in his mouth and lay back. He was so vulnerable, lying there in his underclothes, and yet so brave.

She grasped his arm. "He's ready."

"Not quite." Ceso held out the knife for her to take.

Betta stepped back, even clutched her hands. "I can't. You're the maghiarzo."

"Such a stupid word. This is science, not magic," he muttered. "I need you to cut, so I can insert the corincanto. It will speed up the process, which could mean the difference between life and death."

She looked at her son. Despite his brave words, tears had pooled in his blue eyes, the eyes he'd inherited from his bastard southern father. Anselmo would be nothing like him. Betta had sacrificed everything to ensure that.

Could she forfeit her soul? She believed, and she'd taught her son to as well. The priests made their position on this ceremony more than clear. Heresy, punishable by death. And after, an eternity in the three blazes of Fógo. Bringing him here was bad enough, but to actually perform the deed ...

Anselmo grabbed her hand. Her heart cracked like an egg. If only corincanto could absolve her of this sin. And yet, she would choose it again. Anything to preserve him. Anything to make him strong enough for this world. Anything.

She smoothed his hair back. "You trust me, yes? You know everything I do is because I love you."

The boy's chin shook, but he nodded.

Betta took the knife from Ceso. The weight and heft were familiar; she'd wielded many in her life. The old man moved Anselmo's undergarment and pointed to the center of the groin. His other hand held the first twisted corincanto.

"Here. And be quick. We have to get the thread in immediately so the cotton can heal the wound, or he will die."

She looked at her son, into his blue eyes, so stark against his Rialtano olive skin and dark hair, as deep and boundless as the sky. He held so much potential. He was all of her joy. Her soul was a small price to pay for his future.

Betta took a deep breath, steadied her hand, and cut.

CHAPTER ONE

Ten Years Later

If ever Imelda had need for wings, it was the day of her father's funeral.

The soft whir and creak of the spinning wheel filled Pàre's room as Imelda spun. She wore an old dress just for spinning. It smelled of the rose petals she packed with it, mixed with the sharp scent of blood from the open wound on her palm. She squeezed her hand periodically, pushing blood to her fingertips, turning the gray wool red. Her blood activated the latent magic within the fibers, turning it into crimson corincanto. Wool for strength. Strength enough for the wings to fly her away from her new reality.

It was so easy to get lost in the rhythm of spinning. The sharp smell was always the same. The smooth feel of the age-worn dress the same. The throb of her palm and the whir of the wheel the same. Normally they put her under a spell, and her body fell into the cadence of drafting and pinching with her fingers, feeding the thread onto the flyer, working the treadle with her feet.

But today wasn't normal. Tears mixed with droplets of blood spattering her lap. The voices of the servants in the hall murmured, hushed and reverent. The air in the home hung heavy with the memory of Pàre's death two days before. Her eyes drooped and her hands shook from two days at the spinning wheel. Before she spun wool, she'd spun linen corincanto. Linen, so when they buried Pàre in the sea, when his body sank to the bottom of the ocean, he would be able to breathe until the goddess Rea found him and carried him to Cielo.

His body lay next to her, wrapped in mourning midnight blue. Most funeral shrouds—even those of the nobility—had only a few lines of thread. Imelda had spun so much, crimson striped his entire length. Arturo, her twin, had spent the day before sewing the corincanto until his hands cramped. Even then, he'd pushed on.

Arturo walked in, still in his sleep clothes. Her twin's dark eyes were dry, though she'd heard him weeping during the night through the wall separating their rooms.

"Imelda." He rushed over to her, putting his hands on hers to stop her from spinning. "What are you doing? You could hurt yourself from using so much blood."

"We have to finish the wings." She tried to pull herself free, but she was too weak. "He's going to be in charge of our lives now."

Imelda looked through the windows of her room to the view of the palàso across the grand canal. Palàso Dogal, where their cousin Primo lived. Where he ruled the republic, and now, with Pàre gone, where he would rule their family.

"How long until he marries us off?" She could barely voice the words.

"It won't be today, so you might as well take a break." Arturo fished a knife out of her spinning basket and cut the thread. The end of the string spiraled out of control. "You've done enough for now. We can resume working on the wings tomorrow."

"How long, Arturo?"

He walked to the washbasin and soaked her towel in it. He returned and wiped the blood off her hands and arm, though the cut on her palm continued to bleed. Dark circles sat under his eyes. "No more than a year, I'd guess. We're too valuable to him to wait very long."

"Giore cancaro." Her voice was half cry, half whisper.

Arturo hesitated, his mouth opening then closing, as he pressed the cloth against the cut on her hand. "The military is returning," he finally said.

Imelda's breath hitched in her chest, and her pulse sped up. The throbbing in her hand was strong, but not as strong as the bittersweet hope that suddenly held her heart. The bittersweet hope of a new future. The last two days of spinning were the culmination of years of caring for her ailing father. She'd watched his eyes dim, his skin dull, his body wither. She'd watched him die.

Now the burden of carrying her father's failing health had disappeared, and she could think about herself again.

And Anselmo was returning from four long years at war.

"Why did he write you and not me all this time?" Fresh, hot tears pricked her eyes, and she rubbed at them, smearing blood on her face. She groaned in exasperation, and Arturo gave her the wet towel.

There was a knock on the door, followed by Imelda's maid, Editta. She was even shorter than Imelda, and her hair, pulled into a tight bun at the nape of her neck, was streaked with gray at her temples. She gasped when she saw Imelda's face.

"Mè siora!" Editta wiped Imelda's face with her apron. "It's time to get ready."

"I need to wash and set this batch."

"I will take care of that for you. Let's get you dressed. Mè sior," Editta said to Arturo, "your manservant is waiting for you in your room."

Imelda let her maid lead her from her father's room into her own bedroom.

Half an hour later, Imelda and Arturo boarded the grand ducal barge, dressed in mourning blue. Arturo's doublet wasn't wrinkled, for once, but his hair was as messy as always. Imelda's hand was bandaged. They certainly looked the part of mourning offspring. They were the first ones to arrive and for that she was grateful. Servants carried Pàre's body to a platform at the prow, and she and Arturo stood next to it.

Behind them, the upper level of the barge filled. No one approached them, not yet. They stayed at the back, under the black wool pavilion, helping themselves to the exorbitant spread of food and wine.

The barge left the dock with a surge. Laughter spilled out from under the canopy behind Imelda. She glanced over her shoulder, at the people mingling around the one person who would dare take away Imelda's new freedom—Primo. He didn't need the laurel leaf crown or silver sash to remind everyone of his power, but he wore them anyway. Even at his uncle's funeral.

Someone told a joke, and Primo threw his head back in laughter. Disgusting.

Imelda squeezed her fists, then winced as the cut on her palm opened and hot blood seeped out. So help him, by Rea's holy name, if he tried anything today. It had better be a year, like Arturo had said.

"Sorry, Pàre," she said.

"He's probably laughing, too," Arturo said. He watched an albatross glide across the sky. His head tilted, a sign he was deep in thought.

Snowflakes landed on the dark blue velvet of Imelda's dress, appearing like stars then vanishing. Snow falling on her father's shroud didn't melt. She rested her head on Arturo's shoulder. He stiffened, but wrapped his arm around her back. She poked his side.

"Don't get used to it," he said, though a dimple appeared in his cheek. His teasing dimple, she'd always called it, a sure sign he was holding in a smirk. "You need food."

"I'm fine."

"No, you need some meat. You just spent two days spinning. I'll be right back."

He walked off. Imelda leaned on the silver-painted railing of the grand ducal barge, rocking with every tug of the oarsmen taking the boat out to sea, out to her father's final resting place. The water on the smooth floorboards soaked into the hem of her dress. Cold wind pricked at her face. She breathed in the damp, salty air and fought back tears. The rowing chant from the first deck mixed with the cries of gulls overhead, the sounds of a true Rialto requiem.

Imelda reached her arms over the railing, stretched her tired back and arm muscles. Cold water slapped at the hull, sending a spray across her bandaged hand. A pelican bobbed in the waves, snow collecting on its brown feathers. How she longed to stroke the pelican's wings, to hold them out for inspection. What was her design missing? What was she getting wrong with the wings she and her brother were creating—real wings that could make a human fly? Someday, *someday* they would finish them.

Primo stepped up beside her. His large, straight nose, wide shoulders, and thick mustache—without a beard, going against current fashion—made him identifiable to even the poorest beggars in Rialto.

He pushed a glass of wine into her hands.

She shoved it at him. "I don't want any."

"It'll soften the pain."

He put his hands on the railing and watched the horizon. Imelda tried to fold her arms while still holding the glass.

The barge passed the last of the barrier islands, leaving the peaceful lagoon for the rough waters of the gulf. A lighthouse stood beside the mouth of the lagoon, dim in the murky daylight. The boat rocked as it cut through the waves, and Imelda's feet shifted to keep her balance.

Primo gave a pointed look at Pàre's body. "You shouldn't have made so much corincanto."

"Is it indecent for someone to have so much?" She bobbed her head. "Your Serenity."

Primo's lips pursed at the sarcasm in her voice. "You could've injured yourself spinning that much in two days. You've made yourself weak."

The boat crested a large swell and slid into the trough. Primo managed to keep his footing, but Imelda slipped on the wet floorboards and stumbled into him. She dropped her glass, and he caught her by her shoulders. His hands were gentle, his eyes concerned. His tenderness disrupted her quiet mourning, and a sob caught in her throat. He hugged her. She tensed, the discomfort at such an intimate gesture—especially from him—almost painful.

"He lived a good life, and soon he'll be with your mother." He stroked her hair. "It's up to us now. We have to protect the family legacy."

Imelda pushed herself free. "You mean protect your legacy."

A servant rushed over to mop up Imelda's spill. The wine turned the towel red, like a bandage soaked with blood.

Primo waited until the servant left, then turned to her. "My legacy? Everything I do is for the Albizzi name."

"Oh, so you don't enjoy ruling the republic?"

"Is it so wrong if I do?"

Donatella, Primo's wife, walked up and smiled as sweet as a biscotto. "We're here." Her voice was bright and her inflection high, though the sharpness in her eyes showed she knew she'd broken up an argument. Donatella was large, exquisitely dressed, and far too good for Primo.

The boat slowed to a stop, and the rest of the mourners joined them. The high priest took his place at Pàre's head. The two intertwined circles of the gods and the winged lion of Rialto were embroidered on the priest's chest in spirit rose corincanto. Even with the weak light, his silver robes gleamed.

The high priest, the ducal barge, the expensive wine. Primo had used every piece of his power to make everything perfect for Pàre's funeral. Not out of concern for Imelda or Arturo or their father. It was all to highlight Primo's prestige, wealth, and influence.

The high priest raised his thurible. "Father Giore, bless this gathering. Mother Rea, comfort these mourners. Amen."

"Amen," the crowd echoed. The high priest started the funereal prayer, but his voice grew quiet in Imelda's mind, as if it were floating through murky water. She reached out to Pàre's body, running a finger along the corincanto. Would it be enough? Would Rea come for him soon? Would Mare greet him when he entered Cielo?

The high priest lowered a wide-mouth amphora to the sea, then grunted as he pulled it up, relying on Primo's help to get it over the railing. The priest approached Arturo. He dipped a hand inside the amphora, then sprinkled the water on Arturo's head. "The water of your father's grave, to bind you to him for eternity."

"A-amen." Arturo's voice was thick with sorrow. A drop slid down his shaved cheek.

The high priest moved to Imelda. Her thick hair caught the droplets, protecting her skin from the frigid water.

"The water of your father's grave, to bind you to him for eternity."

"Amen," she whispered.

The high priest repeated the ritual with Primo and his family. Primo had to crouch for the old man to reach over his head.

"Lorenzo's two other sons are abroad, yes? And his niece, Fleet Admiral Dandolo, of course," the high priest said.

Primo nodded. "His eldest sons, Renzo and Donte, have been in the south for a year now. My sister Venezia is leading the military back to Rialto at this moment."

The high priest lifted the amphora. "Keep this water until they return, so they may be bound to the deceased."

Primo motioned, and a servant ran up to take the amphora.

Primo walked to the front of the crowd, and the priest had to edge sideways to give him room. "I have a few words to say. As long as no one minds."

Imelda's suspicions were correct. Primo was about to make the day about him. How could he not? He was the Doxe after all, leader of the republic. Now he would deliver a grand speech, sure to solidify his reputation even further. He was already a perfect father in the city's eyes. Now he'd show everyone what a good family leader he was as well.

Worst of all, he was delivering his speech before burying Pàre. Anger and fear circled inside Imelda like a pair of sharks, devouring her sorrow. She needed to go home and disappear under a pile of blankets, let herself mourn her father. Instead she had to watch her cousin assert his dominance.

Primo widened his stance and clasped his hands behind his straight back. He was turning on his politician's shine. "The one word to best describe my uncle Lorenzo was kind. Once, my cousins and I set fire to the dining room curtains, and rather than rage, he laughed."

His voice wavered, and he paused, running a hand down his sash. The curtain incident happened with Imelda's older brothers in the months leading to her mother's death. Of course Primo would get emotional—or rather, pretend to get emotional.

Donatella laid her hand on Primo's arm, and he curled his fingers around hers. The crowd believed his act, the sycophantic saps. They touched their hearts and dabbed their eyes. Husbands wrapped arms around their mourning wives. Primo was stealing the attention from Imelda's deceased father, same as he'd stolen Imelda's chance to know her mother. All Imelda had of her mother, she'd inherited—her slight build, her wavy, black hair, her rare blood with the ability to spin regular thread into corincanto.

Primo bowed his head, took a deep breath, nodded as if composing himself. "I'm nothing like my uncle. I don't have his gentleness, but I appreciate his influence. He taught me that family is more important than anything—than self or even our great city and republic, La Serenìsima Repùblica de Rialto. Uncle Lorenzo was the final member of his generation, so as the oldest member of the next generation I'm now the head of the Albizzi family."

Primo turned away from the gathering, pinning Imelda and Arturo with his most authoritative gaze. She felt like a mouse, and he was the hawk watching her. "Arturo, Imelda, before your father died, I promised him I would take care of you. Our family has been separated since I was elected eight years ago. I wish for you to live with my family in Palàso Dogal until you get married. Families should be together. Our celestial parents, Giore and Rea, have commanded us. We bind ourselves at death. We should also bind ourselves in life."

Imelda's fingers went cold, and heat rushed to her cheeks. She grabbed Arturo's hand. He gave a gentle squeeze. Move into the palàso. Leave their family home. He *was* going to marry them off soon. He didn't say those exact words, not in front of this crowd of her father's mourners. It didn't fit his image to be that blunt. He was the polite but assertive Doxe. Even commanding them to move was bolder than she'd expected.

But the others didn't see it that way. The idiots nodded in approval. Some even smiled. Primo was nothing but humility, thanking them and stepping aside for the priest.

The priest recited one last prayer. Imelda pressed on her hot, hot eyes. She had to focus. Focus on her father, focus on his funeral, focus on his burial.

A sob clutched her throat, escaped a moment later.

Someone touched her back.

She opened her eyes to a blurry vision of everyone watching her, sympathy tightening their lips and brows. Donatella was the one touching her, with tears in her own eyes. No one realized Imelda was crying not only from grief, but from anger as well.

"I'm okay." Her voice was a rasp, her words a lie.

Primo took her by the shoulders. "Imelda, I promise to help you achieve the best in life." He kissed her cheeks five times, a binding promise. Then he turned to Arturo and repeated the same line, kissing his cheeks five times as well. The crowd murmured in approval.

The high priest gestured toward Pàre's body. "Arturo, Imelda, please take your father on each side. Your Serenity, if you would place yourself at his feet."

Imelda laid her hand on her father's arm. Across from her, Arturo did the same. His fingers trembled, imperceptible to anyone but her. Imelda's breath quivered in her lungs like the death rattle Pàre had sighed in his final moments.

She could make out the shape of his face under the shroud. He was still her father, but he held no power in this life anymore. No power over the family. No power over Imelda's future.

That responsibility rested in Primo's greedy hands.

The high priest moved aside, and a servant removed a body-sized panel from the railing. The water frothed and churned, a hungry sea ready to devour Pàre. Imelda tugged on a stitch of corincanto. It held firm. It would hold him until Rea retrieved his soul from the gulf's greatest depths.

Primo pushed, and Imelda and Arturo joined. They slid Pàre's body to the edge where it balanced for a moment. Imelda's grip faltered. She couldn't do this, couldn't relinquish the only parent she'd known. Panic clawed inside her, and she looked at Arturo for help. He took her hand across their father's body.

Primo gave the final shove.

Pàre plummeted to the water.

The splash seemed too small, too insignificant. Midnight blue bobbed in the waves, then the sea swallowed her father down.

Down where she would never see him again.

Down where she would never hear his voice again.

Down where she would never smell his pipe smoke or curl up next to him or feel his kiss on her head again.

Primo placed his hand on his heart and bowed his head. "Rest now, Uncle Lorenzo. I will care for your children as you cared for me."

Imelda rushed to the boat's edge and squeezed the railing until her fingers ached and the wound on her palm tore open and the bandage turned red with her blood.

CHAPTER TWO

The barge turned around and headed back to the city. The crowd dispersed. Some went straight to the pavilion, to their food and wine, to their laughter and irreverence. Others murmured their condolences to Imelda, Arturo, and Primo. Donatella rubbed Imelda's back before retreating. Even Primo returned to his admirers. Arturo wandered off and returned to the prow with a glass of wine in hand. He drank, the gulls cried overhead, and tears pricked at Imelda's eyes. Tears that should've belonged to sorrow, but instead were fueled by anger.

"That bastard." She kept her voice low. Arturo opened his mouth, but she cut him off before he could begin. "Don't try to say anything rational right now. It was worse than we expected. He's making us move in with him so he can keep an eye on us."

"It was inevitable."

She lifted her wounded hand off the railing. Her blood had smeared on the black lacquer. She wiped it up with the backside of her bandage. "Why does it have to be inevitable?"

"Traditions of our fathers."

"Traditions be damned."

The barge passed into the lagoon, and the city crept into view. Docks jutted into the water, full with galleys and round ships. The outlying islets were the lowest, and the small islands rose in elevation up to the center. The houses were a rainbow of color, the faded reds and purples and blues of the poor islands leading to the bold hues of the homes of the rich. Palàso Dogal stood on Centro, the government island and highest point in the city. Its white walls gleamed above the other buildings, as white as Imelda's breath in the winter air.

"Look." Arturo pointed at three small purple clouds floating toward them over the water. Hemp messages. One descended onto someone in the pavilion, while the other two reached Imelda and Arturo at the same time. Imelda's vision became unfocused and sound faded as the purple haze enclosed her head.

I'm on my way. So sorry I'm late. Venezia's voice echoed in Imelda's mind. Then Imelda's vision cleared and sounds returned.

"Venezia." Imelda smiled, petty and spiteful, savoring the forthcoming showdown between her two cousins. "She's not going to like this."

"There she is," Arturo said. A small galley sped by. The blue flag of Rialto whipped in the wind at the prow of the ship.

A military vessel. Primo had been right when he'd said Venezia was returning to Rialto. She was even going to beat them to the city.

Ten minutes later, the barge pulled up to the dock where Venezia waited. Her Fleet Admiral's uniform was slightly wrinkled and strands of her black hair had fallen out of her low bun. She must have worn the outfit the entire journey home. And not fixing her hair—so unlike Venezia. The several-days' journey on the ship must've been as rough as storm-rocked waves.

But Venezia stood tall as she watched everyone walk down the gangplank. Her sharp eyes and straight nose—same as Primo's—reminded Imelda of an eagle. No wonder men followed her orders into battle.

Venezia nodded at Primo, who returned the gesture. Their expressions were smooth, business-like, as if they were working together in the palàso rather than siblings attending their uncle's funeral. Then she turned to Imelda, and the disciplined admiral softened into the closest thing to a mother Imelda had ever known.

"Imelda, carina." Venezia hugged her and smoothed Imelda's hair as she'd done so many times. She smelled of salt air and damp wool. "I'm sorry I missed your father's funeral."

"I understand." Imelda resisted the urge to bury her face into Venezia's neck, to linger in her arms like an anxious child. She straightened, squared her shoulders, looked Venezia in the eyes. "Primo is—"

Primo passed between Imelda and Venezia, forcing them to step back from each other. "Venezia, I'm glad you're here. Imelda, Arturo, ride with us." He walked on without a pause, clearly expecting them to follow.

The Doxe's góndola was lacquered black like all góndole in the city, but silver inlay lined every edge. The winged lion carved into the pettine at the front was painted in silver leaf. Most góndole had a two-seat sofa for the riders, but the Doxe shared with no one. Floor cushions were scattered on the thick carpet on the hull. Imelda sat on the cushion farthest from Primo, putting Venezia and Arturo in front of her, her line of defense.

"What's going on?" Curiosity edged Venezia's voice, but so, too, did fatigue.

"Primo's making Arturo and me move into the palàso." The words rushed out of Imelda's mouth. Like a child. She resisted a wince and fought to keep her posture. "And he's going to marry us off."

Venezia shook her head and rubbed her temples. She was even more tired than she seemed. "You told them today, Primo? The day of their father's funeral?"

Primo motioned to the gondolièr to pull out from the dock. "I loved your father, Imelda, but he spoiled his children. You two especially. You're twenty-two years old, for Giore's sake, and still leeching off family money rather than adding to it."

"You're only twelve years older than us." Imelda wanted them to see her as the adult she was, but even she could hear the small-girl-pout in her voice. "You can't tell us what to do."

"You know that's not true," Venezia said.

People gathered on the bridges to watch the procession. Normally they'd cheer for the Doxe, but there was no mistaking the color her family wore—midnight blue, the color of mourning. And surely news of Pàre's death had spread by now. Primo lifted a hand in greeting to the citizens. Not a wave, nothing so lighthearted as that. A somber salute from the Doxe to his subjects.

"It's up to me to keep the family in prosperity and power." Though his words were directed at Imelda and the others, Primo kept his attention on the crowd. "We must further strengthen the Albizzi legacy. Your brothers Renzo and Donte aren't merely adventuring in the wilds. They're working. It's time for you two to do the same. At this point, your only option is marriage."

"We don't need to get married." A whine was creeping into Imelda's tone. She squeezed the edges of her cushion and tried to keep her pitch level. "We *are* doing something."

"Ah yes, the famous wings. How long have you been working on those? Four years?"

"Seven." Arturo spoke as soft as the gondolièr's pole dipping in and out of the water, but everyone paused.

His defeated tone made Imelda want to scream. Why was no one helping her? "We're trying to achieve human flight. It's not going to happen in a fortnight."

"There are better ways to spend your time than wasting family money on an impossible dream," Primo said.

Like getting married and having him benefit from whatever connections he gained? Disgusting. "I can't think of a better way to 'ensure the Albizzi legacy.' Our family would have no power if it weren't for chasing impossible dreams."

"If you had succeeded, you *would* be contributing to the family." Venezia's tone was soft, even gentle.

"If you give us enough time, we will succeed," Imelda said.

"No." Primo gripped the arms of his sofa and sat forward. He kept his face impassive, other than a restrained compression of his mouth. His lips were nearly white from the pressure. "No more time. No more money. No more of your nonsense ideas. Italo Albizzi was a singular man. Are you two so prideful to think you could invent something to match the labyrinth? You honestly think you're as smart as the greatest genius in Rialto history?"

"That was unnecessary, Primo." Venezia's reprimand cracked like a whip.

Primo's shift to Venezia was just as fast. He pointed at her. "I invited you to this conversation for your support, not your opinion." Primo spoke every word clearly and deliberately, to deliver the full impact of his displeasure. "I am the eldest of the family. Not you."

Venezia didn't crumble or lower her eyes or give any indication of defeat. She turned from Primo and took Imelda's hand, admiral and mother all at once.

Venezia could handle herself, and Imelda could take Primo's scorn. But no one insulted her twin. "Arturo's not an idiot."

"Imelda, it's fine," Arturo said.

"He's one of the smartest people in the city," Primo said, as if Arturo hadn't just spoken. As if he wasn't even there. "Perhaps even in the republic. Which is why he isn't arguing with me right now." Primo fixed her with a stern look, an *I'm-the-Doxe* look. "You're going to do what I say, or I'll cut you off from all family money."

He could do it. He could do anything with the family now. There was no use arguing. She'd never win in an outright debate. Primo was a politician. Scheming and twirling the truth around his fingertips were his specialty.

Imelda folded her arms and scowled at the buildings sliding by, at the curious citizens gawking at the Doxe and his family, pretending to be sad about the death of someone they'd never met. The funeral procession of góndole stretched down El Canalasso, past the last bend. So many people, most of whom she only vaguely knew. Everyone flaunted their relation, however tenuous, to the powerful Albizzi family.

Primo seemed to remember where they were and who was watching. He smoothed his sash, straightened his crown, and raised his hands to the crowd. Some yelled, "Ave Doxe!" while others shouted their condolences.

Venezia might've been surprised by Primo's timing, but it made sense. The entire city was watching. The family's reputation was at stake. Primo's reputation was at stake.

"We can survive without family money." Imelda turned to Primo. "We'll get jobs."

"I'd rather get married." Arturo stared at the gray water of the canal. His shoulders were slumped, his face was slack. He looked as if his body had gone numb from the cold. Imelda should've known he would fold in on himself this way. He hated confrontation as much as he hated snow.

"There are no jobs worth having without family connections," Primo said.

"We don't need—"

"Where will you live? How will you afford food?" Primo's tone choked Imelda's objections like a sharp, bitter wine. "You'll be begging in the alleys of Sordo before the end of the first week."

Venezia laid a hand on Imelda's arm. "You have time, carina. Enjoy it while you can."

"Not much time. Her fiancè will be here soon."

The boat glided through the water, but Imelda's vision, stomach, heart all twisted and toppled, like silt stirred by oars. She put her hands on her hot cheeks. "I'm already engaged? To who?"

Primo waved toward Venezia. "You tell her. You know him better than I do."

"What?" Betrayal gutted Imelda like a knife and sent a bolt of energy spiraling down her legs. Venezia knew! Imelda jumped to her feet. The boat rocked, and she stumbled, arms wheeling to keep her balance.

Primo grabbed her by the wrist and pulled her back down. "Everyone is watching." His voice was as tight as freshly spun thread.

She pulled her arm out of his grasp and faced Venezia. "You knew all along. How could you?"

"We do what we must for the family." Venezia's tone was stiff, and her eyes flickered toward Primo.

"Who are we engaged to?" Arturo muttered the words into his chest. He was sinking further and further in on himself. He'd acted stoic and reserved during the funeral, but he'd been right when he said he was heartbroken too. Arturo had been treading water before, and now Primo handed him an anchor and expected him to stay afloat.

"I'm still negotiating yours," Primo said. "Imelda, you're betrothed to King Ulisse Contarini."

Imelda rubbed her face, searching for something to grasp. "Contarini? As in the greedy rulers of Eraclea?"

Primo's facade slipped as his eyebrows creased into a glower. "That man is going to be your husband. You will speak more respectfully of him from now on."

The gondolièr pulled up to a mooring. Primo stood and adjusted his crown once again, regaining his composure, then held out a hand for Imelda. She remained seated.

"Don't trust rumors, Imelda." Venezia stepped onto the dock. "Ulisse is a good man. He's a wonderful father, and he was devoted to his late wife."

"He has children?" she asked. "How old is he?"

Primo shoved his hand closer to her face. "Three children. Thirty-three years old." Primo's voice was so civilized, so political, so final. "Now, stop making a scene."

Stop ruining my life. But she couldn't say that now, couldn't say that here around so many people. Other boats tied up and their passengers spilled onto the docks and headed toward the stairs up to the palàso. Imelda took Primo's hand and stepped out of the boat. Primo shifted from annoyed cousin to humble, mourning Doxe, though his grip remained firm in warning. He gave her one last look before turning away to find his family.

Venezia touched Imelda's back. "He has your best interest in mind. He would never do anything to intentionally hurt you."

Imelda spun her pain into anger. "You're a traitor."

Venezia's face hardened and her eyes narrowed. "You know I had no say in the matter." She walked off.

Arturo stepped up beside Imelda. "It will be okay." He tried to sound upbeat, but it was too forced, too contrary to his slouch and downcast eyes. Because he knew it wasn't true. Even if Arturo married a Rialtano woman, it wouldn't change the fact that Primo was shipping Imelda hundreds of miles up the coast, up to the tip of the peninsula, to marry the greedy old Contarini, with three children and a dead wife already. No doubt he'd salivated at the chance to marry her.

Her fiancè wouldn't give up.

Primo definitely wouldn't.

Neither would Imelda.

She just had to figure out a way to fight back.

CHAPTER THREE

It was full dark by the time Anselmo stepped onto dry land for the first time in three days. Three long days at sea followed by the victory procession, sailing through El Canalasso at a crawling speed as the Rialtani rained thread confetti on their heads. He'd ridden the eleventh ship out of fifty. Eleventh, and it was still night when he arrived at Gara, the military island. The soldiers on the last ships hadn't even entered the lagoon yet.

Eleventh out of fifty wasn't bad. But the elite fighters, the Lions, rode on the first ten ships. One day, Anselmo would be on the first of all those.

Anselmo's legs wavered as they adapted back to solid ground again. Three days at sea, and before that, four years at war. Four years without seeing or even communicating with Imelda, after seeing her every day since he was eight. He was to blame; he'd been the one to insist they not write while he was gone. But it had left a hole in his life, not knowing anything of her except what Arturo wrote. And then nothing even from Arturo the last year. Anselmo had been confused until he'd seen the Doxe wearing mourning blue at the procession. Anselmo would bet every ducat he'd earned that Lorenzo had passed away.

He needed to visit Imelda tonight to give his condolences. If she even wanted to see him. Gods, who knew how she felt about him? She'd been angry when he'd broken things off with her. But he couldn't let his oldest friend—friends, because he'd see Arturo too—mourn alone.

Anselmo removed his helmet and pulled out tangles of thread from the crest as he walked across the island. Rows of squat, brick barracks surrounded the islet's piaza and temple. A bright blue flag fluttered on a pole. Giatoro, the one-eyed winged lion, and Ioanna, the woman he loved—the founders of Rialto. Similar flags had flown over Zorzi, but seeing them over his city, over his home, loosened the tension Anselmo had carried for the last four years.

A group of Lions lounged on benches in front one of their buildings. At four stories tall, it was closer to a palàso than a barrack. The elite soldiers of the Lion Guard had been back long enough to clean and change. They wore coats of bright blue with silver lines on the shoulders denoting their ranks. At their sides, they carried swords with silver hilts in silver-leafed sheaths. Everyone recognized Lions. They weren't required to wear their coats but they did, especially when it earned them free drinks in every bacaro they visited.

"Lieutenant Errari," one of them called.

Anselmo approached and saluted. "Yes, Captain."

The Lion nudged the man next to him. "This is the soldier I told you about. Killed twenty men when they ambushed his team."

The other man sipped his wine. "That was only a month ago, correct?"

"Yes, sir," Anselmo said. "It was one of the last bunches of rebels."

"The admirals are sending a group into the labyrinth after Carnevale," the first one said. "You putting your name in?"

"I plan to, sir."

"When's the lottery?" a third said, grabbing a slice of salami from a plate on the bench. The second man frowned into his glass of wine.

"In two days." Anselmo shifted. His armor creaked and rubbed against his skin. "They take entrants tomorrow morning."

"You can go, Lieutenant," the first man said. "With any luck, your name will get picked. We could use more recruits like you."

"Thank you, sir." Anselmo saluted and turned to go.

"Poor bastards," the second man murmured.

"How many died from your group?" the first asked.

"Ten. You?"

"Thirteen."

Anselmo quickened his pace to his barrack, and the sound of other soldiers chatting drowned out the Lions. Two weeks until the admirals trained the next batch of soldiers to become Lions. Two weeks until Anselmo could begin his climb to honor, glory, and—most importantly—elevation of status. The opportunity to become a noble. To become Imelda's equal.

The labyrinth would be terrible, but it would be worth it. His mother had trained him for this, ever since he could remember. It was the reason he'd endured that night of torture ten years ago. He'd finally be able to put himself to the test. With his unique advantages, his risk of failure was slim.

But none of it would matter if he didn't win the lottery.

Anselmo walked into his room and unfastened his cuirass. As a lieutenant, he had his own space. Cramped, bare, but his. It was new, since he'd been promoted while in Zorzi, but someone had moved his trunk in. He set his helmet and breastplate on the table, stripped off his shirt, and scrubbed his face and neck with the towel in the washbasin. Three days of sea grime turned the rag gray. Water dripped through his beard, which had grown unkempt during the voyage. He should trim it. Outside, the temple bell marked the time—seven o'clock. It would take an hour to get to Imelda's home, Cax' Albizzi, but he could spend a few minutes making himself presentable.

The privates returned to their bunks, filling the room attached to his with their clamor. Swords rang as they were unsheathed. Cuirasses thunked onto the floor. Men ribbed each other and cleaned their gear.

"You keep scrubbing, Lieutenant, you'll wipe all the pretty off your face," one of the men called.

"You think I'm pretty?" Anselmo said, tossing the towel at him. "How sweet."

The men laughed. Anselmo shut the door to change. He pulled his nice shirt out of his trunk. It smelled dusty and the wool stretched across his shoulders but it fit well enough. He'd have to start saving for a new one as he continued bulking up.

A slip of paper was tucked inside the lid. Anselmo tensed. He didn't need to unfold it to know what was inside. Dozens of notes over the last decade, and they always said the same thing—a simple command: *Tonight.*

He grabbed his other shirt, then slammed the trunk closed. The lid cracked in half, and a hinge popped off. It was brand new—he'd purchased it just before leaving for Zorzi and it had sat in the barracks ever since. He'd have to buy a new one. Anselmo swore under his breath, changed shirts, and threw on his civilian coat. So much for visiting Imelda tonight. She and Arturo were night owls, as only the rich could be—the poor couldn't justify the cost of candles. But tonight's appointment would outlast even them.

Outside, he crushed the note and threw it into a fire in the piazza. He angled for the bridge, but the islet's temple bell rang four times. Anselmo stopped. He turned slowly. Four bell rings, not at four o'clock, meant one thing: an execution. Privates, officers, and Lions gathered in Gara's piaza, murmurs already starting. The Lions waited on the inner ring, exchanging glances—they clearly knew the offender.

On the temple's steps, acolytes spread straw around the base of an X-shaped cross. A priestess emerged from the doors, followed by two soldiers hauling a man in a ripped Lion's coat. The prisoner's face was bruised, his eye swollen, his lip busted. Fresh blood spattered his pants. The soldiers ripped the bright blue coat off his body, revealing purple and blue across his torso, then tied him to the cross by the hands and feet. The prisoner tugged at his arms, but he was too weak to manage anything else. Anselmo rubbed his wrists. Only one class of heretics warranted such a public, humiliating death.

A class that Anselmo belonged to.

Fleet Admiral Venezia Dandolo, in her singular uniform dress, approached the front of the platform, sorrow echoing with each click of her boots on the wood. Silence fell over the soldiers like a volley of arrows.

"We regret the timing of this unfortunate event," she said, "but justice must be paid. You see before you former Lion Captain Tomasso Polani. Just before leaving Zorzi, he was discovered to have corincanto in his arms. We apprehended him, then administered an anti-corincanto potion to deactivate his threads. We cannot tolerate this kind of heresy in our city, especially in our military. If we did, we'd lose Giore and Rea's favor in our battles. The person who reported Polani has been amply rewarded. You will receive the same if you report any heretics you come across."

The priestess, a surprisingly young woman with an unsurprisingly dour expression, stepped forward. She wore black robes embroidered with red threads. "Giore told us this is heresy. In the third book of Erastus, he declared, 'Corincanto shall be a gift to bring you closer to the gods. In all thy uses, dedicate it and yourselves to the Father and

Mother, and they shall be for thy good. Thou shalt use thread of the spirit rose in the Spirit Stitch to bind thyself to the gods, and the Heart Stitch to bind thyself to one another. To put any other corincanto in thy skin is spiritual death. Such a man sets himself up against the gods, and no son of Giore is he.' All else is abomination. All else is heresy."

The priestess walked around to the back of the cross and placed her hands on Polani's back. The prisoner tensed. She ripped his Spirit Stitch out of his shoulder, and he shrieked like a dying gull. Gasps and murmurs spread through the crowd. They'd known what would happen, but seeing it was a different matter.

The priestess came back around, red thread held aloft. "Cielo has been denied this man. Without his Spirit Stitch, his soul is doomed for Fógo."

She regarded the soldiers, baiting them with a moment of silence. They braced for the next step, pulling the air taut with dread. The priestess approached Polani's left arm. Anselmo glanced around. Wide eyes and shocked faces turned into sneers of righteous indignation. The priestess reached into the bush of hair in the prisoner's armpit, then yanked. Polani's back arched against his bindings, and a long, slick string slid out of his skin. His agonized wail echoed off the buildings. Blood splashed across the priestess's robes. She walked to his other side. Again she tore out the corincanto, accompanied by Polani's scream. The straw at the base of the cross stained red, and the prisoner slumped.

"Heretic!" a man yelled, and the soldiers launched into jeers.

"Torch him!"

"Burn in Fógo!"

The cold air grew hot against Anselmo's skin. His palms began to sweat, and he inched toward the nearest alley. The admirals descended from the platform, and an acolyte passed a torch to the priestess.

"Tomasso Polani, you have suffered spiritual death. Now you shall experience physical." The priestess hurled the torch at Polani's feet. The straw burst into flames. Fire raced across the platform and up the prisoner's body. Anselmo slipped out of the piaza, chased by the man's dying screams and the taunts from the other soldiers.

They'd say the same about Anselmo, were he caught. They'd relish his pain and scream for his damnation. Even if he became a Lion, it wouldn't stop them. It hadn't saved Polani. People were like sharks, quick to attack once blood filled the water.

Like any soldier, Anselmo feared death, but that wasn't what made his stomach turn. It was such a demise, without honor. Laid bare and spat upon. His ashes and their curses rising together, choking the sky. A glorious end in battle was the only death he could contemplate.

Of course, he didn't want to die at all. Not so young, at least. Polani's death reiterated that—Anselmo's years stretching ahead, and the possibility they could end any day. He had to make the most of the time he had now. By entering the labyrinth to become a Lion. And by visiting Imelda tomorrow to see where things lay between them.

Anselmo walked as quickly as he could without garnering suspicion. It wasn't until he'd crossed the bridge over El Canalasso that the indignant cries of the soldiers finally died out. He stepped onto Riga and looked over his shoulder. An angry, orange glow hung over Gara, and smoke clouded the stars above. Were the threads a gift from his mother, or a curse? Would he have grown strong without them? Were the priests right? Not about the gods and burning in Fógo—were the threads a dishonorable thing? To have such an advantage over his fellow soldiers, over his opponents—was there shame in that?

And yet, that was the only way Anselmo could rise above his social station. The world spat on people like him unless they found their own leverage.

Half an hour later, he was on Sordo, pounding on the old man's door. It opened, and Ceso glowered at him.

"You're going to break down my door."

"Then stitch more wool into it."

"If I've done my job well—and I have—no amount of corincanto would stop you." Ceso jerked his head toward the stairs, and Anselmo started climbing them.

Ceso followed Anselmo. "What took you so long?"

"I walked here. Didn't want to spend the coin on a góndola."

"One thing I've learned in my old age is that time is worth money."

"Depends on which you can afford."

"The hubris of youth," Ceso said. "Your time is just as limited as mine is."

"Sure it is, old man."

They reached the room at the top. It looked the same as that first night ten years ago. Worn and bare but clean. A fire burned in the pristine hearth. No grime or stains marred the wood operating table. The old man must wipe it down as soon as he completed each job. Ceso hadn't changed either. The last decade seemed to have no effect on him. He wore corincanto in his clothes, but that wouldn't stop him from aging.

Anselmo stripped his boots off, then climbed onto the table. He didn't need instructions. These maintenance appointments were always the same—untying the knots in his heel to lengthen the corincanto.

Ceso approached, knife in hand and a magnifying glass over one eye. "You're breathing quickly."

"I walked fast."

"Stop lying."

The fire popped. Wind rattled the shutters. Ceso waited.

"There was an execution," Anselmo finally said. He could still feel the blaze on his face, and the man's screams reverberated in his memory.

Ceso grunted. "What was his name?"

"Tomasso Polani."

"Not mine—they never get caught. You don't have anything to worry about."

The old man bent in front of his feet, and Anselmo stared at the ceiling. Ceso cut down the length of Anselmo's foot. The pain was minimal, but it brought back the memories of that night. The bark of the stick against his tongue. His mother pushing his hair off his sweaty forehead. The agony that wracked his body before he passed out. It was impossible not to relive it every time he visited.

Ceso paused. "You'll be fine as long as you keep your mouth shut. You haven't told anyone, right?"

"Of course not."

"Good. Because anyone will turn you in."

"Not anyone."

"Yes. Anyone." He straightened and pointed the knife at Anselmo. "Don't underestimate what someone will do for money, boy. Even someone who loves you."

"You're paranoid."

"And it's kept me alive a long time."

He bent back to his work and twisted the knot. Pain surged in Anselmo's feet and raced up to his groin, where the first knots lay hidden. Anselmo clenched his teeth. The old man pulled on the string, causing Anselmo's leg to spasm. Ceso untied the knot, fed the excess into Anselmo's artery, then retied the strings. Fifteen minutes passed until Ceso tucked the knot into a small pocket of skin with a satisfied nod. He placed a cotton corincanto bandage over the cut, and Anselmo's body knit itself together instantly, covering the knot and erasing all traces of the corincanto. Sweat slicked the table beneath Anselmo. He panted and scrubbed a hand across his face as he sat up.

"You better stop growing; there's not much left." Ceso handed him some water. "How was Zorzi?"

"It was war."

"Spoken like a veteran." Ceso watched him. "Aren't you going to tell me any of your great feats?"

"You know me better than that." Anselmo's hand shook, but he managed to gulp down the entire cup. He held it out for more. "They're sending a group into the labyrinth soon."

"I assume you're planning on entering your name." Ceso refilled the cup from a battered pitcher. "Be wary of the snakes in there."

Anselmo scoffed. "I hardly think any snakes will stop my cotton."

"Not common snakes. They have jade diamond mambas."

The only snakes that could actually injure Anselmo, with venom that counteracted corincanto. He rubbed his beard. "I'll keep an eye out."

Ceso set the pitcher on a shelf. "Your mother would be proud."

Something in his tone stopped Anselmo. "And how do you feel about it?"

"I think it's a good move. But I don't like your motivation."

"Which is?"

"Don't think I didn't pay attention to the conversations between you and your mother when you visited. She wanted a noble's life for you."

Anselmo downed the water, though dumping it over his head was a tempting thought. "You say that like it's a bad thing."

"It is." Ceso took the cup and placed it on the shelf. "You're spending so much time and energy making yourself bigger, stronger, and tougher than everyone else, only to end up a soft nobleman who can't dress himself? It's a waste, boy. You could be so much more."

"Like what?"

"Like I said ten years ago: a god."

"Except you don't believe in those."

"A man who rises above the rest of mortality as someone truly extraordinary is a god. Imaginary beings living in the beyond? That's a farce."

Anselmo scrubbed a hand through his hair. "Why don't you believe in the gods?"

Ceso wiped his knife clean on his apron. "I came across evidence that the holy book is ... not accurate. At the very least, it's been changed."

"By who?"

"The Sacrestano generals that pulled down the empire. They'd sewn thread into their skin to give them an edge. They knew the power it gave them, and were afraid of being thrown from power as well. They changed the holy book to say it was heresy."

Anselmo watched the old man, but he only scrubbed his blade.

"Now lay down and let me do the other foot, and I will make you a real god."

What was the point of being a god if you were alone? Giore had Rea. Giatoro had Ioanna, even if she couldn't love him in the same way. Just stories, but their creators recognized the need. Anselmo didn't want many people, only one. Only one person called to him. Only Imelda could drive him to endure pain at Ceso's hands time and time again.

Anselmo had a lifetime ahead of him, but it could end at any time. Best to make the most of it. There were worse fates than becoming a lazy nobleman with a wife he adored.

If he became Imelda's equal in rank, they could be together. If she still wanted him. Perhaps she didn't. It was a risk he was more than willing to take. He submitted to Ceso's command, lay down, and gritted his teeth through the pain.

Chapter Four

Light blazed out the windows of Ca' Dandolo as Venezia's góndola abutted the dock. What a long day it had been. The messenger with news of her uncle's funeral, preparing a galley to race her there, dinner, the procession, and that awful execution. Plus the three-day journey from Zorzi, which felt like it would never end with how terribly she'd slept on the ship. Her head pounded, and her body ached. She resigned herself to use the gondolièr's outstretched hand to step off the boat. How she hated showing weakness in front of anyone. Then she gripped the rails of the gangway and the stairs to ease the trek up to her home.

Alessia knew she'd be returning tonight. The maid would insist on undressing Venezia and brushing her hair, and it would all take such a long time. Venezia would be fine falling into bed fully-clothed, even though she'd worn the same dress for days and smelled like salt water and unwashed skin.

Venezia entered through a back door, careful not to let it slam shut, and crept up the stairs. More than an achy body urged her on. It had been about a month since her last seizure, which meant one was around the corner. With all of the fatigue and stress of the day, she could have one at any moment. Normally she didn't let the threat stress her, but her body couldn't take much more today.

Additionally, it would alert her husband to her arrival. What a terrible way to end an exhausting day. She made it to the third floor and snuck down the hall. Her husband's door was closed, but light peeked out from underneath. Voices—his and a woman's—leaked out from under the door. Venezia rolled her eyes, but his distraction was well-timed.

She slipped into her room and closed the door. A fire already blazed in the hearth. She pulled her knives from their various sheaths, and they caught the light. Waist, thigh, ankle. Venezia never went without them, and her dress had special slits sewn in for quick access. She pulled the sheets down on her bed, moved the pillow, and placed all three blades in the hole she'd cut into the mattress. She started unbuttoning her doublet. At least she'd get the damned clothes off.

The door opened.

"Mè siora." Alessia pulled Venezia into a tight hug. The stout woman's back had grown hunched in the four years Venezia had been gone, though her dark eyes remained bright. "I'm so happy to see you."

"It's good to be home." Venezia continued undoing her buttons, but Alessia *tsk*ed and took over. Venezia's arms slumped from the weight of the day. "Be quick. I'm exhausted."

Alessia pursed her lips and helped Venezia out of the doublet and started on the dress. She understood Venezia's unspoken warning about a possible impending seizure.

"Who's the new girl?" Venezia stepped out of her Fleet Admiral uniform. A doublet similar to a man's, with a straight, short collar, worn over a simply cut dress. Gray-blue wool for the armada, with bright blue trim for the Lions.

"Kari," Alessia said. "Sior Lazaro bought her a few months ago."

A slave? The man had absolutely no shame. "We don't need any more help." Plus owning slaves was distasteful. Once Venezia had the chance, she would abolish the practice in the republic.

"You're right as always, mè siora, but he insisted." Alessia grabbed the hairbrush from the vanity and sighed. "Your lovely hair is a tangled mess."

"Life on a boat."

"It's like seaweed, and it will be worse in the morning. Please let me brush it."

"Fetch her, then you can attend to my hair."

"Of course, mè siora."

Alessia left. A moment later Venezia heard murmuring in the hall. She changed into her nightgown. When Alessia returned, Venezia sat so the maid could brush her hair. Minutes later the slave girl entered. Kari had yellow hair and smooth, pale skin. She stood by the door, demurely holding a washbowl and towel. But her braid was mussed, and her clothes wrinkled. She was young and pretty, as Lazaro preferred.

A red ring of corincanto circled her tiny wrist. The slave stitch, binding slaves to their masters. Technically against Giore's commandments, but an infraction the priests conveniently ignored. The stitch even used spirit rose. Venezia's lip curled, halfway to a sneer before she caught herself—she couldn't help it, faced with such blasphemy in her own home. Alessia and every other servant in the Dandolo household bore no thread cruelly embroidered into their arms. Venezia paid them, and they returned to their homes every night, heads of their own households.

"Make yourself useful." Venezia nodded at the washbowl. Kari crept forward, seemingly an inch at a time, her fingers barely darker than the porcelain she held. "Put that on the table by the window."

The girl did as told, then remained by the table. She fussed with her hair, then her dress, then wrung her hands. Venezia exchanged a look with Alessia through the mirror. The girl was clearly not a household slave. Lazaro had bought her for one reason only.

When Alessia finished braiding her hair, Venezia walked over to the table, forcing Kari to step aside. Venezia washed herself, the water turning murky when she rinsed the towel. The girl wandered over to the bed and messed with the pillows and blankets. She dropped the pillow and picked up a knife, eyes wide.

"Put it back," Venezia said. Kari threw it in the hole and covered it with the pillow.

"Kari?" Lazaro's voice called from the hall. "Where'd you go?" He walked through the door, and smiled. "Venezia, mè amor. So good to see your beautiful face."

Lazaro had been handsome when they'd married. He'd still had his strength, and salt and pepper hair had made him look gallant, noble. Venezia hadn't loved him even then, but there'd been a thrill when the great Doxe Dandolo turned his charming smile on her. Plus he'd held the allure of what political insights he could give her. Even with her powerful family, no one had expected much of Venezia. Not her father, not her brother, not her sickly mother. No one had expected her to become dogasina at only eighteen.

But the last thirteen years hadn't been kind to Lazaro—and he certainly deserved what he got. His white hair was wispy, his back stooped, his hands and arms marked with age spots. But his teeth were still perfect, and he flashed them at every woman he met. He even kept trying to disarm Venezia with his wit, but she'd long ago found the holes in his politician's glamour.

Venezia offered her cheek to him. He was allowed one kiss and one kiss only. Even though she initiated the touch—even invited it, disgusting as it was to think of—it still took every ounce of control not to flinch when his age-roughened lips made contact with her skin. It was a greeting kiss, but he lingered too long. When he straightened, she could feel a sheen of saliva on her face.

She nodded at Alessia and Kari. "Leave us."

Alessia gave Venezia one last look before leaving. She knew—the entire household knew the truth of their marriage. But Venezia kept up appearances, even for the servants. Quitting would feel too much like defeat, and she had stopped losing long ago.

"Why didn't you attend my uncle's funeral?"

Lazaro put a hand on his chest. "My heart was too weak this morning. I spent most of the day in bed."

Kari closed the door. Of course he had. Venezia opened the window. Cold air burst into the room, cutting through her nightgown. She leaned out and emptied the bowl. The icy touch tickled her skin, but her alpaca corincanto kept it from sinking in. "Did we really need another maid?"

"You've become so busy since your brother appointed you as Fleet Admiral. I wanted to ease some of your responsibilities."

Kari was certainly easing one of Venezia's "responsibilities." That was one duty Venezia was happy to let another woman endure.

"Fine," she said. "You can help me with the next dogal election."

"You're not ready."

"I'm tired of waiting, Lazaro. I'm running this year. Don't try to—" It hit her, sending a chain of tension through her body. The forewarning, like the pressure drop before a storm. As a child she'd described it as the tickle before a sneeze.

It was coming.

A seizure.

She had about fifteen seconds.

Dread tensed her muscles. Slowly, so slowly, she set the bowl on the windowsill and turned around.

"Try to what?" Lazaro held his hands out, waiting for Venezia to continue.

Ten seconds.

Her thoughts slowed. Muddled.

Her breathing grew fast. Shallow.

Anxiety filled her mind, constricting every corner.

Lazaro kept talking, but she heard no sound. Her hearing had cut out.

Five seconds.

She opened her mouth but couldn't form words. *I'm about to have a seizure.* Her brain could string the words together, but her tongue had forgotten language. *Get out*, she wanted to say. *Leave me alone.* He was the last person she wanted to be with right now.

It hit.

All of her muscles contracted. "Seizzzz—"

Lazaro finally understood, but there was nothing he could do. He flapped his mouth and waved his arms and tried to get her to sit.

I'm dying! Make it stop! It wasn't true, but fear ricocheted around her mind. Lying, deceitful fear. Thoughts were disjointed. Scattered. They raced, dripping with terror. She wanted to curl in a ball.

Alessia. She needed Alessia.

She had to focus, had to fight. She walked a ship's rail, and a gale buffeted her, trying to push her over the edge into a full convulsive fit.

She could keep her footing if she could show her mind she was still in control. She opened and closed her fingers, rolled her wrists back and forth. How long had it been? Time stretched and contorted. An eternity and mere seconds filled her.

Alessia and Kari ran into the room. Everyone tried to get her to sit. But she focused on her hands, on her fingers, on asserting dominion over her body. She teetered on the precipice, certain that gravity would pull her down into a churning, hungry sea, but finally the episode faded. Sound returned—a room full of panicked voices—and she could take a long, deep breath.

Exhaustion barreled into her like a monstrous wave. She stumbled toward her bed. Alessia rushed forward with a cotton-corincanto-stitched blanket. Lazaro ripped it from her. Venezia crawled under the covers, and he tucked the healing-empowered quilt around her. He smoothed her black hair away from her face.

"You push yourself too hard, mè amor. You're not as strong as you think you are. What if ..." He glanced at the maids. "Out."

They turned to leave.

"Alessia," Venezia slurred. "Come back in ten minutes."

Alessia forced a smile. "Of course, mè siora."

Venezia yawned and her body sunk into the mattress. It cradled her like a mother's arms. "What if what, Lazaro?"

"What if you had cotton corincanto put in your arteries? Just a bit in each arm."

"That's heresy." She managed to muster strength into her words. "I won't even consider it."

"But these seizures handicap you. They're the reason your body failed to carry our four children." He smoothed her hair again and tucked the blanket around her shoulders. "I hate seeing you suffer like this."

He hadn't minded making her suffer for the first eight years of their marriage. Venezia reached under her pillow and curled her fingers around the hilt of a dagger. She'd finally learned how to fight him off five years ago. If only she could leave permanently, move back into the

Albizzi home. It wasn't culturally sanctioned, but Venezia had never been one to hold to social mores.

But damn it all, she needed him. She'd only married him because, as a former Doxe, he could teach her. He could help her reach her goal, could help her finally best her brother and take the sash and crown for herself. Then she could leave him behind, go live in Palàso Dogal and leave him to his sex slaves in this dreadful house. If she didn't win this election, she'd be stuck with him for four more years. Four years of lies and adultery and feigned love.

But not abuse. Not anymore.

Venezia clenched the knife and pretended to be calmed by her hateful husband.

CHAPTER FIVE

Imelda left her room, a skein of wool corincanto in hand. The sun hadn't risen long before, but the hallway was already full of noise and activity. The frenetic action of packing and prepping the house to be empty. Because after they left, there'd be no one in the Albizzi home until Arturo got married or Renzo and Donte returned, whichever happened first.

They were moving. It was happening. And so soon. Imelda had hoped Primo would wait until after Carnevale. Or at least a couple days. But that had been foolish. Primo wasted nothing, not even time.

Imelda climbed up the stairs to the roof. Arturo had spent the night in the dome up here. It was his spot in the house, more than his own room. He'd put a sleeping pallet on the floor on one side and had a small desk made to fit in here, where he was currently writing in his notebook. Early morning light slanted through windows.

She plopped onto the mattress. "I hate this."

"I know." His voice was as soft as the *scritch* of his quill on the paper. "We did see it coming."

"But not so soon." She looked at the wool corincanto in her lap and bit her lip. "And not to a foreigner who lives so far away."

Arturo put his pen down and stared out the window at the palàso across the canal. "No, neither of those."

"You'll take care of the house, right? Keep Mare's portrait in your room, or maybe the dining room." Perhaps Arturo's future wife would appreciate it. Hopefully Primo would find a good bride for him. She put her head into her hands. "How could he do this to us, especially after killing Mare?"

"Imelda." He didn't say anything because Imelda didn't need to hear his objections. Objectively, he'd say, Primo didn't kill their mother. But his behavior made a sick woman sicker. In Imelda's mind, that was the same thing. If Primo had stopped being a selfish prick, he'd have seen the effect his actions had on Imelda's mother and he would've straightened up. He'd had a choice, he'd chosen wrong, so he was to blame.

A drawing of the wings in Arturo's notebook caught Imelda's eye. A simple sketch surrounded by notations in his small, tight script. "Do we even have time to finish those?"

"I think so. We owe it to ourselves to try." He smiled. "I've had some ideas that we should be able to implement in the next couple of weeks. And if we complete them in time, we could still get out of these marriages. Are you up for spinning more?"

"Always. But who are we going to sell them to?"

Arturo tilted his head, a sly look on his face. "Who makes the most sense?"

Imelda shook her head. "No, not Venezia. She betrayed us."

"Did she actually?"

"Well ..." Imelda sighed. "She can't go against Primo, though."

"Not publicly."

"You think she'd go behind his back to buy the wings?"

Arturo grinned. "I have no doubt. Get dressed. Let's go."

An hour later, they stood in Venezia's parlor.

Venezia walked in, wearing her Fleet Admiral dress. "I'm glad you're here. I want to apologize."

Imelda's heart clenched, the pain fresh again. No, Venezia had had no choice. Not in public. "It's okay. I understand. But that's not why we're here."

"I'm still sorry with how everything happened yesterday." Venezia sat on a chair and gestured for them to take the sofa, which they did. Arturo had brought his notebook and a pen, and he opened it. "Primo was out of line telling you during your father's funeral. But running the family is his responsibility now. It's his—" She took a deep breath. "It's his right." Her voice had an acidic edge to it. Imelda knew the siblings weren't close, but obviously Venezia disliked Primo being over her in the family hierarchy more than she let on. She leaned toward Imelda. "You have to face the facts. Primo is the oldest of our generation. He's head of the family."

"I wish you were the oldest," Imelda said.

"So much would be different. So much." Venezia shook her head with a rueful smile. "I'm sorry. Truly. Do you forgive me?"

Imelda looked at Venezia's hands. Her fingers were long and scarred from her years using the knife, but they were also strong. They'd smoothed Imelda's hair and wiped her tears so much when she'd been younger. Imelda sighed. "Of course I do. Doesn't change the fact that I'm still upset about the situation."

"Marriage ... can be daunting." She tucked a lock of Imelda's hair behind her ear, as she had so many times growing up. "Ulisse is a good man. I promise you that."

"But he's greedy," Imelda said, "selling his soothsaying abilities or whatever they are. And he's Primo's lap dog."

Venezia laughed. "I can assure you, Ulisse is no one's lap dog."

"They're good friends, right?" Arturo said even as he scanned his notebook. He made a thoughtful sound and nodded to himself.

"We've known him our whole lives, yes," Venezia said. "You can trust Ulisse. Marrying him won't be bad. I can't promise he'll be a great husband, but he won't be a terrible one. That's more than many women get. You don't need to worry."

"I'm not scared. I want to be in charge of my own life." She wanted to see Anselmo again, see if he still cared for her as much as he had four years ago. See if he cared as much as she cared for him. Primo's timing was too perfectly terrible. "And I don't want to leave you or Arturo."

Arturo half-smiled.

"That's why we're here," Imelda said.

Venezia arched an eyebrow and folded her arms.

Imelda looked at Arturo. "Will you buy our wings?" he said.

"You think you can finally perfect them?" Venezia sounded more hopeful than her words let on. "In a month?"

Arturo handed his notebook to Venezia. "I've already been toying with new ideas. I'm fully confident we will."

"No one will want just one pair of wings."

"We have two—" Imelda said.

Arturo cut in. "We'll sell the design. But we'll need a lot of money to survive without the family."

Venezia's eyes scanned the page, and she nodded. "Five million ducats for two pairs of wings and the finalized design. You'll be well off with that amount, especially if you invest it wisely."

Imelda pulled Venezia to her feet and hugged her tight.

Venezia took Imelda by the shoulders and kissed her cheeks five times. She then kissed Arturo's cheeks five times as well. The deal was sealed.

Arturo's face split into the biggest grin Imelda had seen in years, and she returned it with one of her own. He looked as confident as Imelda felt. They didn't have time to second-guess. They had to finish the project they'd started seven long years ago, a dream so long in the making. Human flight. Primo scoffed and called it impossible, but if Italo Albizzi could make walls move, Imelda and Arturo could invent wings. They were his heirs in name, and soon they would be in legacy as well.

The time for chasing their impossible dream was over.

It was time to capture it.

Chapter Six

It was hard for Venezia to concentrate as the Secretary of Finance droned on. It had been three hours since Venezia had promised Arturo and Imelda five million ducats for the wings, three hours since she'd sealed her promise with five kisses. If Primo found out she was helping them to rebel against him, he'd be furious. But it wasn't the only way she was acting against him.

She brought her attention back to the Council meeting. The labyrinth lottery was in two hours, and the Council still hadn't voted on the number of captains they'd allow to buy their way in. Two hours left, and they'd been debating all morning. This lot of old men had forgotten the value of time. Forgotten anything beyond the value of their own pockets.

Her foot tapped as the Secretary enumerated the many advantages—most of them financial—the city would glean from accepting more purchased entries. Those were the measurable assets. But the unmeasurable benefits of limiting purchased entries outweighed them. Allowing a noncommissioned officer, born into a lower class, the chance to become a Lion and a noble would provide greater results. That soldier would be grateful to the military in a way no highborn would. They'd be more determined to prove themselves as well. The choice was clear.

Just as her choice regarding the wings had been clear. Clearer, even, because most of the assets the wings promised were measurable. Most, but not all. They'd provide a strategic advantage over any other country in the known world.

That alone was worth five million ducats.

Finally Enrico Lando, Council President, stood. "We will now convene to the voting chamber," he said. The slim man was Primo's biggest ally and, frankly, his biggest sycophant. He even went against fashion and sported a mustache and no beard, same as Primo.

One at a time, starting with Primo, they left the room. Venezia exited third, after Enrico. She walked into the robe room, donning a black hooded cloak, black gloves, and black mask. The mask was not tied on but had a bit on the inside—it was held by one's teeth, thus ensuring silence and anonymity during the vote. She took two stones—one white and one black—from the bowl. Then, with a glance in the mirror to ensure she was completely covered, she entered the voting chamber. The room was plain and dark with no windows. The only source of light was a roaring fire in a large hearth. They lit it no matter the season—voting in the summer was a miserable affair. Even now, at the end of winter, it heated the room to an almost uncomfortable temperature.

Enrico was easy to spot, as the only other person in voting robes. He stood with his back to the room. Primo, as Doxe, didn't vote anonymously, and he only voted if there was a tie. He wore a black robe without a hood and a white Bauta mask, tied on so he could speak freely. Primo's secretary stood next to him, holding the voting bowl covered by a cloth.

Venezia faced the wall and waited. Voting was so tedious this way. Why all the ceremony? They could find a different method to ensure anonymity. To Fógo with tradition. It wasted time and talent. Though when Primo announced that everyone was here and they could turn around, she couldn't help but admire the effect of the black robes and masks. In the dim light, they looked like visions of death. It did invoke a sense of somberness. But that was it—the only benefit from the antiquated practice.

Primo regarded each person in turn. "The proposed number of purchased entries into the labyrinth is nineteen, which will allow one lieutenant to be drawn in the lottery. Cast your votes as Beniamino presents the bowl to you. White is in favor, black is in disagreement. If the opposing side wins, we will reconvene to the Council chamber to discuss a different number of captains allowed to buy access."

Beniamino walked around the circle, and one-by-one the Council members put their stones in. Their gloves hid the color of their stone. Beniamino kept the cloth over the bowl, only allowing enough space for Venezia to drop her black stone in. If she could, she'd drop five black stones to match the intensity with which she disagreed with the proposal.

When the secretary had collected all the votes, he took the bowl to Primo who looked through the bowl to count the votes.

"Seven for, five against," Primo said. "Since there is no tie, my vote is not needed. The Council's decision is clear: we will draw one lieutenant's name in the lottery this afternoon."

They left in the same order as they entered. Venezia shoved her robe onto a peg and dropped her mask on the shelf and her white stone into the bowl. In the hall outside, she waited with arms crossed, staring out the windows of the grand porch.

Fia Pesaro exited the Council chamber and walked over. The buxom woman, smooth olive skin powdered almost faintly, wore at least five strands of pearls and a dress with a meter-long train. "Close call, Fleet Admiral," she said. "We had a few other allies at least."

"We have to find a way to bring more to our side." Venezia drummed her fingers on her arm. "You're a shrewd business-woman, siora. Why did you vote against funds for the city?"

"As you told me, true loyalty is a powerful thing that cannot be bought." Fia would know, as the woman who owned the last remaining slave company in the republic. "How to get the others to understand ..." She pursed her lips as two Councilmen exited the Council chamber. "Leave that to me."

Sior Ruzzini approached them with a smug expression on his ruddy face. "Poor loss, siore." He had the gall to pat Venezia's arm. She jerked it away. "See? So soft. Always thinking with your hearts." He shook his head. "Council*men* put their logic first."

Primo approached, followed by Enrico Lando.

Fia turned on a bright smile for Sior Ruzzini. "Maybe you could enlighten me? Over a full dinner at my house tonight?" She allowed herself to be led away by Ruzzini, flashing a wink at Venezia. She was willing to play the role of the fish-out-of-water female Council member—which was part of the reason she was the ally Venezia needed. She could twist the men to hers and Venezia's motives.

Primo spared a glance for Ruzzini and Fia before turning to Venezia. "I need you to come with me to my parlor. We have a visitor."

Venezia arched an eyebrow. "They don't want to meet with the Council, or even the cabinet?

"It's a sensitive matter, apparently."

This would be interesting. "Which way would you have voted had there been a tie?" Venezia asked as they walked through the spacious yet austere hall, Enrico following them.

"I see the merits of both sides," Primo said. People quickly stepped out of the way as he passed, most murmuring their deferences.

"If you had to choose?" she insisted.

Primo lowered his voice. "Nineteen is an extravagance. Fourteen or fifteen purchased entries would be wiser. But you know how the treasury thinks."

"They also don't want to risk allowing too many lowborns into the nobility."

Primo *hmm*ed in agreement as they left the Senate building and walked to the palàso. When they reached the Doxe's parlor, Primo's secretary hurried to open the doors, then scurried off to retrieve the visitor. Other than the mural of Giatoro and Ioanna, the room was like the rest of the palàso—dark wood paneling with silver inlay. Pretentious in a restrained way. The mural was beautiful, painted by the finest artists in Frenza. The Council room and Doxe's audience chamber needed more of this decoration. Rialto was a world power, and their central building should reflect that. Palàso Dogal should be covered in visions of their many successes. The walls and ceilings ought to be dripping in silver. Once she was Doxe, that would be her first act.

Enrico perched on a chair in front of Primo's desk, as if he didn't want to wrinkle his coat. Venezia lounged on the couch. Primo frowned at her casual composure, but said nothing as he selected a wine from the many bottles along his sideboard. She could push him a bit, but not too much. He couldn't suspect her plans to take the crown and sash from him.

Primo poured a small glass for himself. "Would either of you like some?"

Enrico visibly wrestled with his answer. Drink on the job to please Doxe Albizzi or appear responsible and say no? "Yes, Your Serenity."

Venezia waved the offer away. "Who's the visitor?"

Primo handed a glass to Enrico. "Janus Komnenos, grandson of the late Iliano Emperor Gregorios Komnenos."

Venezia sat upright. "What?"

Primo's eyebrows pinched together. "Don't tell me you still hold a grudge for Gregorios' massacre."

"I just don't understand why he's here."

"Isn't it obvious? He wants the throne back."

Enrico frowned. "Like the Iliani would let him keep it. There's always some power-hungry noble waiting to depose a weak ruler in Ilios."

"But why now?" Venezia asked. Right before Carnevale, when everyone would forget about politics for a week. Janus would disappear from the Council members' minds as quickly as the citizens' morals. He'd never convince anyone to join his side, and the Council wouldn't vote until they reconvened after the holiday. Such terrible timing.

Primo sipped his wine. "Most likely he found some support."

"Who'd be fool enough to align himself with a family that condoned murder?" Enrico muttered into his glass. The Lando family had lost members in the massacre of Rialtani citizens living in Ilios twenty years before.

"Emperor Gregorios let the whims of his people affect his decisions," Primo said. "That's not the mark of a good leader."

Venezia stood and straightened her dress. "This Janus might prove to have a different character."

Primo finished his wine and set the glass on his sideboard. He held out his hand for Enrico's goblet, and placed it next to his own. "He might," he said doubtfully.

Primo's secretary entered, followed by a stout man with the mahogany skin of the Iliano nobility. Ilios descended from Sacresta, the same as Rialto and other cities of the Venetano peninsula, but generations of life in the warm north and intermarrying with peoples from all over the Muriseano had browned their skin from the olive complexion of other Sacresta descendants. He wore a long robe in the Iliano style. But unlike most Iliani, his robe was made entirely of crimson corincanto. A member of the Komnenos family, and the blood monk cult on top of that. He'd never convince anyone to join his cause.

"Janus Komnenos of Ilios," Beniamino said, "heir of the Komnenos family."

"And rightful emperor of Ilios," Janus finished, stepping in front of the secretary.

"Your family was deposed legally, as far as I understand your laws," Primo said. His tone was almost dismissive. Janus would never notice—neither would Lando, perhaps—but Venezia heard it. She'd heard it many times in her life, sometimes directed at her. "Or am I wrong?"

Janus's mouth twitched like a fish on a line. "My family ruled for two hundred years. The Heraclius family has only held the throne for twenty. That is why I would like to present myself before the Council of Twelve. I seek your help in deposing Emperor Rouvin Heraclius." He looked like a fool, laying all of his cards on the table. Venezia folded her arms. He glanced at her and frowned.

Enrico and Primo exchanged a look, one that didn't include Venezia. They were too tight. A Council president and Doxe should not have such a close relationship. They were meant to balance each other.

"Go on," Primo said.

Janus clasped his hands behind his back, but his posture was poor and his outfit too ridiculous for him to pull off the power pose. His voice rose to a commanding tone. He certainly tried to act the part of a ruler, but his red robe was a reminder of his extremist views. "I seek Rialto's military help regaining the throne of Ilios, ending my family's exile and returning us to power. In exchange for that—and ending the schism and submitting your temples to the Iliano high priest—I will give you the following: fifteen million ducats, to be paid over the course of five years, a steady supply of Iliano black bane, and free passage through the Bogasa Strait."

Fifteen million ducats was far too low. Primo would never accept it. And yet, Venezia fought a smile from curling her lips.

Primo laced his hands together. "What was that about submitting to the Iliano high priest?" He kept his voice even, his cadence steady, though it was unlikely he'd allow Janus to present his proposal to the Council. Despite Primo's many flaws, he'd never failed to play the role of politician with perfection.

Janus drew his shoulders up as his expression darkened. "Your priests follow a corrupted form of our religion, Your Serenity. It pains me that so many of my brothers and sisters will not reach Cielo because of the inaccuracy of their teachings. Your spinners run around in their guild rather than submitting themselves to the will of the gods and working as priests and priestesses. The Rialtano high priest would cease his blasphemy and step down. We are Sacresta's heir, in government and religion."

"*We* are Sacresta Unfallen," Enrico said. "We practice as they did in their most glorious years."

"Yes, the republic." Contempt dripped from Janus's voice like blood from a freshly used sword. "And how well did they fare? Meanwhile, the empire continues in Ilios. Divinely-appointed monarchs outlast all else."

Primo stood. "Siori, this is no time for a theological or historical debate. Sior Komnenos, please excuse us as we deliberate."

With a stiff bow and a stiff look for Venezia, Janus left.

Here was the opportunity she'd wanted. She had to play it right, though. She paused for a moment, as if undecided. "I think it's worth considering." Carefully, as if she were still weighing the benefits against the costs. Her tone light, thoughtful. "Even if he is a pious prick."

Primo started to smile but caught himself. He sat at his desk. "It's a terrible idea."

"Agreed," Enrico chimed in like an obnoxious seagull.

Primo didn't want it. Good. She had to make her case, especially in front of Lando—Primo would be suspicious if she didn't. But he wouldn't side with her, which was exactly as she needed. Venezia took her seat. "If we put him on the throne, he'll owe allegiance to us. The entire Iliano Empire will owe allegiance to us. Everything they have will be under our control. The Strait, the Phyriano peninsula, the diamond mines of Sena. Think of all the ships we could build if we controlled the cedar forests of Belanur."

Primo shook his head. "He won't be our puppet. No man so haughty and pious is going to take orders from us. He's a blood monk, Venezia. He believes he has a mandate from Father Giore to reign, while the people gave me my title. Which holds the more immediate power? Sior Lando, do you think he is a man who will be content to be controlled?"

"No, Your Serenity." Did the man have any original thoughts?

Primo nodded. "He has made handsome promises, but I don't want to struggle to maintain control over anyone. His final offer—free access to the Bogasa—I must admit is enticing. However, I have a plan for our ships using the Strait." Primo straightened his posture and lifted his chin, clear signs he was proud of whatever he was about to announce. "I sent an offer of marriage to Imperial Princess Calixta Heraclius for Arturo. She is traveling here to ascertain whether she will marry him or not. As part of the marriage arrangement, Emperor Rouvin will give Rialtano ships a minimal fee through the Strait."

"Brilliant move, Your Serenity," Enrico said.

Venezia stared, as if incredulous. "You could have a galley, but you settle for a skiff."

"Without bloodshed. The sword is not the only tool of negotiation. And war is expensive. You know that better than anyone, Fleet Admiral." He spoke her title sharply, a blade as surely as the ones strapped to her body.

Venezia threw up her hands. "How can you be so shortsighted? We'd be the greatest power in the Muriseano, perhaps even the world."

"The Heraclius family has proven themselves to be strong." Primo stood, his lips pressed tight, his hands tense on the desktop. He looked so much like their father when he took this stance. His voice had grown quiet, but hard. How she hated when he used that look and tone with her. Her stomach writhed, but she wouldn't show her discomfort. "We can make them our greatest allies or our greatest enemies. I've received word that Prince Nikkoforos is accompanying his sister to Rialto—presumably to ensure we don't align with Janus. I prefer to work with the actual ruling family, rather than some spoiled grandson with a grudge. Ilios has never been sacked. Its famous walls have held for a thousand years. I do not wish to throw away the lives of our men on such a gamble. I care more about our citizens than my own greed. And I *am* the Doxe, and you would do well to remember that." He nodded at the knife on her belt. The handle was blue, studded with onyx, and gilded in silver. The ceremonial knife awarded to the Fleet Admiral by the Doxe. "Do not forget who gave that to you."

Of course he'd gone on the defense. It always hurt more than she anticipated, and especially this time, with Enrico present. "My apologies, Your Serenity."

Enrico gave her a smug look. If only she could slap the obsequious bastard.

Primo walked to the door and spoke with Beniamino. He then sat at his desk, and gestured for Venezia and Enrico to stand on either side of him. She tensed her jaw as she complied. How he loved bossing people around. He'd probably rejoiced when Uncle Lorenzo had died and he'd become head of the family.

Janus walked back in.

"We've considered your request," Primo said, "and have decided not to grant it."

Janus spluttered. He looked between Primo and Venezia. "But I've promised you so much. Money. The Strait. Black bane!"

"The sum you promised wouldn't cover the cost of this war. And we have plenty of weapons."

Janus glared at Venezia, his face nearly as red as his robes. She returned it with an arched brow.

Primo waved him off. "Thank you for your time. Beniamino, escort Sior Komnenos out."

The secretary guided Janus through the door. Janus's indignant protests could be heard from the hall.

Primo glanced at Venezia with an amused look. "That's the man you want to work with? Honestly, I thought you had better sense than that."

Primo might think it was funny, but Venezia was right. Primo was overly cautious. He was blowing this chance, just as she'd hoped he would. Venezia was happy to take it for herself. Even though Janus was an idiot, she could use him to her advantage. When she managed to start this war, she could claim the victory for herself and no one else. All of the riches of the Iliano Empire would belong to Rialto, and it would be due to Venezia's cunning. If that didn't win her the Doxe seat, nothing would.

Chapter Seven

Imelda wound her freshly spun wool corincanto onto the niddy-noddy, focusing on the repetitive circles in an attempt to ignore the flurry of packing around her, the slam of trunks and the rustling of dresses.

Editta stepped in front of Imelda holding an armful of dresses. "Mè siora, please, you need to choose. I can't do it for you."

What Imelda needed was to spin as much corincanto for the wings as she could in the next several days. She pulled the corincanto off the niddy-noddy, walked to her wash basin, and dunked the thread in the water. "You can choose, Editta, I trust you."

Editta pressed her lips together. Imelda knew she disliked Imelda using the wash basin for corincanto. "We'll bring your winter and early spring dresses. And your mother's portrait."

"Perfect, grassie."

"Of course, mè siora. I'll wrap the portrait myself." Editta waved other servants over to give them commands.

Arturo wandered in, munching on cheese. "Still packing?"

"You're done?"

He shrugged. "I have less junk than you."

Imelda held up the looped corincanto. "I've been preoccupied." She put the thread back in the water.

He smiled. "That's a beautiful sight. Silk?"

"Wool. I'll do silk tonight."

Downstairs, someone knocked on the door.

Imelda held in a sigh. "Tell them to go away." She pulled the corincanto out of the water and wrung it out. Red-tinted water splashed onto the floor. Editta hurried over to wipe the spill with her apron, then excused herself.

"They're just being polite," Arturo said. "Each family has to send its condolences."

"Every visit reminds me again that he's gone." Since Pàre's death, Imelda and Arturo had entertained a steady stream of guests. They all brought wine or blood oranges or loaves of bread. Generous gifts all, but none would bring her father back.

"I'll tell them you're sick," he said.

"Grassie."

The house steward entered. "Lieutenant Anselmo Errari is here, mè sior and mè siora."

Anselmo. Just hearing his name curled something inside Imelda, excitement and sorrow and anger and love all at once. She'd held his name in her heart like a secret these four years—five really, with their relationship before he left—and now he was back and he was at her home, waiting downstairs, waiting to see her.

Inside, Imelda was a swirling maelstrom. She managed to stay calm on the outside, save for a slight tremble in her hands.

Arturo dismissed the manservant and turned to Imelda. "Did Anselmo tell you he was coming?"

"Of course not." Her words were bitter. She took a breath and swallowed the resentment. "Did he tell you?"

"No. I haven't written him in a while."

Imelda hung the wound corincanto on the iron hook by the fire and gave it a tug. "Now he knows how I felt."

"Not exactly the same, I'm sure." Arturo wasn't wrong about that. He glanced at the door. "Would you like me to tell him you're sick? I understand if you don't want to see him."

"Because of Pàre, or because he didn't write me, or because of our past, or because I'm already engaged?" Engaged. She'd said the word too easily for how much she hated the idea. Not the idea, the fact. The fact that she was engaged before she even got to talk to Anselmo after their four years apart.

"All of them, I imagine," Arturo said. "You don't have to see him. You don't owe him anything."

But Imelda owed it to herself. She needed to know. She'd spent nearly every day of her life with Anselmo, and then nothing for four years when he left for Zorzi. Even if the wings failed and she married that gods awful king, she had to know how Anselmo felt. She tugged on the loop of thread. "I want to see him." She turned around. "Because we're making … because of …"

"The wings." Arturo smiled. She couldn't let herself say it aloud, give voice to her hope. Not when the hope was connected to Anselmo. But Arturo could say it for her. She returned the smile, a small one but genuine all the same.

"I'll tell him you'll be right down." Arturo left.

Imelda rang the bell for Editta, then turned to her bed. The maid hadn't packed all of the dresses yet. She pulled out a deep plum one, made of silk that draped like lines over the side of a galley. As Editta tied a silver belt around the high waist, Imelda combed her fingers through her hair and pulled it over one shoulder.

She walked down the stairs and paused outside the salon. The door muffled Arturo's and Anselmo's voices, but she could tell whose they were. Arturo's was the tenor, a skipping staccato as he followed his thoughts. Anselmo answered in a restrained, resonant baritone.

Four years with no word from him. And now she was going to see him, days after her father's funeral. The day after Primo told her she was engaged. But just hearing that voice, a bit deeper than before but still unmistakably Anselmo's, brought back memories of their time together. As friends and then more than friends. Much more.

No more dawdling. She smoothed her hair, took a deep breath, and entered. Anselmo snapped to his feet. He wore his gray-blue uniform, one line of silver on his shoulder indicating the rank of lieutenant. Someone had finally recognized his skill and promoted him. His clothes were clean, and with his crisp posture, he looked the part of the heroic soldier. But his eyes had grown tight from the things he'd seen, the things he'd done these last four years at war. Gone was the boy she'd known and loved. Instead, a man stood in his place, handsome and tall and so very grown up.

"You're huge!" she blurted, then slapped her hands over her mouth, causing a popping sound that made Anselmo chuckle. Despite his deep voice, it was a quiet sound.

"I'm sorry," he said.

"No. I mean, you look good."

Anselmo laughed again, and Imelda felt herself blush. To hide it, she pulled him in to kiss cheeks. His face was earnest, but gave nothing away. And he wouldn't, not with Arturo here.

"Anselmo's been telling me about Zorzi," Arturo said.

"How was it?" she asked.

Anselmo rubbed his beard. "I survived."

"I'm so glad you did. I mean, obviously, I wouldn't want anything to happen to you." She twirled a hair around a finger and forced her breathing to remain slow.

He smiled, as if despite himself, and there he was—her Anselmo. Under those military blues and weary look, he was still there.

"Renzo and Donte are gone?" he asked.

"To the south on some quest. We sent them word of Pàre's death, but haven't heard back," Imelda said. "It's been several months since their last hemp message. There hasn't even been a written letter."

"Those two always manage to get out of any predicament they're in. I'm sure they're safe."

"Yes, I'm sure." She smoothed her skirt, resisted the urge to play with her hair. It was almost too much to look at him. He was so much … more since she'd last seen him. It created an ache within her, though not entirely unpleasant.

Arturo cleared his throat. "I need to keep packing." Imelda glanced at him, and he waved his fingers by his side to acknowledge the lie. Gods, he was the best. "Good to see you, Anselmo."

"Packing?" Anselmo asked.

Arturo smirked. "Primo's orders. Imelda will tell you about it."

Anselmo gave her a questioning look as Arturo left.

"We're moving into Palàso Dogal for a while," she said. "A short while." They were finally alone. Where to begin? "Stay for dinner. What would you like? I think the kitchen is empty, but I'll send a servant out." Primo probably expected them by then, but she didn't care. He might be able to force her to move in, but she'd take her sweet time doing it.

"I have gulf patrol duty tonight, unfortunately," Anselmo said. "I actually came to ask if you'd like to go for a walk. But if you're busy …"

"A walk sounds lovely." She took his arm before he even offered it. Underneath his wool coat, his muscles were strong and steady. He'd grown taller in the last four years, and yet she didn't feel small around him. It was right, being so close to him. It was also different than before. It felt new, in a way. A new sense of his proximity. A new warmth. A new desire to be even closer. She pulled herself snug against his side. He looked at her in surprise, then placed his free hand on hers, though his posture remained rigid.

"What?" she asked. Had she been too presumptuous?

"The labyrinth lottery is today."

"And that's where we're going?"

He nodded.

"And you've entered your name," she said slowly.

"I have."

She gripped her hair. "Why? Why didn't you listen to me?"

"All those years you lectured me?"

"*Told* you, Anselmo. I told you how dangerous it is."

"You think I don't know? The rumors in the armada are unimaginable. Soldiers who die. Soldiers who come back worse than dead, maimed and unable to fight or make any kind of living for themselves other than begging. But I'm better than them, and I have to take any chance I get." He hesitated, pausing before the threshold. "Do you still want to go with me?"

She led him toward the door. "If it's important to you, it's important to me."

On the street, litters bustled around pedestrians in the afternoon sun. Anselmo joined the river of people.

"I'm sorry about your father," he said quietly. "He was a good man, always treated my mother and me with kindness."

Imelda took a long, shuddering breath and ignored the prickling in her eyes. "Grassie. But I'd rather not talk about it. Everything was in limbo for the last year, and I just want to remember how to live again."

He covered her hand, squeezing it gently. It was tempting, so tempting to lay her head against his shoulder, but it wasn't Carnevale yet. Social mores still held. Primo would undoubtedly hear about this, and he'd have plenty to say on the subject. In fact, she shouldn't even have her arm through his. With a reluctance that was almost painful, she pulled herself free.

He tensed even more, which seemed impossible. "I'm sorry, that was too forward."

"No, please don't apologize. I—" Her voice broke. Damn that they had to be in public. She spoke quieter. "I missed you. So much. But Primo."

"He's head of the family now that your father is dead."

"And you know how he is."

With a long inhale, Anselmo nodded. "He'd never approve. Which is why I have to go into the labyrinth." His tone lifted at the end, and he gave her a hopeful look.

Oh gods, she should tell him about her engagement. But she couldn't, not with that expression on his face. She'd seen it so many times before when he spoke about the labyrinth.

They crossed El Pónte Grando. Sunlight danced on the waters of El Canalasso, and boats slid across the surface. A rainbow of houses lined the canal, bold as spring in the brightness of the day. The chant of galley rowers below mixed with the cry of seagulls overhead.

The streets grew more and more crowded as they made their way across Centro. The air seemed to buzz, everyone chattering to their neighbor. People of the lower classes barely flinched as a cold gust whistled in from the south. Carnevale was coming, bringing the end of both the winter and the year. Servants carried armfuls of fabric for new dresses for their siore and new coats for their siori. A young man pushed a cart full of mask-making supplies—feathers, jewels, paint, and paper. He wore the embroidered vest of an apprentice mascarer. A lady's maid bumped into Imelda with a basket full of ribbons. She bobbed her head, murmured her apologies, and hurried away.

"I don't have any expectations, Imelda," Anselmo said slowly. His gaze anchored her. "I never have. Hopes, always. But you don't owe me anything." He stopped just before the piaza. "I'll be what you want me to be. A friend. Or something more. Or gone, if that's what you want. Because I shouldn't have done what I did. I should have written you, and let you write me. I was wrong."

He watched the street, his eyes tracking the bustle around them. Most people would say it was his military training, but Anselmo had always been that way. He saw the world different than others, saw it the way his mother had taught him, saw it in a way Imelda couldn't comprehend.

Even now, as his words hung between them, waiting for her reply, he watched. Perhaps especially now, while deep in thought. Some people chewed their lips while thinking, others cracked their knuckles. Anselmo watched and missed nothing.

"I was hurt when you ended things," she said, "but that all left as soon as I saw you in my house, home safe from war." The tension in his shoulders eased the tiniest bit. Arturo said he was inscrutable, but Imelda had always been able to read Anselmo. Seeing his relief made her long to put her hand on his cheek, to have him hold it against his face or kiss her palm. "I want more."

He exhaled, long and slow as if he'd been holding his breath, and smiled. It was such a rare sight since his mother died. His eyes brightened, as bright as the sun over the lagoon.

Her heart broke. She shouldn't want more, she shouldn't have told him she wanted more than she was free to give. But this might be the only time they would get, this beautiful afternoon and the week of Carnevale. Even if the wings failed and Primo married her off to the greedy king of Eraclea, she'd never regret the days she spent with Anselmo.

They reached the bustling piaza, filled side to side with people. The crowd gossiped and laughed, but all eyes focused on the palàso's portico. Admirals and politicians chatted in a group. Venezia stood apart from them, watching the crowd. In front of her sat a table with a large glass bowl brimming with slips of paper.

Primo walked out onto the portico, and everyone hushed. His silver crown shone like a blade in the bright sunshine. He welcomed the people and started droning on about the history of the labyrinth, what a great honor it was, and so forth. His voice struck Imelda's every nerve, and she did her best not to roll her eyes. Other soldiers dotted the crowd. Many had girls on their arm as well. Most wore the Captain's armband, though there were more than a few lowborn lieutenants like Anselmo. The highborn captains stood with chests puffed up like blowfish. Overcompensating idiots.

Primo finished speaking, and everyone clapped. Imelda slapped her hands together a few times.

Venezia stepped forward. "We have nineteen captains entering this year. Please come up when I call your name. Sior Rafael Galbani, Sior Luca Moretti, Sior Enzio Colombo, Sior Franco Pugliani, Merchant Massimo Garibaldi—"

Anselmo's hand tensed on his sword hilt. "Nineteen. They let *nineteen* ducks buy their way into the labyrinth. That leaves one slot for the rest of us, and we actually earned the right."

"Ducks?" Imelda asked.

"Lowborn slang for the rich. They have lots of ducats."

"Clever."

"I'm sure your set has less-than-kind names for the rest of us."

Imelda sniffed. "I wouldn't know."

Venezia moved to the bowl. Anselmo's name was in there somewhere. Imelda gripped his sleeve, queasy with worry.

"With so many captains, we only have one slot for lieutenants," Venezia said. "If I draw your name, come up. If the soldier isn't present to accept, they forfeit the opportunity. And a reminder to all candidates that you must secure a patron in order to enter the labyrinth. Best of luck."

Venezia buried her hand in the bowl and stirred the contents. Imelda went as still as Anselmo. So many slips of paper, so many people willing to risk their lives for a chance at glory. Was being a Lion really that great?

Dozens of names in that bowl. The odds of him getting chosen were slim. They'd announce someone else's name. Anselmo would be disappointed, but he'd get over it and then she wouldn't have to make herself sick with worry over the next month and—

"Lieutenant Anselmo Errari," Venezia announced.

"No," Imelda whispered.

The crowd cheered. She gripped the rough wool of his jacket, a plea for him not to go. Up to the portico, into the labyrinth. Deliver himself into Primo's power and the minotaurs' territory. Anselmo removed his arm from her grasp—gently, but there was a definite firmness in his calloused hands. This was what he wanted—more. And the only way to get it. But she still ached to see him walk away, his broad, tall frame blocking her view of her despicable cousin.

People quickly realized who he was and stepped aside. Soon he walked down a corridor of beaming faces, like a galley full of treasure floating down El Canalasso. Men clapped him on the back, and women called his name. None of them knew him. None of them cared about him. None of them would mourn if a minotaur gored him inside out.

On the portico, Venezia gave Imelda a sympathetic look. Primo followed Venezia's gaze and frowned when his and Imelda's eyes met. Imelda turned her attention away, but it was almost worse. The citizens continued to celebrate Anselmo. The people near Imelda congratulated her. Their cheers filled her ears, and she could see nothing but waving hands and Anselmo climbing the steps to salute Primo.

It was too much to bear. She escaped into the nearest alley as Primo started another speech. His voice echoed off the cobblestones and buildings. She leaned against a wall and remembered how to breathe. Damn men and their damn pride. Damn society and its damn rules. She and Anselmo would have a week of Carnevale, and then he'd enter the labyrinth. By the time he came out, her stupid fiancé would probably be here. A greedy king, someone rich and noble and, most importantly, useful to Primo. He didn't care about what she wanted or what would make her happy. Her heart didn't matter to Primo, and since he was in control, it didn't matter at all.

Primo finished his speech, and the crowd dispersed. A few people passed her in the alley, barely sparing a glance. Anselmo found her minutes later. He approached, silent and expectant.

She should send him on his way, save them both the pain. But she couldn't look away, and she couldn't bring herself to utter the words. Her heart did matter. It mattered so very much.

"Do you have to go in?" she asked.

"You know I do. It's the only way to gain the life my mother wanted for me."

"What about the life you want?"

He hesitated. There was so much buried in that pause. "That lies down the same path."

Of course he wanted to go into the labyrinth. He'd talked about becoming a Lion ever since they were little, but it had always been in the distant future. Yes, he just returned from war, but that was so far removed from Imelda. The labyrinth she understood. Its legacy hung over her family, the source of their wealth. Minotaurs that lusted after men's blood. Wild and dangerous beasts. Walls that moved, that could crush a man into dust.

A group of laughing men entered the alley. They recognized Anselmo and rained congratulations on him, casting curious glances at Imelda. Anselmo accepted their well wishes good-naturedly but with short replies. Eventually they got the hint and wandered off, leaving Imelda and him alone once again. But not truly alone, not with the palàso in view. Primo might still be out there, watching for her.

"We could run away." She grabbed his hand, gripped it tight. He needed to understand. "What if you don't come back to me?"

Anselmo watched her in patient silence, face covered in shadows. "I've been training my whole life for this."

"You say that, but anything could happen." She turned from La Piaza del Leon and its view of Palàso Dogal. "I should get home," she said, the words thick in her mouth.

He nodded, and they made the trek back to her house. His face was impassive. She'd crushed his hope, but she could restore it. She wanted to, needed to.

They reached the front door to Cax' Albizzi. Through the windows, she could see the trunks piled up and waiting for a cart to haul them to Palàso Dogal. No servants bustled in the hall; no doubt they were cleaning rooms and pulling curtains elsewhere. The sky had lost the light of the sun, and she still had to move into the palàso tonight. So much time wasted today. She wouldn't waste another moment.

She led him into the garden. Imelda took a deep breath, trying to gather all of her emotions from the last four years and quilt them into words. "Do you remember our first kiss?"

"We were so young." He chuckled. "I was so nervous." His hands moved as if to hold her shoulders again, as they had that night. But he lowered them, and she felt their absence.

"And I told you I'd been waiting for it for months."

A flock of geese flew overhead, their cries echoing off her home. Servants walked by, chatting about the lottery and complaining about their siori. The garden was private, but not private enough in these late winter days. The skeletal trees wouldn't hide them if a neighbor passed by, but she had to take a risk. She took his hands. They were rough from wielding a sword, but they'd always been rough. He'd worked his whole life to better his position in society, but all Imelda cared about was him. It didn't matter if he lived on Riga or Sordo, if he ran a shipping business or worked in the salterns. Her feelings for him would never change.

"And even though you were nervous," she said, "you said you had to try. And look what we had because of that—a wonderful year together before you left for Zorzi. Primo's taken control of the family. I don't know what the next month will bring, but I know I need to seize my chance to chase after what I want." She couldn't tell him about Primo's plan to marry her off. Not yet. After all, it was only that—a plan. She had one too, as did Anselmo. And as she'd said, anything could happen.

"Which is?" His voice was so quiet and hesitant it seemed impossible to come from a man of his stature. He cupped her face, and his thumb smoothed over her cheekbone.

"More." She closed the distance between them. "So much more."

He smiled. "I like the sound of that."

The temple bell gonged eight o'clock.

"Carnevale," she said. "Come back to me on the first night." She pressed a hand against his cheek, and he kissed her palm.

"Of course," he said.

Then she walked out of the garden alone and into her house, as if nothing had happened—in case Editta or another servant was waiting for her. Still, she couldn't resist the smile that pushed its way through. Six days until Carnevale. That's all she had to wait. And yet, she had to wait so long.

Chapter Eight

Imelda sat at her window, watching góndole and galleys floating on the canal far below. Cold rain spattered the window, and her breath fogged the glass. Her room at the palàso didn't have a nice view. The living quarters there all faced the street. This morning she'd awoken to the sight of servants on foot, nobles in seated litters going about their business, and the black monstrosity of the Senate hall nearly blocking out the sky. Just another thing to hate about moving into the palàso.

She'd spun all day the day before, until Arturo told her it was enough and that she needed to regain her strength. But she couldn't stay at the palàso, sitting around with nothing to distract her from the days left until she could see Anselmo again. Or from her engagement. So she'd returned to Cax' Albizzi for the day. The house was mostly empty, though a few servants were still there, readying the house for vacancy.

She turned her attention to the mask in her lap. It was for Arturo, even though he'd resist wearing it. A half-face mask, painted midnight blue and edged in crimson, it was inspired by Pàre's funeral—the dark blue of mourning, the red of the linen corincanto.

Imelda walked to her desk, which was littered with feathers, masks, and paint. Carnevale was only two days away—she needed to finish this mask. She had three others to make. She tapped the side. It needed something else. A silver design around the eyes, perhaps. Nothing too dainty, of course. Not that Arturo would notice.

Arturo walked in. "They're ready." He paused at sight of the mask and leaned over to study it. "Macabre," he said approvingly.

She hid the mask behind her back. Not because it was a surprise, but to keep him from getting distracted. "What are ready?"

"The wings, of course."

"Already? I thought it would be another two or three days."

Arturo grinned and pulled her to her feet. "I paid the seamstresses extra to stay late last night."

They hurried up to the dome on the roof. Two sets of wings leaned against opposite sides of the table. They were both large, though one set was considerably bigger. A patchwork of black leather covered the wooden frames, and red corincanto zigzagged through the leather.

Imelda set Arturo's Carnevale mask on his desk and knelt in front of the smaller pair of wings. "I thought we were using feathers."

"I skipped them for the sake of time."

Imelda sighed. "They're so ugly."

"Beauty doesn't equal utility."

"But I think it could. It seems like a good idea to try to mimic the real thing as much as possible."

"Bats fly without feathers."

She ran a hand across one wing. The leather had been patched together in any which way. That, combined with the red corincanto, created a visual mess. But he was right—they didn't have to be beautiful to fly. "What kind of bird is it again?"

"Albatross." Arturo grinned. "Have you watched one fly before? I've heard they can go months without touching land."

"There's no way that's true."

"It's in Promith's volumes on the natural world. He observed—"

"I believe you." She had to cut him off before he got started, or they'd never test the wings today. She turned around and started putting the harness on. Arturo came over to help. "You think it'll actually work?" she asked.

"Given the trajectory of our experiments so far, I'll be shocked if it doesn't. Cow leather wouldn't even flap. Chicken failed, likely because they barely fly when they're alive. We need a large bird that flies well. What better than albatross? I don't know how I ever missed the idea in the first place. A huge oversight on my part."

He wondered how he'd failed to consider an albatross, but really what he failed to see was the genius in the idea. Who else would consider albatross?

They finished strapping Imelda in, and he helped her stand. Which she could barely do, even with his help. She had to lean on him almost entirely to keep from falling back. The harness dug into her skin, and it was hard to breathe. This wasn't different than any of their previous designs, but it didn't make it less unpleasant. But once airborne, those issues would disappear.

Just like all her problems in life would disappear if these were successful. Venezia would pay them for the wings, and Imelda would be free. Free of Primo, free of the marriage, free to be with Anselmo.

Holy Mother Rea, please let these work.

Arturo helped her outside. A breeze blew but nothing happened. Imelda sighed.

"Wait," Arturo said. "Give it a moment."

The wind blew stronger, swirling Imelda's hair around her face. The wings started to flap. Imelda laughed as she lifted into the air. The ascent lasted for only a few seconds, then she hovered with the wings slowly beating.

"How high am I?" she asked.

Arturo pursed his lips as he studied the gap. "About a meter, I think. They're not strong enough." Disappointment lined the edge of his voice.

"That's twice as much as last time."

"But it's not real flight," he muttered.

A gust cut across the roof top, and the wings jerked into motion, racing her toward the edge of the house.

"Arturo!"

He jumped and grabbed her feet just before she flew out over the street. His weight brought her down, and she landed on top of him. The wings beat against the roof top for a moment, then stilled.

Imelda dragged herself off her brother. "Are you okay?" she began, then stopped.

Arturo was laughing. He stood then helped her to her feet, tears leaking from his eyes. "Now that is flight!"

"But you said they weren't strong enough."

He hugged her tight, even tried lifting her off her feet, which he couldn't do with the wings still attached to her. "And it's a good thing too, or you would've been lost to the wind."

"So they're going to work?"

"Yes!" He helped her out of the harness and together they carried the wings to the dome. "They do need to be stronger, so you'll need to spin more wool. But we'll clearly need a way to control them. I have an idea, but it'll take some time to implement. I'll hurry it as much as I can. Our deadline just got tighter."

"What?"

Arturo picked up his Carnevale mask, turned it this way and that to inspect it. "Primo talked to me before I came over here. He's found a wife for me. Kind of."

She took the mask and held it to her face. "Then the burial-themed mask is appropriate. You can wear it at your wedding. Who's the lucky girl?"

"Her name's Calixta."

Imelda snort-laughed. "The only Calixta I've heard of is that princess in Ilios, and no way you're engaged to her."

"Actually." Arturo retrieved his mask. "Her full name is Calixta Heraclius, Imperial Princess of Ilios and second in line for the throne. She's sailing here as we speak."

"Primo cancaro," Imelda muttered.

Arturo laughed. "Such language. I'd be shocked, if we hadn't learned it from our brothers."

"Why are you so calm? She'll be here in a matter of days, and the wings are far from ready."

"They're not as far as you think. Today was a huge success." He sat on his cot and scratched on his cheek. "But I don't know. I might want to marry her anyway."

"Arturo!" She sat next to him. "The whole point of the wings is to get away from Primo."

"Which is what this marriage will do. You think he'd hold any power over me once I'm a prince of Ilios?"

"The wings are also meant to get us out of these marriages."

"And this marriage might be the best thing to happen to me." He stood and started pacing, mask held behind his back. "I don't want to worry about investing the money Venezia gives us. I want to read and research and invent, not run a business. As long as this princess doesn't mind me doing that, it would be the ideal situation for me. I don't have anyone else like you have Anselmo." He stopped. "Plus, she's a famous beauty."

"Rumors always make people out to be more attractive than they are."

"Primo showed me a portrait."

"And portrait artists are liars."

"I don't care much about that anyway, as long as she's kind."

"I bet she's hideous and cruel."

He smirked. "I'll take that bet. One thousand ducats?"

"Three."

They kissed cheeks five times, then laughed. It felt good, though there was a tightness in Imelda's chest. This joke was one of Imelda's greatest nightmares. "But Ilios is so far. At least five hundred kilometers away."

"Almost a thousand, actually."

She clenched her teeth and resisted strangling him. How could he be so obtuse at a time like this?

"You and Anselmo can visit me," he said. "Or better yet, live in Ilios."

She toyed with her hair. "That's a lot to assume about Anselmo."

Arturo snorted. "Please. He would follow you anywhere."

She looked at the wings leaning against the wall. They were so close, and yet still so far. She scrubbed her face. "You said Primo has 'kind of' found a wife for you. What does that mean?"

"Apparently it's not completely settled. She has to agree to the marriage. That's why she's coming here."

"Must be nice to be in control of your own marriage."

"You do have control. Spin as much wool as you can the next two days. Without hurting yourself, of course. I'll do my part, and we'll perfect the wings. You'll be free to be with Anselmo, and if I marry Calixta, it'll be because it's my choice and not Primo's bidding." Wind rattled at the door and windows, and he shivered. "Plus it's warm in Ilios all year long."

Imelda wouldn't let Arturo's unexpected willingness to marry crush her hope. She couldn't. He was right, after all, about all of it. But it hurt that he would so easily consider moving so far away for a cushy life and pretty face.

But he didn't have anyone, and even though he'd never directly stated that he was disappointed he'd had no romantic relationships, she'd always suspected. She knew him too well to think otherwise. Why did it have to be someone from so far away though? Imelda would have to leave Venezia to stay close to Arturo. It was an easy choice, but not one she wanted to make.

Focus on the wings. Focus on getting out of this wedding to Ulisse Contarini. Focus on Anselmo. Focus on beating Primo at his own game. Focus on Arturo's happiness as well as her own.

The wings had been a simple dream for a while, but now they meant so much more.

And Imelda wanted more.

Chapter Nine

Raucous laughter filled the inn's common room as Venezia entered wearing a cloak with a deep hood. Carnevale was still days away, but the rich could afford to celebrate early, and only the very rich could afford this inn. A consort of viols performed lively music in the corner, and several patrons played nine-men's morris at a table, a stack of coins next to the board. Men would gamble on anything. A group of merchants haggled over the price of cinnamon, their squid ink spaghetti forgotten on their table.

Of course, Janus wasn't down here. No blood monk would associate with this kind of frivolity.

She climbed the stairs to the third floor and pounded on his door. His manservant—also wearing red robes—answered, and she pushed her way in. "You idiot. I told you to wait until I could talk to the Council members first."

Janus turned from the window, where he'd been glowering at the canal below. The infernal man still wore corincanto, still silk, always silk with this man. He'd been wearing it the first time they'd met, and she'd seen him in nothing else since. With that much magic, he should've had women fainting in the streets. But his constant sour expression managed to ruin the effect of the corincanto.

She sat. "I want to speak in private."

Janus frowned. "He's my most trusted man."

"I don't care."

"Go on," Janus said, and the man left.

"You were supposed to wait until after Carnevale," she said. "The Council will soon dismiss for the holiday and won't meet until after. No one will want to discuss politics with me during the week. And you laid all your cards on the table. I told you to be subtle."

"Subtlety is lying."

"You're terrible at politics. How do you expect to rule an empire?"

"There's more to power than manipulation."

She pressed a finger to her forehead. She should just be done with the man. He was too risky. But there was one question she had to ask first. "Did you at least visit Ulisse Contarini like I told you?"

He gave a curt nod. "I will have my throne back."

"How did you phrase your question?"

His expression darkened. "'Will I be emperor of Ilios?' I'm not an idiot."

Janus would be emperor, after all. What Ulisse said, while harnessing the soothsaying powers of sea silk corincanto, always came to pass. Primo was wrong—Janus would make a good tool for Venezia. She just had to figure out how to keep him in line. As long as she stayed close. That would be the tricky part. "Giore must favor you."

"Don't feign piety with me, siora."

That was rich, coming from a blood monk. A cult that flaunted their riches by wearing only corincanto; there was no holiness in that.

"I'm not even sure I should trust him," he said. "He charged me two million ducats."

Oh, Ulisse. He'd charged Janus much more than any other clients. That man never failed to make a spectacle. "Ulisse may have his faults, but he would never lie about the sea silk's prophecies. If he said you'll be emperor of Ilios, then it must be true."

"Which is a relief, since Primo nearly laughed at my terms. Fifteen million ducats wouldn't cover the cost of war."

Venezia had told him such a low amount so Primo would have no reason to accept Janus's offer. But she couldn't let Janus know that. "You're the one who changed the terms. What was that about submitting to the Iliano high priest?"

"What I said earlier today." His voice was strangely stiff. "Sacrestano's religion should be practiced the same all over the empire." He moved to the table and took a bottle of wine.

"Aren't you going to offer a glass?" Venezia said.

Janus's eyebrows creased. "Would you like some wine?" he asked tightly.

"No."

He huffed. As he poured himself a glass, his sleeve fell back, exposing his forearm. The tail end of red thread stitched into his dark skin caught the light from the candle. He noticed and yanked the fabric down. Venezia leapt from her chair and pinned him against the wall. She managed to grab his sleeve to reveal the stitch continuing up his arm. With a grunt, he pushed her off—much too strong for his stature—and she fell to the floor.

She jerked to her feet. "Is that what you blood monks are hiding—heresy?"

"It's only heresy to the ignorant."

"The holy book says—"

"'No son of Giore is he.'" He sneered. "Giore and Rea. I want to spit on their statues whenever I see them. Zitello was the original god, as practiced by Sacrestano's ancestors. Giore and Rea came later from some outside civilization, and then they replaced Zitello and condemned him as a silly trickster. All to persecute Zitello's followers because we were too strong. They killed many of us, but we never lost the faith."

"Blasphemy." She wanted no part in this. And yet, he'd suddenly proved himself to be a much stronger tool than she'd originally accounted for. Him, and all of his blood monk fools. "Show me your other arm."

He pushed the fabric all the way up. His skin on this side was the same.

Bile rose in her throat. It was a disgusting sight on its own, but the pain he would've endured to have all of that stitched in only added to her revulsion. "Your legs and torso too?"

He pushed his sleeves down without a word, but his silence was answer enough. It was bold—and risky—for blood monks to stitch into their skin directly rather than inserting it into their arteries.

Her hands had begun to sweat and her mouth had dried, faced with so much heresy. She could barely stand the sight of the man. And yet, she couldn't stop herself from asking. "Why?"

"How would you feel if you watched your grandfather's eyes and tongue cut out, watched your father killed, watched everything that belonged to your family taken away? What would you do to avenge those crimes?"

Start a war? Yes. Kill? She wanted to say no, but she'd never faced such a dire situation. But to blaspheme the holy father and mother? She wouldn't go that far. She'd never allow herself to.

"Is every member so defiled?"

"Hallowed." Janus looked at his arms as he smoothed his sleeves. "I have more than most."

Which meant he was one of the leaders. She already had a militia, but to add extra soldiers to her ranks. And not mere soldiers, but men and women with corincanto stitched all over their bodies, enhancing their strength. It could tip the scales, even against black bane.

Her thoughts shot to Tomaso Polani, the Lion captain she'd had executed a few days before. Technically Janus deserved the same treatment, but he would be an even better tool than she'd originally planned.

Still, her stomach writhed at the idea of working with such a blatant heretic.

"You could join us," he said. "You could be as powerful as any immortal, the way Zitello intended us to be." He pulled the fabric up to his shoulder. Red lines transversed his skin like veins. "We use corincanto the way it should be—to reach our full potential as mortals."

"I prefer to earn my strength the honorable way."

"Do you want to know why I added that bit about submitting to the Iliano high priest?"

She paused. "He's a member of your cult."

His face darkened at the word cult, but he nodded.

Her hand fell next to her thigh blade, and she tapped it lightly. What a disgusting thought, a man of the gods taking the side of these blasphemers. No one doubted blood monks were rich—who else could afford to wear only corincanto?—but their coffers were even deeper than expected. They had likely paid the high priest to join them.

Venezia had always heard that blood monks were zealous Iliano highborns who wore clothes of corincanto. What a clever front. No one took them seriously, and would continue not to until one day …

"Why not take the throne without war?" she asked.

His lip twitched. "There aren't enough of us."

She swung her gaze, quick as a dagger in the back, to his arms. He couldn't miss the derisive curl to her lip. "I can't imagine why."

"We take only the truly dedicated."

Venezia straightened her shoulders. She'd received her Spirit Stitch when she was eight, as all did. Over twenty years ago, and yet her skin remembered the push and pull of the needle digging through her skin. It had been worth it, to bind herself to the gods. But that had only been five stitches—two for each god, one for herself. These blood monks put themselves through much worse to prove themselves. Dedicated definitely described them, but so did reprehensible.

Janus went back to gazing out the window, arms crossed. The movement drew his sleeves back, revealing the threads once more, and they grabbed her attention like a shark grabbing its prey.

"Everyone in this disgraceful republic commits sacrilege every time they pray to those imposters, Giore and Rea," he said.

The man clearly put too much emphasis on his gifts from the corincanto, and not enough thought into ... well, everything else. To insult the city he was appealing to, the city she loved more than any-thing—she couldn't tolerate it. But she needed him. She needed his claim to the throne, and now she needed his cult. But she had to keep him in line. She approached him. They were the same height, but as she glared at him, he leaned back, despite his corincanto-enhanced strength. "If anyone in here believes in sacrilege, it's the dirty blood monk."

He sneered. "Get out."

"Gladly. I have to visit the temple, after all. The priests will be very interested in what I have to tell them. I think they can get over the schism long enough to relay the news to Ilios about your fellow heretics."

His eyes widened as she turned to go. He grabbed her arm, tight enough that it hurt, but fear painted his face, not anger. She had him.

"You need me," he croaked. "You're the one who approached me."

"Because I heard some fool wanted to take his grandpapa's throne back. But I can find some other ambitious noble to sponsor." Not without alerting her brother, and that was the problem. Janus wasn't wrong when he said she needed him. But she couldn't let him know that.

His mouth twitched, but all he could say was, "Please."

"Apologize."

"For what?"

"Insulting the gods."

His face darkened, though it did not mask the fear. "My sincerest apologies to the holy father, Giore, and holy mother, Rea. May they wrap my soul in the threads of their mercy." His voice was tight—almost as tight as his grasp on her arm, almost as tight as his desperation to stop her.

Lucky for him, his annoyingly-fake apology would suffice. "If we continue to work together, I have two conditions," she said. "First, do *exactly* as I say, or we'll never get what we want. Second, lose the arrogance. No one will work with us if you keep insulting everyone."

"You have my word, siora."

She looked at his arm. His sleeves covered the stitches at the moment. Were they only wool? There was one way to find out. She ripped her knife from the sheath on her hip and slashed the back of his hand. He jerked it away with a strangled cry. It was only a shallow cut, but already it had begun to heal. First, the bleeding tapered off. Then the skin began to knit itself back together.

"Wool *and* cotton," she said. "Your lot isn't completely clueless." More importantly, they weren't useless. Far from it, in fact.

She wiped her blade on his robe and sheathed it. "Remember, do exactly as I say and nothing else, or your name will be in the priest's ear faster than the wind."

His lip curled as he looked at his clothes, but he nodded. "What about the other Council members? You said they won't want to discuss politics during Carnevale."

"I've found out a new piece of information that will entice them." Arturo and Imelda's wings. The prospect was almost too good to be true. Declaring war on Ilios was close to insanity, but with the wings, they'd have a strong advantage.

"What is it?"

"You will find out in time." Unlike Janus, Venezia knew when and how to keep information close to the chest. "I take my leave, Your Majesty." She bowed mockingly, and he saw it for what it was. Rialtani didn't bow—that kind of debasement belonged only to antiquated monarchies.

She left, and the manservant scrambled back inside. She pulled her hood up as she walked down the stairs. She was right—he had no choice but to work with her. And she had no choice but to work with him. She could sail to Ilios to find some other power-hungry noble to sponsor, but it would take too long. Her informants there said all nobles were either happy with the Heraclius family or too intimidated by them to attempt a coup. She'd continue her partnership with Janus, despite his despicable, blasphemous beliefs. As disgusting as they were, they could prove useful. As long as she succeeded in starting the war—and became Doxe—it was worth it.

Chapter Ten

Ulisse Contarini would do anything for Eraclea. His beautiful home had one tradeable resource—sea silk corincanto, and a royal family with the secret knowledge of how to harness its soothsaying powers. Sure, his kingdom had a few other exports: luxury items like pearls, aquamarine, and blood oranges, but not in large enough amounts to bring real wealth. Nothing that paid like foreign royalty demanding to know the unknowable.

The kingdom supported their national industry, harvesting and processing the sea silk, and Ulisse spun it then sold its services as his forebears had done for centuries. People whispered behind Ulisse's back, calling him greedy, but he counted himself lucky. He had a way to keep his citizens safe.

Still, sometimes it would be nice to travel without being known as the King with the Sea Silk. Like today. No sooner had Ulisse walked off the galley, and some Rialtano nobleman had ambushed him—no doubt having received word of Ulisse's imminent arrival—and dragged him onto a góndola and to his caxa. Now Ulisse and his captain of the guard, Arrigo, stood in the nobleman's parlor, waiting for him to figure out how to perfectly word his question.

"Is my business partner—no, wait." The man glared at the floor, muttering under his breath. It was wise to be precise, but this was excessive.

Ulisse folded his arms. "I'll be in Rialto for a few weeks, if you'd like to wait."

"No, no, I need to know now." The man was stocky, well-dressed, and as pretentious as any Rialtano nobleman Ulisse had met. Made sense, if he had the money to afford Ulisse's services. "All right, I have it. How much again?"

Ulisse glanced in his notebook, where he'd taken notes on the man's income and money to be gained from the question to calculate the cost. "Five hundred thousand ducats."

"Giore cancaro." The man motioned to the page behind him. "You Contarini are a greedy lot."

A Rialtano nobleman calling *him* greedy. Ulisse pushed his jaw to the side but resisted a retort. His citizens could only remain tax free as long as he brought in business. So he endured the nasty reputation. "I also accept payments in kind. What's your business?"

"Spice trade."

"I'd take half a million's worth of saffron."

"I'll give you the ducats."

The page brought a contract over to Ulisse, detailing the transfer of money, to be initiated immediately. The girl would find a Council member to sign today, ensuring Sior—Ulisse glanced over the contract as he signed—Paolo Ruzzini didn't skip out on his financial obligation. With the document complete, the page ran off to finish the job. Sior Ruzzini toyed with the rings on his fingers as he mouthed the words to his question one last time.

Ulisse rolled up his sleeve. He'd worn a sea silk armband to Rialto—less conspicuous than the ceremonial stole he wore at home. Then he unsheathed the knife on his belt, cut his palm—and damn it all if it didn't hurt as much as the first time he'd done it. He flipped the blade and offered the handle to the nobleman.

Sior Ruzzini grimaced as he took it. "This is distasteful."

"It's how it's done."

"What's to stop someone from stabbing you and stealing your sea silk?"

"Is that a threat?"

The nobleman drew himself up, but Ulisse continued before Ruzzini could claim to be above threats, or some similar nonsense. "The sword at my side isn't a decoration. He isn't either." He jerked his head toward his captain of the guard, Arrigo, standing in the corner. The man wore his polished cuirass, leather pteruges skirt, sword, and a menacing expression.

Sior Ruzzini *hmph*ed. He finally sliced himself, and they clasped hands. "Is my business partner Franco Gritti embezzling our company's funds?"

Blood seeped out from between their fingers and dripped on the fine Shantzese carpet. The nobleman's gaze followed the droplets to the floor, and his grip tightened, though he didn't let go.

Ulisse's skin tingled, and the world grew fuzzy. A moment passed until the impressions came. Vague images floated around the nobleman. Money hidden under a rock. A contract ripped in half. A sinking galley. Ulisse also heard whisperings in his ear, no words he could understand but the voices were more than suspicious. The answer was clear.

Harvesting, processing, and spinning sea silk were valuable, but this was where the money truly came from. Only Ulisse's family could see the images clearly. Only his family could interpret them. And true, they didn't always interpret them correctly. Ulisse had bungled more than one in his youth, but he'd grown more proficient with time and practice.

He came back to himself, his mind returning to its normal buzz as the images faded. "He most certainly is." Sior Ruzzini's expression darkened. He looked ready to murder this Franco Gritti. Ulisse patted the man's shoulder with his clean hand. "Good luck."

The nobleman pulled a kerchief out of his doublet pocket and wrapped it around his palm. "Shall I call a litter for you?"

"Oh gods no," Ulisse said. "My feet are good enough." A horse would be preferable, but they didn't have any in the city.

"As you wish." Sior Ruzzini managed a stiff, jerky bow as he muttered, "Your Majesty."

Ulisse chuckled as he left the man's house. Rialtani were so bad with royalty—actual royalty, not their elected Doxe. It didn't offend Ulisse in the least. In fact, he enjoyed the spectacle whenever he visited. Bowing and scraping were instinctive all over the Muriseano, but the people of Rialto didn't know what to do with it. It was like making a cat swim.

Outside, it was chilly and cloudy. The last remains of winter. The weather had started to turn in Eraclea, with a warm breeze that blew off the Muriseano. Ulisse liked Rialto, but he tried not to visit in the winter. He'd been planning on coming down to meet Imelda Albizzi after Carnevale and would still be home if Primo hadn't sent a hemp message two nights ago insisting Ulisse come early. So Ulisse had hopped on a ship yesterday morning and sailed south.

Arrigo eyed the crowded street. "Perhaps we should take a góndola across the canal, Your Majesty."

Ulisse started walking in the direction of the bridge. "No one's going to try anything here. And it's a five-minute walk, maybe ten. We'll be there before you know it."

Even with the crowd, Ulisse was right. Less than ten minutes later, he and Arrigo stood at the official entrance to the palàso. Arrigo knocked, then some stuffy old steward answered and led them to Primo's parlor that also served as his office. Rialtani were too practical at times. This huge palàso, and they combined the Doxe's two most important rooms into one.

The room was empty. Arrigo took a post in the corner, and Ulisse walked over to the sideboard which was covered in wine bottles.

Behind him, he heard the door open. He'd just narrowed in on a bottle of red wine from the Frenza region. "Primo, you haven't lost your touch."

"I think he's got a bit of a problem, personally," a woman said.

Ulisse turned. Venezia stood at the doorway. She nodded at Arrigo. "Hello, Arrigo."

Arrigo deeply inclined his head. "Hello, Fleet Admiral."

"Venezia Dandolo." Ulisse grinned. "Rialto's secret weapon. I heard you showed the Zorziani what happens when they try to mess with Rialto."

Venezia closed the door and approached him to kiss cheeks. "They learned their lesson."

Ulisse nodded at the sideboard. "Primo drinks too much?"

"He drinks one, maybe two glasses a day. No, he buys too much."

"And we benefit." He picked up the bottle of the Frenza red. "Think he'll mind?"

She smiled mischievously. "He'll hate it, and you know it."

"Exactly." Ulisse poured a glass and offered it to Venezia. She accepted it, and he poured a glass for himself. He set the bottle down, then held up his glass. "Shall we toast?"

"You're in a good mood."

"I'm in Rialto for Carnevale with some of my oldest friends."

"And you're soon to be married."

"Oh, yes. That too."

She tipped her head to the side, her look surprised yet amused. "Don't tell me you're nervous."

"And what if I am?"

She paused, tapping her finger on her glass. "I'll be honest, Imelda has been . . . reticent about getting married. But once she meets you, she'll see things in a new light. You're too delightful for her not to like you."

"You're patronizing me."

"Not at all. Besides." She clinked her glass to his. "I don't believe a man who swims with sharks is afraid of marriage."

"A shark is either hungry or he's not. A woman, on the other hand. Unpredictable."

She didn't answer, only raised her eyebrows as she sipped at her wine. It had been so long since he'd last seen her. Had it been since his wife Marina's funeral? He'd been too grieved to fully attend to the guests, and the years since had been a blur of routine life. However long had passed since he and Venezia had spoken, they'd been nothing but kind to Venezia.

He grinned, then took a long draught of the wine. It was perfection, robust and dry with a hint of vanilla. "To think, we'll be cousins in a few weeks when once I dreamt of making you my wife."

"A futile dream."

"One you dreamt as well, if I remember correctly."

"Even though we both understood the impossibility."

Eraclea law stated every member of the royal family must marry others with the gift to spin corincanto so their children would inherit the talent as well. Ulisse hadn't minded that restriction until he fell in love with Venezia, a girl without the ability. He'd abolish the law, but that would be foolish. Not to mention selfish.

"It was a long time ago," she said.

He laughed. "Are you calling me old, Fleet Admiral?"

"If I were, I'd be calling myself old as well."

"That would be a crime."

She cut him a sly look. "See? You haven't lost your charm."

Primo walked in. "Ulisse, glad to see you arrived safely." He looked at their glasses, then the open bottle of wine. "I see you helped yourselves to refreshment."

Venezia set her glass down and kissed Ulisse's cheeks. "See you soon."

After Ulisse had met his future wife. He downed the rest of his wine as Venezia slipped out.

Primo pursed his lips, then poured himself a glass from the open wine bottle. "Are you ready to meet Imelda?"

"Doesn't seem to matter if I am or not. Why did you have me come early?"

Primo took a drink. "I thought it best for you two to spend Carnevale together. That way you get over a week before the wedding to acquaint yourselves, rather than a few days."

"Yes, more time for her to regret her decision." Ulisse finished off his glass and refilled it. Two glasses would be perfect, just enough to relax him before meeting his future spouse. He resisted a sigh. He still wasn't sure how he'd let Primo talk him into marrying again, especially a stranger. But here he was, and he wouldn't back down now. After all, Venezia hadn't been wrong when she said he swam with sharks.

Though truth be told, at that moment he'd preferred the company of a shark to the prospect of a reluctant bride. But perhaps he could win Imelda over with his supposed charm. It had worked on Venezia years ago. There was a chance it would work now.

Chapter Eleven

Imelda stood in front of her mirror, turning this way and that to admire her new dress. White with a shockingly deep V, silk corincanto in a small meandros design circling the high waist, and a small train trailing behind. She needed to change for dinner, but the dress had just been delivered. A new outfit for Carnevale. She couldn't wait to wear it in public, but even more, she couldn't wait for Anselmo to see her in it.

She was swishing the skirt back and forth when someone knocked on the door.

"Come in," Imelda said in a sing-song voice.

Editta entered and smiled. "What a lovely new dress. It's perfect!"

"Isn't it?" Imelda twirled once, then faced Editta. "I know. I need to change for dinner."

Editta tightened the side ties on Imelda's dress. "No, mè siora, this dress is perfect for tonight."

"This is for Carnevale. It's far too fancy for dinner."

Editta laughed as she combed her fingers through Imelda's hair. "Has the Doxe not sent you a message? Your betrothal is tonight."

Imelda stepped out of Editta's reach. "My what?" Her shrill voice rose to the high ceiling above.

"King Ulisse Contarini has arrived." Editta tilted her head ever so slightly. "I believe the Doxe asked him to come early. Now let me fix your hair."

No, no, no. Dread weighed Imelda's body down. She could do nothing to stop Editta from pulling her hair over one shoulder and arranging it just so.

She smiled at Imelda in the mirror. "It's okay to be nervous."

"I'm not—I'm not—"

"You don't need to admit it to me. Here, I'll help you."

Editta put her arm around Imelda's back and led her through the halls. Imelda dragged her heavy feet as reality added extra weight.

Betrothed? Betrothed?! Engagement was one thing, with a fiancé hundreds of kilometers away. But officially betrothed before the gods to a king, who was here during Carnevale, the one week Imelda had to work on the wings and spend time with Anselmo. How would she escape to see him? They'd need an escort with them at all times.

They reached the dining room. The doors were closed, and four guards waited outside. Two soldiers were Rialtano, but the others wore unfamiliar armor. They had the same olive skin and dark hair as Rialtani, which meant they were from the Venetano peninsula as well.

Ulisse's guards.

Imelda froze.

Editta gently pushed Imelda. "They're expecting you, mè siora."

Imelda held her ground. "No, please. I need a moment. Just a moment."

"As you wish. I'll tell them you're still coming down."

Editta went inside. Imelda paced, ignoring the guards. She'd come up with a plan. Somehow. Arturo would help. He could be their escort. Maybe she and Anselmo could find a way to be alone. At least once. Gods above, how she needed more than just one visit with him though.

Editta appeared moments later, holding the door open. "It's time, mè siora."

Imelda took a deep breath, wiped her palms on her dress, and stepped inside. She'd expected everyone else to be here, but at the moment, only Primo and one other man stood by the large windows of the dining hall, talking quietly. She slowly walked forward.

"Here she is," Primo said, holding his arm out.

Imelda's fiancé—and soon to be betrothed—turned.

Shock stilled her tongue. She'd anticipated someone like Primo, cold and formal. But Ulisse was neither of those things. He lounged more than stood. His fine clothes and gold circlet were immaculate, yet seemed like an afterthought—something in the way his hair was a bit ruffled and his beard lacked the sharp, precise lines Rialto men preferred. His eyes were bright, his olive skin tanned from the sun, and his smile easy. Behind him stood a large guard wearing a plumed helmet and serious expression.

"Siora Albizzi," Ulisse said with a deep bow of his head, "you are even lovelier than the portrait Primo sent me. That is a rare treat."

"I told you," Primo said.

"I don't believe anything I don't see with my own eyes. You know that."

She accepted his cheek kisses with bewilderment. Such a man was friends with Primo? She'd only seen her cousin with uptight politicians.

"Thank you, Your Majesty," she managed to say. "I—I ..." She floundered as surely as a fish dropped to the deck of a boat.

"And I've rendered you speechless with my good looks, I see." He laughed. "Call me Ulisse. I'm only king because I'm a lucky bastard. Come, sit."

He led her to the dining table and pulled out a chair for her. Imelda looked back at Primo, who had a decidedly smug twist to his lips.

"Lucky?" she asked.

"Born to the right parents," Ulisse said. "All of us are. That's the only thing separating us from the poor wretches in the gutter."

"Where's—" She swallowed, her throat dry as wool roving. "Where's everyone else?"

"I thought it best to let you two meet before starting the ceremony," Primo said. But he'd had no problem completely surprising her with her own betrothal. "I'll wait for the guests outside."

Primo walked out, then Ulisse turned to his guard. "Arrigo, give us some privacy please."

The guard bowed and left.

"I brought you a gift." Ulisse retrieved a velvet sack from his pocket and held it out to her. It was far heavier than it appeared. She pulled out a necklace with a large, pale blue stone surrounded by diamonds. It twinkled in the candlelight, brighter than a star.

"It's aquamarine," Ulisse said. "May I?"

She gave it to him then leaned forward so he could slip the necklace over her head.

"It's lovely," she said.

Lovely and heavy, a weight that pressed against her chest. It had clearly cost a lot of money, money he'd earned selling services like a common merchant. Even Imelda could tell that much. He was obviously trying to impress Primo. True, her cousin wasn't there, but he'd see the necklace in a few minutes. Ulisse was a lackey and a sycophant, and this nice guy routine was clearly a ruse. Primo couldn't be friends with such a man as this king pretended to be.

She'd have to play along. To be able to get away, she'd have to earn his trust. Maybe she'd even let him see the wings, and his greed would let her keep working on them. She'd ask Arturo for his opinion.

But play along, she must.

She forced a smile. It didn't have to be genuine—surely he'd understand her anxiety.

"I'm so glad you like it," he said. "It reminds me of the winter sea at Eraclea. It glistens as the waves do, and the sunlight dances on the water just as the diamonds catch the light. The ancient Sacrestano nobility vacationed on our beaches. The coastline is peppered with their ruins. They called it the Jewel of the Muriseano. I know you'll fall in love with it." He reached toward her, hesitated, then took her hand in his. They weren't as smooth as a king's hands should be. He performed some kind of labor, in addition to shilling himself out.

"I know this is a frightening prospect for you." His voice dropped. "Nothing I say will change that in the next few weeks. But if there's anything you need from me, anything at all, just ask. Your happiness is my only priority."

How about cancelling this wedding? If only she could be so forthright. If only she could dictate her own future in such a way. "Tell me about the sea silk corincanto."

"I'll teach you how to harvest it, if you like. We can take diving trips together."

"I could hire a boat when you're busy."

His hands slipped on hers. "I'd enjoy it more if we went together." His smile returned, not as grand as before. "It would be an excellent opportunity to get to know each other."

The doors opened. Primo, Donatella, their children, Venezia, her husband, Arturo, Ulisse's guard, and the high priest entered. It really was a betrothal. Imelda closed her eyes. She'd stain her soul by being with Anselmo while betrothed to another man. She cared about it, yes, but she cared about Anselmo more.

"It'll be fine," Ulisse whispered. When she opened her eyes, he had a small smile on his lips.

"Of course." Her voice cracked. He helped her stand, then led her to the window where the high priest stood. The others gathered around.

The high priest beamed. He held a large loop of corincanto. "What a joyous occasion to gather together tonight. The gods are pleased with your decision to elevate your engagement to a most holy betrothal, their joy second only to the joy of your upcoming marriage. Your Majesty, please take Siora Albizzi by the hands."

Ulisse did so and smoothed his thumbs over her fingers, seemingly as a comforting gesture. It took everything Imelda had not to pull herself free, though his grip was not tight.

"Betrothal is a sacred union, a declaration of two individuals to honor each other from this point on. Once we place the spirit rose yoke upon you, you promise to remain faithful in deed and in thought to each other until you die. If one of you transgresses this law, you will be held accountable for your sin at your judgment after you pass from this life. If you do not wish to proceed, now is the time to let it be known. King Contarini? Do you swear total fidelity to Imelda Albizzi?"

Ulisse's hands twitched slightly. "I do." He kissed her cheeks six times. The betrothal kiss. Two for each god, one for Ulisse, one for Imelda. The only kiss more powerful was the wedding kiss—eight kisses.

"And you, Siora Albizzi? Do you swear total fidelity to Ulisse Contarini?"

This was supposed to be Anselmo standing across from her. They were meant to promise their lives to each other.

Play along. Play along.

Her breath hitched as she forced a nod. "I do." She stood on her toes to kiss his cheeks. She'd never thought she'd kiss someone's cheek six times. It was hard to push herself past the normal two kisses of a typical greeting. She lost her balance on the fourth kiss, causing her to take a step back.

"I'm sorry, I'm sorry," she rushed to say.

"It's okay." Ulisse squeezed her hands. "I should've held on tighter." She felt herself blush.

The high priest cleared his throat. "Siora, you must start again."

"Oh yes, of course." This time she kissed his cheeks quickly, nearly dizzying herself as she moved from cheek to cheek.

"Wonderful." The high priest gave one side of the corincanto to Ulisse, who placed it over Imelda's head. The high priest twisted the loop once then gave the other side to Imelda. With shaking hands, she reached up to drape it over Ulisse's head.

"Spirit rose corincanto," the high priest said, "in the figure eight symbol of infinity seals this betrothal for this life and beyond. Congratulations."

Donatella hugged Imelda and kissed her cheeks. Primo kissed cheeks with Ulisse. Everyone was happy, everyone except Imelda. She forced back tears that welled in her eyes as they led her to the table, to dine next to her betrothed, wearing a dress she'd intended for a night with Anselmo. The thin spirit rose corincanto lay heavy across her shoulders, binding her to Ulisse and pulling her away from Anselmo.

Chapter Twelve

Venezia marched up to Lazaro's room. His door was closed, and suggestive sounds leaked out from underneath. In the middle of the afternoon. The man had no shame. Any time spent with another woman was less time with Venezia, but he needn't be so contemptible about it.

Venezia put her hand on the doorknob as Kari whispered, "Please." It wasn't in a sensual way. Venezia's breath hitched. The man had neither shame nor compassion.

She threw open the door and marched in. Kari squeaked as she scrambled to cover herself. Such pale, pale skin. Almost translucent. She had a series of tattoos on her right upper arm, three columns of runes of the Southern clans. Bruises ringed her wrists and dotted her arms—Venezia had come in at the right time. Lazaro didn't move except to pull his arms behind his head.

"Yes, mè amor?"

Venezia found a pair of pants on the floor and tossed them at him. "The election is in a month."

"I heard."

"And you didn't tell me?"

"I only found out this morning, while you were meeting with the admirals on Gara. I didn't realize you'd arrived home. I've been busy."

She jerked her head in Kari's direction. "Get her out of here."

Lazaro sighed and glanced at Kari, who cowered behind the blanket. "Go on."

She scrambled out of bed while trying desperately to keep the blanket wrapped around her body, then searched for her dress. Venezia pointed behind the chair. Kari gathered her clothes and made for the door.

"That blanket is merino wool," Venezia said. "Imported from the other side of the Muriseano. You will not drag it down the servants' staircase."

Kari froze, then attempted to dress while still holding the blanket up.

Venezia advanced. "Did you hear my husband? Out."

The girl went still again as Venezia came closer. Finally, she dropped the blanket and ran out, naked as a fish and mumbling apologies. Venezia closed the door with a satisfied smile. She couldn't stop Lazaro from buying slaves, or doing what he wanted with them, but she could intervene at times. As long as he didn't suspect.

"Why do you taunt them?" Lazaro still lay in bed, pants crumpled on his lap where they'd landed.

"Why do you insist on bringing them into my home?"

"I have to find *some* way to fill my needs." He gave her a pointed look. "It's better than the brothel."

True. Who knew what kind of diseases ran rampant on Sordo. But she wouldn't give him the satisfaction of agreeing with him.

She snatched his shirt off the chair and twisted it as she paced. "They scheduled the election early because Primo knows I'm going to run against him. There's no way this was some chance decision by the Council. Enrico Lando must be in the middle of it all."

"Moving the election is a bold move," Lazaro said, still infuriatingly naked.

"I won't let Primo throw me off balance." If he thought this move would, he was underestimating her. "It gets worse. He knows I'm going to sponsor Janus. I don't know how he found out, but I'll discover who told him."

"How did you learn about the election, mè amor?"

She stopped pacing and glared at him. "My eyes-and-ears."

"Who are?"

"Oh no, dear husband, you won't trick me."

Lazaro might be her greatest political ally—as depressing as that was—but even he couldn't know who they were. Beniamino, who had delivered this news, was proving to be the most valuable of all her sources. It had been a gamble to approach Primo's secretary about spying, but it had paid off. Once she was Doxe, she would immediately give Beniamino what she'd promised, what his family had been desiring for years—elevation to the nobility.

Primo had as many eyes-and-ears as anyone, if not more. As well he should, as the Doxe. But she'd ensured no one had followed her when she visited Janus. She'd worn a cloaked hood to hide her face from the inn's patrons. How, in Rea's holy name, had he learned two of her closest secrets?

"How is your alliance with Fia?" Lazaro asked.

"Strong. She voted with me on the lottery." She rolled her eyes. How it galled her to admit he'd given her good advice. "You were right about working with her."

"Of course I was. Which is why you need to keep listening to me."

"Then get out of that damned bed. The Iliani are on their way, and I somehow have to get the Council members to discuss politics during Carnevale."

"Iliani?"

"Heir-Apparent Nikkoforos Heraclius and his sister Calixta." She rubbed her temple. "We need to plan our strategy for the dinner tomorrow night. Now get dressed."

Lazaro pulled himself to the edge of the bed and grunted as he put his pants on. Venezia tossed his shirt over and sat at the desk. She bobbed her foot as he finished dressing. The hair on his back and chest had long ago turned white, but it had been four years since she'd seen it. His stomach puffed out, but the skin hung off his once-muscular arms.

He was taking so long to die. He'd seemed ancient when they got married. She'd been naive, thinking he would live long enough to help her become Doxe and die promptly after. Thirteen years later, Lazaro was still alive, and she still didn't have the sash and crown.

It's not that she'd expected to do the Heart Stitch with him—she'd never anticipated such a rare kind of love—but she'd hoped for some measure of happiness. Not the thirteen years of discontent—and worse—that defined their relationship. She was no stranger to disappointment, but this failed marriage hurt the most. Perhaps because this was the only disappointment she'd had an active part in.

Her fingers drifted to her stomach before she realized it. She quickly shifted her posture and kneaded her temple. "I should've just written Janus."

Lazaro stood and adjusted his pants. "Primo still would've heard about it." He pulled the other chair over, sat, and took her hand in his. "You should wait until the next election, mè amor. You're not ready. Not for an election so soon."

"You say that every time." She ripped free of his grasp and stood to pace once more. "You will help me, Lazaro. Or shall I sell your new plaything?"

He scowled. "What? Will you finally resume your wifely duties?"

She'd never fulfilled them—he'd forced them every time for eight years. But not since she'd tired of that and learned to fight back. She pressed her palm against the knife strapped to her thigh. Never again. "You can haul yourself down to Sordo to satisfy your needs for all I care."

He stood and blocked her path. Even with his stooped back, he had a few inches on her. As he loomed, her heart became nineteen years old again, timid and trembling.

"You agreed to this marriage," he growled. "Agreed to be my wife and everything it entailed."

She couldn't let him see her fear. Confidence was key, even when she didn't feel it. That's how she won battles. That's how she'd win this battle. She stood her ground. "And you promised to help me win the sash and crown."

He glowered, his dark eyes sharp. "I wish I'd known what a gnat you'd turn out to be. I would've found a young bride with a more suitable temperament."

Loathsome man. How had she ever agreed to marry him? If only she'd seen him for the lionfish he was. The very marrow of her bones screamed to run, but she smiled and stroked his cheek. "Yes, my dear, but you would've been bored to tears with a pretty, dumb thing. How many months did you keep the last one around? How long until you tire of Kari? The past thirteen years have been anything but dull."

His glare continued a moment longer, then he shook his head. "How right you are." He even chuckled as he offered his arm. "Fine. Let's plot your rise to power. You can't do it without me, after all."

He was right. So utterly, disgustingly right. She knew military strategy, but he'd centered his life around political maneuvering. She swallowed a sigh as she accepted his arm and allowed him to escort her down to the office.

Chapter Thirteen

The opulent dining hall finally began to fill as dignitaries streamed in. Rialtani arrived on time for temple services, boat launches, and nothing else. The Doxe himself would arrive fashionably late. Anselmo should've realized. He'd been so eager to find a patron, he'd arrived right at eight. For fifteen minutes, he was the only one here. Even then the room remained sparse for another quarter-hour.

People chatted and laughed in the dark, wood-paneled room, and servants wove between them with silver trays piled with wine and appetizers. Their fine clothes rustled, and their jewels sparkled. The candles alone cost a small fortune. This was a life worth living. This was Imelda's world. She viewed Anselmo as her peer, but he wasn't. Not yet.

Even within this society, there were levels. The merchants weren't the equals of the nobility. They brown-nosed the haughty noblemen and women, even though some of their clothes were finer and their pockets deeper. But a few families rose above the rest the way Palàso Dogal rose above the city. The Albizzis belonged to that highest tier. Their family ran the labyrinth, and the government paid well for its elite training grounds.

Anselmo skirted the edge of the party. When he'd arrived, a page—obviously surprised by Anselmo's punctuality—had met him at the door with instructions to mingle. The woman had smirked at him as he stared at the empty room. But now it was full, and Anselmo still hadn't spoken to a soul. How could he mingle with the wealthy elite? Men and women drank and celebrated Rialto's victory over the rebellious vassal city, Zorzi. A victory they had no part in, yet they would profit just the same.

The rich people regarded him as if they knew his humble beginnings. They glanced in his direction, but their gaze slid away as if bored. A lowly lieutenant, nothing more. The other Lion candidates were all nobles or wealthy merchants. None of them first borns, who inherited the right to take over the family business. So their parents had paid for their chance to enter the labyrinth. The candidates lounged at a table together, laughing and drinking. No need to mingle. No need to introduce themselves to potential patrons. They already knew everyone here.

They might have the advantage tonight, but that would all change in a couple weeks. The rings on their fingers glittered in the candlelight, but Anselmo would outshine all of it once the doors of the labyrinth slid shut behind them.

Of course, Anselmo wouldn't be able to enter the labyrinth if he didn't get a patron tonight.

Doxe Albizzi stood on the far side of the room, greeting the party-goers with a nod. The people around him must be the richest and most influential. Anselmo should start with them. He took a breath and smoothed the front of his doublet. It—and his shirt—were almost too tight. He'd left it in Rialto while in Zorzi, and there hadn't been any that fit him at the tailor's that morning. But the velvet was still in good condition. He'd been planning on wearing it on the first night of Carnevale with Imelda. She'd probably appreciate the snug fit.

He needed to focus. Through the crowd was the quickest way to the Doxe. He started across, but a hand on his arm forestalled him.

"Lieutenant Anselmo Errari," Fleet Admiral Venezia Dandolo said when he turned. She didn't wear her military uniform, which was jarring since he was only used to seeing her in a professional capacity. But her dress was still in the colors of the military—gray-blue with bright blue embroidery along the hems. "I was hoping to find you tonight."

Anselmo saluted her, arm across the chest. "Fleet Admiral."

She smiled. "You're friends with Imelda and Arturo, correct?"

"Yes, Fleet Admiral. I'm surprised you remembered."

"You're rather unforgettable." She waved down a servant and retrieved two glasses of wine. "The wine is excellent. Primo selected it himself, as always. You should enjoy yourself tonight."

"I need to find a patron, Fleet Admiral."

"They'll be more likely to accept you if you relax." She nodded at the people around them, then gestured at his drink. He sipped the wine to comply. She tapped her finger on her glass. "I spoke with your mother a few times. She was a unique woman. Very determined. And ambitious, in her own way."

Where was she going with this? But there was no hint of derision in her voice or demeanor. "She was a fighter," he said.

"I could tell. She seemed willing to do anything for you."

Anselmo hesitated. Yes, his mother had sacrificed much for him. Her soul even, if the priests were to be believed. She'd trained Anselmo without mercy, but it had forged him into the man he was today. "She loved me very much."

"It shows." She set their glasses on a passing servant's tray. He'd only drunk half of his, and she'd barely touched hers. The waiter would dump the undoubtedly expensive wine into the canal at the end of the night. "Come. No one will sponsor you if they can't meet you."

She led him into the thick of the party. Now people began to pay attention, though not in any obvious way. Out of the corners of their eyes. Over someone's shoulder. The Fleet Admiral was favoring a lieutenant. Clearly information they could use. Weaponize, even, in the right situation. Who knew a fancy dinner could feel like battle? Rules existed, and Anselmo would have to learn them once he joined the upper ranks.

The Fleet Admiral headed for a group of stuffy old men. One woman, busty and expensively dressed, stood with them.

"Council members," Admiral Dandolo said quietly to Anselmo. "Let me speak for you. All these fools do is talk. Your silence will unnerve them—they won't be able to forget you." They reached the politicians. "Good evening, siori. Siora Pesaro," she said to the woman. Anselmo gave a deep nod to the group. "I'd like to introduce you all to Lieutenant Anselmo Errari."

"Lieutenant, eh?" one of the old men said around a mouthful of cheese. "You must be a Lion candidate."

Admiral Dandolo put a hand on Anselmo's arm. "He is, Sior Cancio. I heard Lieutenant Errari's name several times while in Zorzi. He played an important role in our victory."

That was an overstatement, but Anselmo didn't interrupt. Clearly she was maneuvering. For him, it was clear—she was helping his future success. But for herself, he couldn't guess what.

She nodded at the group. "If you'll excuse me, the lieutenant has many others to meet and dinner is almost upon us."

Admiral Dandolo steered Anselmo away. They angled toward the two admirals of the military. One wore the gray-blue of the armada, while the other sported Lion blue. Both boasted several lines of rank on the shoulders of their doublets.

"I hate politicians," she said, "but unfortunately they're necessary. I'd rather deal with a soldier any day. Men of direct action, like yourself. Men like Admirals Cattaneo and Galbani." Her voice rose at the names, so the men turned to greet them. Anselmo saluted as she introduced them. "Galbani is over the Lions."

"You're the lieutenant who fought off that ambush in the forest outside Zorzi," Galbani said. He wore a tightly groomed beard and barely touched his wine.

Anselmo glanced at Admiral Dandolo, who nodded for him to speak. "Yes, sir," he said.

"What were the numbers?" Galbani asked.

"I don't remember exactly, sir."

"Don't be modest," Admiral Dandolo said. "One hundred rebels to fifty men. Their captain was killed, and Lieutenant Errari took control immediately."

"A natural leader," Galbani said. "You'll do well as a Lion."

"We'll feel your absence from the armada," Admiral Cattaneo said. He stood nearly as tall as Anselmo, with the crisp posture of a lifelong soldier. "You're stealing twenty of our best yet again, Galbani."

"It's my job." Galbani sipped his wine. "My son, Rafael, is entering the labyrinth with you." He gestured at the table where the Lion candidates sat. One man watched them with a curious expression on his face. Obviously the son, evident by the broad stature and square jaw he inherited from Galbani.

Admiral Dandolo's gaze tracked something in the crowd. "The Doxe will speak to the trainees soon, and Lieutenant Errari needs time to meet his fellow Lion candidates."

"Good luck finding a patron tonight," Galbani said. "I'd hate to see you lose your chance at the labyrinth."

Anselmo saluted once more before Admiral Dandolo led him away. They reached the edge of the crowd. The Doxe spoke with a short man who bore a mustache like his along with an unpleasant expression. Admiral Dandolo watched her brother before turning her attention back to Anselmo. "I was pleased when I drew your name this week. Imelda has always spoken well of you. And I meant what I said earlier. Your name was everywhere at Zorzi. Stick with me, and you'll go far. I would sponsor you if I could."

"Thank you, Fleet Admiral."

"Good luck in the labyrinth."

"Venezia." A man emerged from the crowd and kissed cheeks with the Fleet Admiral. He wore a gold crown and an open green jacket. His clothes were every bit as fine as everyone else's, but his casual appearance was jarring against the stiffness of the other partygoers.

Admiral Dandolo smiled. "Ulisse." She turned to Anselmo. "You two should meet. Lieutenant Errari, this is His Majesty, King Ulisse Contarini of Eraclea. Ulisse, this is Lieutenant Anselmo Errari. He's a Lion candidate."

Ulisse's smile was as genuine as the crystal goblets being passed around the room. "I don't know whether to congratulate or console you."

"Perhaps both, Your Majesty," Anselmo said.

Ulisse laughed. "I like him," he said to the Fleet Admiral.

"You always were a good judge of character." She turned to Anselmo. "My brother is preparing to speak to the Lion candidates. Hurry."

Anselmo saluted her, then walked over to the table for the Lion candidates. Several of the men were already drunk. One even leaned back in his chair with his feet propped up on another seat.

Rafael Galbani watched Anselmo with a cool look. "Lieutenant Errari, right?"

"Yes, sir." Ridiculous he had to defer to these ducks. Their mamas and papas had all bought their ranks, just as they'd paid for them to enter the labyrinth. Likely none of these so-called soldiers had actually gone to Zorzi.

"I've heard of you." This from the one with his feet on a chair. He threw an olive and caught it in his mouth. He was still baby-faced, and the scraggly growth on his cheeks barely counted as a beard—far too young to be a captain.

Rafael frowned. "Enzio. The Doxe is here."

Enzio crossed his arms and leaned back even further. "When's dinner going to start? I'm starving."

Rafael turned back to Anselmo. "How do you know the Fleet Admiral?"

The other soldiers perked up. Even Enzio seemed interested. Anselmo tensed his jaw. "What makes you think I know her?"

"She seemed pretty friendly."

"And why would you care about that?"

"Taking you around and introducing you to all the higher ups. Playing favorites. That gives you an unfair advantage."

"You mean the higher ups like your father, Admiral of the Lions? Since we're talking about unfair advantages."

Enzio laughed, and Rafael smacked his feet off the chair.

The Doxe walked over, followed by the short man with the mustache.

The soldiers snapped to their feet with a salute. "Ave, Doxe," they said in unison.

Doxe Albizzi gestured for them to sit. "Welcome and congratulations, soldiers. In one week, you'll begin the process to become Lions. You will be challenged mentally and physically. You've all proven yourself worthy of the task. I have full confidence every one of you will succeed."

He turned toward the crowd. A servant rang a bell. The party goers quieted and faced the Doxe.

"Siori and siore," Doxe Albizzi said, "I present to you the Lion candidates for this year." He gestured for them to stand, and the audience applauded politely. The Doxe held up his hands, and the room quieted again. "Now is the time we ask for your generosity in sponsoring our candidates. As per the rules of the labyrinth, they cannot enter without your patronage. You don't need to cover all of their costs, but each needs at least one patron to cover some cost, even the price of a spear. So please help these soldiers and change the rest of their lives. Admirals and Vice Admirals, remember that you are prohibited from sponsoring any candidates. We will start with Captain Rafael Galbani."

Anselmo and the others sat while Captain Galbani remained standing.

Doxe Albizzi waved toward the captain. "Who is willing to buy this fine soldier new weapons and armor for the labyrinth?"

A stuffy middle-aged man in a maroon doublet raised a hand.

"Sior Ruzzini, grassie. Is anyone willing to go higher? Cover his gear and a quarter of the fifty thousand ducat entrance fee?"

Fifty thousand? Anselmo had saved twenty thousand. That's what the entrance fee was before he left for Zorzi. No one had told him they'd raised it. If his patron didn't cover at least thirty thousand ducats of the cost, Anselmo would never be able to enter.

Another man rose his hand, this one in black. "Sior Gritti," the Doxe said. "I think we can go higher for the son of our esteemed Lion Admiral Galbani. Gear and half of the entrance fee?"

It didn't take long for the man in red to raise his hand. He glared at Sior Gritti.

"Sior Ruzzini." The Doxe's voice turned amused. "Business partners turning against each other." Everyone laughed, except Siori Gritti and Ruzzini, whose glowers pierced each other. "Let's raise it to gear and three-quarters of the entrance fee."

Sior Gritti raised his hand.

"I'll cover it all," Sior Ruzzini said. Everyone laughed again, privy to some joke that Anselmo had no part in.

"Grassie, sior, for your generosity. And congratulations to Captain Galbani. Sior Enzio Colombo, please stand."

And so it went, soldiers getting auctioned off like fish at the market. No one had told Anselmo this was the process for getting a patron, that he'd be sold like a piece of meat. Some soldiers were sponsored by their own families. Some only had one willing patron. Others had bidding wars like Captain Galbani, soldiers who had the most potential to survive the labyrinth. Sior Ruzzini outbid his apparent business partner, Sior Gritti, two more times. It was dizzying to see so much wealth flaunted in such a manner. Dizzying and disgusting.

Anselmo couldn't wait for his turn.

He was the biggest one there and clearly the strongest. The others were not small men, but Anselmo's shirt and doublet strained across his shoulders. Although, perhaps that belied his poverty, that he hadn't been able to order a new shirt for the event. Would that make people disdain or pity him? Or perhaps they'd see it as him boasting his strength. That could be good. These people seemed to love a big ego.

One by one, the Lion candidates received their patrons. It went faster than Anselmo had expected, though not fast enough for the anticipation swirling in his gut. Surely he would incite a bidding war as Captain Galbani had.

"Last, we have Lieutenant Anselmo Errari," the Doxe said, and Anselmo stood. "Who is willing to cover our only lieutenant's gear?"

No one raised their hand. No one said anything. People looked from one to the other, shifted their feet, refused to do more than glance at Anselmo.

"Surely we have one soul willing to help this fine soldier." There was no hope in Doxe Albizzi's voice. He was merely going through the motions.

At the front of the group, Fleet Admiral Dandolo's face was somber, though a glower flickered across her face. King Contarini stood beside her. He looked around the crowd, bewilderment on his features.

"A new sword at least?" The Doxe's voice rang in Anselmo's ears. It was the only sound in the room. There was no rustling of skirts, no pad of servants' feet. Even they had stopped to watch Anselmo's embarrassment. "Lieutenant Errari served valiantly at Zorzi, and I'm sure he'd like an upgrade from his old xiphos to a fine kopis like the captains."

A hand rose.

Anselmo's heart jumped.

But it was only a woman covering a cough.

Doxe Albizzi turned to Anselmo. Anselmo had never felt so small. "Without a patron, Lieutenant, I'm afraid—"

"I'll cover it all." King Contarini's voice rang out across the room.

"Pardon?" Doxe Albizzi nearly shook in surprise. "Are you sure, Your Majesty?"

"I've never been more sure of anything in my life." The King nodded at Anselmo. "Everyone deserves a chance to improve their situation, and Lieutenant Errari is a fine soldier from what I hear."

"But—"

"It's allowed for a foreigner to sponsor a Lion candidate, is it not?"

"It is." Fleet Admiral Dandolo smiled at Ulisse. "Unprecedented, but not forbidden."

"Perfect!" King Contarini slapped his hands together. Everyone jumped at the sound and launched into whispers. Their faces held neither kindness nor joy. The king grinned.

"Very well." Doxe Albizzi's voice didn't agree with his words. He bowed to King Contarini, who was already walking toward Anselmo. "Patrons, please take a few minutes to meet with your soldiers. Dinner will start shortly."

"Grassie, Your Majesty," Anselmo said as soon as the king reached him.

King Contarini still had a huge grin on his face as he clapped a hand on Anselmo's back. "Let's talk away from these blowfish." He led Anselmo to the far side of the room. Everyone watched as they walked away, including the Fleet Admiral who still smiled.

"Why, sir?" Anselmo couldn't stop himself from asking.

"As I said, you deserve it." Ulisse leaned in, and his grin grew. "Plus," he added, his voice quieter, but full of amusement, "as much as I enjoy Rialto, sometimes it's fun to piss off all these stuffy nobles. Actually, it's always fun."

Anselmo laughed. Relief washed over him, making him laugh harder than he normally would.

"Grassie, Your Majesty. Grassie tante."

Ulisse waved over a servant bearing wine and took two glasses, one of which he gave to Anselmo. "Please, call me Ulisse." He held up his wine. "To your future."

Anselmo had almost failed. For a few minutes, he had. But Ulisse had swooped in like a hawk and saved Anselmo. He'd saved Anselmo's future with Imelda. Anselmo would be indebted to Ulisse for the rest of his life. As long as he was with Imelda, it was worth it.

Anselmo raised his glass. "To my future."

Chapter Fourteen

Venezia sipped her wine and controlled her seething. Primo was surely to blame for Anselmo Errari's nearly botched sponsorship. Thank Rea's holy name for Ulisse. People would never believe it, and Ulisse would never admit it, but his heart was as big as the Muriseano. It was a sticky situation, him as Anselmo's patron, with Imelda in the middle of it all. Venezia would keep an eye on it.

The most important thing was that Anselmo would be a Lion. He was someone to watch. His strength, his skill—and the accounts of his success in Zorzi. Anselmo Errari would make his mark on the world. Which meant he was a valuable tool, one Venezia could use to build her legacy.

Now that Anselmo had a patron—he and Ulisse were talking far from everyone else—Venezia needed to focus on one goal: gaining allies. Lazaro had begun making his rounds. He knew the plan, but she could only hope he would implement it. She couldn't be everywhere at once, couldn't whisper in every jewel-adorned ear.

"This party is a disgrace," Janus said next to her, frowning into his glass. He'd arrived just after the auction, wearing the same expression and his ridiculous red robe with his ridiculous titles embroidered along the bottom hem.

"And things were better for you in exile? Did you dine in opulence every weekend?"

He grumbled something about the Illustrious Empire of Ilios and drank his wine.

"I know you think you're above manipulation, but a pleasant expression won't kill you."

"What is there to smile about? Everything was taken from me."

"And I sympathize with you. But we'll never get it back if you glower at everyone."

He gave a tight smile. It was a start.

A servant walked around the room, ringing a bell. Ten minutes until dinner. Venezia angled for Fia, who chatted with a group of wives of the Councilmen. When she saw Venezia, she excused herself from the group and joined Venezia on the edge of the party. She eyed Janus.

"He's fine," Venezia said.

Janus frowned and drank his wine.

Fia raised one shoulder. "If you say so." She lowered her voice. "Ruzzini was delighted at our proposition the other night at dinner. I also sent him off with several of my finest bottles of wine and free use of one of my slaves for a year."

"Good idea." Venezia kept her tone neutral. It was a shame Fia owned a slaving company—the only unlikable thing about the woman.

"I pointed out to him how much his spice business would benefit from free access to the Bogasa Strait."

"Anyone else?"

"Orso Cancio is just about sold. He practically salivated at the idea of no import taxes on supplies for corincanto."

"Yes, the empire has every fiber needed," Janus said.

Fia gave him a flat look. "I had no idea that was the case. Thank you for your helpful contribution."

Janus huffed. He could be such a child at times. He was about a decade younger than Venezia, so he was barely an adult. How much better it would be if he had at least five more years.

"This is all good," Venezia said. "We need to keep focusing on those who stand the most to gain from taking over the empire."

"You mean restoring me to my throne," Janus said.

Venezia waved a hand. "Of course."

The servant rang the bell once more. Time for dinner.

"I'll focus on the politicians and their greed," Fia said. "You keep reminding everyone of your military and strategy prowess." She walked off, returning to her friends with cheek kisses.

Venezia would start with Paolo Ruzzini. Surely he'd enjoy congratulations for sponsoring so many Lion candidates. Not only because it flaunted his wealth, but because he'd won in bidding wars against his former business partner, Franco Gritti. There were few things Rialtani enjoyed more than gloating.

Venezia and Janus wove through the crowd toward the table. People stood clear of her. Or rather, stood clear of Janus. Word had already made its rounds—they all knew who the dour-faced man in the corincanto robes was. His family was still loathed in the city, twenty years after the massacre. Janus had only been a boy when his grandfather had sanctioned killing the Rialtani living in Ilios, but that didn't matter. Not to the people of La Serenìsima Repùblica de Rialto. Family came first, but the republic was a close second. And out in the world, the republic was family.

Venezia had almost reached Ruzzini when Enrico Lando intercepted her. Priggish as always, the Council president wore unimaginative gray.

"Good evening, Sior Lando," Venezia said with a nod. She tried to step around him, but he moved to block her.

"Heading off to plot your bid for Doxe, Siora Dandolo?" The leech stood inches below Venezia. He tried puffing up his chest to seem taller. "The gods do not look kindly upon sibling rivalry."

"I'm well-versed in the holy book."

"Sponsoring this man"—he indicated Janus with a jerk of his head, finally acknowledging the Iliano—"and his wild proposition when your brother has clearly stated his opinion on it is a shameful thing."

Janus shook in indignation. "My family deserves its return to power."

Enrico took a step closer, as if to intimidate her. She refused to retreat—that was not how battles were won. He stepped back, defeated, though holding his arrogant posture as if to trick her. But Venezia knew tricks, and he couldn't fool her.

She arched an eyebrow. "You're not very good at intimidation, sior."

"And you're not very good at choosing your allies," he snapped.

"I happen to agree with Sior Komnenos. His family ruled well for over two hundred—"

"I mean Lazaro," Enrico said. "He's drunk and making a fool of himself. If you can't control your husband, how could you ever expect to control the republic?" He slid away with a smug expression.

"Wait here," she said to Janus. The man folded his arms but did as told.

Venezia swallowed her anger and searched the room. Primo chatted with a group of Council members. The Lion candidates were interspersed through the room with their patrons. Fia still laughed with her friends.

Finally, Venezia spotted Lazaro. Drunk as a youth at Carnevale, glassy-eyed and arm hooked around the waist of a senate member's wife. She leaned away from him, and kept glancing around for someone to save her. Venezia walked over and pulled Lazaro free of the woman. Or rather, pulled the woman free from him. Immediately the woman exhaled loudly. Lazaro, naturally, didn't notice.

"What are you doing?" she whispered in his ear.

"What's the point of a party if I can't enjoy myself?" He took another swig and raised his glass. "You showed those Zorziano rebels, eh Fleet Admiral? I'm merely celebrating my wife's victory."

"And you're sabotaging my next one." Truly, there should have been a separate dinner to honor Venezia and the military's victory at Zorzi. Primo tacking it onto the Lion candidate dinner was another slight. She snatched Lazaro's glass. "Can't you just sit until dinner?"

He saluted her. "At once, Fleet Admiral," he slurred.

What a scene. She helped him into a chair, smoothed her dress, and found Janus. The Iliano stood alone in a bubble, untouched glass of wine in hand. Orso Cancio, of all people, walked over. This could be good. He'd served on the Council for two decades. He held more political influence than anyone other than Primo.

"Please be polite," she whispered to Janus. He didn't smile, but his face went neutral.

She kissed cheeks with Orso. "Sior Cancio, I'd like to introduce you to Janus Komnenos."

"You're the one who wants the Iliano throne." The old man looked Janus up and down. "I hear Imperial Prince Nikkoforos and Princess Calixta will be here soon. Things will get interesting."

Janus glanced at Venezia before answering. "The Heraclius family has ruled for only twenty years. My family held the throne for two centuries before their grandmother Elektra Heraclius dethroned my grandfather."

"Sounds like he deserved it. Damned murderer."

Janus frowned. "I do not condone my grandfather's ... actions. I will use my power wisely."

"But you'll wear that ridiculous outfit. Are you going to make everyone in the city become blood monks?"

Janus bristled. "That name is offensive. We are Giore's Order of Holy Corincanto Monks."

The servant came through again, ringing the bell a second time since no one had actually sat down yet.

"First the lieutenant, and now this foreigner. Such feminine pity you have for the downtrodden. You do the women of Rialto proud." Orso smirked as he looked at Janus. "Good luck. You're going to need it." He wandered off to find his seat.

Damned man had only come over to gloat. Fia would have more work to win him over than they'd thought.

Venezia pointed at the far end of the table. "You sit down there," she said to Janus. "Try not to offend anyone during dinner."

"They're the ones making ignorant statements," Janus said.

"Then keep your mouth shut."

She watched to ensure he followed her orders, then sat next to Lazaro in the center of the long table, across from Primo. Lazaro had remained seated, but he laughed loud enough for the entire room to hear.

"Don't you have an image to uphold as former Doxe?" she whispered in his ear, smiling as if they were sharing a private joke.

"I did my time acting respectable." He grabbed wine from a passing servant. "What about you, cozying up to that lieutenant a few minutes ago?"

"He's an old family friend."

"Wasn't his mother your uncle's cook?"

"Where he started doesn't matter. What is important is where he ends up and what he does for the republic."

"Shrewd, mè amor."

"I had a good teacher."

He smiled and took her hand, his wrinkled fingers curling around hers. They were wet from wine he'd sloshed out of his cup. She resisted the urge to pull free.

Ulisse was seated next to Primo. He gave Venezia an expression that said *lucky you*.

Now that the Lion candidates had their patrons, the rest of the night was about Venezia. Primo had seated no strong politicians close to Venezia. And if that weren't on purpose, she'd swallow an entire mudcarp.

During the second course, Fia stood and raised her glass. "To Fleet Admiral Dandolo, on her victory over the Zorziano rebels."

Everyone at the table held their wine up. "To Fleet Admiral Dandolo," they said in unison. Venezia inclined her head in thanks.

She caught Primo's eye before dessert. He'd talked with those around him the whole meal, but finally he looked her way. This was the first time they'd met since he'd found out about her bid for Doxe. She'd never been close with her brother, but they worked well together. What would it be like until the election?

He tipped his head and raised his glass. People around them noticed. In a wave down the table, everyone toasted Venezia again. She held her wine up, a fake smile on her lips. Of course he'd pretend everything was fine. Save face, that was Primo's mantra. Just like their father. The late Giovanni Albizzi had presented the image of a perfect family, but it had been a lie. Estranged spouses, a favorite son, an ignored daughter, and unhealthy expectations all around.

Primo stood, and the room fell silent. He smoothed his sash, no doubt to bring attention to it. "Siori and siore of La Serenìsima Repùblica de Rialto, thank you for celebrating our victory together. I'd like to recognize our admirals and generals. Their bravery and cunning played an important role in subduing the Zorziano rebellion. And of course, our Fleet Admiral, my sister Venezia Dandolo. Her strategies proved the key to our success."

The guests applauded and cheered. Lazaro kissed Venezia's cheek. She backed up her chair to stand for her speech, but Primo continued.

"I was the youngest Doxe ever to be elected. Only twenty-five years old, I knew I had to prove myself. I needed to show the Council that their faith in me was not misplaced. I also wanted to continue the strength Doxe Dandolo had established before me. I kept much of his cabinet for the first years, including Fleet Admiral Anafesto, may he rest in Rea's holy arms."

Everyone repeated Primo in hushed voices and touched their heads then hearts. Head and heart, Giore and Rea, the sign of the gods. Lazaro murmured something about relieving himself and slipped away. Venezia tapped her foot as she waited for Primo to finish.

"My sister had since risen to vice admiral in the armada. I've always known she was intelligent, but her success in the campaign at Cinyras proved her keen, strategic mind. Because of her, we now control both of i Occi de Zitello. Appointing her as Fleet Admiral was, in my mind, the only choice. Many people questioned my decision, but it didn't take long for them to realize my wisdom. She's proven herself time and again as my second-in-command. We make a great team. Rialto will continue to flourish as I serve as Doxe and my younger sister Venezia as the Fleet Admiral."

More applause. Venezia ground her teeth behind her smile. How she'd like to tear his never-ending, self-aggrandizing speech to shreds. And he still wasn't done.

He raised his hands in her direction, as if inviting her over for a hug. Oh, how that would dance on the hearts of the dinner guests. "Before she speaks, I want to say thank you. Thank you for serving me so well. Thank you for keeping our republic safe for me. Thank you for being a great advisor and a great sister. The floor is yours."

The guests jumped to their feet with applause and cheers. Donatella dabbed at her eyes. Ulisse eyed Venezia as he clapped.

Venezia controlled her seething and stood. "Thank you, Your Serenity, but the honor is all mine. I wouldn't have succeeded without the brave—"

Lazaro stumbled up to the table and fell into Fia Pesaro's lap. "Me scusa, Siora," he slurred. He kissed each of her cheeks, then, after a moment, kissed her on the mouth. Fia's eyes went wide as she shoved him back. He pushed himself to his feet, using her breasts as leverage, then took her goblet.

"To my wife!" he cried, holding the glass aloft. Wine spilled over the rim and onto Fia's dress. The Councilwoman glared at Venezia as everyone reluctantly toasted.

Venezia opened her mouth to speak, but the room had already erupted back into conversation. Lazaro's toast had ended her speech. Janus sat at the far end, arms crossed as no one engaged him. Lazaro stumbled back to his seat, then drew Venezia into his lap. She clenched her fists as he chatted loudly with the senate member next to him, something about gambling together during Carnevale. She jerked herself back into her chair. Across the table, Donatella offered a sympathetic look. Ulisse glared at Lazaro.

And Primo just smiled.

Chapter Fifteen

La Piaza del Leon had already started to fill with revelers as Anselmo made his way to Palàso Dogal. Firelight from torches danced across the white marble walls. Anselmo skirted the front of the building and turned down the side. The Doxe's living quarters were on the opposite side of the official government wing. Without a large portico, this part of the building was less grand than the state section, but only slightly less. The dark wood door towered heads above Anselmo, with a large silver handle and matching knocker. Anselmo smoothed his coat, took his white Bauta mask off, and knocked.

A severe older man opened the door. He looked Anselmo over, clearly unimpressed by Anselmo's dark gray wool coat, black wool pants, and plain mask. "How can I help you?"

"I'm here to see Siora Imelda Albizzi and Sior Arturo Albizzi," Anselmo said. "My name is Lieutenant Anselmo Errari."

The butler looked skeptical but led Anselmo to the foyer. If such a room could be called a foyer. A huge staircase descended from the second floor, wide enough for four soldiers abreast. The ceiling arched above, tall as a temple, and massive portraits of past Doxi covered the mahogany walls inlaid with silver. Forty-eight men and two women glared at Anselmo, with lifted noses and down-turned mouths. Further along the hall, doorways branched off and led to other, no doubt equally impressive rooms. The thick Shantzese rug squished under his dusty boots. He frowned. He'd polished them that morning—as he always did—but the streets had gotten them dirty. The leather had gone thin from years of daily shining. He should've bought new shoes before tonight.

"Anselmo!" Imelda glided down the stairs. She wore a purple dress that accentuated her dark eyes and held a matching half-mask with pheasant feathers. Her dark hair fell over one shoulder, tied with a black ribbon. He barely resisted pulling her into his arms as she kissed his cheeks.

"You came," she whispered.

"I wouldn't consider any other option."

She bit her lip and smiled. "Can you help me?" She held her mask to her face and turned around. What a shame to cover her soft cheeks and delicate nose. The smell of roses drifted up as he tied the ribbons, taking him back to their first kiss five years ago. She'd worn rose water then, and it was as intoxicating now as before. They'd kissed in a sotopòrtego under a merchant's home. The light had been dim, and water had dripped in the corner. They had many such stolen moments in the year that followed, but that memory remained one of his favorites.

He brushed her neck as he finished the bow. She shivered and looked at him over her shoulder. How soon could they leave?

Arturo trudged down the stairs. He held a mourning blue mask trimmed with red corincanto.

"That's dark," Anselmo said.

Arturo waved at Imelda, who pretended to pout.

"It's artistic." She broke into a grin and took Arturo's arm. "Let's go." She practically pulled her brother out the door.

Outside, Anselmo slid his mask on. Imelda narrowed her eyes as she scrutinized him.

"What?" he asked.

"I don't like your face covered up."

"Imelda," Arturo muttered. "This isn't exactly private."

"Fine. But I'm making you a new mask, Anselmo."

"As you wish, siora," Anselmo said, and Imelda laughed.

They reached the square. Music played somewhere, pipes and drums, and people danced in the center of the crowd. On a wagon in front of the temple stood an effigy of Zitello, Trickster King of Winter. A silver-painted crown perched askew on his straw hair. He wore robes of wool, and keen eyes had been painted on his face. No other features, for the eyes of Zitello were second only to his mind. If he turned his eyes on you, bad luck would befall your family.

The wagon was covered in red-dyed thread, which people grabbed hastily before wandering off in search of food carts. Everyone wore masks, some the square-jawed Bauta like Anselmo's, others the half-face Colombina like Imelda's. There were the beaks of the Crow and the oversize ears of the Fool. A few skeletal Deaths dotted the crowd, shrouded in midnight blue and refusing to dance.

"What first?" Arturo said.

"Threads," Imelda said.

Anselmo nearly jumped, until he realized she meant the secrets tradition.

They walked over to a cart beside Zitello where a black-robed lesser priest sold hemp corincanto. The red threads at Zitello's feet were only imitations, and those were offered for free. True hemp corincanto was available at a hefty price. A rich, saturated crimson, unlike the plain thread, which was a pale coral color beside it.

Imelda turned to the priest. "How much?"

"One hundred ducats per strand."

"We don't need real hemp," Anselmo said. "Our secrets will release no matter which kind of thread we use."

"But real corincanto is more fun to burn." She handed over two hundred ducats, and the priest gave her two strands.

"I can buy my own," Anselmo said. Although he only had one hundred ducats in his pocket, and it was an entire week's wage, even as a lieutenant. He wouldn't have any left over for food, and he'd planned to buy it for her.

"My treat." Imelda tied a thread around his wrist. A hair had fallen free of her ribbon. His fingers itched to tuck it behind her ear.

"You still don't participate?" Anselmo asked Arturo.

Arturo shrugged as his gaze wandered around. "I still don't have any secrets."

Imelda held out her wrist to Anselmo, and he tied a string around it. "Shall we get some food?" she said when he'd finished.

They wove around people until they reached the edge of the piaza, where vendors hawked their wares, anything from toys to sweets to masks. Anselmo picked a cart selling peeled blood oranges and hard cheeses.

"My treat," he said, even though the food was overpriced due to the occasion. But he could splurge this one time, for her.

She smiled. "Fine."

After a short search, they found a fairly empty spot under a veranda. An alley branched off, and numerous couples enjoyed themselves against the edge of the building. Arturo leaned against the wall and watched the crowd, nodding to himself every so often. Anselmo had missed that, seeing Arturo lost in thought. It had been a part of his everyday life, one he'd taken for granted until he left for Zorzi.

Imelda popped a slice of orange into her mouth. "What is your secret, Lieutenant?"

Anselmo's secret every year, of course, was the threads in his legs. For the last four years, he hadn't worried about anyone asking. This Carnevale, he'd have to resume the old familiar lie. "You'll have to wait until the end of the week to find out."

"And then you'll go into the labyrinth." She sighed and stared at the rest of the fruit in her hands. "Do you really have to do it? Can't you just … back out?"

It was the only way Anselmo could make a decent life for himself. But Imelda didn't understand. She couldn't. She'd been born into a life of silk and roses, of alpaca corincanto to stave off the cold. "I want to be a Lion. You know that." He bit into the cheese and took his time chewing it. "What about you? Are you willing to spill your secret so early?"

Imelda turned her attention to the crowd. "Isn't it wonderful how we're all the same with masks on? Nobles and peasants, soldiers and politicians. We all look alike."

Anselmo glanced out at the sea of people. That was the idea, wasn't it? No social hierarchy during Carnevale nights, not while you wore a mask. You left your old identity at sunset and became someone new, someone with no future worries, someone who cared only about present pleasure. But the classes were still there. Sure, the highborns pretended not to see rank during the week, but it was all an act. Not Imelda, which was one of the things he loved most about her. But one day, she would. She couldn't live in her world and keep her naiveté.

Anselmo saw the hierarchy clear as a sword's edge. Elaborate masks meant someone with money. Peasants bundled up in cloaks and gloves, while the rich defied winter with their fine wool embroidered with alpaca corincanto. The cold was there now, in Anselmo's bones, while Imelda flaunted her bare shoulders. Not that he was complaining. Her skin was smooth and perfect as silk. Not like his battle-worn hands, made rough to win the life he wanted.

"I found a patron last night," he said.

Imelda pressed her lips together. She'd painted them red as pomegranates. "Am I supposed to congratulate you?"

"Imelda. Please."

She sighed. "I'm happy for you because I know it's what you want. Who is it?"

"The king of Eraclea."

"What? No!" She dropped her food on the ground. Anselmo resisted a grimace at the oranges on the dirty cobblestones.

"What's wrong?" he asked.

She shook her head and fled into the piaza.

Arturo jumped suddenly. "Sorry, my mind was wandering. What happened?"

"I just told her my patron is the king of Eraclea, and she panicked."

"Oh. *Oh*." Arturo nodded. "Go talk to her."

What in the three blazes was going on? Anselmo shouldered his way through the crowd to keep up with her. Snow began to fall, and the people cheered. Imelda wove through the laughing throng until she reached the edge of the island—opposite from Palàso Dogal.

Anselmo reached the edge of the island and pushed his mask onto his head. Imelda walked between a building and the drop, not even glancing at the inches between her and the nearly twenty-meter fall to the canal. Once she reached a narrow walkway, she sat with her feet dangling. No one mingled here. The sounds of the crowd were distant, and it was quiet enough to hear her breathing. Anselmo stood a meter away. They were alone, their only company gondole drifting along El Canalasso.

She watched the boats as snowflakes landed on her velvet hair. "I'm betrothed." The announcement puffed into the air with her breath, so light it dissipated immediately. But the words were as heavy and sharp as a sword thrust through Anselmo's chest.

"Let me guess—"

"I'm marrying Ulisse."

The anxiety in his chest twisted further. "Does he know about us?"

"No, of course not. Did it seem like he knew who you are?"

"No." But Anselmo had never met the man before the dinner. Ulisse seemed like an honest man, the sort that was easy to read, but Anselmo had no way of verifying that.

Imelda remained silent.

Anselmo sat beside her. "Why didn't you tell me at the lottery?"

"I was only engaged then. And I thought I had time." She looked at him. "I thought we had time." She wiped at her cheeks. "This night has gone all wrong. I wanted to be with you and forget about it, but I can't."

The clouds parted, and for a moment, moonlight illuminated the snow falling around them. Illuminated her face, and the tears and melted snow on her cheeks. He took her hand as the clouds converged, covering them in darkness.

"Some things are like the moon," he said. "They follow you wherever you go. Even on a swiftly sailing galley, it chases you."

She finally looked at him. "What chases you?"

Imelda had been his moon. Her face had followed him across the sea and through the streets of Zorzi. He wasn't worthy of her, but there'd always been the hope that one day he'd become a Lion—and therefore a noble—and he would finally deserve the woman he loved. And now that hope was gone, stolen by a king with golden coffers and deep blood.

"Desire," he said.

"For what?"

"Glory. Honor." He swallowed and brushed her cheek. "You."

Imelda pressed his palm against her face. The temple bell rang ten o'clock. Two hours left in the day. Two hours and six days left until he entered the labyrinth. She pulled her mask off. The effort plucked the ribbon out of her hair. The breeze grabbed it and sent it spiraling toward the water. Her hair danced around her face as he cupped her soft, damp cheeks with both hands. She was strong and delicate, flawed and perfect. And she was to marry someone else. She was to lie with someone else, bear someone else's children, experience joy and heartbreak with someone else. She would spend the rest of her days with someone other than Anselmo.

"Did Primo arrange it?" he asked, his throat thick.

"Of course he did." Her voice was bitter and resentful. She set her mask on the ground and pulled herself to sit sideways in his lap, then tossed his Bauta next to hers. His arms wrapped around her as she ran a finger down the side of his face, along his jaw.

Her rose perfume enveloped him. He closed his eyes, immersing himself in her touch on his skin, her body in his arms. He'd imagined it countless times the last four years, and here it was in real life. A moment that should've been sweet, but was tinged with bitter.

"Look at me," she whispered. He complied. The wind pushed her hair across her face, and he gently moved it out of the way. She draped her arms around his neck, and pulled him close, her lips almost touching his. She paused, watching him.

He pressed his forehead against hers. "I wanted more," he said. So much more.

"I did too."

Finally, she kissed him. She tasted like blood oranges and went straight to his head like the strongest wine. He pulled her closer. She was magic, gift of the gods, and he would never deserve her. That wouldn't stop him from trying. Even if she were meant for someone else, he had to make himself worthy of her love. He would brave the labyrinth for her, cross oceans and battle armies for her.

His life would never be the same. He could feel it in his bones as they kissed beneath the falling snow.

CHAPTER SIXTEEN

Imelda's heart danced as she stood on the roof of the Albizzi home. The night before with Anselmo had nearly ended in disaster, but instead had turned into a dream. Had they really kissed in the falling snow on the opening night of Carnevale? It was like something from a story, and yet it truly happened. She touched her lips and smiled.

Arturo cleared his throat, bringing her back to the present. "Focus, Imelda."

The cold pricked at her fingers as the wind blew around her. Thank goodness for alpaca corincanto, or she'd be freezing right now with no way to warm up. No one had been to the home in days, other than Imelda and Arturo. Everything was boxed up or covered in sheets.

But the wings were still here. And at that moment, the smaller pair was strapped to Imelda's back. Arturo had made a crude rope-and-pulley system to control the wings. She gripped the ropes to keep the wings closed as the wind blew around her. The sun shone in a sky patchworked with clouds.

Arturo held up his hands to shade his eyes as he looked across the rooftop. "Good thing we didn't add the extra wool yet. If this pulley system doesn't work, the wind would steal you away if the wings were stronger." He turned to Imelda. "I don't know why I fixed the pulleys to *your* wings." Imelda couldn't miss the sadness in his tone.

"You'll get to fly next time."

"Yes, of course. Now, don't open the wings until I say."

He knelt down and tied two ropes around each of Imelda's ankles. The ropes were tied to the legs of Arturo's chair from his room in the dome. He double-checked the knots on her legs, then sat on the chair. "All right." He took a deep breath. "Release them."

Imelda slowly loosened her grip on the ropes. The wings snapped open. She had to clench her fingers to keep the ropes from ripping through the pulleys all the way, and her palm stung from rope burn. The wings started flapping, sending her into the air until the lines around her ankles tightened. With the wind and the strength of the wings, the front legs of the chair lifted. Arturo gripped the edges of his seat and planted his feet firmly on the ground.

"Pull one of the ropes," he said through clenched teeth.

Imelda tugged on the right rope. The right wing folded in, causing her to dip to the side. If she'd been free, she would've changed the direction of her flight.

Arturo whooped and popped to his feet. The chair whipped into the air, and Imelda once again found herself flying toward the edge of the roof. She yanked at both ropes with all her strength, and both wings pulled closed, sending her back to the roof.

"Keep your grip tight!" Arturo ran over. He laughed yet again as he rolled her over and unfastened the harness. "They worked!" He pulled Imelda to her feet and swung her in a hug. "We're finally going to succeed!"

Imelda hugged her brother tight. He'd done it. He'd saved her, and she would be free soon, free from her betrothal, free to be with Anselmo. "Let's show them to Venezia."

"Not yet." He wiped sweat off his forehead. "I have a blacksmith working on better parts for the pulley system. And we need to sew the wool in. Venezia won't buy them if they can only keep us a few feet off the ground. That's next to useless."

"How many days?"

"The blacksmith said a week at least."

Imelda felt herself crumple. "But that's so close to my wedding."

"It'll be fine. I promise. I'll go later today and pay him extra to prioritize our proje—A hemp message?"

A purple cloud of smoke drifted in across El Canalasso. Without anyone to catch it in a hemp-corincanto-stitched cloth, it floated directly to Arturo and encased his head. His eyes unfocused for a moment, then he blinked.

"Who was that?" Imelda asked. Who in the three blazes would send Arturo a hemp message?

"Primo. I'm supposed to meet him in the salon, and apparently change into nice clothes." He looked down at his ink-splattered sleeves and doublet dusted with feathers. He arched an eyebrow at Imelda and left for his room.

"Wait!" She dragged the wings into the dome, one at a time. After, she met him outside his room. He wore a dark violet satin doublet, but his hair was the usual display of disarray. He combed his fingers through in an attempt to subdue it.

Imelda caught up to him. "What does he want?"

"Isn't it obvious?"

Oh no. They hurried out of the house and to the closest public dock to hire a góndola to take them to the palàso. Once there, they made their way to the salon. Beniamino, Primo's secretary, waited for them. He was tall and skinny, a few years younger than Imelda. His father was a member of the upper merchant class, but their family had been vying for nobility for a few generations. She didn't know him very well but had seen him at social events for years.

Imelda gripped Arturo's sleeve as Beniamino opened the door. Primo wore the silver crown and sash of his station. The wall behind him was covered in a mural of the founding of Rialto, Giatoro with his one eye and wings, flying over the marshes with Ioanna on his back. Beside Primo stood a man and a woman. Both had cool brown skin and wore clothing in the Iliano style, long bejeweled-robes with their titles embroidered along the bottom. The man had well-coiffed black hair and a beard, a rakish smile, and a swagger in his posture. The woman, with long, sleek black hair and a delicate facial structure, radiated more confidence than anyone Imelda had ever met.

Arturo's potential fiancèe. The woman's beauty, her grace, her title—her very existence—hit Imelda like a bucket of cold water from the gulf. This woman represented all of Primo's terrible plans for Imelda and Arturo. She wasn't here merely to court Arturo. She was here to steal him away. Imelda couldn't stop herself from putting her hand on Arturo's arm to steady herself. To keep him safe, to keep him in Rialto, to keep him by her side and in her life always.

No, it was what he wanted. And Imelda would move to Ilios. It would be okay. She'd make the wings, marry Anselmo, and they'd live in Ilios, where Arturo would be with his princess.

Gods above, the woman was gorgeous. Arturo's heart stood no chance.

Primo gestured to Arturo and Imelda. "Imperial Prince Nikkoforos Heraclius, Imperial Princess Calixta, may I present my cousins Arturo and Imelda Albizzi." Arturo made a jerky bow, and Imelda curtsied.

Calixta kissed Arturo's cheeks twice. There were even more jewels strung in her hair, and a long veil billowed behind her when she walked. "I'm so happy to finally meet you, Arturo."

Arturo smoothed his hair. "Um, yes." Calixta waited as he searched for something else to say. "Me too."

She pursed her lips to hide a smile and moved to Imelda. She added a hug with the cheek kisses. Imelda couldn't help but stiffen under the woman's embrace. They were not family. And yet Calixta held her as dearly as a sister, though surely she felt Imelda's apprehension.

"I'm so happy to meet you as well, Imelda. I hear you and Arturo are close. I'm glad for it. It's said a man treats his wife only as well as he treats his mother—or sisters."

"Well, we're twins, after all." Imelda would not like this woman. She refused to, even if the princess practically glowed. It was all those rubies and sapphires. That's all. She'd ignore the warmth and musical lilt in Calixta's voice. Even her Iliano accent was charming.

Nikkoforos gestured, and a manservant walked over, holding a large basket full of golden apples. Imelda hadn't even noticed him, she'd been so distracted by the prince and princess. The manservant handed the basket to Imelda.

"The famous Iliano golden apples," Nikkoforos said. "A gift from our family to yours."

Arturo perked up. "Are there any golden apple spiders with them?"

Calixta laughed, a sound as playful and charming as a dolphin riding the waves. "I don't want to put your life in danger, dear Arturo."

"I would love to study them," Arturo said.

Nikkoforos *tsk*ed good-naturedly. "And learn the secret behind black bane? I think not."

Imelda forced a grateful smile as she struggled to bear the weight of the basket. "Grassie, Your Highnesses."

Primo took the basket and placed it on the table.

Calixta led Arturo to the sofa. "Your portrait didn't do you justice at all, and I'm sorry to say I know almost nothing about you. Come tell me about yourself, so I can fall madly in love with you. His Serenity says you're an avid reader. What's your favorite book?"

Arturo tilted his head as he considered his answer. "Kohaavisiya. Probably. It's a treatise on math and astronomy by the ancient Kipa scholar Kohaavis."

"I'm afraid I haven't heard of it."

"I have three copies. I can lend you one."

"I'd love that. But I've never had much of a mind for astronomy. Maybe you could read it to me and help me understand."

Imelda twisted her lips as the princess pulled Arturo out of his shell. By the gods, this woman was magical. Clearly she knew it, and Arturo was completely blinded by it.

Nikkoforos moved to the sideboard and looked through the bottles. "I understand you're recently betrothed, siora Imelda. Are you excited for your upcoming nuptials?"

Imelda glanced at Primo, who seemed perturbed at the prince helping himself to his personal wine collection. "I'm adjusting, Your Highness."

"Call me Nikkos. We might be brother and sister soon." He poured himself a glass of wine. "I imagine that's normal, the adjustment. I've been unofficially betrothed since my birth, and officially since I was ten, so I grew up with the fact. I tend to take it for granted and even forget about it at times." He took a drink and nodded in approval. "Excellent choice, Your Serenity. Who's your sommelier? I want to steal him away."

"I select my wines myself. A small hobby."

"Well then, maybe I'll hire you sometime." He chuckled and clapped Primo on the shoulders as if they were old friends. Primo pressed his lips together, but in a flash, the tension was gone as he turned back into the Doxe.

Imelda resisted a smile. The prince and princess were quite a pair. Except Imelda wouldn't like them. She couldn't let herself.

"Who's the lucky man to claim you, siora?" the prince asked.

Primo stepped up beside her in a strangely protective gesture. "The king of Eraclea."

"Good man, Ulisse." Nikkos moved to the window. He tapped the cup as he watched El Canalasso below. "I'm looking forward to spending Carnevale in your city, Your Serenity, though I'm sorry to have missed opening night. I've heard quite the rumors about Rialtano celebrations."

Imelda tuned them out and turned toward the couch. She opened her mouth to say she and Arturo should get back to work, but froze. Calixta was whispering something into Arturo's ear. He laughed. Calixta took his hands, and he made no move to pull them back. The look on his face was more than amusement. Was it ... delight?

"I think he likes her," Primo murmured.

So did Imelda, unfortunately. Arturo falling in love was part of the plan, but now that it was actually here it was far more terrifying. With a foreign princess, no less. A woman who would whisk him hundreds of kilometers away, days of sailing on rough seas. And a woman who could cloud his mind, make him forget the urgent need for the wings. This was bad. This was so very bad.

Calixta stood and walked over to take Imelda by the hand. "Let's go for a walk. You, Arturo, and I. It's lovely outside."

Imelda resisted a scoff. It was cloudy and chilly. No way this princess from the north actually considered this weather to be pleasant.

In the hall, Calixta took Arturo's arm. "Shall we go out to the balcony? I simply cannot get over the view."

Not only was it chilly, but wind blew from the north. It held some warmth—the promise of spring—but it must have cut through Calixta's silk robes.

"You must be cold, Your Highness," Imelda said. "I understand it's much warmer in Ilios."

"We have perfect weather year-round. Luckily, my maids sewed alpaca corincanto into my ... clothing." Calixta flashed a smile at Arturo, who blushed. She wouldn't say her underclothes specifically, but it was clear what she meant and she had the gall to flirt with Arturo over it. "Now, tell me about the beautiful mural in the Doxe's salon."

"It's the founding of Rialto," Imelda said. "Giatoro, the lion, was a part of the Sacrestano gladiator shows. He loved Ioanna, a noblewoman who often came to watch. When the city fell, Giatoro prayed for a way to save Ioanna. Zitello promised to intervene on his behalf. He kept his word, and Giore gave him wings, but Zitello took his eye as payment. Giatoro rushed to Ioanna. Her husband was dead, as was her child, but she went with him. They led the survivors out of the fallen city and into the marshes to build our city."

"How romantic," Calixta gushed. She stroked Arturo's arm with one hand and gestured at the city with the other. "And look at their legacy."

"It's only nonsense," Arturo said, cheeks still pink.

"Even if it is, it's beautiful nonsense."

Arturo stared down at the canal. "I've heard so much about Ilios. El Palàso d'Oro, the Hanging Gardens, La Baxélaga d'Oro. Everything must be gold."

"Yes, all of Ilios is gold and white. And the Hanging Gardens. Words can't do them justice. You would love them, Arturo, I just know it. The irrigation system will fascinate your brilliant mind."

Imelda stepped between them. "Perhaps we will visit one day."

Calixta slipped her arm into Imelda's, as if she'd planned it all along. "Oh yes, dear Imelda. Please promise you'll visit us one day."

Primo opened the door. "Imelda, I need to speak with you."

Imelda hesitated. Arturo looked as if he wanted to shake his head, but had the sense to refrain. Calixta smiled as she pulled her arm out from Imelda's. Primo cleared his throat.

With an eye roll, Imelda walked away from her brother and over to her cousin, who wrapped his thick fingers around her upper arm and pulled her back inside. She leaned away from him, and after a moment, he noticed and relinquished his hold.

"They need to get to know each other," Primo said.

Imelda put her hands on the window sill. "She might not like him."

"That is a possibility, but it's not the most important matter. She'll choose him because we're their biggest threat. They need to secure us as allies."

Imelda gave him a dirty look. "Nothing more romantic than international politics."

"Romance is for Carnevale, not marriage," he said, then returned to his office where the prince must've been waiting.

Imelda turned around. The opposite wall held a map of the Muriseano. She walked over and touched Rialto, at the center of the sea. She then walked her fingers north by northeast to Ilios, almost one thousand kilometers away. So far north, where it was always warm and never snowed. Where they spoke Venetano with a different accent. Where they ate golden apples instead of blood oranges, rode horses instead of gondole, and rained black bane down on their enemies.

She brought her finger back to the peninsula, to Eraclea at the northern tip. A land of waves that assaulted the craggy coastline, unlike the gentle waters of the lagoon. Everyone said Eraclea was beautiful, but she would never find beauty there. Not where her betrothed ruled, a king who sold his services like a merchant at market.

Outside, Calixta had threaded her arm back through Arturo's and was leading him down the porch. Her laughter was infectious, and even the cadence of her voice was charming. Imelda couldn't hear what they were saying, but Arturo replied easily to her remarks. He even smiled.

The princess was cunning. As was Primo. According to him, Ilios and Eraclea were Arturo's and Imelda's futures. Ilios, fine. But not Eraclea. Imelda couldn't let that happen. She wouldn't be separated from her twin, wouldn't let half a sea come between them. And she wouldn't lose Anselmo. She'd do anything to avoid Primo's plans for her.

Imelda's palms throbbed from the rope burn. It would ease by nightfall, but by then, she'd be with Anselmo. She wouldn't forget her goal. Arturo wouldn't either, once he left Calixta's magnetic presence. Once Imelda reminded him what was at stake.

Chapter Seventeen

Anselmo stepped onto the dock of one of the biggest caxe in Rialto. Arturo got off the góndola and walked up beside Anselmo. They'd met at Arturo and Imelda's home, where Arturo had given Anselmo a gift from Imelda—a mask to wear for the night, unlike any he'd seen. It was Giatoro the Lion, missing his right eye. The socket was black, the rest of the mask covered in gold leaf. The thing must have cost a fortune for her to make, probably half a year's worth of his wages.

Arturo faced the house and sighed.

"Grassie for this," Anselmo said. "I know you hate parties."

"I want to help in any way I can."

Anselmo checked the knot of the ribbon on the back of his head and smoothed the front of his doublet.

"No one will notice if your clothes aren't completely straight," Arturo said.

"They won't notice your clothes, but I'm a stranger."

Arturo tilted his head. "Good point."

"If anything," Anselmo said, "it would be strange if your clothes weren't wrinkled."

Arturo laughed. A group of people pushed by them toward the house. Unlike Cax' Albizzi—a solemn, dark spot in the night—light spilled out of the windows of this home. Balconies dotted every story, and one ran along the entire second floor. Even from outside, the smells of meat and pasta filled the air.

Imelda rushed down the dock toward them. "You wore the mask!" She kissed cheeks with Arturo, then Anselmo. "It looks even better on you than I'd hoped."

"It's truly amazing," Arturo said. "You outdid yourself."

She beamed. "What do you think?" she asked Anselmo.

"It's a work of art."

"Grassie." She dropped a small curtsy. "And mine matches."

Her mask was a silver-leafed Ioanna, with sparkling tears on her cheeks for Giatoro's death. She wore a white dress with a silver design along the waist and a tantalizingly deep V-neck. A large amethyst necklace rested between her breasts.

It took everything in him not to kiss her right there on the dock.

"Whose house is this?" Anselmo asked.

"Ca' Galbani," Imelda said.

Anselmo stopped. "As in Admiral Galbani?"

Imelda shrugged. "He won't be here. The old folks will be partying somewhere else."

"But his son is the host, right?"

"Your mask is crooked." She reached up to straighten it, then tugged on his shirt sleeves and smoothed the shoulders of his doublet.

Arturo coughed. "Less touching, Imelda. We're in public."

"Fine." She combed her fingers through her hair. "As far as the party goes, think of it as an opportunity to make friends."

Anselmo grunted. Rafael Galbani, heir to this extravagance of a house, would never deign to befriend a lowborn like Anselmo. But there were hundreds of people here—it was unlikely Anselmo would see him.

Imelda took Arturo's arm, and Anselmo fell in behind them. Before they reached the house, she looked back and smiled at him.

"It's going to be hard resisting you all night," she whispered.

He appraised her again, that tantalizing dress and those lips like pomegranates. Tonight would be a new kind of torture. "You're not the only one."

Arturo cleared his throat loudly, then led them inside.

The house was practically painted in silver. Crystal was everywhere—wine glasses, vases, and chandeliers. Arturo and Imelda led him up the stairs, weaving around groups of people. There was no mingling of classes here. Technically anyone could come, but from the finery it was clear only the rich attended this party. Shimmering silk, glistening jewels, corincanto-embroidered dresses—it was as ostentatious as the state dinner, but more relaxed. Less dignified. There, the nobles and merchants kept their voices easy, their demeanor proper. Here, people threw their heads back in laughter and made suggestive propositions without caring who heard. Even the Lions, in their bright blue coats, spilled wine as they wrapped their arms around the waists of the siore or siori next to them.

"I'm going to find Calixta," Arturo said when they reached the top of the stairs.

"Who's that?" Anselmo asked.

"My bride-to-be." Arturo grabbed a glass of wine from a server and held it up as if in a toast, though his expression was sardonic.

"*Potential* bride-to-be," Imelda said.

Anselmo looked between them. "What does that mean?"

Arturo took a long draught of his wine. "It means she has to decide if I'm worthy of her or not."

"Don't let him fool you," Imelda murmured. "He likes her."

"Don't let *her* fool you," Arturo said. "She likes Calixta too. Be back soon."

One huge ballroom dominated the second floor, with several doors branching off. Musicians played on a small stage in front of a wall made of mirrors, and windows covered the opposite side. Rialto was aglow as everyone found their own ways to celebrate. Several tables boasted an array of wine and rich foods. Salumi, fried fish, ravioli stuffed with lamb and cheese, and blood oranges everywhere. Masked revelers filled the room, laughing, chatting, dancing. Sofas and divans had been placed throughout the room, and more than one were employed by amorous couples. People eyed Anselmo as they walked by, but not in a suspicious way as the politicians at the dinner with the Fleet Admiral had. Their gazes were interested, some more than others. A few women and men trailed their hands across his chest as they walked by.

Imelda pulled Anselmo to the opposite side of the room. A servant walked by, bearing wine. Imelda grabbed a glass and gulped it.

"Slow down there." Anselmo took his own cup from the servant. The glances his way didn't stop.

Imelda glared around them. "You'd think they'd never seen a handsome man before."

"It's not like I'm going to take anyone up on their offers."

Imelda smiled, but took another goblet from a passing servant. "I'm going to need as much of this as I can to get through tonight without clawing anyone's eyes out."

Arturo appeared minutes later and led them to a door with uproarious laughter spilling out. A group of people sat inside, including several of the captains going into the labyrinth. A guard with dark brown skin stood in the corner, gaze sweeping the room for any sign of a threat.

"Your secret, Your Highness," one of the men said, "is that you sew silk corincanto in your underclothes."

A woman in the center laughed, and all the men and several women in the room swooned. "This is all natural, sior." She turned as Arturo walked in, and popped to her feet.

"Have you figured out Arturo's secret yet?" one captain called.

The woman slipped her hand into the crook of Arturo's elbow. "That's simple. He's wildly in love with me." Arturo blushed. She turned to face the room. "As are all of you." They burst into laughter again, though the truth in her words was clear. This woman knew the power she held, and wielded it well. She waved at her guard, who came to her side. "I must take my leave and find my brother. Siora Gaetana, you can have my turn."

Gaetana rubbed her hands together as she eyed the room. She pointed at a man. "Enzio, your secret is that you're an asshole."

Everyone laughed, some even falling off their chairs.

Anselmo and the others went back into the main hall. Now Anselmo could see the woman more clearly. She had the same cool brown skin as her guard. She wore an elaborate white and gold dress, and her Colombina mask looked like it had been made of red stained glass set between bands of gold rather than lead. A large fan of feathers rose above the mask.

"How do I look?" she asked Arturo. "I considered a full-face mask, but it's a little unnerving."

"You—you look amazing," Arturo managed to say.

Calixta laughed and took his arm, then looked back to Anselmo. "You must be Anselmo."

"Yes, of course." Arturo held out a hand toward Anselmo. "Calixta, this is Lieutenant Anselmo Errari, our good friend. Anselmo, may I present Her Imperial Highness, Princess Calixta Heraclius of Ilios?"

An Iliano princess? Anselmo hastily bowed. "I'm honored to make your acquaintance, Your Highness."

"And I'm delighted to meet you." Calixta held herself differently than the Doxe did. He possessed certainty, but in the princess, it was more innate. She'd been born with the right to rule in her blood, and it showed. "A friend of Arturo's is a friend of mine. Please call me Calixta."

"Of course, Your Highness. I mean, Calixta."

She laughed and batted at his arm. "Let's find my brother. He'll be delighted to meet you."

They meandered through the crowd, passing more than one closed door. The walls were dotted with so many doorways, it was clear that the space had been designed specifically for raucous Carnevale nights. Imelda kept her distance from Anselmo, but glared at anyone who looked his way. He brushed her fingers with his, and her face softened as she looked up at him.

The floor had grown sticky, and the hall was beginning to smell of too many bodies crammed into one space. Voices and music bounced off the mirrored walls, a cacophony made worse by the alcohol in Anselmo's body. When they reached their destination, a small and quiet side room, he breathed a sigh of relief. Five tables sat on plush Shantzese rugs, surrounded by richly upholstered chairs. Men and women played cards while a few onlookers crowded around. The room smelled fresh compared to the hall outside, and the people spoke quietly.

Rafael Galbani approached. "Imperial Princess Calixta, Sior and Siora Albizzi. And Lieutenant Errari!" He grinned and kissed cheeks with everyone. If the man's rosy cheeks hadn't given away his drunkenness, the wine on his breath certainly did.

"He's our guest," Imelda said, stepping a little in front of Anselmo in a protective gesture.

"What a wonderful surprise! You'll have to tell me one day how you two know each other. Maybe in the labyrinth." Rafael jerked his head toward the far side of the room. "I'm about to play corteo with your brother, Your Highness. Please join us."

Rafael took Anselmo by the shoulder and led everyone to the farthest table. A dealer sat on one side of the square table, shuffling cards. And across from him, another Iliano with a guard close by.

"Imperial Prince Nikkoforos Heraclius, this is Lieutenant Anselmo Errari," Calixta said. "Arturo and Imelda's friend."

Anselmo bowed. The prince nodded but didn't bother to stand. He wore a red coat as decadent as Calixta's dress, a shiny white mask, and a ring on each finger. A woman sat on his lap, masked and wearing a slip of fabric that barely qualified as a dress.

"Call me Nikkos," he said. He gestured at the table where Rafael now sat. "Join us."

Anselmo held up a hand. "I'd rather not, Your Highness."

"I've never met a soldier who didn't enjoy a gamble every now and then."

"Begging your pardon, Your Highness, but how many soldiers have you met?"

Nikkoforos smirked. "Don't let these baubles fool you. I know my way around a battlefield. We need another player, and I doubt Arturo is interested in cards."

Arturo stood at the sideboard, loading a plate with food. "Not even a scintilla." Calixta joined him. She peeled an orange and fed him a slice.

What a flirt. Anselmo wouldn't have guessed Arturo would normally find that attractive, but the way his eyes lit up at Calixta's touch said otherwise. And she seemed earnest. Perhaps sincerity was what Arturo had needed all along—something no one had been willing to give him in all their years growing up. Not that Anselmo had attended upper-class events with Imelda and Arturo—a few Carnevale parties as they got older, but nothing more—but Imelda had always told him how everyone treated Arturo like an oddity. A rich oddity, the mark of more than one person's romantic scheme, but an oddity all the same.

Anselmo turned back to the table. The dealer, Rafael, and Nikkoforos watched him, waiting for his answer. Anselmo could practically feel the cards in his hands. Nikkoforos wasn't wrong—few soldiers turned down the opportunity to gamble. Anselmo loved the risk of laying it all out on the table. It was the closest thing to battle. But that was with privates and lieutenants, men like him who'd grown up poor. They knew the value of a ducat, what it meant to lose ten or fifteen. This glittering prince, with his fancy siora on his lap, wouldn't think twice about a hundred or a thousand. Rafael would be betting high tonight as well. They were all ducks, with no concept of the real world outside their own fantasy land.

Still they watched him. It was so tempting. The idea of beating them—what a rush that would be. But his pockets weren't that deep. They wouldn't be any time soon. One day that would change, but not tonight.

"Another time." He turned to walk away.

"Squid," Nikkoforos said nonchalantly. "That's what you Rialtani call cowards, isn't it? Are you worried about me clearing out your savings too soon?"

The prince's words climbed up Anselmo's spine, hitching his shoulders up as if he were preparing for battle. He spun around—not missing Imelda's glare—and sat. "Deal me in."

Nikkoforos clapped him on the back. "That's what I like to see."

The dealer finished shuffling the deck. "You know the law, siori—masks off." He dealt each player three cards, then placed four face up on the table. "The game is corteo, and coins is the high suit. Lieutenant, start us off."

The betting started reasonably with twenty ducats. Nikkoforos lounged in his chair, tossing cards onto the table or even consulting his siora on what play to make. Rafael sat upright, carefully considering each move though his eyes were a bit glassy from drink. The bets climbed to seventy-five by the end of the round, which Rafael won. Rafael raked the ducats toward himself, and Anselmo's coin purse already sat lighter on his belt.

"Haven't you ever played before, Your Highness?" Rafael asked as the dealer collected the cards.

"We have a different version in Ilios," the prince said. "I must admit—I have a bit of a learning curve ahead of me."

Rafael leaned back in his seat. "I'll try not to take advantage of it too much."

The woman on Nikkoforos's lap whispered in his ear, and he laughed. "Well, you've got nothing else to occupy your mind, Sior Galbani. After I win, you'll be poorer *and* lonely."

"After I win, she'll leave you for someone better looking."

Nikkoforos looked around the woman, who trailed her fingers across his shoulders, to Anselmo. "Nothing from you, Lieutenant?"

"Some people are good at talking, some people are good at winning," Anselmo said.

Both Rafael and Nikkoforos laughed. They continued to banter about losing money, but never made comments of that sort to Anselmo. They knew, everyone in the room knew. It was so obvious. He was poor, a lowborn lieutenant. Not some rich nobleman whose father had bought him a captain's rank. His doublet, though his best, was nowhere near the fine wool, velvet, satin, and silk the men in the room wore. There was no red corincanto along his hem, as there was on theirs—all of it either alpaca or silk. His clothing was plain black, barely dyed, while everyone else in the room wore colored apparel. Nikkoforos boasted the brightest of them all, a bold crimson with pearls on the collar.

It was disgusting.

It was motivating.

The game continued, and the bets grew steeper. Anselmo had brought quite a lot of money with him tonight, but his coin purse was nearing empty. He won more than his fair share of rounds, but even that wouldn't cover the sums Rafael and Nikkoforos would escalate to. But Anselmo couldn't back out now. To fold was to forfeit all of his winnings. If he lost, everyone would be talking about it. The poor lieutenant who tried to keep up with the highborns and gambled away his money. But if he won ...

By the last round, everyone was all in. Anselmo had bet six months' of salary. He'd survive without it, but he could practically feel his savings depleting. He'd been foolish to let himself get so caught up in the game.

Nikkoforos looked at his cards, at his own depleted pile of coins, and pursed his lips.

"I'm afraid I didn't bring enough money with me tonight."

"You may bet items of value," the dealer said.

"Put Armina on the table," Rafael said. Everyone laughed, including the woman on the prince's lap.

Nikkoforos trailed a finger down her arm. "A woman this beautiful is too rare to risk losing. I'd rather play with something far less valuable." He removed one of his ruby rings and threw it onto the pile.

The dealer took the ring and inspected it, hefting its weight and holding the gem close. "My informal appraisal is four thousand ducats."

Nikkoforos looked pleased with himself as he placed a seven of swords on the table.

"Damn it," Rafael said, throwing his cards down.

Anselmo couldn't match four thousand ducats. Not in ten years, at his current income. Not even in three as a Lion. Nikkoforos had played the perfect card for Anselmo to win, but Anselmo had nothing left. He began to fold his cards together.

Imelda's amethyst necklace landed on the pile of money, dwarfing the ring. The crowd chattered. Imelda put her hand on Anselmo's shoulder and smiled smugly at Nikkoforos. Anselmo looked back at his cards as he resisted crumpling them. This was worse than defeat.

Nikkoforos gave Imelda an approving look. "This just got fun."

The dealer inspected her necklace. "Informally, I value it at eight thousand ducats. Do we have any more bets?"

Nikkoforos shook his head, attention on Anselmo. He didn't look concerned or worried at all. In fact, he seemed to be having the time of his life.

"Lieutenant," the dealer said, "your move."

Anselmo glanced at his hand, then at the cards on the table. Even with Imelda's humiliating move, he couldn't help but smile as he pulled out the ace of coins and flashed it at the prince. "Corteo," he said, capturing the five cards on the table.

"Game," the dealer called. "The lieutenant wins."

Everyone cheered and clapped. Nikkoforos laughed, bouncing the woman on his lap, as if he hadn't just lost over twelve thousand ducats. The dealer put the money and Nikkoforos's ring in a bag, but offered the necklace back to Imelda. She took it then grinned at Anselmo as she slipped it over her head.

His good mood spoiled at the sight of the necklace. The dealer had even recognized it belonged to her and not him. Anselmo put his cards on the table and stalked out of the room. He found a pair of doors that opened onto a veranda overlooking the canal. A couple kissed against the building, just outside of the light spilling through the windows. He ignored them and leaned on the railing.

Imelda came out a minute later, carrying a large clinking bag and his forgotten Giatoro mask. "You left your winnings."

Anselmo shrugged. The railing started to crack under his grasp. She thrust the purse at his chest. He turned away. At least the quiet air smelled fresh out here. The windows provided a buffer to the sounds and aromas of the merrymaking inside.

"Are you mad?" she asked, coming around to face him. "You just beat that pompous prince."

"Because of you."

"So?"

"I accepted the consequences when I agreed to play."

The other couple muttered and went inside.

Imelda stared, disbelieving. "You're embarrassed." When he didn't reply, her expression grew angry. "Admit it!"

"And why shouldn't I be? Rich Imelda Albizzi coming to the low-born lieutenant's rescue."

"You could be grateful." When he didn't reply, she shook her head. "You're being an ass."

"That's what everyone thinks now that you 'saved' me. What kind of impression will that make?"

She pushed her mask onto her head. "That's what you're worried about? All those idiots in there?"

"I've told you that before."

"And you've told me I look beautiful and that you love me. This was never about having a fun time with me, was it?"

She *was* beautiful, even with her hair mussed from the mask on her head. Her dress shimmered in the light from the windows, and the glistening chain of her necklace accentuated her collarbone. But this whole party had been nothing except a reminder of how forbidden she was to him. Here they were, at a Carnevale party, and they had to pretend they were friends. They'd been fooling themselves all week.

"I should've stayed at home and prepared for the labyrinth."

Imelda clenched her fists. "You've prepared your whole life! That's all you've done, as long as I've known you. 'I can't play, my mom wants me to practice hitting dummies with swords.' 'Sorry I can't make your birthday dinner, I have to shovel salt day in and day out.'"

"Imelda—"

"It's Carnevale, Anselmo! The best week of the year, our one chance to be together, and you've got an oar up your ass. Why are you always so serious?"

"Because I'm poor!" Anselmo regretted yelling as soon as he opened his mouth. Imelda didn't crumple or weep. That wasn't her style. Her glare hardened, her arms crossed over her chest, and she retreated to the other side of the balcony to pout. This night was a disaster.

"I see money everywhere I go. I can't ignore it, even for a holiday." That was one of his mother's lasting lessons. She'd trained his awareness of the classes so he'd never settle for second best. "Fun is a luxury."

"Now you can afford some. Enjoy." She shoved his winnings and mask into his hands, then went inside.

Imelda didn't understand. She couldn't comprehend that her peers, these people she'd known her whole life, judged Anselmo differently than her. If she misstepped, they'd tease her about it. But if

Anselmo screwed up, it would only provide evidence that he didn't belong with them. That he didn't belong with Imelda.

He squeezed his fingers. The Giatoro mask creaked, and he immediately let go. It clattered to the floor. The gold leaf caught the light as he picked it up, making the black of the missing eye seem even darker. She'd made this mask and her matching one, bought a coordinating dress, all for this party. All of that money spent on a night out with the man she loved. And he'd fouled it up. He was indebted to her, while she owed him nothing. She could be with any of these pretty rich boys, and she chose the son of her family's cook, a boy who'd grown up to be nothing more than a lieutenant with a chip on his shoulder.

He tied the mask back on, tucked his money in the crook of an arm, and returned to the party. The room had thinned out a bit. It was easier to weave through the throng, though the remaining people were even more raucous than before. Every flash of white caught his eye, but after a few minutes, he hadn't found her.

Then he heard Arturo's voice, louder than usual. Anselmo made his way toward the sound. Arturo was talking animatedly with Prince Nikkoforos, even slurring a bit. Anselmo had never seen Arturo this drunk before, yet he still managed to spout off impressive historical knowledge. Calixta waved at people who passed, calling them by name. Nikkoforos rolled a ring—unadorned gold but thick as ship line—across his fingers absentmindedly. Imelda stood by the group, her face impassive. She glowered when Anselmo walked up.

Nikkoforos dropped his ring but didn't bother to retrieve it. "Lieutenant!"

Anselmo picked it up. "This fell, Your Highness."

"Keep it, keep it." Nikkoforos waved good-naturedly. "Add it to that wonderful clinking bag in your arms. It's an exciting thing to win. Seeing a friend sweep the game is almost as fun."

"I agree, Your Highness." Anselmo cringed inside at the lie. Maybe it was fun for someone as rich as Nikkoforos not to win, but for someone in Anselmo's position, it could be devastating. As surreptitiously as possible, Anselmo loosened the rope around the bag and slid it in. He wouldn't make a show of the prince's generosity.

Calixta and Arturo slipped away. Imelda glared at Anselmo with her arms folded.

"Are you going to buy Siora Albizzi something nice?" Nikkoforos said. "She seems upset. A lovely trinket might cheer up your dear friend."

"I do owe her for saving me back there," Anselmo said.

"I was glad to do it," Imelda said between her teeth.

Nikkoforos grinned. "If you'll excuse me, I have to find my beautiful companion. I'm afraid she got lost on her way to the wine table. I'll leave you two to patch things up." The prince disappeared into the crowd.

A servant passed bearing wine, and Imelda grabbed one—only one—and took a long draught. "At least you're wearing the mask again."

He sighed. The bag felt like an anchor in his arms. "You were right. I was being a jerk."

She softened and set the glass on a nearby couch. "You were just thinking about your future." She nodded at the money. "Going to spend it on anything fun?"

He laughed. "If you actually think I'm going to spend this, you don't know me at all."

"Straight to the bank, I know." She smiled, made as if to take his arm, then pulled back as her smile saddened. "I'm tired. Escort me to the dock?"

Anselmo glanced through the party as Imelda led him out. Calixta had worked her way into Arturo's arms, the jewels in her hair glittering as she laughed. And Nikkoforos had found his siora, who looked more than pleased to have her prince back.

Meanwhile Anselmo had to congenially walk Imelda down to the gondole so she could return to the palàso and her betrothed, the king, after which he would go home to his empty barracks, alone save for his new bag of coins.

Anselmo had been right before: fun was a luxury, like everything else worth having.

Chapter Eighteen

Arturo sat at his desk, making notations on his latest schematics for the wings. He paused to stare out the window. Outside, people dragged themselves around the city, despite the sun sitting high in the western sky. It was almost midday, and yet everyone was still feeling the effects of their Carnevale celebrations the night before. Arturo felt them as well, his head uncharacteristically fuzzy. That was part of the reason he didn't like to partake in the raucous parties. The other was the sheer mass of people. It made him itch to be close to so many people, especially strangers. He rolled his shoulders just thinking about it, then sipped his wine.

The temple bell began to ring the eleventh hour. He tilted his head to the side. Wasn't there something he was meant to do now? By the tenth ring, he jumped up. Calixta—they were going to tour of the city, or something like that. And get to know each other more. That part seemed unnecessary. Surely she could decide whether to marry him based on the benefit to her empire. It made the most sense to secure Rialto as an ally, or else it would only be a matter of time before the republic made a move against Ilios. The Bogasa Strait was too valuable to leave untouched.

He snatched the closest doublet, combed through his hair, and hurried out the door. Calixta waited in the foyer, along with Nikkos and Imelda.

Arturo buttoned up as he trotted down the stairs. "Sorry! I lost track of time."

Nikkos clapped him on the back when he reached them. "I'm going to a play tonight. You all should join us."

"What play is it?" Arturo asked.

"Don't recall the title. It's about a foreign goddess who eats souls, I think."

"*The Song of Fate.* I've seen it." Imelda half-shrugged. "The theater, Your Highness? How will you dazzle everyone in the dark?"

Nikkos grinned. "I dazzle plenty in the dark."

"Nikkos." Calixta gave her brother a pointed look.

But Imelda wasn't offended. It took a lot to upset her. "Is that what they say? You think they'd actually tell the Imperial Prince of the Illustrious Empire of Ilios anything different?"

Nikkos continued grinning. "So that's a no on the theater?"

Imelda frowned. "I have a dress fitting."

Nikkos turned toward him. "Arturo?"

Calixta put her arm through Arturo's. "We should stay in and get to know each other. You can't talk during a performance."

Nikkos *tsk*ed. "That's awfully forward, sister."

She swatted his arm. "That's not what I meant, and you know it."

Arturo felt himself blush. Imelda looked out a window and toyed with her hair.

A servant opened the door to announce the arrival of their litters. Imelda headed out. Arturo turned toward Calixta, but Nikkos had taken her shoulder and spoke with her quietly. Calixta waved him to go on.

Arturo joined Imelda, who waited outside by the second litter.

"What's that about?" she asked.

Arturo shrugged.

"They're conspiring against us," she said.

He helped her into her litter. "Why are you so suspicious of her?"

"Isn't it clear?"

"It's clear you're determined not to like her."

Imelda frowned. Calixta emerged from the palàso and joined them.

"So sorry." She combed her fingers through her hair, which didn't seem to need combing. But the effect was mesmerizing as black strands floated in the wind like kites. Or, what Arturo imagined kites looked like based on his readings about them. He ought to try making one sometime.

"Sibling talk," Calixta said. "You understand, of course."

Arturo glanced at Imelda, then held out his hand for Calixta. "Of course."

She stepped into his litter, easily settling herself into her seat. Arturo climbed in next to her and chanced a look down at his doublet. Great—he'd smudged ink on his buttons. What an impression he was making. Had he gotten it on her hands? He tried to surreptitiously inspect her skin.

He wasn't that subtle. She laughed. "What are you looking for?"

"Umm ..." He rubbed the side of his nose. "Ink."

She splayed her fingers, turning her wrists this way and there. "None there. But." She gently wiped the spot on his nose he'd just touched. "Just a smidge here."

"I'm hopeless."

"Not with my help." She winked.

Ulisse walked out the doors, followed by his guard. "Wait up!"

Arturo glanced back in time to see Imelda's posture tighten. Arturo could practically feel her urge to sigh.

Ulisse frowned at the litter, then climbed on next to Imelda. "Primo said you have an outing planned. I need to get out of that dark palàso." He turned to Imelda. "Is that all right with you?"

"Of course." Imelda forced a smile, though only Arturo would be able to tell.

The litter bearers started off. Ulisse's guard followed behind. Clouds hid the sun, yet Arturo barely managed not to squint. A chill breeze blew through the streets. At least it wasn't snowing.

Calixta pressed the back of Arturo's elbow. "Now you'll fall madly in love with me."

He gave her a bewildered look.

"I heard that if someone touches you right there," she said, "they'll fall in love with you."

"What an audacious fallacy." But he felt himself blush *again*. Gods above, he was a fool. He felt even more so as she clearly hid a smile.

"Have you ever considered growing a beard?" she asked.

"I had one." He rubbed his cheek. "It itched."

"Too bad."

"I'm not very fashionable. Much to Imelda's dismay. She always wants us to coordinate."

"Geniuses don't need to be fashionable," Calixta said.

He couldn't resist a smile, just a little one. Most people laughed at his eccentricities, but she seemed to enjoy them. Of course, it could be an act. But it was nice not to be the butt of jokes for once.

"Still." She lowered her voice. "I've always hoped my husband would have a beard. Sometimes friction can be a very good thing."

He coughed. Gods, she was forward. Not that that was a flaw. Just surprising. "Interesting hypothesis," he managed to say.

Calixta laughed and took his arm. Her laugh was as warm as her skin against his. He didn't mind her so close to him. That was a first. He noted that and tucked it away for future reference.

Calixta tapped his wrist. "Why does everyone wear a red string but not you?"

"Carnevale tradition. The thread represents a secret."

"And you don't have any?"

"None that I'm aware of."

"You sure about that?" She nudged him with her shoulder. "Aren't you going to ask what my secret is?"

"Do you want to tell me?"

She *hmm*ed. "Maybe later."

They toured the islands of the nobility, Monte and Riga first. The caxe were a burst of color against the gray sky and water—reds, yellows, blues. Calixta doted on the extravagant houses, throwing compliments around like thread confetti at a military procession. If only it were summer, and she could see how they gleamed under the summer sun.

What a silly thought. But it would be interesting to see the delight on her face.

"I know your cousin wrote on your behalf, and this proposal isn't your idea," she said. "What are your thoughts?"

He breathed a sigh of relief. Other people found conversation about silly things fun and distracting, but he never felt so awkward as during small talk. No point sailing around aimlessly. Best to get to the heart of the matter.

"I figured he'd marry me off once my father died. And our republic is a beneficial ally to your empire, due to our rate of growth over the last two hundred years and the value of the Bogasa Strait."

Calixta nudged him with her shoulder. "But how do you *feel* about it?"

"I haven't considered that." That wasn't entirely true. Perhaps he did have a secret after all.

"What do you look for in a spouse?" she asked.

Arturo tilted his head. "What I most want, I guess, is a wife who will let me work on my ideas and who won't laugh at them."

"I promise I will never laugh at you or stop you from pursuing your genius theories."

He smiled, and she returned it. Gods above, it was a beautiful sight.

When they reached Cax' Albizzi, the bearers paused. The windows were curtained, unlike the other houses which were open for everyone to see the rich wares inside. The house's purple facade seemed to sag like a melancholy face, despite the happy memories that filled it.

Arturo looked at the caxa for a moment, then glanced back at Imelda, who seemed to be blinking back tears as Ulisse awkwardly patted her shoulder.

"Keep going," Arturo said to the litter bearers.

When they crossed over El Canalasso, Calixta gaped again at the huge canal and the white stone bridge, covered in shops and tall enough for galleys to sail under with room to spare. He couldn't help but feel a little proud of his city. It was something special, a place like nowhere else in the known world.

Calixta asked to stop in front of a jewelry shop on the bridge.

"If you don't mind," she said to Arturo.

"It's your tour."

Imelda got off her seat slowly. "I'm going to wait by the water."

Calixta weaved her arm through Imelda's and dragged her inside. "I'll buy you a present."

Ulisse raised his eyebrows at Arturo, then followed the women inside. Arturo trailed behind.

Calixta took her time looking at the jewelry. The shop owner followed her around patiently, offering to let her try on this necklace or that ring. His Rialtano accent was so thick, she often had to rely on Arturo to translate.

Imelda murmured to Ulisse then slipped out as a case full of red and green tourmaline distracted Calixta. Imelda walked across the bridge to the opposite side.

"Imelda was feeling overly warm and stepped out," Ulisse said. "Let us know when it's time to go." He left and joined Imelda.

Calixta frowned. "Does she think I'm taking you from her?"

"It's … complicated." That was the safest way to put it. He couldn't give away his sister's secrets, after all. They were for her to reveal, and no one else.

"A present probably wouldn't do anything for her, would it?"

Arturo shrugged, then shook his head.

"Is this about Anselmo?"

"What? No."

"Arturo."

Arturo scratched at his cheek. "We've been friends with him almost our whole lives. And she just found out he's going into the labyrinth."

Calixta inhaled sharply. "That's incredibly dangerous, yes?"

Arturo nodded. "She was hoping he wouldn't make it in, but they pulled his name. Then there's the complication of patronage."

"Which is …?"

"Even if a soldier gains entry into the labyrinth, they can't go in unless they have a patron and can afford the entry fee."

"I'm guessing Ulisse sponsored Anselmo?"

Arturo smiled. "You're quite smart, you know that?"

She half-shrugged, her expression coy. "Yes, but you can point it out whenever you like." She arched an eyebrow. "And they're friends?"

"Yes."

"I see." She gave him a knowing look before returning to her shopping.

Arturo had managed to tell the truth without revealing Imelda and Anselmo's secret. However, Calixta was smart and likely saw through his sidestepping, that they were friends but also more.

Great gods above. Arturo needed some wine.

In the end, Calixta bought a diamond necklace and a set of matching opal rings. "The necklace is for my mother and the rings for my sisters," she said as the shop owner placed the jewelry into velvet bags. Calixta retrieved the money from her coin purse and handed it over. "Io is still young, but she can wear the ring on a chain until she grows big enough to fit it."

"I'm sure they'll love the gifts." He wandered over to the case she'd been enamored with earlier. He pointed at one of the tourmaline rings. "You liked this one, right?"

"I love it."

The shop owner held it out to Arturo. Calixta held her hand out, palm down and fingers splayed. Arturo took a small breath and slipped it on without jabbing her. She admired the stone, turning it side to side to admire its glitter in the sunlight through the window.

"This is gorgeous. Grassie, Arturo." She kissed his cheek. A real kiss, not the airy kisses Rialtani used as greetings. "I'm going to check on Imelda."

"Bill the Albizzi family," Arturo told the shop owner as she walked outside. He touched his cheek where she'd kissed him.

This was what it was like to be interested in someone. People had flirted with him at Carnevale parties, but he knew it was only because he was an Albizzi. It had been tempting a few times, to engage with a woman and see what the fuss was all about. But he didn't want his first time to be so meaningless, nothing more than an experiment. That wouldn't be fair to himself or the other party. There was no way in the three blazes he was going to get involved in a mess like that.

Plus none of them had been ... well, magical like Calixta. No, not magical. Magnetic. No, that wasn't quite right either.

She opened the door, and his attention snapped straight to her. "Are you coming?" she said, a playful lilt in her voice.

Bewitching. That was the perfect word to describe Calixta.

They continued to Centro, ending the tour with the grand temple, El Casteo de Giore. The veined marble contrasted with the stark white of Palàso Dogal across the piaza. The symmetry was admirable, though Giatoro's statue in front of the palàso threw it off. Only a bit, though. Enough to overlook.

Inside, a choir of women chanted behind the altars. Arturo blinked as his eyes adjusted. It was nice to be indoors, but even with the colored light from the stained-glass windows, it was too dark in here. And smoky with the incense.

Candles illuminated and cast shadows across the effigies of the gods. Imelda approached the statue of Rea, Ulisse at her side. The goddess held a sword in one hand and her heart in the other. Wings protruded from her back, flared out to either side—two sets, one for each god. Imelda touched the statue's marble foot.

Arturo looked up at the statues. Giore wore robes in the ancient Sacrestano style—similar to Iliano formal robes. His beard was trim, his mouth stern, his arms strong. Somehow, the sculptor had manged to capture the god's wisdom and ingenuity. Admirable.

Rea stood on Giore's right. Her face was at once intense and loving. She gripped the sword and heart in each palm with equal force. Love and death were under her dominion. Every line of every feather had been carved in exact detail. Arturo could practically feel the wind coming off the beating wings.

Giore and Rea stood close enough to almost hold hands. Another thoughtful detail.

Calixta intertwined her fingers with his and walked to the side to look at a stained-glass window depicting Giatoro helping Ioanna out of the burning, fallen city of Sacresta.

"I love this story," Calixta said. "Even if it's not real, it's not non-sense. It's truth."

Arturo tilted his head. "Human truth. Love and loyalty."

"Exactly."

The choir continued to sing, their voices intertwining in a peaceful harmony. It conveyed a deep sense of truth—outside of gods and goddesses—that resonated deep within him. His brain quieted, but didn't still. In fact, he thought more clearly. He ought to visit more often.

"What do you think of me?" Calixta asked. "As a potential wife?"

"I think, of everyone Primo could've chosen, you're the best."

She smiled, then looked down. "I'll tell you my secret if you promise not tell anyone." She rubbed the corincanto tied around her wrist in a bow. "I have to choose a husband, and I want one that will stand by my side. A man I can trust, who I can allow to see me at my worst. I've never had anyone like that in my life, other than my family. And I'm not close enough to any of them to reveal everything in my heart." She looked up at him, her expression earnest. "I live inside my mind out of necessity—keep up a strong facade for the family. But I long to speak all the thoughts in my head. It's torture keeping them tied up all the time. I want a husband who will listen to it all, the good and bad, and still respect me." She breathed a sigh that almost sounded like relief.

Could he be that close to someone? He'd only ever had Imelda to listen to, and he doubted he was the best confidant for her. But it was inevitable in marriage. A healthy marriage, at least.

"I could be that for you," he said.

"But could you, really?"

His eyes roved around the room as his head tilted. "We all have different sides. Some are good. Some are not so good. Even the gods have their flaws. Giore is often too rigid. Rea sometimes reacts without thought. And they both allow Zitello free rein during the winter." His gaze returned to her. "You promised not to laugh at me. It would be unfair for me to not extend the same courtesy to you. If we marry, we'll fight at times, of course. Even Imelda and I disagree. But it always works out because we care about and respect each other. I think you and I would have a marriage built on the same principles."

"I think we would too." She kissed his cheek. Her eyes flicked over his shoulder. "Your sister and Ulisse have left."

Arturo looked behind him. Imelda and Ulisse were nowhere to be seen.

Calixta pulled Arturo farther into the temple, along the wall to the far corner, past even the altar. It was dark here—no candles, the only light source a dimly-lit window. Ioanna knelt at Giatoro's side as he died.

Calixta hugged Arturo's arm and laid her head on his shoulder. "I didn't know he died."

"Saving Ioanna's life, as the story goes."

"How do you feel about me as a wife? Truly?"

"You've discovered my secret." A crooked smile lifted the corner of his mouth. "I like you. Quite a bit, in fact."

"I like you too. Quite a bit."

She moved to stand in front of him, wrapping her arms around his neck and kissed him. Panic shot through Arturo's veins. He didn't know how to kiss! But the warmth of her lips melted his anxiety away. He held her waist, and she pulled him closer. Her mouth traveled along his jaw, leaving a trail of kisses on his skin that sent shivers down his body, until she reached his ear.

"Shall we get married?" she whispered.

He couldn't speak, only breathlessly nod, and she laughed. He'd never heard a purer sound. He could spend months working on finding the perfect harmony to match it, and it would be time well spent.

But all thoughts of music and math flew out of his head the moment she kissed him again. There was nothing but the sense of touch, her breath mixing with his, her hands tangling in his hair. He'd always imagined the study of the natural world would lead to the highest levels of knowledge and understanding. How wrong he'd been to underestimate the other side, that of sensations and emotions and desires.

Now, as he and Calixta kissed in the dark corner of the temple, the stained-glass window glowing above, the ethereal voices of the choir echoing off the stone walls around them, he could perceive truth clearer than ever.

Chapter Nineteen

It was the last night of Carnevale. Finally. Lazaro had managed to talk Venezia into attending Orso Cancio's party. How in the three blazes he'd managed that, she didn't know. But here she stood on the edge of the crowd, trying not to glower. From the way people avoided her, it was clear she was unsuccessful.

Fia Pesaro sat on a couch with other members of the Council, all of them laughing so hard they were falling over. They grabbed new wine glasses whenever a server walked by, then sloshed it on the carpet as they exchanged jokes. A complete loss of decorum. She was still Venezia's best chance. Lazaro may have offended Fia at the celebratory dinner, but Venezia wouldn't let that stop her. She could bring the woman back to her side.

On the other side of the room, Primo wove through the crowd, greeting everyone he passed. The insufferable man wore his sash and crown of all things. He could've chosen to wear only his sash, which was somewhat discreet. But no, he wore both. With his height, the crown reflected the light of the candles and shone like a beacon. It was almost as powerful as his weapon of a speech the other night. Cunning man. But Venezia was sly too.

She took a glass of wine and offered it to Janus next to her. He accepted it, but the drink did nothing to improve his expression. People glared at him in his ostentatious crimson robe, then looked away with sneers.

"My damned grandfather," he muttered.

Venezia arched an eyebrow. "Are you sure it doesn't have anything to do with your clothes?"

"That wouldn't matter if my grandfather hadn't allowed the massacre. He practically opened the door for the Heraclius family to sweep in. He deserved his maiming, but my father didn't deserve to die, and our family didn't deserve to lose our power."

"And you'd already be on the throne," she said. "Or next in line, at least."

"And I wouldn't have to work with you. No offense."

"The feeling is mutual."

He actually smiled. Venezia returned it and clinked her glass with his.

Nikkoforos Heraclius swaggered over. The prince had ditched the ridiculous Iliano formal clothes in favor of red pants and a long, white jacket. It was still extravagant, heavily brocaded in gold and dotted with rubies along the collar and cuffs, but at least he looked less stuffy.

"Fleet Admiral Dandolo, you are looking exquisite tonight." He removed his gold half-mask and gave it to the guard behind him. "And how nice of you to let little Komnenos tag along with you. Janus, I'm so glad you could make the trek all the way from Zorzi. What a financial sacrifice that must've been." Janus glared as Nikkoforos looked him up and down. "I heard you were a blood monk. It's a good look. You should visit my family's palàso; I think some of the lesser nobles are members of your cult."

Janus's face darkened as he drew himself up. "You mean *my* palàso, you imposter."

Nikkoforos laughed and patted him on the shoulder. "How lucky you're no longer a citizen of the empire, or I'd have you hung for treason." He turned to Venezia and flashed a smile no doubt meant to send her heart fluttering. It didn't work. "Join me on a walk, Siora Dandolo?"

"Janus, why don't you head back to your inn?" Venezia said.

Janus held his ground.

Nikkoforos made a shooing motion. "Run along, little Komnenos."

With a huff, Janus pushed his way out.

Nikkoforos swept his arm toward the exterior doors. "Shall we?"

Venezia fell into step beside him as they wove through the crowd to a private balcony. The prince stood at the rail and looked out over the city. "I've never seen Carnevale parties with so much delightful debauchery. The masks only add to the appeal." He looked at Venezia. "Rialto is an amazing city. And the secrets tradition. How entertaining. I noticed you're not wearing a red string."

"I don't engage in games."

"But no doubt you have your secrets."

"We all do, Your Highness."

He smirked. "Too true. Come to the railing and enjoy the view. I cannot get over it."

Venezia stayed by the doors. "Are you here to buy me off?"

Were Nikkoforos more like Primo, he would've been offended at the potentially insulting question. The prince only smiled then turned back to the view. "Your brother assures me Janus won't win the vote. He says the Komnenos family is too hated in this city."

Venezia walked closer to Nikkoforos. Not too close, just enough to indicate she'd hear him out. Not that she'd ever accept his terms. They couldn't possibly be good enough to entice her to even consider changing her mind. "It's been decades since the massacre. You'd be surprised what people will forget when there's money to be gained."

"What would it take for you to forget Janus? Ten million ducats?"

"That's quite a sum." No doubt Ilios earned at least that amount from the Bogasa every year.

"It's cheaper than war, siora."

Venezia folded her arms. "I want three-quarters of the taxes from the Strait every year."

Nikkoforos laughed. "Primo didn't tell me how funny you are."

"It's one of my lesser-known traits."

"Then I'm honored." He leaned against the rail and ran a thumb along his jaw in mock thoughtfulness. "So many colors. Every house a different hue. Streets of water. Boats instead of horses and carriages. A thriving economy and booming population. Wouldn't it be terrible if something were to happen to your home?"

"No doubt you're about to tell me what could happen."

He grinned. "I like you, you know that?"

"Just give me the threat and be done with it."

"As you wish. As soon as I hear the results of the vote, I will send a hemp message to my father. I have two written already. One says Janus lost, and we can continue our mutually beneficial alliance. The other says he won. Our armada is ready and awaiting the command—they'd be here in a week. Yes, that gives you time to prepare, but nothing will protect your ships from Iliano black bane. Nothing will protect the islands and citizens. Nothing will protect Rialto." Nikkoforos lounged with his foot on the bottom rail, gazing over the city.

Venezia could imagine it clearly—black bane-covered ships sinking in the lagoon as sailors attempted to swim to safety. Those fortunate enough not to have any acid eating its way through their bodies, anyway. Then, nothing to stop the Iliano armada from advancing. The poverty-stricken outlying isles would go first, acidic tar corroding the buildings, streets, and piaze. The Iliani would advance island by island, until even the white walls of Palàso Dogal melted into the lagoon.

Could she really risk the lives of eighty thousand people? Everything she'd worked for, disappearing into the water. The screams of children and wails of mothers. Some people would survive, but not enough. They'd lose their territories and be lost to history as a broken civilization.

So much to lose. And yet so much to gain. The riches that would pour into the city once they conquered Ilios and took over the Strait were enough to keep her on course. "It's war either way."

"War at your gates is different than war on foreign soil. That's quite a gamble."

"I have confidence in my city."

"Admirable. Truly. My courtiers could learn a lot from you. When your old husband dies, you should visit my city. I'll find a fine Iliano for you to marry."

She lifted an eyebrow. "You're quite funny yourself, Your Highness."

He spread his hands and inclined his head. "I try." He waved at the guard, who brought over a large clinking bag. "Consider this a pre-payment and gesture of good will. Choose wisely, siora."

Venezia accepted the money, but didn't heft it to give him the satisfaction. She merely held it like it was a fish, and a small one at that. She'd seen greater sums than this. "Have a good night, Your Highness."

He adjusted his ruby-encrusted cuffs. "I have no doubt I will."

With a nod, he re-entered the party and disappeared into the crowd. Venezia turned toward the city. She had to face this, to see all she was risking. Was it worth it? Were those people and their homes worth the gamble? What would the gods say? Giore's wisdom told her no, but Rea's passion urged her on. They had both blessed her abundantly, despite her childhood experiences. Every day she thanked them for her intelligence, her ambition, and her vision. She saw so much while everyone around her saw so little.

She hefted the sack of coins. This was no small amount of money. Most Rialtani would never see this amount in their lifetimes. But the money from the Strait would benefit everyone. With those taxes flowing into the city, once she was Doxe she would launch much-needed municipal projects. Tax breaks for the spinning, mascarer, and gondolièr guilds. Welfare programs for the poor. Paint for the buildings on the outlying islands. These would give the people pride and uplift them. They'd work harder, and domestic problems would drop. The city already enjoyed a measure of stability, but it could always use more. And Ilios would provide it.

That was a gamble worth making.

Chapter Twenty

Ulisse would never understand Rialtani. It was the last night of Carnevale, the last night for them to let loose and actually enjoy themselves, and some noblewoman had dragged him into what appeared to be the library to ask a question of the sea silk. And it had been such a stupid question, something about her supposed best friend spreading rumors of infidelity behind her back. She paid one hundred thousand ducats to learn she was terrible at choosing friends.

These people had too much money and too much time at their disposal.

That didn't mean he wasn't happy to take their money. Quite the opposite. Eraclea needed it more anyway.

He also didn't mind their abundance of time either. Tonight's party had started in the late afternoon. The sun hung low over the eastern skyline. Apparently the Rialtani liked to celebrate the final night of Carnevale for as long as possible.

Primo entered the library as Ulisse was cleaning and bandaging his hand. He wore his silver sash and laurel crown. Of course. Only Primo would wear his regalia to a Carnevale party.

Ulisse turned to Arrigo. "Why don't you scare the partygoers for a while?" The man glanced at Primo, bowed, and left.

Primo watched Ulisse wrap his palm. "Why do you insist on that charade?"

"It makes people squirm, which I find highly amusing." Ulisse tied off the cotton corincanto wrap. "Truth is, my family started doing it because people didn't believe us without it. It seemed too simple. Bring in a little blood, and suddenly they're raining coins on your head."

"That's rather dark."

Ulisse shrugged. "People believe darkness more than light." Wound taken care of, he rolled his sleeve down. "I heard Venezia's vying for Doxe."

Primo frowned. "An annoying development."

"You want to ask who will win? I'll have to charge you since it's a personal question."

"Why would I throw away thousands of ducats when I only have to wait a couple weeks to get the answer?"

"It would actually be millions of ducats for a question of such importance." Ulisse grinned. "Most people don't have your restraint. Still, didn't hurt to ask." He opened the door, and the clamor of the party invaded the room. "Are the Iliani here?"

Primo tensed. He'd always been easy to goad. "Don't antagonize them, Ulisse."

"Wouldn't dream of it." Ulisse tied on his mask, some plain white thing he'd picked up between the palàso and the party. "You're not coming?"

"I only came to make an appearance." And clearly remind the politicians who was in power. Primo straightened his doublet. He was leaving, and yet he still wanted to look presentable on the way out. It was admirable that he was so meticulous. He probably couldn't help himself. He turned toward the door then paused. "Can I ask why you sponsored Lieutenant Errari? Him, of all the Lion candidates, a lowborn with no prospects?"

Ulisse put his coat on. "One day when I was a boy, my family was at our private beach. A flock of seagulls was pestering us for food, as usual. But I noticed a small one standing apart from the others. I decided to feed it. I had to scare the others off, but it managed to get the sardine I offered. After that, I came down to the beach every day to feed it. After a while, it grew into the biggest seagull in the flock." He shrugged. "I have a soft spot for the underdog."

"Sometimes the underdog is that for a reason."

"You know me—I like to take chances."

Primo shook his head in long suffering then bowed, as naturally as any non-Rialtano. Primo and Venezia were the only ones in the city comfortable with royal formalities, having spent their summers with Ulisse's family in Eraclea. "Your Majesty."

Primo left, weaving his way through the crowd. Ulisse waited a moment, then headed back to the party. Arrigo had been waiting outside the door, and followed him immediately. More people had arrived while he was away, and the room echoed with their voices. A couple passed him, on their way to the room he'd just vacated. Vaguely familiar faces filled the hall, though it was hard to tell with everyone wearing masks. He'd met a few nobles in his years visiting Rialto, but luckily, no one approached him—probably due to Arrigo. Then Ulisse would have to try to remember their names.

Nikkos and Calixta stood by the windows, chatting with the people around them. Imelda stood with them, holding her mask rather than wearing it. She looked tired and, worse, bored. Ulisse turned on his brightest smile for her. She returned it with a reluctant one of her own.

"Are you okay?" he asked.

"I'm a bit tired. Do you—" She toyed with her hair. "Do you mind if I go back to the palàso right now? I'd like to spend time with Arturo."

"Of course, of course." He hesitated before kissing her cheeks twice. "Tell him I say hello."

She bobbed a quick, stiff curtsy then disappeared into the crowd.

"Carnevale can be a long week," Nikkos said. "It tests the endurance of even the most enthusiastic."

"Imperial Prince Nikkoforos." Ulisse bowed. "How is your evening so far?"

Nikkos bowed and pushed his mask onto his head. "Well enough, though I'm hoping to find something a little more exciting soon."

Calixta bid goodbye to the woman she had been talking to, then stepped forward. She didn't remove her gold mask, but her dark eyes conveyed her displeasure. "Your Majesty, I heard you gave your services to Janus Komnenos. Why?"

Ulisse bowed. "Last time I was in Ilios, princess, you were scampering through the tree tops in your family's orchard. You've grown bold in the last ten years." He laughed, which seemed to irritate her. "We maintain a neutral stance in international politics. And I sold my services. I don't give sea silk prophecies away for free."

"Except your debt to Rialto."

"Except that."

Calixta lifted her chin. "Seems like an excuse to take whoever's money is most convenient."

"Gold is gold, Your Highness. Especially for a humble city-state such as mine. We don't have a vast array of resources like your illustrious empire. Only one, and it's up to me to sell it."

"More like shilling cheap wares like a traveling peddler. Don't you think that's beneath a king?"

"I'd sell eel oil if that's what it took to keep my people safe. Wouldn't you, princess?"

This only irritated Calixta more. Normally Ulisse would've continued to irk her merely because he could. It would've been much too fun, and people revealed themselves when provoked. But Ilios was the greatest power in the Muriseano Sea. It was best not to poke a lionfish. He'd done that before, and the lionfish had poked back in the most terrible way.

He shrugged. "If it makes you feel better, I charged him an absurd amount of money. The man is odious, and I prefer your family on the throne. I have no doubt your brother will be as fine an emperor as your father."

Nikkos clapped him on the back and gave him a glass of wine. Calixta's eyes remained narrowed, and her mouth pinched. "What exactly did he ask you?"

Ulisse shook his head. "My family has a practice of strict confidentiality."

Much as he'd like to tell them. He'd hoped the information would get to them somehow, but Janus was as tight-lipped as he was unpleasant. The prospect of Janus as Emperor of Ilios was not a pleasant one. But he couldn't ignore the answer he'd given, or the images he'd seen floating around the man—half of the Iliano crown, scores of ships, and a horse with wings, of all things—one of the strangest visions he'd ever seen. But one thing was certain: Janus would one day rule the Iliano Empire.

Ulisse took a long drink to distract himself from the dreary thought. "Don't you think it's funny that in a few months we'll be siblings?" he said. "Never thought I'd have a sister so much younger than me."

"Youth and wisdom are not mutually exclusive."

"Not at all. I've proven that many times in my life."

Calixta sighed and rolled her eyes, no doubt a calculated move. She turned to her brother. "I'm going back to the palàso." With a deft curtsy in Ulisse's direction, she left.

"You'll be hard pressed to shock my sister, Your Majesty. She's put up with me for twenty-three years." Nikkos scanned the crowd. "This party is tamer than others, but surely I can find a card game in one of these rooms. I'm itching to make a risky gamble."

"I'd be careful about poking your head into dark corners tonight."

Nikkos laughed. "Wise advice." His expression sobered and he gripped Ulisse's forearm in the Iliano greeting. "If the Council votes with Janus, will you lend your troops to them?"

"If they ask me, I have to." Eraclea was in the unfortunate position of being in Rialto's debt, thanks to clever maneuvering on Rialto's part two hundred years ago. "But I hope he won't win this one."

Nikkos considered this. He didn't look entirely appeased, but finally he nodded. "Have a good night," he said and disappeared into the crowd.

Ulisse wandered through the party, exchanging pleasantries with people and regretting his decision to stay. He should've gone back to the palàso with Imelda rather than remain here with all these strangers. But he couldn't leave, not when there was the chance someone might need to ask a question of the sea silk.

He *was* as bad as a cheap peddler. People weren't wrong about that. But they were wrong about his motivations. Surely it couldn't be called greed when all he wanted was the prosperity of his people.

Professionally speaking. And personally? All he wanted was someone to love him.

Was that too much to ask?

Granted, his track record was not the best. Things had gone well with Marina at first, but three children took their toll on a marriage. And then, it all ended with the catastrophic boat ride. Next thing he knew, he was wearing mourning blue at her funeral with no body to drop into the sea, promising himself he'd never marry again.

Finally, he came across the only person he actually knew at the party, the first woman to break his heart. Venezia moved through the crowd, her presence commanding a bubble around her. She was the only person in the room without a mask, and the only woman wearing a knife in her belt. Strangely, she held a bag that looked full of coins.

Ulisse placed his hands on his hips and smiled wide. "Venezia Dandolo, how lovely it is to see you tonight."

Venezia arched an eyebrow and dipped a curtsy. "Your Majesty."

"Oh, don't." He kissed her cheeks twice, then looked around. "Where's your husband?"

She waved in the direction of the food tables. "Getting something to eat, I think."

"Then he won't mind if I steal you away for a bit."

"Not at all, Your Majesty." Her lips pursed in amusement, ever-so-subtly.

He snorted. "You of all people don't need to worry about formalities." He held out his arm, which she accepted. "I've heard an interesting rumor recently about you and the upcoming election."

"A rumor that's actually true for once."

"Always doing things your own way. One of the many things I like about you."

"Perhaps because you see that trait in yourself."

He laughed. "How true, siora. How true. You've got bigger balls than a minotaur."

"I'll take that as a compliment."

"As you should."

"Who do you want to win?"

He *tsk*ed. "You won't bait me into taking sides." He lowered his voice. "Though it would be interesting to see you at the helm. Quite the change in pace."

"I will win." Her eyes darted in the direction Lazaro had gone. "I have to."

"Venezia against the world, as always."

Ulisse steered them through the party to a door leading outside. This house—he'd already forgotten the host's name—had a deep balcony that jutted precipitously over El Canalasso. Gone was the stench and cacophony of drunken revelers. Arrigo remained by the door as Ulisse led Venezia to the railing. What an amazing view, the floating city lit from shore to shore for the final night of Carnevale. He breathed in the clean, quiet night air and whistled the beginning of a tune. "Remember that song?"

"You used to play it on the viol."

"I played it for you." He whistled a few more bars. "I'm sorry. I stole you from the party to make you listen to me whistle like a loon."

She smiled, but there was ... a tightness to it that hadn't been there when they were younger. He didn't really know her anymore. "I don't mind. It's nice to visit with an old friend."

"'Old friend.'" Ulisse gave her a dry, knowing look. They watched a galley slip by below. Some merchant hoping to take advantage of the fine weather and get a head start on the spring trading season. The chant of the rowers echoed off the rainbow houses lining the canal.

"You'll be happy with Imelda. She reminds me of Marina," Venezia said.

He frowned and rubbed at his beard. He would be happy with Venezia. He shouldn't think such a thing, not when he was betrothed to her cousin. But now that the thought was there, he couldn't get rid of it. It was true.

Not that she was available, with that ancient husband of hers. Surely she couldn't be happy with him.

Life could be a real pile of shit sometimes.

"Does it still hurt to talk about Marina?" Venezia asked.

"It's not that." He didn't release Venezia's arm, and she didn't pull it free. It was a comfort, something to remind him he wasn't alone. "Am I a fool, Venezia?"

"Why would you say that?"

"Your cousin doesn't want to marry me. Here I am, a king come to steal her away from her home and family." He scrubbed his hair. "Maybe I'm being greedy. All three of my children can spin. I had eleven good years with Marina. That's more than most people get."

He leaned on the railing. He shouldn't have said anything. He hadn't intended to, but it had all come pouring out.

A door opened behind them to let out a drunken couple. The laughter and music of the party spilled out as well.

Venezia turned to the two women. "Go back inside." She sounded like a slightly softer version of the Fleet Admiral, her tone authoritative and one that demanded obedience. The women grumbled but complied.

"You're not greedy for wanting happiness. If anyone in this world deserves it, you do. However." Venezia put her hand on his forearm. "I do have something unfortunate to tell you. Please know I don't want to cause you pain, but you need to know. Arrigo, can you give us some privacy?"

Arrigo looked to Ulisse, who nodded.

She waited as the captain left, then hesitated.

"Gods above, woman," Ulisse said, "you can't stop after that. Tell me."

"Imelda and Anselmo Errari have a relationship."

The spinning in Ulisse's mind slowed and stopped. The sounds of the party faded away. Even the cold on his cheeks disappeared. "A Carnevale fling?"

"More than that. They've known each other almost their whole lives. His mother was their cook. Before he left for Zorzi, they became romantic. And it appears they picked things up when he returned."

His heart churned; his stomach writhed. "I am a fool." A horrid, horrid fool. He gripped the railing and stared up at the stars. Another chance at love ripped away.

Ulisse hadn't felt so angry in years, since learning of Marina's fate. He saw her last letter to him sitting on his pillow, saw himself opening it, saw her boat dashed on the rocky shore, saw his children at her funeral, dressed in mourning blue. At least they wouldn't bear the burden this time. At least they wouldn't have to see their father made a fool.

"You are no fool, Ulisse Contarini." Venezia's voice turned Fleet Admiral again, one that wouldn't allow for disagreement. "I told you because you can do something about this," she continued in a softer tone. "Anselmo goes into the labyrinth tomorrow, so you'll have Imelda to yourself. Remember what I said when you arrived, that you're too charming for her not to like you? Show her who you are. Help her with the wings she's working on. Then she'll be happy to meet you at the altar. Which, might I remind you, is in a matter of days, well before Anselmo returns from the labyrinth."

Somewhere, a temple bell rang five o'clock. Someone knocked on the glass door. Ulisse glanced back. It was Venezia's husband. He waved at her impatiently. She pressed her lips together and held up a hand to forestall him. Ulisse joked about being old, but that man truly was. It was a shame Venezia had married him.

"I meant it when I said you deserve happiness more than anyone I know. But you're going to have to work for it." Her husband knocked on the window again, and a glower flashed across her face. She kissed Ulisse's cheeks twice. "Good night, Ulisse."

The door clicked shut behind her. Arrigo knocked softly at the door, but Ulisse waved him away. He needed to be alone. Even though it felt like he was always alone, even at a crowded Carnevale party.

Imelda had a relationship with Anselmo. Was it love? Best to assume it was. And Anselmo, the man Ulisse had sponsored. Had he known who Ulisse was at the dinner party? Had he known that the man offering to be his patron was betrothed to the woman he loved? Had he knowingly betrayed Ulisse's good will?

"Gods be damned." He wanted to yell but had to restrain himself, so the words came out in a growl. He slammed his fists onto the railing. The view had been so glorious before, but now the darkness seemed a weight on the brink of smothering the lights of the city.

Venezia was right, as always. She was the only one whose logic and cleverness outmatched his own. His wedding was in a few days. Anselmo was going into the labyrinth tomorrow and would be there for at least a week, likely two. By the time he emerged, Ulisse and Imelda would be in Eraclea, hundreds of kilometers away.

Although once Anselmo did emerge, who was to say he wouldn't come to Eraclea and abscond with Imelda? She seemed not to care for their betrothal rites. Would she care for their marriage vows?

He could always break off the betrothal, reveal her betrayal to the world.

And yet, he couldn't. He wouldn't do that to Imelda, wouldn't embarrass her in such a way.

Wouldn't make her the fool.

Ulisse scrubbed his face, then straightened his posture. Venezia said he could do something about it. It seemed futile to try, but he would anyway. After all, there was no shame in hoping for happiness. Would Imelda ever come to love Ulisse instead of Anselmo? Would Imelda provide the kind of companionship Ulisse wanted? Would he provide what she needed? He would try his best. After all, that was all he could do.

As long as she stayed, there was hope. Hope for friendship, at least. That could be enough. It had to be. It was more than he had at the moment.

It probably didn't matter, in the long run. Marrying another spinner, whether it was Imelda Albizzi or some other woman, whether she loved him or not, was best for his country. Anything for Eraclea. Anything.

That was enough of a pity party for one night. It was time to go inside and get drunk.

CHAPTER TWENTY-ONE

Arturo spent the last day of Carnevale in his room, overseeing the seamstresses as they sewed the last of the corincanto into the wings. Not that he didn't trust them—he couldn't even tell if they were doing a good job or not—but this was his and Imelda's life's work finally coming to fruition. He couldn't *not* watch. Besides, the blacksmith had the pulley design, Imelda was at a party with Ulisse, and Calixta was off tending to political matters, so what else was there to do but stay home and work?

Everyone had laughed at them and called them obsessed. Arturo preferred dedicated. Or passionate. The only difference between a passion and an obsession was success. If—no, *when* they finally managed to fly, everyone would stop laughing. Instead, they'd praise the twins' dedication. They'd go down in history as Arturo and Imelda Albizzi, inventors of human flight.

The seamstresses finished and packed up. Arturo crouched in front of one of the pieces, lifting a feather to trace the stitching in the leather. It seemed good.

Imelda walked into Arturo's room and gasped. "Why are the wings here?"

"We don't have time to go all the way home to work anymore. Your wedding is only days away."

"But now everyone will know. Primo will find out!"

He sighed as he stood. "How many times must I tell you—everyone already knows."

"But they don't know about our plans for them."

Imelda was dressed to go out, in as nice a dress as he'd ever seen her in. She'd worn something else to the party with Ulisse, hadn't she? But now she was home and had changed, which meant she was going out with Anselmo. And she hadn't asked him to accompany them. There could only be one reason.

"Anselmo's going into the labyrinth tomorrow," he said. He'd been so preoccupied with the wings and his upcoming nuptials, he'd forgotten about his sister's emotions. Nothing unusual, typically, but she would be feeling a lot right now, and he'd neglected to check on her. "How are you, umm, handling it?"

Imelda toyed with her hair and turned her attention to the wings. "The feathers look good. I'm glad we added them." Imelda looked at the wings, running her fingers along the gray and white feathers. "When will we be able to test them again?"

"The pulleys should be ready tomorrow, and it will take me a day to attach them. Oh, and I need to buy more rope." He scrubbed his face. So much to do. "Did you use all of the wool roving?"

"There's actually quite a bit left. Do you need it?"

"No." He tilted his head as he considered the wings. "No, I think we're fine."

"Why did you ask?"

"Habit, I suppose."

The temple bell rang seven o'clock. Imelda narrowed her eyes at him. "Nice beard. I never thought you were the type to fall for a pretty face."

He rubbed his cheek across the three days' growth. It hadn't begun to itch yet, but it would soon. "Imelda—"

"Admit it, Arturo: you like her."

"And why shouldn't I? She's kind. She's done nothing but encourage me. She's asked me about my interests, and nobody but you has ever been that polite to me. I know you like her too. She's been exceedingly nice to you, so why are you so determined to hate her?"

"Because she's got her hooks in you!" She took a breath. Arturo braced himself—this clearly wasn't going to be good. "I'm worried she's only trying to get the wings for herself."

He rubbed the back of his neck as he turned away from her. "You're saying a beautiful princess couldn't possibly be interested in me for no other reason?"

"No, of course not, Arturo—" But she had no rebuttal. And maybe she was right. Behind him, Imelda's dress rustled as she moved. Her hand rested on his shoulder. "I've been with you this whole time, working toward this moment. *Our* moment. I don't want it ruined."

"Go, Imelda. Enjoy the last night of Carnevale. Don't worry—I'll be a good brother and stay home to finish the wings so you don't have to marry the big, bad king."

Imelda huffed and left, muttering under her breath. Arturo dropped into his chair. He'd told the truth. He always told the truth. Arturo would finish the wings before Imelda's wedding because, as far as he could see, she was getting the smallest boat in the fleet. Primo had betrothed her to an older, widowed king with children—though Arturo truly liked Ulisse—while Arturo would marry a young and beautiful princess. Once it was all done, and Imelda was free, she'd forget their argument. She'd finally drop this vendetta against Calixta, and rejoice with Arturo in his good match. She'd get to be with Anselmo—at some point, hopefully—and they could visit him in Ilios, where it was warm all year and no one would dare laugh at the Imperial Princess's odd husband.

Speaking of Calixta and marriage, Arturo reached under his mattress to retrieve his current read, something too shocking to leave out so maids would see it. A book on, umm, human procreation. But nothing so dry as that. Arturo's cheeks warmed even as he opened the book. But he needed to learn as much as he could before his wedding night. Calixta was too precious to risk going into the situation uneducated.

A knock came at the door. "Arturo!" Calixta said, sweeping in. The room, impossibly, seemed to grow brighter at her presence. "What are you reading?"

Arturo threw his book under the bed and jumped to his feet. "Just some boring math stuff."

She tilted her head. "I've never heard you describe math as boring."

"Umm ..." He scratched his cheek.

She laughed and pulled him in for a kiss. She trailed her fingers along his jawline. "I like your beard."

"That was the, umm, goal." He couldn't stop his eyes from flicking toward his bed.

Calixta laughed and turned toward the wings, holding his hand. "How I've longed to see these! They're incredible, Arturo."

"They're coming along."

"What's the next step?"

"Putting the pulley system together and attaching it to the wings. We have to finish before Imelda's wedding."

"Why before then?"

"Because she's moving to Eraclea after that, and I'll leave with you for Ilios."

She studied him, lips pursed slightly. She could clearly see through his half-truth.

He glanced away to stare at the wings, his cheeks growing warm. Normally he'd relish her attention, but not right now. Not with her perceptive look. "How was the party?"

She half-shrugged. "Well enough, but lacking my favorite Rialtano." Her tone was mischievous enough that he looked back to her. She didn't wear any of her normal refinement, just an off-white wool dress and simple earrings. No jewels in her hair or on her dress, no elaborately embroidered camisia, no gauzy veil down her back.

"Would you like to go outside?" he asked.

"What a fabulous idea. But first." She pulled something from her pocket and offered it. A golden apple, like the ones she and Nikkos had brought on their first day in Rialto. She put it in Arturo's hand. "My father calls me his golden apple. And I thought it could represent our upcoming marriage. Now I'm *your* golden apple."

"Excellent symbolism."

She beamed and hugged his arm. "I knew you would love it."

He set the apple on his desk, grabbed the thick blanket off his bed, then led her to the hall and up the stairs. But as they climbed through the palàso, he berated himself. What if Imelda was right? What if Calixta *did* want the wings, and not Arturo, and she was only feigning interest in him? What if she took them, and Imelda had no way to buy her freedom?

So many questions. Normally he enjoyed questions. They meant he was thinking and searching. But these questions weren't about systems and theories. People ... they were a different kind of problem, one he didn't relish spending his time on. They thought him oblivious, or unthoughtful, but really, he just hated dealing with it all. People were messy. Truth was absolute. The heart made no sense, while logic never failed.

None of this stopped him from guiding Calixta to the roof. Because he wanted to see her reaction. Because he wanted this moment, even with all of the messy moral quandaries. Because the heart made no sense, but sometimes it was infinitely more interesting than logic.

Maybe Imelda's hypothesis was right. But there was an equally good chance it was wrong.

At the top of a narrow staircase, he opened the door and beckoned for Calixta. She raised her eyebrows coyly as she walked past him and through the door. The sun hung low over the eastern horizon, reflecting off the water in the distance. The canals had turned into orange twists and turns. Galleys sailed through the lagoon, and birds took flight from clay rooftops. Her gaze turned to wonder as she took it in. Arturo barely even registered the view. He could see nothing past the light in her eyes.

She shivered as the breeze blew. He wrapped the blanket around her, and she smiled gratefully at him.

"You're dressed simply," he said.

"Simply?"

"No jewels in your hair or on your dress."

She tilted her head, waiting for him to continue. Waiting for him to make sense.

"All of that finery is your armor. Being charming and making people love you is how you fight for your empire. But right now, you're letting me see you as just you."

"And how do you feel about that?"

"I'm honored."

She stepped closer. One hand kept the blanket tight around her. "Everyone says you're oblivious, but you're not."

"I tune out all of the extraneous, but when something's important, I notice every detail."

She brushed his cheek with her fingertips, ever so lightly. "Why are we on the rooftop, Arturo?"

He coughed and nodded at the city. "I, uh, thought you'd like the view?"

"I love it." Her eyes reflected the light of the setting sun, and the brilliance of it crushed and remade him. No one had ever looked at him that way before, like he was a mystery to be discovered. For the first time, he understood all the songs and stories about love, how it drove men to reckless behavior and questionable decisions. Standing on this roof, beside the setting sun, with this bewitching woman when he should be laboring on his invention—surely this was a questionable decision. But he didn't care.

The sun touched the horizon. Its golden rays stretched across the city, turning the clouds pink and purple. He'd been right before—beauty didn't equal utility. But that didn't mean it held no value.

Calixta took his hand as they watched the sun disappear in the east. Twilight enveloped them, though enough light remained to see the delicate planes of her face.

Her gaze remained on the city, but she squeezed his fingers. "Do you think about our future?"

"A little," he admitted. "Moving to Ilios. The wedding. Never dealing with snow again."

"I've thought about it for days." Her expression turned hopeful and wistful. "You'll see my city, meet my parents, and, at our wedding, we'll wear beautiful gold and white robes. You can stay up late reading every night, and I'll help my brother rule. We'll take long morning walks along the palàso walls. And in the future, children. Babies to rock and love, toddlers tumbling around the gardens, feasting on golden apples. They'll play around your feet as you work on your next brilliant invention." She brushed his hair back from his face. "I hope at least one will inherit your keen eyes, your disregard for anything unimportant, your fascination with the impossible."

"My messy hair and inked fingers?"

"Those most of all." She sighed and laid her head against his shoulder.

He fumbled for a moment before putting his arm around her. "And the rest will have your grace and charisma."

"You can be charming too."

"I hardly think stating the obvious qualifies."

A lull fell between them. Not uncomfortable, though—far from it. Seagulls flew past them, calling out to each other. Calixta nestled into his arm, and he held her tighter.

"You'll be far from Imelda," Calixta said quietly.

"She'll visit. Eraclea's not as far from Ilios as Rialto is. The journey should be easier."

"Mm-hmm." She turned to face him. Above her silken hair, the first stars appeared in the ink dark sky.

She seemed to be waiting. He took a breath, then kissed her. It was even better than the first time in the temple. A small breeze swirled her hair around their heads, and night birds sang in the distance. She dropped the blanket to wrap her arms around his back, pulling him close. A hunger opened within him. He became aware of her whole length pressed against his body, her scent—cinnamon and apples—filling his lungs, making him drunk.

Suddenly she pulled back, a coy look on her face.

"What?" he asked. What had he done wrong? Had he been too awkward? Oh gods, this was mortifying.

"I saw what you were reading earlier, Arturo."

"Oh." Oh gods, oh gods. He retreated back a step. "I just ... don't want to ... disappoint you on our wedding night."

"You won't disappoint me." Her tone was concerned as she took his hand to pull him to her. "You won't ever disappoint me. In anything."

"It's inevitable that I will."

She half-shrugged, then wrapped her arms around his neck. "Cares for another day."

Her lips found his, and her urgency matched his hunger. Her fingers roamed across his chest, around to his back, onto his shoulders. Her fingers dipped under his collar, warm and tickling on his neck.

"Wait." He pulled back, took in her appearance again. A simple dress with no camisia over it, no jewels to get tangled in her hair. "Did you ... want to ..."

She laughed. "You think I came to seduce you?"

"I mean ... maybe?"

"Oh, you're too adorable." She kissed his cheek. "You're not ready—"

"I'm not. I'm sorry."

"No, that's fine. I was saying you're not ready, but also there's no rush. We have our whole lives. And the more we know each other, the better it will get. However." Her tone turned playful. "I *am* tired from standing all night."

He straightened the blanket on the ground. Then they lay down, he on his back and she on her side next to him. She walked her fingers up his chest then caressed his cheek before laying her head on his shoulder.

"There's the elephant." She pointed out a constellation directly overhead. Her hand moved to a different portion of the sky. "And the tiger."

"We call that one Giatoro."

"I will never tire of that story."

"Then I will never tire of telling it to you."

She rolled on top of him, pulling her side of the blanket with her. Heat soon filled the space between. "We'll make our own story."

The next kiss was like lightning, light and heat all at once. How had he been so lucky to find himself betrothed to such a woman? She was more beautiful than the stars, more charming than the sea, more ... more ... just more than he ever thought he'd ever find.

She was truth.

She was Arturo's truth.

Calixta was right—there was no need to go farther than he was comfortable tonight. Soon he'd be ready, and there would be no reason to worry about disappointing her. But for now he was happy to memorize the softness of her lips, the smell of her skin, and the way her hair created a curtain between them and the rest of the world.

Chapter Twenty-Two

Imelda rushed through the busy streets. All around her, the revelry had already started. The last night of Carnevale, the last night of the old year, and everyone's final chance for celebration. She wove around people dancing, laughing, and quite a few couples kissing against buildings. All well on their way to drunkenness. Men and women pulled her in for a spin or a sloppy kiss on the cheek. She shoved them away, and quickened her step.

She was late for her meeting with Anselmo at La Piaza del Leon. After leaving the party with Ulisse, Imelda had quickly changed at the palàso then rushed to the guild island, Paglia, where she'd bought a small skein of spirit rose corincanto. Though it weighed nearly nothing, it felt like a gemstone in her purse.

In her rush, she took back alleys. There were far more amorous couples, but they kept to themselves. Oh yes, it was certainly the last night of Carnevale. People usually reserved that kind of behavior for indoors during the rest of the week, but at the end, it all spilled out. Everyone had to enjoy themselves while they could. Tomorrow was the day of rest. Tomorrow they could sleep. And tomorrow they began their fast. The last of the winter stores were about to spoil. They'd endure meager portions and bland foods until the first fruits of spring. Tonight was a night of feasting and celebration.

Imelda crossed the bridge to Centro. She shouldn't have snapped at Arturo. All the hope she'd harbored for the last week and a half was coming to a head. All the hope, and all the fear. In only a few days, her fate would be sealed. It was impossible not to be afraid. But he'd always been there for her. This time would be no different.

La Piaza del Leon was filled edge-to-edge with people. The crowd churned happily, laughing and chatting as they waited for the crowning moment of Carnevale. Highborn and lowborn intermingled easily, a sight only witnessed during the holiday week. Music rolled across the space, a lovely backdrop to the revelry. An army of candles illuminated El Casteo de Giore, shining over Zitello's effigy and across the square. The light reached Palàso Dogal, which reflected it back. The space was as bright as morning, all the masks and laughing faces rendered in crisp detail.

Anselmo was easy to find, even wearing his Bauta mask, watching the mob from the side. Her heart leapt, and she couldn't stop a smile from pushing through. His shirt stretched across his strong shoulders. More than one woman glanced in his direction. A few even approached him, but he quickly turned them away. He was beautiful, and he was all hers. She put a hand on the spirit rose corincanto in her purse, and pushed her way over. The revelers didn't part easily. She had to get to him. This was their last night; she couldn't waste another moment.

"Let's get out of here," she said when she reached him.

"Don't you want to see the ceremony?"

"I saw last year's. They're all the same, right?"

"I ..." He grimaced. "I want to start the year off right. Since tomorrow is the labyrinth. I just ... want to make sure I do everything the correct way."

"Are you nervous?"

"No. I'm ready. Excited, even. But it still doesn't hurt to please the gods beforehand."

"I admire your confidence, but wish you were more cautious." She could wait a few minutes, but that was it. "I understand. But we're gone as soon as they light the bonfire."

A high priest climbed a scaffold next to Zitello's effigy. The roar of the crowd diminished to a murmur as he raised his hands. "Please join me in prayer." He bowed his head. Everyone followed suit. "Father Giore, we thank you for this season. For the cold and the dark, the lean and the barren. In your wisdom, you have taught us that winter is a gift. It strengthens us, physically and mentally. It makes us appreciate the beauty of spring, the warmth of summer, and the bounty of autumn. We are a strong people, carving our life in the swamp and out of the sea. Without winter, we would not have the fortitude for this life. We would not know how to weather the emotional winters of our life, times of sickness, mourning, uncertainty, and poverty. Thank you for winter. Thank you, even, for the trickster winter king, Zitello. Help us to remember your lessons all year long. This we pray. Amen."

The word rippled across the gathering. The high priest held up his hands for their continued silence, though he didn't need to—everyone knew what came next.

"Five minutes," Imelda whispered. Anselmo took her hand in his, hiding their grasp in the folds of her skirt.

The high priest continued. "It is now time to announce this year's Torch Bearer. They exemplify various traits from year to year, but one thing is constant—they have accomplished great things for

La Serenìsima Repùblica de Rialto. This year's honored citizen is a woman who displays strength, determination, and intelligence in abundance. Not only did she defeat the rebellion in Zorzi, but she orchestrated a surrender that benefited our city most advantageously. I have known her since she was a baby, and it's my honor to call her my friend. Siora Venezia Dandolo, Fleet Admiral of the military."

Venezia, holding a torch, climbed the stairs to the platform. Despite the frigid temperature, she wore a drapey black dress with modest silver embroidery and red alpaca corincanto along the neckline, sleeves, and high waist. She glittered in the firelight as she kissed cheeks three times with the high priest. Lazaro beamed beside her.

Anselmo nudged Imelda. "Did you know about this?"

"I haven't seen her much lately. She's probably been busy garnering support for her bid for Doxe. I barely pay attention to that stuff."

"What do you think about?"

"You." She squeezed his hand. He squeezed back.

"Thank you, High Priest Esposito." Venezia turned to the crowd. "I'm honored beyond words. I've dedicated my life to the republic. We live in the greatest sovereignty the world has seen, greater even than Sacresta, from whence our ancestors came. With my leadership, I will strengthen it even further. We will not go down in history with greatness—we will continue our legacy far into the future." She held the torch aloft. "For Rialto!" Everyone cheered. She threw the fire onto the kindling at the effigy's feet, and the flames sprang to life.

"We now banish you, Zitello," the high priest intoned. "May Father Giore allow you to return to us after a bountiful harvest."

Music started as he, Venezia, and Lazaro descended from the scaffold. People made their way to the pyre, untying the red thread around their wrist and tossing it into the blaze. Hemp corincanto tinged the smoke purple, casting a woodsy smell over the piazza.

Imelda undid the red string around her wrist. "Let's burn these and get out of here."

They wove through the crowd to the bonfire. The effigy was ablaze, its clothes melting against the straw and its eyes hidden by the flames. Heat stung Imelda's cheeks as she threw the thread in. It ignited immediately and curled in on itself as the flames consumed it. Purple smoke mixed with the gray smoke and ash from the wood, and together they rose into the sky. Her secret, released into the night.

Anselmo still wore his hemp, his mouth uncertain. Imelda untied his lopsided bow. "You're supposed to burn it."

"I know," he grumbled. "I just feel like I'm throwing away a hundred ducats." But he tossed the string in.

"What's your secret, Lieutenant?"

Anselmo gazed at the blaze, orange and yellow reflecting in his eyes. He smiled as he looked up. He kissed her cheeks, pausing on the second one to whisper, "You are."

Her head swam, and she tugged at his shirt. "Let's go."

They started across the piaza, weaving through the congregation.

"What's your secret, siora?" he asked.

She touched her purse with the spirit rose corincanto. "I'll tell you at my house."

Home was quiet and cold when they slipped in through a side door. Moonlight shone through the windows, making her home cozier and grander than she remembered it. Anselmo came up behind her, wrapping his arms around her waist as he kissed her neck. "So? What's your secret?"

"I—" She turned, and faltered. "Meet me in my room. And start a fire."

He gave her an amused look, but did as told. She went to the kitchen, retrieving a bottle of wine and two glasses. Her fingers trembled. Was it right to do this? The Heart Stitch was a sacred, binding act, saved only for the strongest of love. It wasn't her love she doubted, but the future felt so uncertain. What if they didn't complete the wings in time? Primo would marry her off to Ulisse, yet she'd be forever bound to the man she loved but would never see again.

She made her way to her room. Anselmo stood in front of the glowing hearth, arms crossed with one hand at his mouth, lost in thought. She paused in the doorway, watching the light dance across his face. The wings wouldn't fail. They couldn't. She had to be with this man who held her heart. Her soul would accept nothing else.

Her thirst for wine disappeared, replaced by a greater need. She set the bottle and glasses on the floor and walked to him. "I want to do the Heart Stitch with you. Tonight."

His face ran through a series of emotions. Surprise, joy, tenderness, and finally settling on sorrow. "We can't."

Her heart stuttered, and she grabbed his hands. She'd never considered he'd react this way. "Don't you want to?"

"Of course I do." He scrubbed his hair. "But there's no point. You're getting married next week."

"I'm not. Remember the wings, the ones Arturo and I have been working on for years? We're going to finish them and sell the design to Venezia. They're almost done, and you should see them. They're magnificent. Arturo said they'll be ready in a few days, and Venezia has agreed to pay us well. It won't matter if Primo cuts me off from the family money because I'll have my own. I'll be free to do what I want." Her voice dropped to a whisper. "I'll be free to wait for you to conquer the labyrinth. I'll be free to be with you."

"And if the wings fail?"

"They won't." She pulled the spirit rose corincanto from her purse and held it up like an offering. "Do you trust me?"

"Of course."

"And do you love me?"

He pressed a kiss to her forehead. "More than anything."

He sat on the floor as she went to her desk. She cut the skein in half, setting one half on the desk, then grabbed a needle. She knelt in front of the fire to hold the needle and the knife in the flames. When the needle burned her skin, she gave the knife to Anselmo and set the needle in her lap. She pulled the strap of her dress off her shoulder, freeing her left arm. The top of her left breast was exposed. The dress she'd worn to the party had revealed more with its deep V, but she felt so much more vulnerable. Anselmo's gaze was soft, almost reverent as he pulled her into his lap. He ran his thumb along her skin.

"I can take it all the way off," she whispered.

He rested his forehead against hers. "Keep it on. I can barely focus as it is."

She put her hands on his cheeks and stared into those blue, blue eyes. The world fell away, lost in the darkness outside the circle of firelight. She kissed him, clutching at his shirt. His hands went to her knees, hesitating for a moment before traveling under her skirt and up to her thighs. She shivered and pulled his shirt off. He was all muscle, sculpted from marble like an ancient god of war. She kissed his neck as her fingers explored his torso. Across his pecs, down his abs, skirting along the waistband of his pants.

He put his hand on hers with a laugh. "You have to stop if we're going to do this."

She obliged with a mischievous look. He took the knife and sliced himself above his heart. Straight and shallow, no more than an inch long. Blood seeped out and dripped down his chest. Imelda cut herself in the same spot, whimpering at the sharpness of the pain. She was used to cutting herself to spin corincanto, but her palm had grown desensitized over the years. This skin, flush with the heat from the fire and her heart, was unused to injury. She threaded the needle, and began to stitch up his wound, leaving plenty of spirit rose at one end. Anselmo didn't wince or flinch as she wove the yarn in and out of his skin. He sat still as an island, his breath even. She tied the suture off, and re-threaded the needle on the other end of the corincanto.

Anselmo took a shuddering breath. "I don't know if I can do this."

"Don't you know how?"

"I've stitched up fellow soldiers. But this is different. It's you."

She gave him the needle, then wrapped her hand around his. He pushed the needle through, and she gasped. Tears came, her palms sweat, and she had to bite her lip as he continued. And yet, despite the pain, she felt as though she already wore wings. She watched Anselmo, his brow pinched with concentration. She memorized his face in that moment, his care and focus, the orange glow on his cheeks, the texture of his beard, the line of his nose. The tenderness of his face softened the pain in her chest, sweetened it, purified it. She'd never forget this moment, as long as she lived.

Finally Anselmo tied off the stitch. A long, crimson string connected them, running from her heart to his. She ran her finger along it, careful not to pull on it. The throbbing in her chest bowed before her wonder. Blood seeped into the lining of her dress, and magic pulsed along the thread. It tingled where the corincanto touched her skin. The feeling radiated from the spot above her heart, up her neck, down into her arms, across her torso.

And another sensation. Anselmo's presence sat in her mind. She could feel his closeness, both with body and mind. If he stood across the world, she knew she could close her eyes and point to his exact location.

"I love you," she whispered.

The kiss that followed tasted of promises and the future. She lost herself in it. Her heart pounded, magnified by the feel of his pulse through the thread. She could live forever in that moment, in the feel of his lips on hers, in the warmth of the fire, and the security of his arms.

Anselmo finally pulled himself free to cut the spirit rose, which he gave to her. She threw it in the fire, and it puffed into a red ball of smoke.

"We're bound," he said.

"In this life and the next." She smoothed his hair back from his face. "There's something else I want—you."

He traced the stitch in her chest. His fingertips dipped beneath the edge of her neckline, and she shivered. "Are you sure?" he asked.

"I've never been more sure of anything."

"But I might die in the labyrinth."

"Oh no, Lieutenant, I won't let you talk me out of this like you did four years ago." She climbed onto his lap, draping an arm around his shoulder, her other hand on his chest. "I won't let you resist me this time."

"I willingly surrender."

He kissed along her jaw and reached under her skirt to caress her hip. She'd thought she'd lost herself before, in the moments after the Heart Stitch, but that was nothing compared to the blaze across her skin now, the sweet and wild sensations of lips and hands across the planes of her body. The flames in the hearth crackled, and Imelda burned.

Anselmo laid her down, then settled next to her, smiling as he stroked her cheek.

"What?" Imelda asked.

"I'm savoring this moment. I've dreamed of it for so long."

"Don't savor too long." She laughed. "If I have to wait any longer, I might burst."

"Mmmm." He pulled her dress off slowly, his knuckles brushing the length of her body. She'd never known such exquisite torture could exist, never known she could lose herself in the physical and find herself in the frenzy. He nuzzled her ear as his fingers tangled in her hair. "And I haven't even gotten started yet."

Chapter Twenty-Three

Despite Nikkoforos's threats, tonight had been a triumph for Venezia. Yet she sank onto the chair in front of her vanity with a sigh. Her feet ached, and her head throbbed. She pulled the knives from their sheaths and set them one by one on the tabletop. Her hair hung loose, and in the mirror, she could see dark circles lurking under her eyes.

What a long Carnevale it had been. Long and frustrating. She'd approached the Council members during the last week, and all of them scoffed at the idea of supporting Janus. Two had even laughed directly in her face.

Shortsighted fools. They couldn't get past their hatred to see the opportunity—they were more narrow-minded than she'd anticipated. La Serenìsima Repùblica de Rialto was on the path to becoming one of the great world powers, and controlling the Iliano Empire would lend wind to its sails. Yes, Ilios was not the dominant empire it once was, but it still spanned well over a thousand kilometers. Control of the Bogasa Strait and the income that came with it made it even more enticing. And it held so many resources—diamond mines, sources for every kind of thread fiber, hundreds of miles of the spice road. All of that could belong to Rialto.

Everyone had a price. She hadn't found the Council members' yet, but she would.

If only the celebratory dinner had gone better. Her disgusting husband's outrageous behavior had decimated her chances of winning. Had he done it on purpose? He rarely drank himself to sloppy drunkenness. She unsheathed her Fleet Admiral's ceremonial knife and twirled it. The blade caught the flames from the hearth, then the candle on her vanity, reflecting the light this way and that. Such a pretty knife, and one not intended for use. What a waste.

If only Ulisse were from Rialto. No doubt he would side with her. If he had been born here, he would've been free to marry whomever he wished—which meant they would probably be husband and wife. Tonight he'd stood on the balcony with her, as close as he had long ago, laughing at his own self-deprecating humor. He had a great laugh, full-bodied and unashamed. The wind had tousled his hair even further, and the cut of his unbuttoned coat had accentuated his physique, molded from years of swimming and swordsmanship. He'd mastered the look of nonchalant refinement long ago. Fourteen years ago, she'd fallen for it as only a girl can. It didn't inspire jellyfish in her stomach anymore, but she still appreciated it, especially after years of the stiff polish of Rialtano politicians.

What a match they could've been. They could've ruled the world.

Venezia walked to her bed and deposited the knives in the hole in her mattress. There was no point in dreaming about what could've been. That kind of dream had no use, no value. The only tools worth considering were what was and what could be.

She'd hated telling him about Imelda and Anselmo, but someone needed to. Plus, if he did help Imelda with the wings, then they'd get done sooner and Venezia would have them sooner as well. She hadn't found the Council members' monetary price, but surely the wings would be enough to entice them.

She rubbed her temples, at the headache that brewed behind her eyes. It had been a long Carnevale, but only two weeks since her last seizure. She should be fine for another couple of weeks.

A knock sounded on the door, and at Venezia's command, Kari stepped inside, nodding in deference. "Sior Lazaro requests your presence, mè siora."

Venezia sighed, but complied. She found Lazaro in his room, holding two glasses of wine. He pushed one into her hand, which she eyed warily.

"What's this about?"

"I want to celebrate the Citizen of Honor."

She snorted. "My one victory this week."

"It's no small win, mè amor. The people love you."

"The people don't elect the Doxe."

He sat on his bed and pulled her into his lap. She was too tired to drag herself from his grasp. "Not directly, no. But they elect the Senate, who elect the Council, who elect the Doxe. You could easily find a hundred fifty or so senators who would support you."

"But that would be after the Dogal elections." She ignored him as he rubbed her back. "I don't want to wait another four years." Which meant four more years of enduring Lazaro's presence. He might not even have four more years left in him, and then how would she win?

"You'll be thirty-six, still one of the youngest Doxi to reign. Have patience."

"And where was this advice four years ago?"

"You were twenty-eight. I had no idea you were planning on running so young."

"Primo was twenty-six when he was elected."

He *hmmed* and started playing with her hair. She didn't have time for this. She clinked her glass against his and downed her wine. "You're drunk, and I'm tired. I'll send in your plaything."

He was right, but she'd never admit it to him. He'd offered sound political advice, and that was the reason she'd married him. But he'd offered it too late. She'd consider the tactic after the Dogal election—if she needed to. She couldn't count herself out this early. There was still time.

Kari waited in the hallway. Venezia jerked her head toward Lazaro's door. As Kari hurried inside, Venezia went to her room, got in bed, and fell asleep.

⚬—✕—⚬

She awoke suddenly, gasping for breath. Lazaro straddled her, kissing her neck, fondling one of her breasts. She struggled against him.

"Lazaro." She pushed against his chest, but he didn't budge. How was a sixty-year-old man this strong? "Go find Kari."

"I don't want a slave," he murmured in her ear. He grabbed her hair and pulled her head back. "I want my wife."

His lips mashed against hers. She didn't kiss back, and he didn't notice—or care. He tugged at her gown, pulling it down over her shoulders and exposing her chest to the cold. She bit down the trembling that threatened to overtake her, refused to give into fear. For a moment, she was nineteen years old again, petrified on her wedding night. If only he'd been patient. If only he'd been kind and understood that inside her tough exterior, she shrank from every touch. He'd always insisted she'd come to enjoy it, even learn to love him. How wrong he'd been.

But it had been thirteen years, and she'd learned a few tricks. Doing her best to ignore his mouth on her chest, she reached under her pillow ... and found nothing. Her knives, where were her knives? Both hands searched now, but the blades were gone.

Terror lanced through her heart, quickening her pulse and weakening her resolve. She had to go inside, that was her instinct—to find that place deep inside herself so this became a distant memory. It was tempting, oh so tempting, to pretend this was only her body, that it wasn't *her*.

Lazaro grabbed at her skirt, yanking it up, until he could squeeze the bare flesh of her thigh. His fingers continued to grope, rough and demanding. She squeezed her legs together, but his hand squirmed in. There was no pleasure in this, only bitterness, and it jolted her into action. She didn't have knives, and she wasn't stronger than him, but she was a fighter. She reached down and took hold of his testicles, giving them a slight twist. Enough to discomfort him, and enough to show her intention.

"Get off me," she said, voice low and dangerous.

Lazaro grunted. With his free hand, he tried to break her grasp. His body might've been stronger than hers, but not his grip. Eight years of sword training had strengthened her in more ways than one.

"You think you'll actually maim me? You'd be jailed in a heartbeat, Fleet Admiral or not."

"I'll blame Kari."

"No one would believe she has the guts."

She pulled on his wrist to get his fingers out of her, but he dug his nails in. Pain flared, sharp and exact. She twisted his testicles further as sweat broke out along her hairline. They stared at each other, locked in their suffering. Finally, Lazaro spat on her face and hauled himself off her.

"Such a hateful wife," he snarled. "No wonder Rea never blessed you with children."

That wasn't the reason why, but now wasn't the time to ponder on that. Venezia waited until he closed the door behind him, then ran and locked it. Her knives sat on her vanity, useless. Not that she could do anything now. One day she'd use him up and dispose of him like leftover fish. But she needed him for now, so he still wielded power over her. Even after everything she'd accomplished, he held her in his wrinkled old fists.

Fear finally flooded her veins, causing her hands to tremble as she covered her face and wept.

CHAPTER TWENTY-FOUR

Anselmo waited at the dock on Porto, so early the sun hadn't risen yet. Fog covered the city, muffling all sound. The other soldiers mingled with their patrons, fitting their new cuirasses, swinging their new swords.

Anselmo had no cuirass, no sword, no shield, not even a spear. Ulisse hadn't shown up yet.

And if he didn't, Anselmo would have to enter the labyrinth with nothing but the shirt on his back and the boots on his feet.

"Time to go," a vice admiral said. He stood by the gangplank to a naval galley.

"Ten minutes more, sir," Rafael said. "Lieutenant Errari's patron is running late."

"Three minutes," the vice admiral said.

"Five. Please."

"Fine. But not a moment longer."

Anselmo nodded at Rafael, and Rafael nodded back, though concern dug a crease into his forehead.

It grew quiet as everyone waited to see if Ulisse would show up.

Minutes passed in silence. The vice admiral waved for the soldiers to board the galley.

"Wait!" a voice called from down the canal. A góndola, going faster than Anselmo had ever thought possible, raced up to the dock. Ulisse climbed out, followed by his guard. Ulisse held a sword and shield, while the guard carried a spear and cuirass.

Ulisse rushed over to Anselmo. "Please forgive me," he said quietly, waving his guard over. "I'm afraid I overslept. Last night of Carnevale, you know."

"Yes, Your Majesty. Of course, no problem." Anselmo put the cuirass on and barely refrained from running a hand along the perfectly polished bronze. It was thicker than his normal one, though not too weighty to be unwieldy. Even the leather pteruges of the skirt had been polished enough to shine in the dull pre-dawn light. The guard tightened the straps of the cuirass as Anselmo slung the sheathed sword across his body.

"I hope the quality is to your liking," Ulisse said.

Anselmo unsheathed the blade and swung it through the air. A kopis, recurved for hacking, unlike his leaf-shaped xiphos in his room, which was a thrusting weapon. But even with the unfamiliar weight balance, Anselmo could tell it was a finer weapon than he'd ever held before.

"Thank you, Your Majesty. This is beyond anything I expected."

"A soldier needs three things before going into battle: a sharpened sword, plenty of food, and a good night's sleep."

Something in Ulisse's voice made Anselmo look up from the sword, but the man's face was relaxed.

"Wise words, Your Majesty."

Ulisse chuckled. "My father was fond of the saying."

"Time to go," the vice admiral called.

Ulisse waved at his guard, who offered the shield and spear. Anselmo sheathed his sword and accepted them. "I've heard you'll be gone in a few days."

"I'll be back in Eraclea when you emerge from the labyrinth. And I know you will emerge. Good luck, Lieutenant." With a nod, Ulisse returned to his góndola. Anselmo and the others boarded their ship.

The galley cut through the early morning fog like a shark through a school of fish. Anselmo stood at the stern as the boat crept closer to the labyrinth—a vague darkness in the mist, which slowly took shape until a fortress loomed ahead. The lowing of a minotaur echoed across the lagoon. In front of him, the other soldiers were silent. Anselmo inspected their cuirasses and shields from where he stood. Their gear was all fine, but none of it matched the craftsmanship of Anselmo's, his gift from Imelda's betrothed.

Guilt twisted his gut. He hadn't known who Ulisse was when he'd accepted Ulisse's patronage, so he hadn't betrayed him. And even if he had, Anselmo knew he wouldn't have rejected Ulisse's offer. He wouldn't be about to enter the labyrinth without it.

Maybe Anselmo was dirty. But he needed every advantage he could find. To survive, to reach nobility, to marry Imelda.

All thoughts of Ulisse faded. Imelda. Anselmo had woken early, extricating himself from Imelda's arms and kissing her forehead before slipping out. He could've woken her, but they'd been up late and she had nearly as big a day ahead of her as he did. She had to finish those wings, those impossible, wonderful wings. He could feel her presence in his mind. He knew the direction she lay in, but it wasn't enough. He could've woken her, and he'd wanted to. Wanted to look into her eyes once more, tell her what she meant to him, kiss the Heart Stitch on her chest and promise again and again he'd return. It had been painful, leaving her like that.

Almost as painful as it had been to lie to her. He'd wanted to tell her about his threads, but when the moment came, he failed. He couldn't go back on a lifetime of caution, of his mother's words drilled into him day after day after day. Tell no one. Trust no one. Stay alive. The knots were hidden, so there was no need to take the risk by telling anyone. He could trust Imelda, but Ceso's words rang in his mind. *Anyone will turn you in.* Not Imelda, surely not her. But it was too late. He'd tell her as soon as he emerged from the labyrinth. As soon as they could be together.

As long as she escaped marriage to Ulisse first.

His chest throbbed, though not from pain. They'd used cotton corincanto-stitched cloths to heal the wounds, leaving only the threads. How was this acceptable while his threads from Ceso were heresy? According to Ceso, it was once acceptable. But Anselmo had been a child, and his mother had led him to a potentially fatal ceremony. And the pain in his chest—that did not compare. Last night had been a jellyfish sting. His threads ... nothing could be more painful than what he'd endured getting those. He'd broken the bite stick before finally passing out. He could see his mother's face now, tears in her eyes and a determined twist to her lips as she'd brandished the knife. She'd hurt him more than anyone ever would, and he thanked her every day for it.

All of that led up to this moment. Even the night before with Imelda was part of his preparation. She was his reason for going through the labyrinth, and he needed to focus. As pleasant as it was reliving the last hours together, the distraction would get him killed.

The boat pulled up to the beach, and the soldiers disembarked. Rafael led the way, with Anselmo—as lowest ranked—bringing up the rear. The walls of the labyrinth loomed before them, nine meters tall and disappearing into the fog on either side. Guards stood on towers about fifteen meters away on each side. The great metal gates were carved with scenes of men battling hulking minotaurs with rippling muscles, topped by an engraving: *Enter as a soldier. Emerge as a Lion.* Doxe Albizzi, Fleet Admiral Dandolo, Admiral Galbani, two Lion Vice Admirals, and the high priest waited on a wooden platform. Four soldiers stood behind the Doxe, who wore the silver crown and sash of his station.

And Prince Nikkoforos, with his own guard behind him.

No other nobles stood on the platform. No doubt the prince had been given special permission, considering his status and relationship with Rialto. A reminder that his empire was richer, bigger, and more powerful.

And rather than wearing one of his fancy jackets, Nikkoforos wore an elaborate military costume—there could be no other way to describe it. A white camisia with an abundance of corincanto stitched along the bottom hem, shiny chain-metal tunic and skirt, bright red cape, and tall boots studded with rubies. He made even the Doxe, in his formal black doublet, look like a pauper.

"Welcome, soldiers. And Your Imperial Highness." Doxe Albizzi clasped his hands behind his back. He glanced at the prince and a frown rippled across his face. "First of all, I commend your ambition and bravery. You are the reason we have such a formidable military. Without men like you, we would not be the Muriseano power that we are. The next several days will test you to your utmost. Your strength, your intelligence, and your strategy will all reach their limits as you battle your way through the labyrinth. When you find yourself at your weakest, remember why you're doing this. When you emerge successful, you will be a Lion, one of the world's elite. Those of you in the merchant and lower classes will be automatically raised to nobility. This is your chance to weave your name into the tapestry of glory."

The Doxe cleared his throat and shifted his feet the smallest bit. The frown returned. "Second, our esteemed guest, Imperial Prince Nikkoforos Heraclius, shall accompany you through the labyrinth."

What was this bullshit? Rage exploded in Anselmo's heart, and his blood vessels carried it to every corner of his body. He dug his heel into the dirt, feeling the knot under his skin press against his muscles.

The soldiers didn't respond verbally, but cuirasses creaked and boots shuffled in the dirt as they exchanged glances. Their annoyance filled the air, thick as the morning fog. They might not have earned entry honestly as Anselmo had, but at least they'd paid. But the fancy heir of Ilios could walk right in by birthright alone. Up on the platform, he looked excited—the same expression he'd had when Imelda had thrown her necklace into the pot at the Carnevale party. He pretended to ignore the soldiers' frustration, but Anselmo could see his eyes moving through the group.

"I know you will all perform to your utmost ability." The Doxe's voice hardened, showed his true message: Protect the prince at all costs. "I wish you all the best of luck."

Fleet Admiral Dandolo moved to the front. Her arms were far more muscular than any woman Anselmo had seen. Women on the middle islands had stout arms from scrubbing pots and washing clothes, but none boasted the defined curves of the Admiral's biceps—evident even through the sleeves of her jacket. His mother's had been the same when he was younger, strengthened through her years as a mercenary. She'd been as tall as the Fleet Admiral as well, and as ambitious. He was surprised by how similar they were.

"As you know, many men have died in the labyrinth," Dandolo said. "You are entering of your own free will. You may relinquish your opportunity until we close the gates. But know this: if you quit, you will never be allowed back in. This is your one chance to become a

Lion. Our elite team can have only the strongest, in body and mind. You have two outcomes facing you: survive and pass, or die. We will not open the gates until you complete the objective. If you attempt to leave the labyrinth by any other means, you will be executed on the spot." She turned to Prince Nikkoforos with an incline of her head. "Except for you, of course, Your Highness."

"Fleet Admiral." Nikkoforos stepped forward and put a hand on her shoulder. "I am no coward, and I know none of these fine soldiers are either." He gestured toward the group. "We'll all exit together, victorious."

Dandolo smiled tightly. "I have no doubt of it, Your Highness." She shifted away from him, just enough to free herself from his grasp. He folded his arms as if he'd intended the series of interactions.

"We, the other admirals and myself, will watch your performance from the sentry posts. Do not forget that. We will see everything, the good and the bad. How you fight, but also how you work together. Inside, rank ceases to exist, though I do suggest picking a leader. How long you stay in the labyrinth is entirely dependent on your performance. Once you emerge from the labyrinth, you are never to speak about your experience. The labyrinth's success as a testing and training ground is partly due to its secrecy.

"Last, and most importantly, we have hidden a sword in the labyrinth. It is a Shantzese jianò with a lion-head hilt, made by the finest smiths in Shantze. Within the steel, they've embedded strands of wool corincanto. The already exceptional metal is indestructible and will never need sharpening. When you exit the labyrinth, you will elect one candidate to be promoted to Lion captain. That person will get the sword. Does everyone understand the terms?"

"Yes, Fleet Admiral," they said in unison.

"I would appreciate the same confidentiality from you, Your Highness," the Fleet Admiral said.

Prince Nikkoforos put a hand on his chest. "You have my word."

"May Giore favor and Rea bless you."

The high priest stepped up, his silver robes glistening. He opened the holy book and started reading. Anselmo resisted the urge to shift his feet. Enough with all of the pomp. They just needed to get in. The sooner he entered, the sooner he could emerge victorious—and the sooner he could marry Imelda. He felt the city at his back, still slumbering after the last night of Carnevale. Imelda needed to return to the palàso before anyone noticed her absence, so she was probably already awake. Fixing her hair, slipping on the dress he'd slid off her the night before ...

Aselmo gripped his shield, honing his attention on the stiff new leather of the handle. He had to stay focused. Even with the prince making a show of removing his crimson cape and putting on a helmet. Even with the priest leading them in prayer. Even with his heart stitch pulsing in his skin, in sync with his own heartbeat.

Finally, the gates groaned open, and the priest lit his incense. Purple smoke drifted out of the thurible, pooling in front of the entrance. The priest placed both hands on his own forehead. "May Giore grant wisdom." He touched his chest. "May Rea confer power." Last, he held his fingers in front of his eyes. "May Zitello not turn his trickster eyes upon you."

Nikkoforos hopped off the platform and walked to the front of the soldiers—without his guard. Primo hurried over to the prince.

"Your Highness, I urge you to bring your guard with you."

"Nonsense." Nikkoforos checked his sword sheath at his side. "No need to put his life in danger."

Or the prince's pride. Anselmo bit down a grunt.

Nikkoforos approached the incense. He made the sign of the gods—head and heart—and walked through the smoke. One by one, the men filed through. Anselmo's muscles tensed. They should be rushing through those gates, spears and shields held high as they readied for battle. Instead they had to appease the gods—gods who didn't exist, according to Ceso. So much ceremony, with so few to watch.

Fleet Admiral Dandolo took Anselmo by the elbow. "Keep him alive at all costs." Her voice was low, for his ears alone. "If he dies, we lose everything. Ensure he lives, and I will reward you no matter who gets the sword."

He nodded, but she'd already walked away.

Anselmo finally entered, hastily touching his head and heart. He may be the last one in, but he wouldn't be the last out. As he walked through the hemp cloud, Admiral Dandolo's voice spoke in his mind. *"Your objective is to find the sword and bring it out with you. Think sharply, act quickly, and live."*

Finally, the open gates stood before him. The other men waited inside, on a barren strip of dirt that strangely sloped downward toward the interior of the labyrinth. He joined them. Another set of gates—these plain metal—stood before them. Anselmo looked back. Rialto floated in the distance. The palàso penetrated the fog, its white walls shining in the sun. Imelda was in there, with corincanto sewn into her skin, connecting her to him. His own chest pounded, and the Heart Stitch pulsed. Anselmo would return to her. She would finish her wings, he'd emerge as a Lion—even with the ridiculous addition of keeping the prince alive—and nothing would keep them apart.

Chapter Twenty-Five

The outer gates closed with a thunderous clap. Only the sound of their breathing and the waves crashing on the shore outside broke the silence. The soldiers shifted, their cuirasses creaking. Some stomped their feet. Anselmo's palms began to sweat.

The plain interior gates groaned open.

"Ready, men," Nikkoforos said. The others gathered around and behind him.

The opening widened, large enough, surely, for a minotaur. But nothing charged. Nothing even moved except wind through the trees and across water covering the ground. Was Anselmo seeing that correctly? Yes, as the gates fully opened, the labyrinth revealed itself as a swamp. Hence why the ground sloped down. He saw strange trees with roots jutting out of the water and some kind of gray plant dangling from the branches. Frogs hopped on small mounds of mud, and though the fog didn't reach into the labyrinth, the canopy of the trees was thick enough that visibility was twenty-five meters at most.

Anselmo straightened out of his defensive posture in surprise, but no one else looked shocked. Instead, relief flashed across their faces. Some grinned at each other.

Even Nikkoforos didn't register any shock. Someone had prepared him for what lay ahead.

They all knew. The secrecy of the labyrinth was nothing but a lie—for highborns at least. But lowborns like Anselmo had ignorance heaped onto their pile of disadvantages.

The ground rumbled.

"Walls moving," someone murmured.

Some men started down the dry dirt hill toward the water.

Rafael quietly cleared his throat. "We need to pick a leader."

"Good memory, Captain," Nikkoforos said. He stuck his spear into the dirt in front of him. "I'd like to be considered, if you good men wouldn't mind following a foreigner."

Anselmo stuck his spear into the dirt at his own feet. "No offense, Your Highness."

"None taken." The prince's voice was casual, as if he actually meant it.

The other soldiers looked between the two men before adding their spears to Nikkoforos's. Once everyone else voted, they turned to Rafael. He threw his spear next to Anselmo's. Rafael didn't say anything, but his posture shifted toward Anselmo ever-so-slightly, and Anselmo nodded.

"That's settled," Nikkoforos said. He pulled his spear free. "I'm honored that you trust me to lead you. No hard feelings, Lieutenant?"

"No. Sir." Except Anselmo would've been the leader if the prince hadn't bullied his way in here through his power and influence. But rather than taking charge, Anselmo had to remain the lowest ranked soldier in here. He bit back a grunt.

Nikkoforos started down the hill and the others fell into formation, Anselmo in the rear. As they hit the water, soldiers complained. All except Rafael and the prince, who held their composure from what

Anselmo could see. The dirt turned into mud that squelched and sucked at his boots, until Ansemo reached the water. It was frigid and soon reached almost to his knees. No wonder the highborns complained. They'd never had to wade through a high tide in their life.

A small school of fish darted through his legs. The edges of their fins ripped at his skin, and his blood seeped into the water. Men shouted and some jumped.

"Hush, you fools," Anselmo said. He might not know the secrets of the labyrinth, but he knew enough for that.

Nikkoforos turned. "Yes, as the *lieutenant* suggested, we must maintain our silence." He gave Anselmo a long look before advancing.

The message was clear. *I'm the leader, and you fall into rank and keep your opinions to yourself.*

The trees rustled, but there was no wind. Nikkoforos held up a fist and everyone stopped. Water lapped at their legs and the men breathed.

Birds shot out of the treetops. Falcons by the look of them, and not very big. But they weren't diving for prey. They dove straight for Anselmo and the soldiers. The cold water made Anselmo's legs clumsy and he wasn't able to feint, but he brought up his shield to block a bird at the last minute. The bird thudded against the shield with a crunch, the sound of bones breaking, and fell into the water. Anselmo grabbed the bird. Its beak reflected the dull light and looked like metal.

"Bronze beaks!" the soldier next to him yelled. The others were pulling their swords out of sheaths or batting away the birds.

After the initial attack, the birds retreated out of the soldiers' reach. As they flapped their wings, feathers shot at the soldiers, flying like a volley of arrows.

What in Giore's holy name? Anselmo kept his sword in his sheath and hurled his spear at a bird. It hit the falcon in the wing and the animal plummeted to the water. The other soldiers followed his example, and soon dead birds littered the water as the rest of the flock retreated.

"Fish that sting and birds with metal beaks." Nikkoforos washed at a cut on his arm with the murky swamp water. "This place has more twists than the islands of the cyclopses."

"You've been?" a soldier asked.

Nikkoforos sheathed his sword and took his spear out of the water. "We launched a campaign there to retake the islands, since the Gregorios family lost it from the empire. Fierce warriors all of them, but it would take a fierce warrior to carve out one of your own eyes. Come to the front with me, and I'll tell you about it."

They continued their advance into the labyrinth. Rafael waited by the side until Anselmo passed then fell in step beside him. Up ahead, Nikkoforos spoke quietly with the soldiers around him, regaling them with tales but also taking time to ask them questions about themselves.

"Someone told him about everything in here," Rafael said, quiet enough that only Anselmo could hear.

"He's not the only one, apparently."

Rafael paused from scanning the trees around them. "No one told you?"

Anselmo grunted for an answer.

"I thought Imelda would at least. Well, for that I'm sorry. It's unfair."

"She ... wanted to." Imelda hadn't said so but he knew her. If she could've told him, she would've.

"I'm not judging her. I've known her my whole life. I know she's a good person." Rafael nodded at Anselmo's new shield, though the swamp water and bird blood had dulled its shine. "Looks like King Ulisse's patronage is paying off."

"What do you want, Rafael?"

Rafael lowered his voice even more. "I don't love the prince leading us any more than you do. But he needs information that only I have."

"Like what?"

"Signs of the minotaurs."

"Your father told you even more than anyone else, didn't he?"

Rafael grimaced. "He said he didn't want his oldest son dying in the labyrinth before I have the chance to make some family heirs."

Anselmo looked at Rafael. His eyes scanned the trees, the water, everything, but his lips were turned down in an almost imperceptible frown.

"Why don't you tell the prince yourself?"

Rafael shifted his grip on his spear and seemingly unconsciously moved his shield in front of his chest.

"You don't want him mad at you for breaking rank," Anselmo said. "Just walk up there and tell him."

Rafael stopped and turned to face Anselmo. "All my life I've been trained to follow orders. You try going back on that kind of conditioning."

As much as he hated to admit it, Anselmo knew that feeling. His mother's training had helped him get further in life. There was a stiffness in Rafael's posture, in his expression, that said it was the same for him. Skills gained, but some wounds inflicted as well.

Anselmo resumed walking. "What are these signs?"

"Nests in the trees."

Anselmo glanced up. "Nests? We're talking about minotaurs."

"Yes, nests. Minotaurs don't look like the scenes on the labyrinth gates."

"What do they look like?"

"My father wouldn't say. He said we'd know when we saw them."

Well that was great. "Other signs?"

"Tall sticks leaning against trees, at least two."

Anselmo looked at Rafael.

"Apparently they use them as ladders."

So they could attack from above. Anselmo looked up. There didn't appear to be anything that looked like nests in the canopy, nor did he see any ladder-like sticks leaning against the tree trunks.

"Last," Rafael said. "Bark removed from the trees. They rub it off with their horns."

Anselmo nodded, and they continued in silence. The day wore on, and even though it was cold, it didn't take long for the effort of slogging through the water to drench him in sweat. They had another attack from a small flock of bronze beaks, and then Nikkoforos called for a rest on a large mound.

"Look at this egg," one man said, kneeling in the mud. He picked up a large egg. The thing looked to be made out of silver. "Just one of these would make me richer than my father."

"That's not saying much," another man muttered, and the soldier next to him laughed.

"That's a cockatrice egg, Enzio." Rafael walked over and took the egg, placing it back on the ground. "It's not worth dying over. You'll earn back your family's money another way."

Anselmo fished out some hard tack from his rucksack. A few bites, just enough to keep his energy up.

"What's your rank in your military, sir?" a soldier asked Nikkoforos.

"General, naturally." The prince had lain back on his shield and had his ankles crossed. He kept one hand on his spear which lay at his side.

"Not commanding general?"

"I can't lead full time. And I prefer to be on the battlefield rather than in the back, strategizing."

"I'll bet your father hates that," another man said.

"Actually, no. The Gregorios family stopped personally leading their armies generations ago, and the people despised them for it. I, however, have the respect of my soldiers. My father did the same before he inherited the throne."

Men nodded and murmured their agreement. It was a sound leadership principle, and Anselmo was willing to bet good politics.

"My chariot racing, on the other hand." Nikkoforos laughed. "He absolutely deplores."

Anselmo glanced at Rafael, who tilted his head and pressed his lips together. No one else noticed—they were staring adoringly at Nikkoforos.

"You'd think they'd never seen a handsome prince before," Rafael murmured.

"Actually, they probably haven't," Anselmo said. "I mean, other than at your party when I kicked his and your asses and took your money."

Rafael chuckled. "Fair point."

"When you soldiers get a break," Nikkoforos was saying, "you should visit Ilios during the chariot races in the spring. I'll have you seated in the imperial box at the hippodrome."

Anselmo tuned out the quiet conversation, all centered around the prince, though he did a fair job of turning questions back to the soldiers. The man knew something about connecting with people. But whether he could actually lead once they faced the minotaurs ... that remained to be seen.

After an hour, Nikkoforos stood. "I see a fork ahead. The maze begins. Does anyone know how to get through it?"

"The walls shift constantly, so it's hard to say," Rafael said. "We need to head inward, but that's all anyone knows."

"A true challenge." Nikkoforos grinned. "Let's get on, then. Lieutenant Errari, I'd like you up front with me."

Rafael took Anselmo's upper arm and mouthed *minotaurs*. Yes, the signs of minotaurs. If Rafael would man up, he would join them and tell Nikkoforos himself. But instead he fell in somewhere in the middle.

"So, Lieutenant," Nikkoforos said as they trudged through the water, "did you take my advice and buy Siora Albizzi something sparkly to ease her mood?"

"Imelda has plenty of jewels. I took that money to the bank."

"Wise. But, of course, a man in your situation has to be strategic to rise as you have." He nodded at Anselmo's new shield and sword. "You're playing the game well."

"I play no games."

The prince didn't answer. They reached the fork. To the left, they would continue to walk along the outer wall of the labyrinth, making no progress to the center of the maze. So the right was the obvious choice. However, Anselmo noticed a stack of large sticks leaning against a tree.

"Which way do you suggest, Lieutenant?" Nikkoforos asked.

"Left."

Nikkoforos tilted his head with a look of warning on his face.

"Sir," Anselmo said.

"Captain Galbani said we need to push deeper into the labyrinth." The prince turned to the rest of the group. "We go right."

"Sir, I really don't think we should."

"I've already asked for your opinion, Lieutenant. If I want it, I'll ask for it again."

They went to the right, and it didn't take long for the stick ladders to grow in numbers. Soon, Anselmo noticed bark missing from trees.

"Sir, I think we're getting close to minotaurs."

Nikkoforos looked angry but he kept his voice under control. "And why do you think that?"

"There are signs. Captain Galbani told me about them."

"Such as?"

"Bark rubbed off of trees from their horns. And see those sticks there and there and there? The minotaurs use them as ladders to get into the trees to reach their—oh shit." There, above one set of sticks was a large, circular gathering of branches, mud, and the gray plants that hung from the trees. "It's a minotaur nest."

A man screamed behind them, and they whipped around. A minotaur had jumped out of the trees and gored him with its horns. Some of the soldiers stabbed it with their spears, while others backed away. One man tripped on a tree root sticking out of the water and fell under the water.

Rafael had been right—the minotaur looked nothing like the depictions on the labyrinth gates. This creature had arms and legs, but that's where the similarities ended. It leaned on its long arms, turning in circles on all fours, and muscles rippled under its thick black fur. Its shoulders were huge, and above that, an enormous head of a bull with horns one-meter long each that ended in wicked points. Tusks jutted out of its mouth from its bottom jaw, tusks that looked thick enough to snap a man's thigh in two.

The minotaur grunted and snorted as it watched the soldiers. It grabbed a spear out of its massive arm. Black blood covered the spearhead. Then the minotaur stood on its powerful back legs and pounded its chest as it roared.

The air filled with the sound of minotaurs in the trees. Deep, resonant bellows that rippled across the surface of the water.

"Phalanx formation!" Nikkoforos called, already hefting his shield. "Two-sided! Come to me, soldiers!"

Anselmo fell in beside the prince, and soon the other men were with them. The soldiers hustled into position, kneeling in the water, overlapping their shields, and readying their spears to thrust through the openings. It was dark inside the phalanx. Fish swam away from the minotaur through their legs, cutting and stinging Anselmo's skin. His feet sunk into the muddy ground.

The men around him smelled of sweat and blood. The smells of battle.

The smells of fear.

And soon, the smells of death.

"Whatever you do, hold formation until I say," Nikkoforos said.

The minotaur pummeled its chest again. Minotaurs leapt from the trees. One crashed into their phalanx.

"Ricci, Colombo, kill it," Nikkoforos called. "Everyone else keep formation! Treat this like a normal battle."

But the minotaurs didn't attack like a human army. There was no slow progression until you were close enough to thrust your spears between the spaces between the shields. The minotaurs rushed forward. Anselmo was able to get a few with his spear, skewering one through its eye, another in the chest.

Yes, the minotaurs were animals, but they were not dumb animals. They soon learned to stay out of reach of the spears and started throwing rocks at the soldiers.

The beasts were testing them, looking for weaknesses. A few even grabbed long sticks and held them in mimicry of the soldiers.

"This is never going to work," Anselmo said. A large rock hit his shield and rattled his teeth.

"They're keeping their distance," Nikkoforos said. "Stay in formation."

Which meant Anselmo and the others were on the defense. They needed to rush and kill the animals, not hide in the phalanx all day.

An especially large minotaur ran toward Anselmo. If it hit the phalanx, it would destroy the formation, and there was nothing to stop it.

Which meant there was no reason to hold formation any longer.

Anselmo raced forward, spear out. Behind him, Nikkoforos yelled his name.

The minotaur swung and knocked the spear out of Anselmo's grip. Anselmo rolled through the water to avoid another blow. He jumped to his feet and unsheathed his sword. The minotaur rose onto its legs. It had to be three meters tall at least. But the posture left its chest vulnerable.

Anselmo thrust his sword into the beast's chest. The minotaur roared in pain. The recurved blade made stabbing more awkward than the leaf-shaped xiphos he was used to, but with his strength it was easy to adjust.

The animal swung, catching Anselmo on his side. He groaned as a rib cracked. He ripped his sword free, feinted to the left. Grasping the sword with both hands, he swung for the minotaur's neck. This was where the true power of the kopis lay. Its hacking ability, and Anselmo's strength, sliced straight through the minotaur's neck. The beast fell to its knees, head hanging on by sinews and skin.

The sounds of the battle rushed back to Anselmo. Men screaming, beasts roaring. Anselmo spun. He had enough time to see the chaos, men swinging their swords at animals, minotaurs charging cornered soldiers.

A minotaur ran into his back. Anselmo fell into the water. His fingers squished into the mud as he pushed himself out of the water before the beast could pin him down.

His sword was gone. The minotaur rose its fists to smash his head. He caught its wrists in his own. They were an even match, but Anselmo had water in his lungs. His knees started to bend. Normally he'd bring an opponent in this position close enough for a head butt, but that bull's skull looked much harder than a human's.

As the beast pushed Anselmo farther down—and got closer to him—Anselmo caught his chance. He brought his knee into the creature's groin, smashing into its testicles. This had the same effect on the minotaur as it would on a man. It stumbled back, bellowing in pain.

There was a tree to Anselmo's right. A large stack of tall sticks leaned against it. Anselmo grabbed one. It was hollow and ridged at regular intervals. But it felt sturdy. The minotaur had recovered and was charging again. Anselmo mustered all of his strength and stabbed the blunt-tipped wood into the creature's stomach.

Black blood squirted from the wound, slicking the beast's dark fur. It fell into the water with a weak bellow. Anselmo took his shield in both hands and smashed it over and over against the minotaur's head until it stopped moving.

His chest heaved. The ache of his broken rib—or ribs—filled his awareness. But the sounds of the battle had stopped. Minotaurs lay dead all around, and the rest were retreating through the canopy.

All of the soldiers looked like Anselmo felt. Winded, injured, shocked. But only one man was down, groaning on a mound of mud. Spears floated in the water, and a few shields stuck out of the surface of the swamp.

Anselmo searched for his sword on the muddy swamp bottom. It hadn't gone far. When he retrieved it from the water, it was perfectly clean, glistening even in the dank light. No blood, no mud, no signs of battle. He sheathed it, grabbed one of the floating spears, and walked over to where the other men had gathered around the fallen soldier.

The man's stomach had been ripped open. He wept openly, trying to hold his intestines in. All around was the stink of feces and metallic blood. These were the smells of death. One other scent sat in the air, acidic enough to scratch his throat. He sniffed at a smear of black minotaur blood and gagged. Everything about the labyrinth was horrible.

"What do we do?" one soldier asked.

"Leave him," another said. "He'll be dead before long."

"We can't let him suffer."

"Do you want to murder him?"

Nikkoforos walked up. "It's not murder—it's mercy." He turned to Anselmo. "Lieutenant Errari, unsheathe your sword."

"What? You're the commanding officer."

"And if my tactics had gotten him into this situation, it would be my fault. But you went against my orders. He's mortally wounded because of you. So finish the job."

Anselmo kept his hands at his sides. No one said anything.

"Do as I said, soldier, or I will kill you myself for insubordination, since we're not in a position to report you to the fleet admiral."

Rafael nudged Anselmo in the back.

Anselmo unsheathed his sword.

"I recommend beheading," Nikkoforos said, "if you can do it in one hit."

Anselmo didn't want to take this man's advice a second more, but he couldn't deny the logic. And Anselmo could do it on the first time. He positioned himself next to the man's neck and raised his sword.

The soldier cried out for mercy, but Nikkos wasn't wrong—this *was* mercy. It just wasn't Anselmo's to deliver.

He pulled his sword down in a strong swing. Anselmo barely had time to register the resistance of skin, muscle, and bone before soldier's head fell from his neck. The cut was clean, sharp, and precise. It had taken so little of Anselmo's considerable strength.

And yet, his knees shook and his head swam.

He'd never killed a man other than in battle before. Meeting as enemies, Anselmo's life or the other soldier's. There was no time to think about the person on the other side, what their life was like back home, who they loved and who loved them.

Anselmo stared at the man's face, eyes gazing sightlessly at the treetops. He recognized him from the party. The soldier had been in the room where he'd met Calixta, guessing each other's secrets.

Nikkoforos turned to Anselmo. "Give me your sword."

Anselmo hesitated then gave it to the prince. The man might lead with a dominant authority, but surely he wouldn't push a line he had no need to cross.

"Lay your hands out, palms up."

Again, Anselmo hesitated, but did as he was told. He glared at Nikkoforos, daring him to do something rash. But the prince was pure, constrained anger as he wiped the blood from the sword onto Anselmo's palms. "His name was Ciro Ricci, and he was soon to be married. His blood is on your hands. If you hadn't broken formation, he would probably be alive."

"If I hadn't broken formation, we'd still be stuck in phalanx. Your fear kept us stuck in defense."

"We were all afraid! And right to be. But I was buying myself time to analyze their movements and adjust my strategies." Nikkoforos shoved Anselmo's sword at him. "You may have just been promoted to lieutenant, but I have almost a decade of battlefield strategy, and twenty years of off-field training. When I don't know what to do, I at least know how to figure it out quickly."

Nikkoforos's rage had him speaking slow and deliberately, and he bit off the end of each word.

"Furthermore, if you'd warned me about the minotaur signs earlier, we wouldn't have been ambushed! The other man who died—Reniero Colombo—is at your feet for that as well."

"You told me not to give my opinion."

"Because you do it with such insolence!" Nikkoforos paused to take a deep breath and regain his composure. "You only need to ask permission. I'm not a despot. Men, fall out." He continued in the direction they'd been going. "Lieutenant Errari, you bring up the rear. And Captain Galbani, keep an eye on him."

As the men filed past, they glared at Anselmo. Some even spat at his feet. Rafael shook his head but said nothing as Anselmo fell in beside him.

CHAPTER TWENTY-SIX

For all of Ulisse's self-assurance that friendship with Imelda would be enough, he couldn't deny that he wanted more. He'd spent the night pacing his room, unable to sleep until the temple bell rang three in the morning. That was the reason he'd slept in. Not because it was the final night of Carnevale—though he had gotten plenty drunk. But because he'd learned that his betrothed was in love with another man.

Which was why he couldn't stop himself from telling Anselmo that bit about a good night's sleep. Imelda had not been at the palàso when Ulisse returned. Ulisse might be a fool when it came to love, but he was not dumb. It was clear where she'd spent her evening. Or rather, with whom she'd spent it.

But Ulisse had meant it when he told Anselmo good luck. He truly did not want him to die.

He also didn't want Anselmo to steal Imelda from him.

Though it could be argued Ulisse had stolen Imelda from Anselmo. Unwittingly stolen, but stolen all the same.

Poor Imelda, caught up in the middle of it all.

The fact remained, though, that Ulisse had pledged his allegiance to both Imelda and Anselmo, and he would not fail either of them.

He'd done what he could for Anselmo, providing him with the finest weapons and armor in Rialto. Their contract was complete.

Now Ulisse could do something for himself. Hopefully. Maybe. Potentially.

Ulisse approached Imelda's door and hesitated. It was after lunch. Surely she'd be back by now. He ran his hand through his hair, noticed a crumb on his sleeve and flicked it off, then knocked.

Imelda cracked the door open. She opened it farther when she saw it was him. "Oh, good morning."

He inclined his head. "Good *afternoon*, siora."

She laughed uneasily. "I suppose I slept in quite a bit." She looked tired, but she was dressed for the day, her hair in a simple braid over one shoulder. She bit her lip, her gaze darting away for a minute.

Ulisse cleared his throat.

"Oh, sorry," she said. "Still sleepy I guess. Would you like to come in?"

"Actually." Ulisse walked into her room and turned to face her. "I was wondering if you'd like help working on your wings. I can have a spinning wheel brought up, or I could sew or—"

"We don't need your help. I mean ..." She toyed with the end of her braid. "Everything is nearly finished. There's no spinning left, and Arturo hired seamstresses."

"I can't wait to see them." He started cracking his knuckles, caught himself, and dropped his hands. "As a backup plan, would you care to accompany me to Porto?"

"Backup plan?" she said slowly.

"I thought we might spend the day together. Since our wedding is this week."

"Oh yes. Good—um, good idea. Let me put some boots on."

"I'll wait for you at the góndola dock."

She met him five minutes later, and the gondolièr started down El Canalasso. Rialto lacked the dramatic landscape of Eraclea—the rugged cliffs and crystalline water—but the canals, bright caxe, and shiny gondole created a different beauty. The city was quiet this morning as the rich slept off their final raucous night of Carnevale.

"Such an interesting festival," he said.

Imelda jumped. She'd been watching the buildings slide by. "Pardon?"

"Carnevale. We let go of all social mores and indulge our every sensual whim. All our other holidays are about honoring family. Isn't that interesting?"

Imelda blushed and turned her head, seemingly attempting to cover it. Ulisse winced inwardly and resisted from rubbing his eyes. He hadn't intended to remind her of last night's activities.

Oh gods, now he was thinking about it.

"Take Zitello, for instance," he said quickly. "There's an interesting fellow. He's a trickster that opposes the gods, yet they allow him to rule as king of winter. Isn't that strange? And then we burn his effigy. What does that say about us as a people?"

Imelda looked ready to jump into the canal. "I haven't really thought about it."

"Blood monks believe Zitello was the original god worshipped in Sacresta, until they conquered the land that is now Ilios, where the people worshipped Giore and Rea, under different names of course. The Sacrestano liked the idea of a loving father god and mother goddess more than the capricious Zitello, and switched allegiance. There's some evidence to support this, though the sources are questionable. But if it is true, I can't blame them. I pref—"

Imelda laughed quietly. "You sound so much like Arturo."

Ulisse half-smiled and rubbed his beard. "I hope that's a good thing."

"It's not bad." She trailed a hand in the water. "You two should talk sometime."

"We'd probably never stop."

"Probably not." She smiled and seemed to relax. Ulisse's chest loosened. She might not enjoy his particular topics of conversations, but she didn't hate him.

They arrived at Porto. Ulisse helped Imelda off the góndola. Large galleys filled the docks in front of them, bearing flags from Rialto, Eraclea, Ilios, and all other countries from the Muriseano. Ulisse held his arm out for Imelda and led her along the rows of ships toward the smaller sailboats.

Imelda eyed the docks. "What are we doing?"

"I thought we'd go sailing."

She looked up at the sky, half covered by clouds, then at the water dotted with whitecaps. "Sounds lovely." Doubt edged her voice.

Ulisse resisted a grimace. It was not ideal sailing conditions, but any time on the water was time well spent.

Arrigo waited for them toward the end of the island. "This way, sir." He led the way down the gangplank to the floating docks, pausing at a slip that contained an eight-meter sailboat. Perfect size.

"Have you ever been on a sailboat?" Ulisse asked Imelda as he helped her onto the boat.

Imelda settled into a seat. "Just galleys."

"You're in for a treat." Ulisse untied the dock lines and used an oar to steer them into open water. "No matter where you are on a galley, you can hear the rowers chanting. But on a sailboat, there's just the water and the wind."

Imelda *mmm*ed noncommittally.

He hoisted the main sail. The block was farther up than Ulisse was used to, which made raising the sail awkward. The wind caught before he was ready and pulled the line through his hands, burning his palm. Wonderful. The wind whipped, and they cut through the water at a decent pace, even with only one sail raised.

The lines weren't as nice as his back home. They were rougher, and errant strands stuck out here and there. Unsurprising, given that the boat was a rental, but irritating all the same.

Ulisse coiled the lines on the deck, took the tiller, and turned to Imelda. She was staring at the labyrinth. It loomed in the distance like a dark mountain rising out of the water. He could say something. Here on the water, where there was no one to hear his accusation. It could be something between the two of them. No need to embarrass her by calling her out publicly. A good marriage was built on communication.

But they weren't even married yet. She would resent him if he brought it up now. Gods above, it was so complicated.

Speed. He needed to make the boat faster.

"I'm going to hoist the headsail," he said. "You'll need to hold the tiller while I'm on the foredeck."

Imelda moved to sit by the tiller. "What do I do?"

"Just keep it steady."

She nodded, and he went to the fore. He hoisted the sail, and the boat really took off.

Ulisse returned to the stern with a satisfied smile. He took the tiller. "Hold on tight. We're going to do something called beating to windward. This is where it gets really fun—are you okay?"

Imelda was hugging herself as she shivered. Wind whipped her hair around her face. "I forgot to put on something with alpaca corincanto stitched in."

Damn it. "I'm so sorry. We'll—we'll head back." He turned the boat away from the wind, and back toward Rialto. He paused. The headsail sheet had a tangle in it.

"I have to go back to the prow. Can you handle the tiller again?"

"I think so," Imelda said. The water was rough enough, and the wind strong enough, that her knuckles were white from keeping the tiller steady.

"I'll be right back," he said. "Hold tight."

She nodded.

Ulisse quickly made his way to the foredeck. As he worked on the tangle in the line, a galley raced by. Its wake soon caught up to them, rocking the boat. Imelda lost her grip on the tiller, and their little boat spun dead downwind. The boat jibed hard to port, sending the boom swinging across the boat. Ulisse lost his footing, though he managed to grab the railing before he fell off. The boat lurched, tumbling Imelda to the deck and spilling the coiled lines. One caught Imelda in the face. She yelled in pain and slapped a hand to her eye.

Damn it all to the three blazes and back. Ulisse gripped the railing and crawled back to the stern. He took the tiller and fought to regain control of the boat. Finally, it righted itself, and he turned into the wind to stop the boat. They drifted as the sails luffed uselessly.

"I'm so sorry. Can I see it?"

Imelda lifted her fingers. Tears leaked out of her eye, which was already swollen and turning dark. "Is it bad?"

Ulisse grimaced. "Nothing cotton corincanto can't fix. I'm really, so very sorry. Here." He pulled his coat off and helped her into it. "Let's get back."

He lowered the head sail and turned the boat around toward Rialto, at a slower, more reasonable pace. They didn't speak again for the rest of the trip back, except for Ulisse's constant apologies.

Imelda kept one hand on her eye, her posture hunched as she stared listlessly across the water. Her other hand clutched his coat closed, though she still shivered.

So much for making her like him. At this rate, she might not ever come to love him.

Unsurprising. One thing life had taught Ulisse was that he was about as lovable as a black eye.

CHAPTER TWENTY-SEVEN

The sun had been high in the eastern sky when Venezia began to write her speech. Now stars twinkled outside her office window. She set down her quill and rubbed her eyes. Between the arduous mental work and getting little sleep the night before, she was losing the wind from her sails. Her bed beckoned, but she still hadn't perfected her proposal. Tomorrow, she and Janus would present to the Council, and the Council members would vote immediately after.

Normally she'd push through the exhaustion until she was done, but she'd be sluggish and dull in the morning. She massaged her temples as a yawn escaped. When was her last seizure? It had been three weeks … hadn't it? The Council didn't meet until late morning. She'd go to sleep now, then wake up early. The quiet of the morning would energize her, and rest would sharpen her mind.

She climbed the stairs to her room, unsheathing two of her knives. She clenched them as the night before rushed back into memory. Lazaro. He was the reason she was so tired. Not only for the interruption, but the energy it had taken to fight him off. If she'd had her knives, it would've been a quick ordeal. It hadn't been a coincidence her blades had disappeared. Of course, he hadn't moved the weapons himself. That was beneath him, especially when he had a slave to do his dirty work.

She put two blades under her pillow then rang the bell.

Alessia appeared moments later. "Are you ready for your nightcap, mè siora?"

"I want Kari to assist me tonight."

Alessia blinked in confusion but recovered quickly. She walked into the hallway. Venezia sat at her vanity and waited. Kari knocked on the open door and slipped in, head down.

"You called for me, mè siora?"

"Let my hair down and brush it."

The girl hurried over and started pulling pins from Venezia's hair. Venezia removed her third knife from her calf holster and set it on the table. Kari flinched and stopped.

"Keep going," Venezia said.

Kari resumed her work. Venezia watched her through the mirror. The girl trembled and glanced at the knife constantly. As she pulled the pins out of Venezia's hair, the neckline of her dress shifted. A fresh bruise, made even darker by the contrast with her pale skin, marred her birdlike collarbone. No doubt Lazaro had taken his frustrations out on Kari. Venezia gritted her teeth.

"Where are you from originally?" Venezia asked.

"Dǫnska, mè siora." Kari's voice was quiet and timid.

"Speak up," Venezia said. "I don't want to strain to hear you."

Kari blanched but raised her voice. "Dǫnska, mè siora."

"You're far from the southern reaches, yet you speak Vèneto extremely well."

"A warring clan attacked my village and sold me into slavery when I was twelve. I was brought to the peninsula four years ago."

"And how old are you?"

"Nineteen."

Venezia pursed her lips. The girl had been in captivity for a third of her young life. "I was nineteen when I married Lazaro. I was young and naive, but you're not naive, are you? You've experienced a hard life."

Kari rubbed her lips together, clearly considering the best way to reply. "I've faced my share of difficulties, mè siora."

"Challenges only make us stronger."

The tension in Kari's face disappeared as she finished with the pins and started brushing. She stopped looking at the blade quite so much.

Venezia tilted her head and smiled. "You have such pretty yellow hair. Like a flower in spring. No wonder you're Lazaro's new favorite."

Kari's face slipped at the mention of Lazaro. She brushed softly at Venezia's hair, far too gentle to do any good.

"I don't hold it against you," Venezia said. "You're doing me a favor."

Now the girl looked confused.

"You're thinking I'm his wife and that should be my job, aren't you? People marry for different reasons. Brush harder, girl. My hair is thicker than yours."

Kari winced and pulled the brush with more strength.

Venezia watched her in the mirror, fingers drumming on the vanity. "Yes, I'm his wife, not his slave. He can't force me to do anything I don't want."

She picked up the knife and turned it. The blade reflected the light from the fire in the hearth. Lazaro couldn't force her anymore, at least. Last night had proven that.

In a way, she had Lazaro to thank. After eight years of his abuse, she'd had enough. She'd learned to fight. At first it had merely been a way to defend herself, but the training had provided a faster path to the

Doxe seat than she could've carved on her own. Leading in the military was far quicker than merely serving on the Council. Quicker and more satisfying. She never would have discovered her talent for strategy if it hadn't been for Lazaro. But that didn't mean she was grateful.

Many would be happy to have risen so far. Not Venezia. Ever since she was a young girl eavesdropping on her father's lessons with Primo, she'd aspired to great heights. She swore to herself she'd wear the sash and crown one day. That desire still pulsed in her heart, clinging to her as only a child's promise could. She would be Doxe one day. Maybe she would rise even beyond that. Then no one, not her father nor her husband nor her older brother would hold power over her.

Venezia's head throbbed. Sleep beckoned. Kari pulled down the bedsheets, her eyes lingering on the pillow before she moved to tend the fire. Venezia folded her hands at her waist and watched the slave girl.

"How much did Lazaro pay for you?"

Kari gaped at the bold question. "I—I'm not sure, mè siora."

"Get him to spill it, somehow. For my thanks, I'll pay a stipend—a small stipend—every week. Over time, you'll have your own money to spend on anything you like."

Like her freedom. By the way Kari's eyes widened, Venezia knew that's what the girl was thinking. A small smile fought its way onto Kari's lips, though she clearly tried to bite it down.

"Now help me out of my dress."

"Of course, mè siora." She hurried to comply, unbuttoning Venezia's dress, then slipping the sleeves off Venezia's strong shoulders and arms. The girl's limbs were tiny, her upper arms small enough for Lazaro to wrap his fingers completely around. The bruises on her wrists had turned brown, and no doubt bruises dotted her skin under her plain wool dress as well. Venezia's arms were scarred from sparring, but her deeper scars still remained. Though they would never fade, they would provide her with the strength she needed to unseat Primo and outlast Lazaro.

She'd protect Kari as best she could, but Venezia's safety came first. There was no other way to survive. A lesson Lazaro had inadvertently taught her.

Kari helped Venezia into her nightgown. The silk fluttered as Venezia moved, a freeing sensation after wearing her constrictive uniform dress all day.

"That's all for tonight," she said.

Kari bobbed her head, scurrying to the door.

Venezia walked to the vanity and picked up her blade. "Kari?"

Kari turned. "Yes, mè siora?"

"You're a sweet girl, but if you ever touch my knives again, I'll pull that pretty yellow hair out of your head strand by strand. Understood?"

Kari's pale face lost the little color it had. "Yes, mè siora, of course. So sorry." She turned, and in that instant another bruise at the base of her neck caught Venezia's attention. Kari ran into the hallway and nearly slammed the door shut.

Damn Lazaro. Just when Venezia didn't think he could get any worse, he proved her wrong. One day he'd burn in the three blazes of Fógo, but there would be no punishment for him until then.

Venezia held back a sob as she threw the blade under her pillow, where it clinked as it landed on the other two.

CHAPTER TWENTY-EIGHT

The Council Chamber was like others in Palàso Dogal, dark wood panels inlaid with silver. One ring of seven chairs, and behind it a ring of six—the second row on a raised surface—faced an open area for presenters. The Doxe's seat sat in the middle of the first row of chairs. It was large and impressive, amply padded in bright blue with silver piping. The room was imposing, but also dull. Rialtani were not a dull people. At least the ceiling was high, and the windows on one side stretched from floor to ceiling. Light streamed in, illuminating particles of dust that floated in the air and landed on Venezia's dress.

She'd hoped a good night's sleep would help sharpen her mind, but sleep hadn't come easily. It had barely come at all. Every time she drifted off, she'd jerk awake, her fingers automatically curling around her knives under her pillow. Her hands had been shaky all morning, even though she hadn't seen Lazaro. She'd finally calmed herself by the time she arrived at the palàso, but now her limbs and mind were sluggish.

She could still win. She'd won battles with less sleep.

But such little energy meant she wouldn't be able to visit the labyrinth to watch the soldiers. She probably wouldn't have time any-way. Between Imelda's wedding and the upcoming election, she didn't know how she'd be able to escape for a whole day at the labyrinth. She'd have to rely on reports from Admiral Galbani. Such a shame.

Primo entered and greeted Venezia with a kiss for each cheek.

"Are you still determined to do this?" he asked.

"I see an opportunity."

"Can't you see some opportunities aren't worth the risk?" He sighed and rubbed his temple. "I suppose you're still planning on running against me as well."

"Don't pretend, Primo. We've never been close."

"One of my biggest regrets. I should've paid more attention to you, and by the time I did, it was too late. Think of what we could accomplish if we actually trusted each other."

She looked at him askance, gauging his sincerity. For a moment, she pitied him. Giovanni, their father, had wanted his son to be Doxe, so Primo's grooming had started from birth. Rough grooming, at that, which was why Primo had rebelled for a time and gone to live with Uncle Lorenzo and Aunt Giulia. Giovanni valued authority and logic, strength and austerity. Who could blame Primo for becoming what everyone trained him to be?

But Giovanni had treated Venezia like a sickly simpleton. Her mother had been weak and timid, so he'd assumed Venezia was as well. She'd risen above it, risen above Lazaro and his abuse. She hadn't let anyone define her. Why should Primo?

"It's too late," she said.

"Yes," he said, voice tired, "I suppose it is." The door opened, and the Council members entered. "Let's get this done with."

Everyone took their seats. Beniamino sat at a desk by the door, quill and paper at the ready, and Enrico Lando stood.

"Siori and siore of the Council, I hope you enjoyed your Carnevale. I heard Orso enjoyed the festivities quite enthusiastically." They all laughed as Orso waved good-naturedly. Venezia had missed that bit of gossip, but it wasn't hard to imagine what it entailed. The lech.

President Lando continued. "We have several items of business to discuss, naturally, after such a long break. First, His Serenity the Doxe has asked that we attend to the most important topic: Sior Janus Komnenos's petition to the Council. Once he, his sponsor,"—his eyes cut to Venezia—"and the opposition speak, we will convene to the voting chamber. Beniamino, bring in Sior Komnenos."

The secretary slipped out, returning with Janus a moment later. The man was as stiff as ever, though his red robe held so many jewels it must've weighed twenty pounds. His meticulous beard framed a somber, arrogant mouth.

Enrico sat and gestured for Janus to speak.

"Council members," Janus said with a bow of his head, "I thank you for allowing me to present my offer. As you know, my family ruled the Illustrious Empire of Ilios for two centuries. During that time, the empire enjoyed strength and stability. Twenty years ago, Electra Heraclius usurped my family, blinding and disfiguring my grandfather."

"A punishment fit for a murderer," Paolo Ruzzini called.

"Let our guest speak," Primo said.

Janus glowered at Ruzzini and cleared his throat. "My family was exiled to Zorzi, which was once an Iliano territory until your city captured it from us. I was there during the rebellion, and was impressed by your military. I've been planning to reclaim my family's throne for the last decade. As you know, the Tedosiano walls of Ilios have never been breached, but the military of La Serenìsima Repùblica de Rialto is the strongest the world has seen since the golden days of Ilios—which were under my family. Rialto possesses the might to restore Ilios to its proper governance. It will succeed where many others have failed.

"In exchange for your help, I will give you twenty-five million ducats, to be paid over the course of five years, and free passage through the Bogasa Strait. I mentioned Iliano black bane to the Doxe, but without much detail. Here's what I will provide: five golden apple spiders, a priest with the knowledge of how to make Iliano black bane, and three ballistas."

"Why not teach us how to make it?" Lando asked.

Janus gave him a withering look. "I refuse to answer stupid questions."

Venezia resisted rolling her eyes. Why did she have to work with this man, of all people? She'd never met anyone more arrogant, which was quite a feat. She'd be impressed if it didn't affect her plans. At least he'd increased the amount to be paid.

Fia scoffed. "Only three ballistas?"

"I assume the great Rialto would have the technology to make their own. Perhaps I am incorrect."

Orso Cancio bristled. "You pompous—"

"Orso, let's not insult our guest." Primo leaned forward. "At our original meeting, you mentioned something about ending the schism in our religion. I believe you used the phrase 'submitting your temples to the Iliano High Priest.' Even if the Council votes with you, that will not be part of the agreement."

Janus drew himself up. "Sacresta's two greatest progenitors should practice its religion."

"We do," Enrico said.

Janus opened his mouth to retort, but Primo held up a hand. "We understand your request, Sior Komnenos. Thank you."

The secretary opened the door for Janus's dismissal. Janus stared between the door and Primo. "I want to hear what your sister has to say."

"All Council meetings are classified. We will inform you of the results."

Janus glared for a second longer, then stormed out.

Enrico turned to Venezia. "The floor is yours, Fleet Admiral."

Venezia walked to the center of the room. She'd had a dress made just for today, high-waisted, short train, silver embroidery on the shoulders to mimic her lines of rank. A softer look than her uniform but in the blue-gray of the armada and bright blue of the Lions. Let the Council see the colors of her station. They would remind them of everything she'd accomplished in the face of tradition. Sponsoring this war was another manifestation.

"Five hundred years ago, our ancestors fled the fallen city of Sacresta and headed south in search of safety. The gods led them here, to a swamp riddled with pests and vermin. 'Make a life,' the gods said, and our ancestors did." Venezia walked to the left, making eye contact with each Council member. "They built a city on marsh grass, but they intended so much more for Rialto. We are heirs to that legacy, one of endurance in seemingly impossible situations. In the last five centuries, Rialto has grown from a cluster of survivors to a thriving metropolis beyond our forefathers' dreams. We dominate the salt trade, and our vessels are hired by companies all over the Muriseano. Our three territories have only increased our riches. We are a world power.

"But we could be more." She hit her fist against her open palm. "We are chained to the coast. We'll never experience our true potential without reaching inland. The Illustrious Empire of Ilios spans over a thousand kilometers. If we only control Ilios and the Bogasa Strait, we'll be unstoppable. Free access is tempting enough, but think of how much money Rialto stands to gain from passage tax. How much will our people benefit from the extra income? How much will you and your businesses benefit? Add to that all of the resources of the empire—diamonds, spinning fibers, control of the spice road—and you can see why I advocate for this so strongly. Money would pour into our city and our pockets. Money we could use to extend our control over the entire Muriseano."

She paused to allow them to create their own fantasy. Some remained stoic, but others smiled at the prospects. Their greed would win this vote for her. "Janus Komnenos is a prick. We can all agree on that." The members laughed, though Primo didn't even smile. "He thinks he can set the terms, but we are in a position of power here. We could put him on the throne, accepting his offered payments, or we could sew a slave stitch into his wrist and make him dance for us. If he refuses to cooperate? We do it the Iliano way, and find another noble eager to be emperor.

"Yes, this is a risk. But so is building a city on water. Our ancestors could have shied away from the challenge but they didn't. When I consider Janus's proposal, I see a glittering metropolis. The white walls of Ilios have waited for a thousand years for an opponent worthy enough to breech them. That opponent will be us."

The Council applauded as she sat. Some reluctantly, but more than a few nodded in agreement. There was a chance. Somehow, there was a chance. That was not her best speech. Her limbs felt heavy enough to drag her to the bottom of the lagoon. Her hands started trembling, and she gripped the chair arms to steady them. She couldn't show weakness at such a critical moment. She could barely keep her attention on the Council chamber and the members. All she could see was Lazaro's face smashed against hers.

Primo stood, smoothing his sash and straightening his crown. Venezia was imposing, but as she sat there under his stare, she knew she had nothing on him. She didn't have his broad shoulders and tall stature. He clasped his hands behind his back and paced slowly as he spoke.

"My sister presents a convincing argument with her pretty words. She is well-intentioned, but she's wrong to risk the lives of our soldiers, or the money it would take to assemble a larger armada and fund this war. All for a shrinking empire. No one has taken Ilios because no one wants Ilios. Not anymore.

"I could never trust a member of the Komnenos family. Emperor Gregorios proved they have no love for Rialto. Who's to say his grandson won't turn his swords on us the second he gains the throne? Taking that much territory would stretch us too thin. Why do you think the Iliano Empire has declined in the last centuries? They grew too greedy and grabbed more than they could control.

"What is more, by marrying my cousin to the Imperial Princess Calixta, I am already increasing our power. Our ships will enjoy a vast discount on passage through the Strait, and we'll see those returns immediately. It is slower than war, but such things are best accomplished slowly. Slow is steady, focused, dependable. Blacksmiths do not rush because of customers' demand. A good sword takes hours of long, hard work. Rialto as we know it didn't spring up overnight. It has taken half a millennium for our city to become the blade that the Muriseano fears.

"Last week, Venezia met with Imperial Prince Nikkoforos, heir to the Iliano throne. He issued a threat in no uncertain terms. If we vote yes on this preposterous proposal, Ilios will launch warships. They'd be here in six days. War in faraway lands is bad enough, sending our brave men and women to die on foreign soil and be buried in unknown water. But think of it in our lagoon. Soldiers raping your wives. Your children trapped in your homes while black bane consumes them. The Iliano ships will be loaded with black bane. It eats stone and wood, blood and bone with the same ferocity. There would be no survivors. I can think of no greater tragedy."

No one applauded. Their faces were gray and somber.

Venezia seethed. "You speak as if Rialto were weak."

"Even if we win," Primo said, "countless citizens will die. Rich and poor, black bane kills the same. Our bodies will fill the canals and turn the water red." He continued pacing. "We face a choice: certain war or peaceful, steady growth. If we vote for Janus, we won't even get our ships out of the gulf before the Iliano fleet arrives. If we vote for Janus, we're already out of time. Rialto will plummet into the lagoon from whence it rose. What would that say about our regard for our ancestors' legacy?"

Primo returned to his seat and Sior Lando stood. "We will now convene to the voting chamber."

Venezia waited for her turn to go into the robing room. Some of the Council members whispered to each other. Others gazed into the distance. Fia Pesaro drummed her fingers on the arm of her chair with one hand, the other toying with her strands of pearls. The secretary called for Venezia. She walked into the robe room, quickly put on the black hooded cloak and black gloves. She took the black mask in her teeth, entered the voting chamber, and faced the wall. The others entered one at a time. Finally, Primo, wearing his white Bauta, called for them to turn around.

Beniamino, the secretary, took over. "The proposal is to support Janus Komnenos and his bid for the Iliano throne. Cast your votes as I bring the bowl to you. White is in favor, black is in disagreement.

This vote took much longer than most, as many people vacillated when Beniamino reached them. One person voted quickly—clearly Enrico Lando. But the others were torn. That was a good sign. If only Venezia could see the color of the stones they cast. But the room was too dark, and the secretary was too good at keeping the bowl covered. Ten minutes passed before Beniamino retreated to the fireplace to give Primo the bowl. He counted the stones, then counted again. Venezia tapped her foot.

"Eight against," Primo finally said. He paused, just to rub it in Venezia's face. "And four in favor. The Council's decision is clear: we will not accept Janus's proposal to declare war on the Iliano Empire."

She gripped her voting robes as everyone filed out. She'd never failed so miserably in her life. And it was all Lazaro's fault. She'd worked so hard the last five years to rid herself of the anxiety he caused, and he'd refilled it in one night. Even if he was still an asset to her in the long run, she couldn't live with him much longer. If he didn't die soon, she might have to help him on his way.

After his attack on her the other night, she could.

It hit her like a bolt of lightning. But it was true. All she had to do was remember his wet mouth on her breast, his wrinkled hand on her thigh, his hoarse whisper in her ear—and her fingers itched to ram a knife through his throat. Her stomach writhed, yet her heart burned at the idea. To never have to hear him with another woman, or see his marks on his sex slaves, or worry that he'd steal her knives again and force his way into her bed. To finally be free of him, permanently and completely.

And to have it be at her hands.

What a terrifying thought.

What an enticing thought.

But she had to win the election first. Once she no longer needed him, he'd hold no power over her. She'd use him, then drop his body into the lagoon without a tear in her eyes.

Chapter Twenty-Nine

Anselmo watched the swamp fill with light as the sun rose. He'd had last watch for the night, and it had been a cold one. Still, the watch hadn't been bad. Overnight watches would get worse as he spent more time in the labyrinth and became exhausted and worn down. For now, though, his threads were keeping him in good condition. Other than the cracked ribs. Even with his quick healing from his cotton corincanto and the structure improvement from the silk, it would be at least a week until those completely healed. But he'd survive. He'd survived much worse.

They'd been rerouted a few times the day before, thanks to moving walls. Throughout the night, the sound of walls shifting had echoed through the labyrinth. Luckily none close by, so they'd been able to stay in one place for the night. Anselmo had a feeling that would change as they pushed deeper into the labyrinth.

Something bit his arm. He slapped at it, looked at his hand, and groaned.

Mud fleas. Great.

It wasn't long before several were on his arms, legs, and crawling under his cuirass.

That's what this torture arena needed: pests.

A man jumped up with a yelp, slapping at his skin. "What in the three blazes of Fógo?"

Soon they were all awake, scratching, complaining, growling.

Even Rafael, who'd slept next to Anselmo, muttered under his breath as he scratched viciously at his arm. "Everything here is awful."

"They're mud fleas," Anselmo said. "Rialto has them too."

"Where? Sordo?" one man said. "You lived with these things? Gods, how poor are you?"

"I grew up on Croce before we moved to Giuffa."

"And Croce's only one step above Sordo. You really are a gutter slug."

"Enough." Nikkoforos pulled himself to his feet. His fancy clothes had already paid a toll. The white camisia was stained with black and red blood, rubies had fallen out of his boots, and his chain-metal tunic had lost its shine. Small, red welts dotted his skin. "Lieutenant Errari has made mistakes and has his faults, but his background is not one of them. I will not tolerate insults among my team. Eat a quick breakfast, then we're heading out."

The men continued to complain about the mud fleas as they chewed on hard tack and dried meat.

"Gods be damned, are we going to have to deal with these the whole time?" one yelled.

"Keep your voices down," Nikkoforos said.

They finished their food and filed out, Anselmo and Rafael in the back. Nikkoforos was silent, no longer chatting amiably with the soldiers around him. He steered them away from the mud mounds, sticking to the water. But the men continued to mutter as they waded through the swamp. Occasionally one would get a particularly bad bite and shout in frustration.

It wasn't long until Anselmo heard the snort of a minotaur behind him, along with a loud splash as it landed in the water. He whirled around. A solitary beast, but bigger than most of the ones that had attacked the day before. Instead of completely black fur, it had a patch of silver on its back.

It stayed back from them, still on all fours, swinging its horned head back and forth as it bellowed. Probably trying to call others to join it.

Anselmo readied himself to launch forward. He threw his spear, aiming for the beast's head. The minotaur swung at it, and in its moment of distraction, Anselmo leapt forward, sword in both hands. One, two, three leaps through the cold water, and he was soon there, swinging his sword into and across the minotaur's stomach.

He didn't make it all the way through the minotaur's body, but enough to incapacitate the beast. It grunted in pain as it collapsed into the water. Anselmo thrust his sword, point down, into the back of the creature's neck. The minotaur went still.

When Anselmo turned around, everyone was staring at him. One man whistled in appreciation. Another muttered, "Rea's holy name." Rafael looked ... well, impressed.

Others watched him with narrowed eyes and a suspicious twist in their lips.

"Impressive, Lieutenant, and well done," Nikkoforos said. He turned, and they continued on.

"How did you do that?" Rafael asked after a while. "That thing was huge."

"I was on alert," Anselmo said, too quickly. That would sound suspicious, and he needed to put them at ease. He slowed down his speech. "Everyone was so loud. I knew we'd attract a minotaur sooner or later."

"But the way you sliced through it." Rafael shook his head.

"I worked at a saltern before joining the armada. Shoveling salt day in and day out for years builds more muscle than you'd guess."

"Maybe I'll try that once we get out of here."

"I bet your father would love that."

Rafael half-smiled, then turned his serious. "He's not a bad man. Just strict."

Again, something Anselmo understood. "My mother was the same way."

"I guess we have something in common."

Anselmo snorted, but smiled. "One thing, at least."

"Sunshine," a man said. Light was making it through the thick canopy onto a large mound of mud.

Nikkoforos glanced around their surroundings. "Let's take a quick break."

Everyone had been relaxed the day before, but twenty-four hours in the labyrinth had changed them. They still lay on the mud, heads on shields, or leaned against trees, but the arrogant expressions were gone, replaced by grimaces as they scratched at the mud flea bites and watched the swamp around them.

Some even grimaced when glancing at Anselmo.

Great. Not only did they hate him, but because he'd displayed his unnatural strength in killing the minotaur, they likely suspected he had threads. Yet if he'd held back against that minotaur, it would've taken longer to beat it and he would've sustained more injuries.

The sun felt good on his face, and he hadn't slept since midnight. He leaned back and closed his eyes. A few minutes wouldn't hurt, especially when everyone else was watching the trees.

Something moved under his back, then hissed. Anselmo jumped to his feet and unsheathed his sword. A snake lay coiled where he'd lain, a black snake with green diamonds along its back. A jade mamba, the snake with the venom priests used to make anti-corincanto potion. The snake with the venom that could disable Anselmo's threads.

The snake pulled its head back as if readying for a strike. Before it could leap, Anselmo cut the coiled serpent in half.

"Shit, man, it's just a jade mamba," the soldier closest to Anselmo said.

"What? Oh. Right." Anselmo walked down to the water. "I guess I'm jumpy after that minotaur this morning." He could feel everyone looking at him as he washed his sword.

"You have threads, don't you?" the man said.

Anselmo turned and gave the man a killing stare. "That's ridiculous."

"He'd be a fool if he did," Rafael said quietly.

Anselmo took a moment to give him a puzzled look. "Exactly."

"Prove it," the other man said.

"And how do I do that?"

"Eat the snake. The whole thing. Muscles, bones, and venom glands."

Others called their agreement. Nikkoforos didn't intervene. He merely watched the situation from where he leaned against a tree.

"If you don't have threads, it won't hurt you," the man said.

"If I eat the snake, will you leave me alone?"

"As long as you're fine. Otherwise ... well, I guess the venom will take care of things."

Anselmo walked back to the mamba that lay in pieces. He picked one, stripped the skin off, and removed the muscle from the bone. He couldn't even cook it first. Even if smoke weren't a hazard, there was nowhere to find dry enough wood or tinder for kindling. The snake hadn't been big, about half a meter, and the piece he held was around a third of that. Still, a lot to eat raw.

He took a bite and grimaced. It tasted like chicken ... but chicken that had gone bad. Chicken that had tiny bones in it that crunched and poked his gums as he chewed.

"Feeling sick?" one of the soldiers called.

"Tastes like shit." Anselmo put the rest of the piece in his mouth. "Slimy shit."

"Venom gland too."

Anselmo picked up the head of the snake. "And how am I supposed to find that?"

The man shrugged. "Not my problem."

Anselmo started tearing the snake's head apart. Finally he found what had to be the venom gland, a liquid-filled sac. Luckily it wasn't big, about the size of the tip of his thumb. He took a deep breath, popped the venom gland in, and swallowed the vile thing whole. A moment later he heaved, though he managed to keep everything down.

The soldiers all laughed and relaxed.

Anselmo kicked the rest of the snake out of the way and lay back in the sun. Other than the foul taste in his mouth and a few straggler bones stuck in his gums, he felt ... well, he felt fine. Maybe he hadn't eaten enough. Or maybe eating it didn't affect him. Relief coursed through his veins as he closed his eyes against the warm, bright sunlight.

Soon Nikkoforos called for them to move. Anselmo stood. His knees almost gave way. He noticed in time and recovered without anyone noticing. His vision swam as he picked up his shield. His stomach churned. His head pounded, and his heart burned.

No.

Oh gods, no.

If anyone noticed, he was dead.

If anything attacked, he was dead.

He might be dead from the venom anyway.

With deep, deliberate breaths, he made his way into the water, staying a bit behind Rafael. At least he was in the back. The one upside to Nikkoforos's punishment the day before.

Also, for the first time, Anselmo was grateful for the water. Everyone sloshed through it awkwardly, so no one noticed the trembling in his thighs.

Lights flashed across his vision. His muscles quivered. Every step sent pain shooting through his feet, pierced his brain, made his teeth rattle.

Rafael paused until he was next to Anselmo. "You okay?"

Anselmo saw Polani burning at the cross all over again, heard the jeers of the crowd, felt the heat radiating off the bonfire. "Of course." Anselmo fought to keep his voice even.

"You're sweating."

"We're walking through a damned swamp with all our gear on. Of course I'm sweating. I don't have threads. If I did, wouldn't I be laying face down in the water right now?"

"Yeah." Rafael rolled the word around in his mouth. "True."

Anselmo bit down as the pain from his broken ribs grew, but when one of the bones slid against its other side, he couldn't stop the groan. Not only was he sick, but his corincanto was losing its power.

"You really don't look okay," Rafael said.

"The minotaur yesterday cracked some of my ribs. I think my fight this morning lodged one out of place."

"Why wasn't it bugging you earlier?"

"Have you ever cracked a rib before?"

"No."

"Well, they don't always hurt." That could be completely false, but Rafael didn't know any better. If the lie saved Anselmo's life, it didn't matter if he was wrong or not.

The sound of rattling filled the swamp. The soldiers froze, watching the trees with wide eyes.

"Cockatrice," Rafael said quietly.

The rattling grew louder and closer.

Nikkoforos turned to Rafael. "Would a phalanx work against it, Captain?"

"I don't think so, sir, not until we know where it will attack from. It's much bigger than a minotaur."

"How much bigger?" Nikkoforos had to yell for anyone to hear him over the rattling.

"Considerably."

"Form a circle, men, shields up in defense. The first one to see the beast, shout."

They hustled into place, fell in beside Nikkoforos, then each other, curving to create a circle. Anselmo pushed himself to move as quickly as them, even though his body threatened to collapse at any moment.

After a minute, they'd formed a complete circle. All except Enzio, who was pulling a cockatrice egg out of his pouch. He gently placed it on a knot of tree roots. Fool.

The rattling suddenly cut off. Cuirasses creaked as the soldiers shifted uneasily. Anselmo split his attention between the swamp and his sickened body. He flexed his fingers on the spear handle. His knee trembled against the muddy bottom of the swamp.

The trees in front of Anselmo shook. A creature drew up, covered in shadow. It rose higher and higher until it hung six meters above the ground. Bird head with the body of a serpent—an incredibly large serpent—and a rattle on the tail. Silver scales gleamed in the low swamp light.

"Shields up!" Nikkoforos called. "Cover your heads!"

The soldiers threw their shields up as the cockatrice cried out. Through the gaps, Anselmo could see the fangs lining the creature's beak. It cried once more, then dove into the group. Their circle exploded. Anselmo tucked and rolled away from the creature.

The beast pinned down one of the merchants with its beak. His screams were quickly swallowed by water as the creature ground him into the mud below. The cockatrice ripped the shield from the man's grasp and tore his body apart. An arm flew one way, one of his legs the other.

"Out of the water!" Nikkoforos was already on a mound, motioning with his spear while keeping his shield in front of himself. Anselmo and the others scrambled through the water, but the cockatrice blocked him, Rafael, and four others from the rest of the group.

Two of the soldiers rushed toward the creature. Anselmo hung back, shifting from foot to foot, observing the cockatrice's movements. His stomach twisted like a snake about to strike. His vision doubled. He focused his eyes until the images formed back into one. The soldiers stabbed at the beast, and it swung its head around to snap at them.

The cockatrice whipped Rafael with its tail. He flew into a tree next to Anselmo. A silvery liquid dripped down his arms, blistering his skin. The cockatrice cried out as a soldier landed a hit on its back.

It was fast, and it kept its head up as much as possible. It was attacking, but also managing a defensive role as well.

Anselmo pointed at Rafael's arms. "That poison came from the scales?"

Rafael nodded with a grunt as he pulled himself to his feet.

"Don't let it touch you!" Anselmo yelled, but Nikkoforos couldn't hear over the cockatrice's rattling. Anselmo couldn't even see him clearly, only the tops of helmets as they moved into some sort of formation.

Anselmo turned to the men with him, but they didn't hear either. They shouted at each other and screamed in pain as they discovered the poison the hard way.

"Spears aren't going to kill that thing," Anselmo said.

Rafael scrubbed his arm against moss growing on a tree to try to get the liquid off. "But getting close is difficult."

"Grab its attention. I'll take care of it."

"Your ribs are broken."

"I'm fine."

Two of the four men that had gotten cut off with Anselmo were down. The others retreated back to Anselmo and Rafael. "I need you three to distract it so I can kill it."

The cockatrice had forgotten about them, fighting instead with the main group.

"Why should we listen to you?" It was Enzio, the one who'd taken the eggs. "We all outrank you."

"Because I know what to do."

Enzio spat at Anselmo's feet, then he and the other man both ran off, trying to find a way to Nikkoforos.

Rafael exchanged a look with Anselmo, then ran toward the cockatrice as he beat his spear against his shield and hollered. The creature turned to face Rafael. Anselmo stuck his spear into the mud, gathered his remaining strength, swallowed his bile, and rushed to the beast's neck. He would slide under the beast and stab the soft part under its mouth when it dove for Rafael.

He stumbled his way around the beast's flailing tail, unsheathing his sword. His dizziness made him veer off course, and suddenly he and Enzio collided. Anselmo's legs slammed into the creature. Even in the water, the poison on its scales burned his skin. He dropped his sword, and his double vision made it impossible to find it on the murky swamp floor.

He came up for breath in time to see the beast rising above him. It had forgotten about Rafael. With no sword or spear, Anselmo had no way to kill it. He might be able to catch its beak, but the poison would burn his hands. Not to mention the issue of his increasingly weak muscles.

He was dead after all.

Would Imelda know when he died—would his presence disappear from her mind? Hopefully she'd still finish the wings and save herself.

He gathered what little remained of his strength, and prepared to fight to his death.

A soldier rushed into the space between Anselmo and the beast, stabbing his spear into the cockatrice's belly. As the cockatrice shifted its attention, someone grabbed Anselmo and dragged him out of the way. The soldier unsheathed his sword and thrust it into the cockatrice's jaw as it dove. It skewered itself on his sword, its strength so great that the tip of his blade burst through its eye.

The cockatrice had raised half of its length into the air. It came crashing down. All of the soldiers jumped out of the way, but Anselmo was still down. Its head collapsed onto Anselmo, pinning him to the mud. Bubbles leaked from his mouth as he struggled to lift it. But without his wool corincanto, he didn't have the strength. Men shouted, their voices muffled, as they ran over to free him. They pushed the dead creature off him, and someone helped him out of the water.

It was Rafael, who sighed in relief. "You're crazy, you know that."

"I'm a survivor." Anselmo leaned against a nearby tree and sheathed his sword as the others shouted in relief. A man lay wrapped in the serpent coils, skin completely bubbled up from the cockatrice's poison. It was Enzio.

Anselmo's legs burned where the poison bubbled his skin. But the blisters weren't as bad as Rafael's. The snake's venom hadn't completely deactivated his corincanto, just crippled it. With luck, the effects would wear off over the next several hours. Until then, he'd have to hide his weakness and pray for no more attacks.

"Who killed the beast?" Anselmo asked.

"Nikkos. Speaking of."

Nikkoforos walked over, helmet tucked under his arm. A man behind him washed the prince's sword in the water.

"Now you're almost getting yourself killed," Nikkoforos said. "You're too unpredictable, Lieutenant."

"It would've worked if Enzio had listened to me."

"He would've listened to you if you'd earned his respect." He shoved his helmet back on then retrieved his sword from the soldier who'd cleaned it. "Damn it, Errari, you're a great soldier, but you'll never advance in the military if you don't learn basic leadership skills. The men don't trust you because you don't listen to your commanding officer—"

"They don't trust me because I'm poor!"

"Do not interrupt me, soldier!" Nikkoforos's voice took on a commanding tone like Anselmo had never heard, and it echoed across the swamp. "Your pride has killed two men. From now on, you're up front with me. Move out!"

Anselmo gritted his teeth through the snake's effects—pain, weakness, dizziness, and nausea—things he hadn't experienced since he was a child. He rested his spear on his shoulder and fell in behind the prince. The prince who'd stolen his opportunity to lead here in the labyrinth. But if obedience was what it took for anyone to like Anselmo ... well, he'd do what he had to.

Chapter Thirty

Imelda stared at the front of her dress as the maid finished lacing it up. Dark purple, a seemingly endless train, and a ridiculous amount of silk corincanto pomegranates embroidered all over the skirt. The needlework was incredibly fine, no rough patches or errant threads as Imelda smoothed her hands down the sides. The silk folds were voluminous, yet somehow managed to show off her figure. It was incredible, and it was awful.

Imelda wore her wedding dress that she would again don tomorrow for her marriage to Ulisse. Less than twenty-four hours were left until she was expected to board the wedding barge.

Yesterday, Anselmo's presence in her mind had weakened and fluttered. It hadn't disappeared completely, but something had happened. It had been noticeable enough she'd lost all sense of where she was for the moment, so distracted by the upsetting sensation.

Yes something had happened. But even without knowing what, she knew it had been bad.

She played with her hair and tried not to throw up.

Donatella beamed and clapped. "Imelda, look at yourself. You're gorgeous."

Imelda turned to the mirror. Gorgeous didn't come close. Imelda had always thought herself pretty, but at that moment she was radiant. A work of art created by the greatest painters in Frenza. No one's face could be this symmetrical, no one's skin this smooth. Her hair was so shiny it seemed to produce light rather than reflect it.

But of course she was stunning. A rockfish would look beautiful with this much silk corincanto. It crept along the edges of her one-shoulder neckline and down the back into the train.

She wanted Anselmo to see her in this dress. Let him be the one to admire her as they walked together to the altar, not that greedy king Ulisse.

If she and Arturo didn't test the wings today, she'd find herself a married woman and queen besides, on her way to her new home in the north.

"Imelda, carina, do you like it?" Donatella hovered uncertainly, hands clasped at her breast.

Imelda forced a smile. "It's incredible."

"I'm glad we went with the deep purple. It suits you well." Donatella beamed. "I bet all the brides this year will be wearing it."

Donatella had outdone herself. Truly. The dress was amazing. Imelda had known it would be—Donatella had impeccable taste. But Imelda hadn't expected to actually wear it. She'd thought the wings would be done by now, sold to Venezia for five million ducats. She'd thought she'd be free, waiting for Anselmo in a foreign city somewhere. Her hair tickled her neck, and she tugged it out of the way.

Donatella batted away her hand. "Stop messing with your hair; you'll rough it up. Oh, I didn't show you the slippers!" She knelt and held them for Imelda to slip on. Rubies covered nearly the entire surface of the shoes, complementing the red corincanto embroidery in the dress. The voluminous dress covered them. How silly to spend so much money on something no one would see. Except Ulisse on their wedding night. Imelda closed her eyes as she wavered. Hands were on her in an instant.

"What's wrong, carina?" Donatella asked.

Imelda shook her head. "I'm just tired, and the dress is heavy. I should probably change now. Don't want anything to happen to it before tomorrow."

"Of course. It's time for the pampering anyway. We're going to completely spoil you, and La Canson is tonight. It's going to be a wonderful day."

"Actually, I'd like to spend time with Arturo."

"But it's tradition!"

"Please," Imelda said.

Donatella saw the desperation in her face and sighed. "Very well. You're the bride after all. Do you have any thoughts about your hair?

After fifteen minutes of changing out of the dress—a tricky maneuver as Imelda had to hide her Heart Stitch without anyone realizing what she was doing—and fussing about this and that, they left, Donatella promising to come up with a hairstyle worthy of a queen.

Imelda ran her fingers over her heart. She could feel the heart stitch through the thin wool. She couldn't fail Anselmo. She rushed to the door and opened it to find Calixta about to knock.

"May I come in?" the princess said.

"Oh, of course." Imelda gestured for Calixta to enter, even though her heart skipped in her chest. She needed to keep this quick. "How can I help you?"

Calixta closed the door. "I know about you and Anselmo."

Imelda's cheeks grew hot as her feet went cold. She resisted playing with her hair and tilted her head in mock confusion. "We haven't hidden our friendship from you or anyone."

"Imelda." Calixta gave her a flat look. "I'm not an idiot. Don't treat me like one."

"How do you know?" Oh gods. Imelda rubbed her arms, shaking her head in disbelief. "Did Arturo tell you?"

"Of course not," Calixta said quickly. "You know he wouldn't. I figured it out. By the way you two look at each other, it's quite obvious."

"Are you going to tell Primo?"

"I'm not a telltale. I'm here to tell you what you're doing is wrong."

"Wrong!" Imelda couldn't stop herself from yelling. She covered her mouth, took a deep breath, closed her eyes. "Primo is the one in the wrong. Anselmo and I promised ourselves to each other years ago."

"With what hope for the future? He's a lowborn. You two can't marry."

"Why do you think he went into the labyrinth?"

"It's too late now." Calixta's voice softened, and she took Imelda's hands. "You're betrothed to Ulisse, who's a good man. You need to stand up to that commitment and marry him."

Imelda snatched her fingers free and stalked to the other side of her room. "A good man? I know he drives you crazy. It's obvious! You wouldn't marry him if you two were stuck on a deserted island together."

Exasperation flickered across Calixta's face before the cool-headed princess returned. "If it were in my empire's best interest, I would." But her voice sounded strained. Even in theory, it was evident the woman hated the idea.

"Why do you care anyway?"

"I want what's best for our political allies."

Imelda snorted. "This isn't best for anyone but Primo. It's all about him getting what he wants. He doesn't care about me or Ulisse or anyone but himself. And I'm tired of being his puppet." She stormed past the princess, out the door, and into Arturo's room.

He sat on the floor in front of his pair of wings, inspecting the pulleys that controlled them, a glass of wine beside him.

"We have to try the wings," she said. "Right now."

Behind Imelda, Calixta cleared her throat.

He lifted his head slowly, glancing between Imelda and Calixta. "What's going on?"

"I'm getting married tomorrow!" Imelda's whisper was high and tight. "We have to show Venezia today so she has time to get us the money."

Something snapped. He yanked his hand back with a curse but didn't look at her.

Imelda turned to Calixta. "Please give us some privacy, Your Highness."

Calixta rolled her eyes, but turned and left, closing the door behind her.

Imelda sighed and sat beside Arturo on the floor. "I'm sorry about what I said the other night. I panicked. I do think Calixta genuinely cares about you. She'd be a fool not to."

He fiddled with the hinge for another moment, then set his tools down. "And you're right—we have to show Venezia the wings today. I let my anxiety get in the way." He half-smiled, but it faltered as he glanced at the wings.

"Still worried?" Imelda asked.

"I've dreamt about this my whole life. I'm excited, but it's hard not to be nervous." He fiddled with the tool in his hands.

"You don't have to fly across the sea. Just show Venezia they work. She's with us."

His jaw moved side-to-side as he considered. Finally, he pushed himself to his feet and pulled her into a hug. He even kissed the top of her head. "I love you, you know that? And I'm proud of you. These wings are just as much your accomplishment as mine.

She smiled. "What's this about?"

"If these don't work, you're getting married tomorrow. There will be no time for a quiet moment like this."

It had been ages since he'd spoken so candidly. They were going to achieve human flight, Venezia was going to pay them, and in a few days Arturo would sail to Ilios with Calixta. For the first time in her life, her twin brother would be gone. She'd walk into his room to find it as empty as Pàre's, sheets covering the furniture and only the lingering smell of books in the dark.

"I'll move to Ilios," she said. "There's no way I'm missing out on being the best aunt in the world."

"Children. Giore cancaro. How did we get here? I feel like yesterday we were running barefoot in the gardens with Anselmo."

"And Pàre reading on the balcony. Speaking of, I'll bet you're excited about the Ilios library."

"That's the second thing I'm most excited about." He smirked then nodded at the door. "Come on, we're running out of time."

He went to his wings.

Imelda grabbed his sleeve. "I want to try."

"You did the last two test flights."

"I thought you were nervous?"

He shrugged, his look rueful. "I still want to fly."

"Then I'll fly another day."

"Of course you will." He grabbed his glass from the floor and finished the last of the wine. "Okay. I'm ready. I'll call a servant to help me get the wings to the roof."

"And I'll get Venezia."

Calixta waited in the hall when Imelda opened the door. Imelda gave her a cloyingly sweet smile, then hurried down the hall, leaving the princess in her wake.

Seven years of work. Seven years of dreaming and planning and spinning. So much thread, so much paper, so much blood they'd used chasing after this moment. Even if they weren't using the wings to save Imelda, it would be a momentous day. But the implications for her personal life made it that much sweeter.

The spirit rose thread in her chest tingled, and Anselmo's weight in her mind urged her to hurry her steps to find her cousin.

CHAPTER THIRTY-ONE

Arturo glanced over the edge of the palàso roof, and immediately regretted it. The góndole below looked like small fish. Cold wind drove dust into Arturo's face, and gray clouds obscured the sky. He wiped at his eyes with shaky hands. He'd never been afraid of flying before. But today he would actually take to the sky, as long as all went to plan. People would be watching. There was plenty to make him nervous.

"Where's Venezia? She told me she'd be here after her meeting." Imelda glanced at the door, then turned back to him. "You look nervous." She grabbed the harness. "Here, I'll wear them."

He pulled the straps from her. "The harness is too big for you, and your wings are downstairs. There's no time to get a servant to bring them up." Not to mention, he was technically older—by fifteen minutes—and therefore the risk fell on his shoulders. Or back, as it were. He scratched at the five days' growth on his face. He'd told Calixta he didn't like beards because they itched, and he was right. But she liked them, so it would be a long time before he'd take a razor to his face. Maybe never. "I need wine."

"After, when we celebrate our victory."

The door to the roof opened, and Venezia rushed out. "Did you finish them?"

"We did," Imelda gushed.

"Good. The Council will be here in a few minutes."

The Council? Why couldn't Venezia just relay the information to them? It did make the most sense to have them attend the demonstration, but he didn't relish the idea of so many eyes on him. He breathed in the frigid air so he wouldn't vomit. One thing the blasted cold was good for.

Venezia touched a wing to admire it. "What bird is this from?"

"Albatross." Imelda clutched Venezia's hands. "You're to buy them, right? Today?"

"If they work. But I invited the Council because they might be willing to pay you more than five million ducats."

Imelda hugged Venezia with tears in her eyes. "Thank you," she whispered.

Arturo smiled. He'd done it. He'd saved his sister, in his own way. Money may be the ultimate power in this city, but intellect was powerful too.

"They're amazing," Venezia said. "I'm so proud of you two."

"Let's just make sure they work," Arturo said.

Imelda beamed as she helped Arturo into the harness. He tried to keep his hands from shaking, but it was no use. Two successful flights, that's all he needed. Once he proved they were safe, they'd sell the design to the Council and he could finish Imelda's wings. She'd love flying. She'd been the one who'd dreamed of soaring in the sky. For Arturo, the only thrill he sought was inventing what no one ever had. And a fine wine. And Calixta's lips.

He would've let Imelda run the test flight, but he couldn't let her take the chance of things going wrong. He swallowed his fear, which tasted a lot like bile, and checked the straps once more. It was worth it. To see his sister happy. He took a deep breath and focused on that thought. The tremor in his hands didn't stop, but it did lessen.

Until the door opened, and the entirety of the Council of the Twelve filed out. Then Calixta and Ulisse followed them. Great. This was all great. His hands started to shake all over again.

It was going to be fine. He would succeed. Arturo had considered every angle over the last seven years. His nervousness was merely a natural response to the height. He did not doubt his own mind. Never. He wouldn't have agreed to the test flight if he'd had even an inkling the wings weren't ready.

Calixta walked over and kissed his cheeks. "I'd rather give you a more thorough good luck kiss, but I don't think these stuffy politicians would appreciate that."

"After," he said. Rea cancaro, her forwardness was rubbing off on him.

She winked as she backed up to stand beside Imelda and Ulisse.

Her confidence, Imelda's excitement, and Venezia's anticipation soothed his nerves. As he pulled the cords and the wings sprang to their full width, his fear disappeared.

"Outstanding," one of the Councilmen said.

They truly were. The wings would take him into the air and help him conquer the sky. Arturo would be the first man to fly, but, most importantly, he wouldn't be the last.

The politicians watched with hungry eyes. Venezia's were brightest of all. Even Calixta raised her eyebrows in interest. Maybe she did want the wings after all—they would benefit Ilios as much as Rialto, if not more—but she'd made it very clear the other night she wanted Arturo too.

The wind activated the corincanto and awakened the leather's memory of flight. Quicker than the last test, the wings began to flap, lifting Arturo off the ground. This was nothing different than last time. The real test came not in the ability to fly, but the ability to control. The pulley system had worked fairly well last time, but that was with less wool corincanto. He'd had the seamstresses sew meters of wool into the wings. Surely they would take him into the wild sky.

Before lifting too high, he pulled on the left cord. The corresponding wing tucked in slightly, turning him to the left. Imelda grabbed Venezia's arm. The wind blew, and the wings flapped harder. He started to climb, higher and higher with each beat. Below him, everyone cheered. He laughed as he ascended through a low-lying cloud, condensation sprinkling his face.

Venezia shouted for him to come down. Imelda pointed at the temple bell. But he didn't need to descend—not yet. There was time enough for him to enjoy himself a little longer. He only needed five more minutes. Strange that he had always dreamt of human flight, despite his fear of heights. But this was the purest thing he'd ever experienced. He ignored the cold stinging his eyes, and flew on.

His legs dangled, clumsily. He'd need a bar to rest them on. He didn't have the strength to hold them behind him, so he tucked them in to reduce air resistance. He flew past the city to the lagoon. A góndola would've taken an hour to get to outlying islets. In a litter, it would have been closer to three to get to through the cramped streets. But with wings, he was there in minutes. There were no barriers. No restrictions. The hard lines of streets fell away into nothing but scribbles in a notebook. The silence of the sky replaced the clamor of the city. Men like Anselmo fought to become like gods by rolling in the mud and sticking each other with swords. Here, Arturo truly was a god.

A god who could fly.

Rain pattered on his face, bringing him back to reality. A reality that seemed more like a dream. He pulled on a cord, turning right as he descended, and headed back home.

Keeping hold of the cords was a problem as well. For these to be truly effective, the hands needed to remain free to carry things. But he'd figure it out. He'd learned how to fly—how hard could transportation be? Of goods or weapons—he didn't care. That was for the politicians to decide.

The rain fell harder. The wind picked up, and the wings beat faster in response. Good, he could get home sooner. But they continued to speed up until the water blurred.

It began to pour, and the onslaught blinded him. He wiped at his eyes as the city rushed closer, and yanked at the cords to regain control, to slow his flight, to stop.

He needed to stop.

The wings didn't respond. They were caught in a frenzy from the gusting wind. He raced over the first islands. The few people out didn't see him, hurrying with heads down against the rain. His elevation dropped with every second. He tried to scream, but the rushing air stole it from him.

Palàso Dogal appeared. The storm dulled its white marble, and it seemed to grin cruelly at Arturo as he rushed toward it.

Gods above, he needed to stop.

He wasn't high enough. He jerked at the cords. They flew out of his hands, burning his palms as they split his skin open. The ropes tore out of the pulleys and plummeted from the sky. Blood from his fingers fell as well, as if in slow motion. Drip drip drip, down down down, until they splattered on the cobblestones far below.

That wasn't right. He couldn't see that far down. But all he could see at that moment was his blood on the street. All he could feel was the pinprick of rain against his face. All he could hear was Imelda shrieking his name. His gut twisted with the sound of her voice, his lungs ached to tell her it would be okay.

He needed to stop. But the wings couldn't. They wouldn't until they hit something.

Until he hit something.

The cords-and-pulley system had been a useless detail. The wings flew well without it—too well. They beat furiously, speeding him on to death.

If only he could write that observation in his notebook.

The streets blurred. People's shouts rushed into one pounding scream, drowning out Imelda's cry. The one sound he wanted in these final moments. Stolen from him.

He should've been a better brother. Should've hugged her more. Should've told her he loved her more.

Should've should've should've.

He'd never thought he'd die with so many regrets.

The palàso grew taller, like a giant rising out of a mountain.

The people on the roof came into view. Imelda lunged forward, arms outstretched. Beside her, Calixta also reached for Arturo.

There was nothing they could do to save him.

There was nothing he could do to lessen the impact.

He could only hope the end would be quick, hope the pain would be quick.

There were only seconds left in his life. It was enough time to pray, if he could remember how. He made the sign of the gods with bloody, burning, trembling hands.

Thank Rea I didn't let Imelda wear the wings.

He reached for Imelda, and the wings crushed his body against the white stone palàso.

Chapter Thirty-Two

Imelda gripped Arturo's hands, straining to pull him back over the edge.

"Help me!" she screamed.

"Imelda, let go." Arturo's voice rattled in his throat. The wings continued to move, twitching here and there, twisting his body.

"I can't, I can't." She dug her heels in and tried to take a step back. The soles of her slippers began to tear.

Arturo coughed, spattering blood on his lips and her fingers.

Another cough shook his body, made him groan in pain.

He coughed again as the wings dragged him and Imelda closer to the edge.

Another cough splattered her face with blood.

He continued to cough, and now the convulsions were pulling him down the wall and pulling her with him.

"Let go!" he said.

Imelda shook her head even as her feet inched toward the edge. She leaned back as much as she could. She couldn't let go, and soon they'd be in a heap on the ground below. She could feel her body losing balance.

She wheeled forward, and soon she'd plummet to the ground with Arturo. An arm caught her from behind. It jerked her back just as she lost her balance. Arturo disappeared over the edge of the roof.

"No!" she yelled, scrambling to free herself.

"Don't look." It was Ulisse's plaintive voice in her ear, his arms around her. She elbowed him in the chest, wriggled free, and ran to the edge of the roof. Dozens of meters below, Arturo's body lay in a tangled heap. Everything was broken, the wings, his bones, his face. And the blood. Even from up here she could see blood pouring out of his body, pooling in the cracks between the cobblestones. Beside her, Calixta screamed.

Imelda pulled at her hair and face. Cold, wet blood covered her cheeks, her forehead, her nose as she grabbed at her skin.

Venezia reached Imelda, wrapping her arms around Imelda's waist and pulling her back. She smoothed Imelda's hair, whispered empty words meant to comfort, but Imelda could only scream. She couldn't stop, even as her throat burned. Arturo was dead. His body lay broken on the street, and it was her fault.

"Let me see!" Imelda tried to break free, but Venezia held tight. Her cousin was too strong, and Imelda too small. She sagged in Venezia's arms and sobbed. "Let me see him!"

Venezia scooped her up like a child and carried her down the stairs. The palàso was a maelstrom of panic. Imelda cried and begged to see Arturo. Primo waited in the hall, his face pale.

"Giore and Rea's holy union," he said, touching his head and heart. "What have they done?"

Venezia passed Imelda to Primo. Imelda's screams quieted as he carried her to her room and laid her on her bed. He stroked her hair and wiped the blood off her face with a wet cloth. After a while, Donatella replaced him. She held Imelda for a long time, singing lullabies through her own tears.

"Let me see him," Imelda whimpered.

Donatella only hugged her closer. She turned to Primo. "We need to get his body wrapped immediately. I'll send a hemp message to Renzo and Donte."

Venezia stayed the whole time, sitting beside the bed, smoothing Imelda's hair. She kept her face calm, but every now and then her gaze drifted out the window and she flinched. Ulisse appeared a while later. He whispered to Venezia, then told Imelda he was sorry. He watched her cry, a helpless look on his face. Primo stood watch, Venezia held her hand, Donatella hugged her. No one could bring her comfort. No one knew what to say.

No one would let her see her brother.

At some point, a servant brought up food. Donatella relinquished her hold, and Imelda bolted. She had to see Arturo. Primo grabbed her at the door. She railed against him with fists and feet, but he withstood her blows. Eventually she lost the strength, too weak to extricate herself from her hated cousin's grasp.

"Please," she sobbed. But he wouldn't let go.

Calixta came in sometime later. Imelda sat curled up on her window seat, staring at the street below. They'd already cleaned it, scrubbed it free of any trace of Arturo.

"Could we have some time alone?" Calixta asked Primo and Venezia. Donatella had left earlier to tend to her children, and Ulisse had left before dinner.

"I'll keep a man outside," Primo said quietly. Imelda pretended she couldn't hear. "Just in case."

Calixta silently joined her at the window. Her jewels were gone, and her eyes were puffy and bloodshot. The heartbreak on her face was too much.

"I'm sorry," Imelda whispered. Guilt raged inside Imelda, devouring her heart like a ravenous shark. She took a long, shuddering breath. Imelda allowed the princess to hold her as she blinked back more tears. How did she have any left? "Why won't they let me see him?"

"It's too much, Imelda. They won't even let me in. It's—it's horrible, from what I understand. We'll remember him healthy and strong."

The way he'd been that morning, sipping wine and working on the wings. Laughing as he began his ascent into the sky. The way he'd arch his brow and smirk as he withheld biting remarks. That was how Imelda should remember him. But she could only see him smashing into the palàso wall, again and again and again.

Calixta left. Cinzia, Primo's sweet young daughter, entered and climbed into Imelda's bed and snuggled in her arms. She cried with Imelda until Donatella retrieved her.

Imelda slept for a time. She was alone when she woke. The sun had set, and stars glittered in the windows. She stumbled to her spinning wheel. She needed linen roving. Rea wouldn't find him if he wasn't wrapped in linen corincanto. His body would lay on the sea floor, slowly eaten by crabs and fish. She hadn't saved his life, but she could save his soul. She grabbed at the baskets around her, rummaging through the contents, then overturning them and digging through the supplies on the floor. She'd finally found some roving when Venezia entered.

"What are you doing?"

"I have to spin his linen corincanto."

"We're taking care of it."

"It has to be me! I killed him!"

Venezia picked her up off the floor. "You did no such thing."

If only Imelda had told Primo about the wings. She wouldn't have had to push Arturo. She'd whined and insisted, and now her brother was dead. If she hadn't acted so selfishly, he would be alive. She'd be marrying Ulisse tomorrow, but at least her brother would be sitting with her right now, sipping his wine as he read and she spun.

He'd hugged her today, even kissed her. The last time that had happened was when Pàre had died. Her dear brother. Her best friend. The dreaded day had finally come—the day they could no longer be together.

She couldn't stop replaying that moment. His fingers slipping from her grasp. His body disappearing over the edge of the roof. The wings, shredded and broken. His sightless eyes turned toward the sky. His blood on her face, her hands, and the street. Over and over, the screams reverberated in her mind. She killed him. It didn't matter what the others said. She killed her twin brother.

Venezia opened a window, then sat next to Imelda. She tucked a blanket around Imelda's shoulders and hummed a melancholy tune. Imelda's wedding dress hung on the wardrobe door, fluttering in the breeze. The dress she'd been meant to wear tomorrow, the dress that had driven her to rush to Arturo. The corincanto embroidery popped against the violet silk. The red threads didn't look like pomegranates anymore; they looked like veins.

Someone smoothed her hair and called her name. Imelda blinked as her eyes focused on Donatella's face.

"The funeral is soon," Donatella said. "Do you want me to help you dress?"

Imelda wore the same dress she'd worn to her father's funeral. It had been packed away in a trunk, laid to rest with lavender. They tried forcing her to eat, but she refused.

Soon she boarded the empty dogal barge. There were no tables full of food, no bottles of wine. This was no celebration of a long life well lived. It was the ache of a thread cut short.

"Where is everyone?" she asked.

"I thought it was best to leave the family to mourn in peace," Primo said.

For once, Imelda agreed with him.

She stood under the canopy, watching the water slide by with dull eyes. Finally she could go see him. She approached the bow slowly, his body laid out on the platform. It was tempting to think this wasn't Arturo, that it was just a dead body shrouded in mourning blue. Someone had put his body back together, and they'd wrapped it tighter than normal.

To keep everything in place.

Salt air danced across her skin and pulled strands of hair out of her braid. The sun shone in a cloudless sky, even cast some warmth on her cheeks. So different from Pàre's cold funeral, but it fit Arturo. He was like an early spring day, cool mornings and warm afternoons. Tears pricked her eyes, and she blinked them away.

Finally the boat stopped. Venezia approached. "It's time."

The rest joined them—Primo and his family, Lazaro, Calixta, Ulisse. They watched her as the high priest's voice droned on, mixing with the sound of water lapping against the hull. Then Primo's voice, and Venezia's. They looked at her expectantly, but she shook her head. She had no words left.

At last the high priest pulled the bucket over the railing. He drizzled the cold water on her head. It dripped down her face, and a drop slipped under her dress, sliding down her back.

"The water of your brother's grave, to bind you to him for eternity." The priest's voice seemed to echo from the depths of the sea.

"Amen." Her throat was hoarse and dry.

The high priest directed her and Venezia to take Arturo's arms, with Primo at the feet. The door in the barge wall slid open. Imelda grabbed Arturo's fingers. She knelt and kissed the fabric. Her tears rained over his shroud. Even through it, she could feel the brokenness of his bones. They grated against each other, moved in ways they shouldn't. She did this—she had destroyed him, had broken his bones one by one.

"I'm sorry," she whispered as the high priest spoke the final prayer. "Forgive me."

She was still holding tight when her cousins pushed him toward the edge. She held on as long as she could, until Primo's last shove sent Arturo into the murky water below.

CHAPTER THIRTY-THREE

The soldiers wandered for two days without any action other than moving walls constantly making them reroute. Anselmo's stomach was nearly empty and mud flea bites covered his arms. He could feel them crawling in his hair and under his cuirass.

The snake's venom had worn off by the night after Anselmo had eaten it. Normally bug bites would heal in a single day, but here he was constantly getting bitten. At least that masked his threads' healing abilities. Especially since Anselmo was stuck up front with Nikkoforos the whole time. The prince had stopped chatting with people while they walked, and they never stopped for more than ten minutes except at night. He took them farther inside the labyrinth whenever they reached a fork, but every time it seemed they'd made progress, a wall would move, forcing them back out. What were they even looking for? Ultimately, the sword, but surely it wasn't hidden in a tree trunk in the swamp.

The fleas grew worse, and the soldiers' scratching grew more intense. Even Anselmo found his sanity pushed to the brink as he tried to reach an itch in the middle of his back by shoving his spear handle down his cuirass. It didn't help.

"Sir." Rafael sloshed up to Nikkoforos and Anselmo in the afternoon. "The water is moving now."

Nikkoforos held up his fist for everyone to stop. Anselmo looked down. Sure enough, the water streamed in one direction. Now that he'd stopped, he could feel it moving across his skin. Slowly, but still moving.

"The land is sloping down." Nikkoforos started in the direction the water flowed. After ten minutes, the swamp bottom took a serious decline and the water sped up.

"Stay on alert," Nikkoforos said even as he walked faster. Behind Anselmo came the sound of swords being unsheathed. Anselmo wanted to ditch his spear in favor of his sword, though that would be foolish. Their surroundings didn't seem any more threatening than before. Birds still sang. There was no rattling. No shadows moved through the treetops.

But it was different. And in the labyrinth, that could mean a new kind of danger.

"Look how many trees there are," Nikkoforos said quietly to Anselmo. "The walls here don't move."

The trees were also closer together. They wove through the strange swamp, the ground sloping gently toward what Anselmo guessed was the interior of the labyrinth. After half an hour, through the dark of the swamp, Anselmo saw a change in the landscape.

"Gods above," a soldier groaned. Anselmo glanced back. The men had all sheathed their swords and were scratching at their arms and legs. Even Nikkoforos was clearly clenching his teeth as he scratched at angry, red bites on his skin.

"Sir, there's some kind of construction ahead," Anselmo said.

"I see it too." Nikkoforos slapped at his arm. "Scout it out."

Nikkoforos called for the others to stop, and Anselmo went ahead alone. Anselmo stepped between two trees into a small clearing beside a wall. Another wall, gods be damned. But a large circular-shaped stone sat beside the wall, like a giant trough of some sort. Steam rose from it. Anselmo crept forward slowly. Water filled the stone construction. Anselmo leaned close and sniffed, then dipped his hand in. It was hot and smelled faintly of rotten eggs.

Not a trough. A hot spring.

Anselmo went back to Nikkoforos. "There's a dead end and a hot spring, sir. Everyone needs to get in."

Nikkoforos's brows knit as he glared. "Are you giving an order, lieutenant?"

"The hot water will kill the mud fleas."

"Kill those bastards?" someone said.

Nikkoforos grunted and itched his leg. He nodded. "Everyone in."

The soldiers ran to the hot spring, throwing their shields and spears on the mud then jumping in fully clothed.

"What in the three blazes?" Rafael slapped at his skin. "This is worse!"

Anselmo pulled his cuirass off and set it on the mud. "You're trapping the fleas against your skin. Take your shirts off and scrub them in the water."

No one hesitated. Cuirasses clattered onto rocks and shirts came off. Nikkoforos looked around at the trees before pulling his chain mail tunic and shirt off. He wasn't crazy to be reluctant. Anselmo had never been naked in a hostile environment, and it gave him a feeling of vulnerability he had never known. Other than when he ate the jade mamba, but he'd been so preoccupied with surviving and fooling everyone else, vulnerability had been an afterthought.

Still, when he stepped into the hot water he couldn't ignore the way his muscles relaxed. He'd been cold ever since wading into the labyrinth's swamp, but now it fled.

He also couldn't ignore the way Rafael watched him as he sat. A little too closely. Like he was looking for something. He'd defended Anselmo to the others about not having threads, but that could've been a cover. And he'd asked his own probing questions about Anselmo's strength and abilities. The man was smart and he paid attention. A dangerous combination.

Anselmo rolled his shoulders and leaned back against the wall. "Felt like I'd never be warm again."

Rafael leaned his head back. "Mmhmm."

One man rubbed at his arms in the water. Dead mud fleas floated to the surface. "I should've sewn alpaca corincanto into my tunic before I came."

"You should've prepared better, Moretti." Nikkoforos pulled his shirt out of the water and held up the hem. Red stitches dotted the arms and neck of the garment. "One of the first things I thought of."

"You're not used to the cold, sir," Rafael said.

Nikkoforos laughed. "True enough. I had alpaca added to all my clothing before I came to Rialto."

The ground rumbled, and they all froze. A wall moving. But the sound was distant and soon stopped. They all exhaled at once.

"All I need now is a glass of wine and a siora by my side," Moretti said. "Feels like Carnevale was weeks ago, not days."

"You're too ugly for any siora, even with a mask on," another man said.

Everyone laughed.

"Keep your voices down," Nikkoforos called, then he smirked. "There's hope for you, Moretti. I hear Lion blue is as effective at improving your looks as silk corincanto."

"First thing I'm doing when I get out of here is proposing to Lucia," a soldier said.

"First thing I'm doing is going to the brothel," Moretti said.

"Say hello to your mother for me."

Anselmo couldn't help but laugh with the others.

"I don't care what you say about my mother. I'm in the labyrinth. I'm not exactly her favorite, now am I?"

"I thought becoming a Lion was an honor," Nikkoforos said.

Moretti leaned his head forward to scrub his hair in the water. "Only because we're not first-borns, the heirs to the family businesses. In Rialto you either work for your oldest sibling or figure it out on your own."

"Except for Rafael," another soldier said. "Heir and Lion."

Rafael grunted as he rubbed his shirt against the rocks. "The Galbani inheritance is surviving the labyrinth."

"Don't sound so sour. You'll be running the Lions once your dad retires."

"If I want to."

"You don't want to be admiral?"

"Not if it means leading your sorry asses."

"And you, Errari, you'll be made a noble for going through this hell?" Nikkoforos asked.

Anselmo took his time wiping dead fleas off his arms and shoulders. "I have no other reason to subject myself to this."

"After we get out, first thing *you've* gotta do, Lieutenant," one man said, "is marry rich."

They all laughed.

"I've got a few available cousins. You like men or women?"

Anselmo folded his arms and leaned his head back. "Save your cousins. I've got my own money."

"Not enough to buy a house on Riga or Monte, I bet."

"Enough to get me there eventually."

The men continued to talk quietly. Anselmo looked up. The clearing was big enough that he could see the sky, an early spring blue dotted with white clouds. As long as Imelda was successful with the wings, he wouldn't need his money to live on Riga. Not that he'd accept any more from her than he had to, but he wasn't so prideful as to blind himself to the facts. Imelda was rich and, for the time being, he was poor. But not for long. Not for long.

"This water stinks, but at least the mud fleas are dead," said a man by the wall. He put his hands behind his head and leaned against the stone. "If only we could stay here and—"

The ground rumbled and the wall swung open and away from them. The man fell back, and all the water flowed toward the opening.

"Grab your shields and clothes!" Nikkoforos yelled.

Anselmo and the others scrambled, but the water was moving too quickly. Another section of wall opened, and the water washed Anselmo away before he could reach his shield. He poured over the edge and down. He fell for a second then landed in cold water, deep enough that he had to swim up to the surface. Around him, shirts floated and men treaded water. Anselmo wiped water out of his eyes as he gasped for air.

He appeared to be in a lake surrounded by tall stone walls. This was probably the interior of the labyrinth, perhaps even the center. He couldn't see much beyond water in every direction and distant walls stretching around him. The walls were tall, and the section right above held the opening they'd fallen through.

"Shore, over there!" someone called, pointing to the right.

"Swim for it!" Nikkoforos called. "Grab whatever you find floating in the water."

Anselmo checked his chest and side. His sword sheath was still slung across his chest, and his sword was still sheathed. At least he wasn't defenseless. He swam in the direction the soldier pointed, grabbing shirts as he passed them.

"Can you help, Errari?" It was Rafael, coming up beside him. He had an arm around another man, holding him up. The man's eyes were wide and rolling, and his whole body shook. "He hit his head. He won't make it on his own."

Up ahead, one man stood up on the beach. He waved both arms over his head, then pointed at the water behind them, yelling something.

"What's he saying?" Rafael asked.

"Can't tell," Anselmo said.

The man pointed more insistently, then unsheathed his sword. Several meters ahead, another man was swimming. Suddenly, he disappeared under the water.

"Faster," Anselmo said.

To their left, another man disappeared.

Something brushed against Anselmo's legs.

The man he and Rafael held was snatched under the water.

"Sirens!" Nikkoforos yelled. "Get to the beach!"

Anselmo let go of the tunics and swam as fast as he could. Rafael kept up. Around them, dark figures darted through the water. Men screamed in the distance.

A figure popped out of the water in front of Anselmo and Rafael. It was female but not quite human. Her eyes were too large and black as the sands of Zorzi. She was naked, revealing her breasts, but she had bony, featherless wings tucked behind her. She rose out of the water, flapping her bare wings and revealing scaled bird legs.

"Anselmo Errari, Rafael Galbani," she said, her seductive voice in stark contrast to her monstrous appearance.

Anselmo unsheathed his sword and swam toward the siren. She dove under the lake's surface. "Go, Rafael!" he said. Swimming with the sword was a struggle, but Anselmo didn't dare put it away.

As Rafael swam away, something pulled Anselmo underwater.

He held tight to his sword and opened his eyes, already kicking for the surface. A siren floated right in front of him. Gone were the bat wings and bird legs, the uncanny eyes. She was an elegant, gorgeous woman. Blue eyes, slim build, skin as dark as coal.

"You don't want Imelda," she said. Her appearance shifted and she had blond hair, ivory skin, and curves as soft as the clouds above a sunset. "You don't want nobility. Those trivial cares belong to the cruel world on land. Stay here, where the water softens the light and the current cradles you. Forget about the harsh rays of the sun and the pain of your lungs sucking in air."

She sang a wordless melody as she came closer to Anselmo. It was the most beautiful sound Anselmo had ever heard. She was the most beautiful thing Anselmo had ever seen. She changed again so her hair was short and black, her cheekbones high, stature tall and commanding.

He flinched away. Her appearance began to flicker constantly. It was a lie. Her words were a lie. She was a lie. She darted for him. He couldn't feint effectively in the water, but he managed to thrust his sword through her chest, tearing her skin open and dyeing the water red. She cried out like a dying gull. Anselmo pushed himself up through her blood until he reached the surface. He sheathed his sword and swam to the shore as fast as he could.

"They're not coming out of the lake." Nikkoforos walked over. Blood seeped from scratches on his chest, mixing with the lake water to run down his skin. "Rest. I'll keep an eye out."

Anselmo collapsed onto dry sand. The sun slowly set as the sounds of screaming men and crying sirens filled his ears.

Chapter Thirty-Four

Imelda sat on her window seat, blanket wrapped around her as she watched the street. One day after Arturo's funeral, two days after his death, and everyone continued their business as if nothing had happened. Politicians walked in and out of the Senate hall, talking and laughing. Street vendors sold what little food was left after Carnevale, and servants carried nobles in ornate litters. Down below, Venezia left the palàso and headed south, no doubt on some Council or military errand. She still wore mourning blue. Others might have as well; Imelda hadn't left her room all day, so she had no idea. She'd slept in her dress, and had refused Editta's attempts to change her clothes.

Somewhere to the north, Anselmo fought in the labyrinth. Completely ignorant of Arturo's death. She could send a hemp message, but the news would distract him. Right now, the only thing he needed to focus on was survival. She wrapped the blanket tighter around herself, imagining it was his arms instead. She would cry as he held her, as she had done for him when his mother died. Her lips quivered, and she mashed them together as she leaned her forehead against the window.

Someone knocked.

Imelda hesitated. "Yes?"

"It's Ulisse. Could I come in please? I brought something to eat."

She scrubbed her face. She had a perfectly acceptable reason to say no, but her stomach grumbled at the thought of food. "That's fine." She stayed by the window, even remained wrapped in the blanket.

Ulisse left the door open and set a plate of salumi and cheeses on the desk. Then he dragged her chair over and sat. "How are you?"

She shrugged and rested her head against the glass again. "I'm alive." Her throat constricted, and tears pricked her eyes. She blinked them back as she pulled the blanket tighter. She hadn't cried since that morning. No way she'd let herself do it now.

"Sometimes that's all we can ask for."

"So you came to check on me?" It came out more defensively than she intended. "I mean, it's kind of you ... grassie."

"I keep thinking about the terrible irony of it: yesterday we were meant to marry, and instead we attended a funeral. Life is bitterly cruel." He leaned forward, elbows on his knees, as a sad smile appeared on his lips. He clasped his hands together, and looked at them as he spoke. "We're not married yet, but a healthy relationship requires a strong foundation. I confess, my motives aren't completely selfless. My advisors have sent hemp message after hemp message, hounding me about returning to Eraclea. Boring decisions to make, people wanting to ask questions of the sea silk, and on and on. Nothing dire—despite their panic—but I do need to get home sooner rather than later. I'm leaving the exact date up to you. It's all dependent on our wedding. If you prefer to get married here, I can wait a week at most. But if you like, we could get married in Eraclea. We'll leave within the next few days, and then you can take your time planning the event. Eraclea is beautiful in the spring, and the change of scenery might be beneficial."

"Here," she said immediately. "It's my home." Plus, Anselmo might pass the labyrinth before then. He was the only hope she had left. The wings had proven to be a terrible, terrible failure.

Not that Imelda deserved Anselmo. She'd pushed Arturo to his death. What about Anselmo, fighting in the deadly labyrinth? He'd entered for her. She hadn't asked him to—in fact, she'd begged him not to—but his love for her had driven him there. Never mind that she'd be with him even if he were a beggar on Sordo. He wanted to marry her, which meant fighting to rise in the social hierarchy. If he died, his blood would be on her hands as well.

Ulisse nodded. "Primo thought you'd choose Rialto."

She glanced at him. He wore a mourning blue shirt and his gold circlet. Despite the gloomy color of his shirt, and the formalness of his crown, he had the same casual air from the day they'd met. There was kindness too, mixed with the sorrow on his face.

She expected him to leave. He'd come to check on her and discuss the wedding date, and he'd accomplished both those tasks. Instead his gaze shifted out the window, watching a flock of pelicans flying in a V formation, but at that moment they looked like an arrow piercing the sky.

"My wife drowned," he said. "I'm not sure if anyone's told you that. We never found her body, so I wasn't able to spin linen for her." He cracked his knuckles, one by one, as he stared into the past. "Grief is a strange thing. People say you get over it, but that's false. You just learn to live around it, around the hole that person left in your life. 'Remember the good times,' they say, but I can't let go of the guilt. If I hadn't taught her how to harvest sea silk. Or if I'd found a more trustworthy person to take her. She'd had no interest in sailing her own boat, but maybe if I'd taught her, she would've been able to handle the weather that day better than the oaf I'd hired. If I'd done one thing different, perhaps she'd still be here with me today."

Imelda toyed with a lock of hair. Maybe he wasn't so bad. Maybe she could trust him. She still didn't want to marry him, but she could give him the benefit of the doubt. "I feel guilty," she admitted.

"That's a natural feeling, I think. We'll always ask what if. But." His voice changed, grew more certain. He straightened. "Just because it's natural, doesn't mean it's true."

He might believe that, but with Arturo's death, it was true. Imelda had killed him.

Ulisse stood. "I'll leave you alone now, rather than forcing you to listen to my ramblings any longer. Anything else I can bring you? More food? Wine? A way to change the past?"

She forced a smile then leaned her head against the window again. "I wish I had his wings."

Ulisse cocked his head to the side. "But they're a wreck."

"It would be something of his, something of ours." Even though they killed him. Perhaps that was a better reason to keep them—to remind herself of her guilt.

Ulisse scratched his beard, then nodded to himself. "I understand."

Awkwardly, he put his hand on her shoulder. It was bandaged across the palm.

"What happened?" she asked, nodding at it.

"I spun the linen for Arturo. Clearly they weren't going to let you do it, and corincanto bought from the guild isn't the same. There wasn't much I could do for you, but this was something. I hope I didn't overstep."

"Grassie." And she meant it. It had been a kind, thoughtful gesture. "Why is it still bandaged?"

"I didn't use cotton corincanto to heal it. I figured it would be a greater sacrifice."

Imelda bit down the threatening sob and nodded. Ulisse patted her shoulder, again awkwardly.

Someone knocked on the door, and Imelda bade them in. It was Ulisse's guard, whose muscles were as big as Imelda's legs, his expression as serious as a churning sea. "A Siora Priuli is here requesting your services."

It had only been two days since her brother's death, yet Imelda's so-called fiancè was still accepting clients. Absolutely disgusting. She hugged the blanket tighter, covering her entire body, and turned away from him.

Ulisse grimaced as he turned to Imelda. "I am so sorry. This is terrible timing. I will—I will visit again soon."

But he didn't leave right away. His gaze shifted out the window again. "I barely knew Arturo, but watching him fly was amazing. Those wings ... he was a genius, wasn't he?"

"Smartest person I knew."

"The world lost something special."

Finally he left, his guard on his heels like a well-trained dog.

Imelda slammed her fist on the window seat. She'd been right—he was a greedy, greedy bastard. He did want the wings now that he saw them. Why wouldn't he? On the day they met, he said he'd do anything for his kingdom. Luckily, even if she managed to get Arturo's wings, they were ruined beyond repair. She'd have to find a way to hide hers. Maybe she should burn them before he could get to them. The wings had been for the world. They were meant to save Imelda. They didn't deserve to be stolen by a greedy king.

Whatever his motives, Ulisse was right about one thing: Arturo had been special, a gift from the gods to their poor, wretched world. And he'd been even more than that to Imelda. He'd been her rock, her light, her counter-weight. And she'd ushered him off to his death.

Imelda buried her face, and the blanket slowly grew wet with her tears.

CHAPTER THIRTY-FIVE

Sleep was impossible. Though the sand was soft, and Anselmo was able to fully dry off for the first time since entering the labyrinth, it was still freezing. The soldiers had to huddle together for warmth. The sirens cried all night, calling each man's name over and over, pleading for them to go to the water. Anselmo spent the night between Rafael and another man, hands pressed against his ears to drown out the lovely, enticing voices of the monsters in the water.

Nikkoforos sent out two scouts at first light when the rising sun revealed their surroundings. They were in a large, circular bowl, surrounded by the high interior walls of the swamp portion of the labyrinth. A lake filled most of the area. The strip of land they stood on was half beach, half bushes and scrub trees filled with scurrying rabbits. It curved about halfway around the crater. And in the middle of the lake, two towers stood on a small island. That must be where the sword was.

It was so open. And bright. After the crowded trees of the swamp, Anselmo's eyes stung in the direct sunlight. Still, when a rabbit came close, he dove for it and managed to catch it. He broke its neck and skinned it.

"I'll gather wood and kindling for a fire," Rafael said.

Nikkoforos stood not far off, staring at the castle. He seemed to struggle keeping his face impassive, because every now and then a look of panic would flash across his features.

One of the scouts returned and reported quietly to Nikkoforos, who listened as the soldier spoke. The scout wore a tunic, but Anselmo did not. Some had washed ashore during the night, but none were big enough to fit Anselmo. The prince didn't wear one either, though surely one of the few tunics they'd retrieved could fit him. He'd made sure to give them to the other soldiers first.

Naked and in a hostile environment. Really and truly this time, because in the hot spring their clothes were within arm's reach. They didn't even have shields or their rucksacks. And a siren-filled lake separated them from the sword and their escape.

Nikkoforos whistled for them to gather. Anselmo sheathed his sword and carried the rabbit over.

"There's a boat not far from here." Nikkoforos nodded at Anselmo. "Good thinking, Errari. Everyone catch rabbits while we walk to the boat."

"A boat?" Anselmo said to Rafael. "I don't trust it."

"The admirals have to give us something once in a while," Rafael said.

"I don't trust it."

They reached the boat after a half hour. It was a rowboat and looked to hold eight to ten people. It was also brand new, judging by the condition of the wood.

A few of the other soldiers also caught rabbits. Nikkoforos set them to skinning the animals and the others to find wood for a fire. One man returned with an armful of dried out boards—from a former boat.

Rafael constructed a tripod for a spit to cook the rabbits on. He glanced at the broken boards. "That bodes well," he murmured.

Just another reason the boat was a bad idea. Anselmo grabbed a stick off the ground and sharpened the tip with his sword. Then he shoved it through the rabbit's back. He grimaced and shifted. He'd sat on a rock and it was digging into his bare ass.

The second scout returned. He spoke to Nikkoforos. The prince checked his sword, then turned to everyone.

"There's another way between the lake and the swamp. I'm going to check it out, make sure we can use it to leave this area after we have the sword. Keep catching and cooking rabbits. We'll need our strength to cross the lake later."

Anselmo stood. "We shouldn't use the boat."

Nikkoforos turned, one brow arched. "And why do you say that, Lieutenant?" His voice was as stiff as the look on his face.

"Because it's a bad idea." Anselmo pointed at the old boards from a former boat, which now crackled in Rafael's fire. "The lake is crawling with sirens. And if there are two ways from the swamp to the lake, there must be two ways to the island."

"Yes, there are two ways—take the boat or swim. We only lost three men when we were dumped into the lake and ambushed by sirens. I'm confident that in a boat we can handle them. And might I remind you." Nikkoforos walked over to Anselmo and got in his face. There were about five centimeters between their heights, but Nikkoforos's regal air made up for it. Anselmo felt like he was facing his equal. "The reason we were unknowingly dumped into a cold lake while naked and without shields is because you suggested we get in the hot spring. I'm done listening to your ideas."

"Your leadership has gotten us where we are. Leadership you only won because of your title, Your Highness." Anselmo sneered. "If you hadn't pushed your way into the labyrinth, I would be the one in charge."

"You think these men would have voted for you?"

"I know they would've."

Nikkoforos scoffed. "And you think you'd do better in this environment?"

"Give me the chance."

"Fine." Nikkoforos stepped back and spread his arms. "We'll put it to a vote. If the men vote for your plan, I'll step down and let you take charge. Soldiers, whose plan do you favor? Mine to take the boat to the island, or Lieutenant Errari's to waste time trying to find a second way to the island that probably doesn't exist?"

Within seconds, eleven swords were stuck in the ground at Nikkoforos's feet. There was not a single one in front of Anselmo. Neither he nor Nikkoforos had voted.

Neither had Rafael.

Anselmo took his cooked rabbit from the spit. "You're all fools."

"You know what your problem is, Errari?" The prince said each word precisely, wielding them like daggers. "It isn't your background or your lack of money. You don't know your place. You think you're superior to us. You think you're smarter and stronger and better than everyone else here. You think you don't need us, but I saved your ass from that cockatrice. You're the same as us, but you refuse to acknowledge it." The other men grumbled their agreement. Nikkoforos walked up to Anselmo and poked his chest. "And because of that attitude, it doesn't matter what you do, here in the labyrinth or out in the world after. You'll never get Imelda Albizzi. She's marrying an actual king while you're nothing but a lowborn desperately clawing his way to the upper classes. But when you get out, it will be in vain because she'll be married to another man, and you'll never see her again."

Anselmo punched Nikkoforos in the face. "You asshole."

Men rushed to the prince, but he shrugged them off. When he straightened, blood dripped from a split on his cheekbone, and his eye was already darkening. He spat blood on the sand. "You are your own problem, Errari. But I'm through with you being my problem. Leave now."

Anselmo didn't need another moment. He turned around and walked off. Nikkoforos's face would only hurt more as the day wore on, but Anselmo's hand felt fine. Anselmo thought he was stronger than all of them because he truly was. Stronger in body and will. He'd get that sword and leave them all to fight their way back through the swamp without his help.

CHAPTER THIRTY-SIX

Ulisse finished bandaging his hand as the siora left the parlor, holding back tears as she dabbed her face with the handkerchief he'd given her. Several times a year, clients would ask about the fidelity in their marriage. Their instincts to ask were almost always right—his answer was almost always yes. He'd watch their faces crumble with heartbreak. These were the only clients he'd offer cotton corincanto bandages to, often wrapping them himself. Their pain was too palpable. Ulisse didn't care about most clients—except those in ruined marriages.

He glanced at Arrigo. "I hate those questions."

Arrigo hesitated. But he knew Ulisse wanted his true thoughts—not empty platitudes—so he said, "That's to be expected, Your Majesty."

Ulisse grunted. He'd given many sad answers over the years, but these were the ones that hit hardest, like a shark ramming into its prey. These were the ones that folded his heart in on itself.

Damn it all. That was the one thing he didn't want to dwell on. Not now, not ever.

And the terrible timing of this client visiting while Ulisse was mourning with Imelda just put gold filigree on the whole situation.

That surely made a fantastic impression. He was the epitome of the doting fiancè. She was swooning right now, he just knew it.

"What time is it?" he asked Arrigo.

"The bell just rang eight o'clock, Your Majesty," Arrigo answered immediately. He knew that when Ulisse was experiencing a vision, he lost all connection to the outside world.

Perfect, dinner should be wrapping up. He wound through the halls of the palàso—almost as familiar as his own—and happened upon Venezia and Lazaro leaving. Imelda wasn't present, unsurprisingly.

"I need to borrow your wife," Ulisse said.

Lazaro snorted. "Talk some sense into her while you're at it."

Venezia arched an eyebrow as her lips tightened. Ulisse may not know her very well anymore, but he remembered that look. She'd leveled it at him more than once when they were younger. Sometimes he'd even deserved it.

Ulisse scoffed. "Trust me, I am the last person to give sound advice to anyone. Especially the Fleet Admiral of La Serenìsima Repùblica de Rialto."

"I'll see you at home," Venezia said to Lazaro, already turning away from him. She started down the hallway before the old man could respond. All her husband could do was glare after her.

"Uh, enjoy your night," Ulisse said, but Lazaro did the same as Venezia—stalking off without responding, though in the opposite direction.

Ulisse caught up to Venezia. Her hand rested on her knife hanging from her belt.

"No doubt he will enjoy his night," she muttered. "Though not as much as he'd like."

Lovely, a marriage quarrel—though certainly not a lovers' quarrel. Not between Venezia and Lazaro. Oh gods, now he had the image in his head.

"Why did you marry him?"

"That's quite a personal question."

"I'm a personal kind of guy."

She laughed. "And how many names of people in Rialto do you know?"

"Doesn't matter."

She stopped abruptly, glancing in the direction Lazaro had gone. "He was useful."

"Not anymore?"

"Maybe, maybe not." She folded her arms. "What did you want to speak with me about? Do you wish to give your condolences on my loss in the Council vote?"

"Oh gods no. You're crazy to want a war against Ilios."

"I thought you said you like that about me."

"Indeed I do. But not if it involves blood monks and black bane." Servants walked past them. He paused, waiting for them to turn the corner. "I need to find Arturo's wings and bring them to Imelda."

"Now you're the crazy one. That will only torment her."

"She asked for them." Kind of. Perhaps bringing them would ease the discourtesy of taking a client while mourning with her. Perhaps it would help her warm up to him. It would be nice to have his future bride actually like him.

Venezia tapped her finger against her knife. "Follow me."

Ulisse fell into step with Venezia.

"How's your hand?" she asked.

"It was almost healed until I had to cut it again for a client just now."

They reached a set of narrow, curling stone stairs that descended to the first level of the palàso. Torches lit the way. It felt like a dungeon, especially compared with the mahogany paneling and silver inlay upstairs.

"A merchant asking about the best place to buy linen?" she asked teasingly.

"No." He patted his breast pocket where he kept handkerchiefs—it held one only a half-hour ago, and now a poor, jilted wife was using it to dry her cheeks. He'd managed to forget about her question, forget about the grief that had emanated from her as strong as a flame when he answered, but now it was back. Gods be damned. He flexed his hand and felt the cut break open. Hopefully her husband would get herpes from whomever he'd been cheating with. Or, better yet, syphilis.

Ulisse was not above pettiness.

They reached the basement. The first room was a wine cellar, a very large one with an extensive collection. How many bottles did Primo buy every year? Not that Ulisse was complaining. It was one of the things he most looked forward to when visiting Rialto. They passed through the cellar, then entered a dusty storage room. In the corner, lurking like a ghost, sat Arturo's broken wings.

Venezia stopped as soon as she walked in. "Primo wants to burn them, but I can't bear the thought. I guess I understand why Imelda wants them after all." She sighed shakily. So unlike her to show weakness. Even in their youth, she'd been slow to reveal any tender emotions. If it hadn't been for Ulisse's disarming charisma, they never would've enjoyed the time they had together. It had been short-lived, but he'd counted himself the luckiest man in the world.

"We always want some part of those we lose."

She looked at him. "What do you have of Marina?"

The last letter she'd written to him. Like Imelda and Venezia with Arturo's wings, despite the pain its existence caused him daily, he couldn't bring himself to burn it. It sat in his desk drawer, buried under quills and parchment and ink bottles. Three years later, he remembered every word.

"My children," he said. "And what will you have from Lazaro when he finally dies?"

Her hand drifted to her knife again. Was she aware how often she touched it? "Nothing I want."

Her attention turned back to the wings. Torches lined the walls, and the flickering flames painted her profile in light and shadows—her straight nose, perfect posture, sleek black hair that she, tragically, always wore in that uptight hairdo.

She was no longer the girl he'd fallen for over a decade ago. Even though she'd been reticent to show vulnerability back then, her features had been softer, her lips quicker to smile. Her years commanding soldiers had given her a new kind of grace—that of strength and survival.

"You're beautiful," he said.

She closed her eyes. "You shouldn't say such things to me." The quiet resonance of her voice in the darkly lit room swept him back fourteen years. She had whispered back then. She didn't seem to be the type to whisper anymore. He relished the sound of it, like the hum of his viol after he'd pull his bow off the strings.

He tried extricating his thoughts back from those short-lived months, but the memories pulled him down as surely as the strongest riptide. "Someone should." His voice felt sticky and raw. He coughed to clear it of any lingering emotion. "I don't think your husband does."

"He did, once." She took a step toward the wings. "Let's get these to Imelda."

Ulisse called Arrigo in, and together they carried the wings back to the main floor, Venezia leading the way. Night had descended on the city, and servants rushed down the hall to light candles.

Venezia paused in front of the staircase leading up to the second floor. "Do you regret sponsoring Anselmo Errari?"

He didn't even need to think before answering. "Not at all. He deserves the chance as much as any of those rich kids."

"Why did you sponsor him?"

Why had this surprised everyone? But instead of the desperate question Anselmo had asked, or the accusatory disbelief from Primo, Venezia sounded curious.

He'd given two different reasons to Anselmo and Primo, and both were true. But this reason—this was the truest one. "To help you."

She blinked in surprise. "What?"

"I saw you leading him around, introducing him to people. It's clear you want him to succeed. When no one was choosing him, I knew you were disappointed, and I couldn't take it."

"Was I that obvious?"

"Only to someone who knows you well."

She smiled. A real, actual smile. Not a full grin like Ulisse's, but a true Venezia smile. No tightness, nothing held back. "Grassie tante."

"I'll leave you to take these to Imelda." Venezia kissed Ulisse's cheeks. Not twice, but three times. Was it gratitude for helping Imelda? Or something more—something he shouldn't want? No, even if Ulisse was a despicable bastard, Venezia was faithful to her cousin.

With a nod, she walked away.

Ulisse watched her go for a moment before picking up his end of the wings. "Let's get these upstairs."

He and Arrigo hauled the wings to the second floor. He was sweating by the time they reached the top of the stairs. He was too old for this; he should've grabbed a servant to help Arrigo. Blood had started to seep through his bandage. He'd have to change it as soon as he returned to his room.

His palm was in bad shape, but not as bad as the wings. Up here, in the brightly lit living quarters, he could see they were much worse than he'd originally assessed. Frames broken in at least a dozen places, tattered feathers and shredded leather hanging from the wood. How could they comfort Imelda? Perhaps he shouldn't give them to her after all. He could haul them back down to the cellar, leave them for Primo and Venezia to decide their fate.

But Imelda had witnessed Arturo's death—she knew the state of the wings. And she wanted them. He'd meant it when he told her that her happiness was his only priority. That was only days ago, and yet it felt much longer. It was amazing how grief stretched time.

The sound of crying caught his attention, coming from the door on his right. If he wasn't mistaken, it was Calixta's. With a glance to Arrigo, he set the wings on the floor and knocked.

"Who is it?" Calixta's tone was sharper than he'd expected.

"It's Ulisse. I heard you crying and—"

Calixta whipped the door open. Her face was tear-stained, and she wore none of her normal jewels, but the look on her face was anything but sad. Pinched eyebrows, sharp eyes, stormy-sea frown. By the gods, she was angry.

"What are you doing here?" She hurled the words like a dagger.

"Me?" Did he sound as dumbfounded as he felt? He must have, because her glower deepened, and she stalked into the hall.

"How dare you." She jabbed a finger in his chest. "How dare you try to console me."

"I'm sorry, but would you rather mourn alone?"

"I'd rather mourn with anyone other than the man responsible for my fiancè's death."

"I'm responsible?" Surely he'd misunderstood her.

"You, Your Majesty."

No, he hadn't.

Arrigo stepped up beside Ulisse. Ulisse put his arm out to stop him. "And how in the three blazes of Fógo is Arturo's death my fault?"

"You grabbed Imelda instead of him."

"I—what?"

"You could've pulled him onto the roof. Or you could've held on long enough for me to help you pull him up, or I could've undone the straps of his harness. Your mistake cost Arturo his life!"

"My correct action saved Imelda's life!" Ulisse ran his hand across his beard and brought himself back under control. He lowered his voice, though it seemed too late. It was a miracle no one had come out already. "If I hadn't acted immediately, if I hadn't done the *only* right thing at that moment, we would be mourning two people right now instead of one."

"But Arturo—"

"Was doomed the moment he hit the palàso. Those wings were incredibly heavy. There was no way I could've lifted him onto the roof. It's a miracle I was able to save Imelda as it is, she was holding so tight. Gods damn it all, I could've gone over the edge with her and Arturo, but I got lucky. Arrigo, let's go."

He turned to pick up the wings. Behind him, Calixta gasped. "What are you doing with those?"

Ulisse held in a sigh as he turned to face her.

"You're sick," she said.

He motioned for Arrigo to take the wings. He waited until the captain disappeared around the corner, and put his hands on his hips. "Imelda wants them."

"Why would you listen to her? They're going to torture her. I can barely stand the sight of them myself."

"Imelda wants them."

"Then you're an idiot."

"And you're crazy."

"Don't talk to me like that!"

"But you can talk to me however you please, because you're the imperial princess and I'm the peddler king?" Her glare hardened, and he shook his head. "Have you lost anyone close to you?"

"I lost Arturo too."

"I mean someone you actually loved."

"I didn't have time to love him. But I would've, soon."

"It's not the same. Otherwise you'd understand. You're out of your league here, princess."

She stepped close, got in his face. The scent of apples and vanilla permeated the air around her. "I see the way you look at Venezia." Her voice was a weaponized whisper. "This marriage is as doomed as your last one."

He was through being baited. He turned and walked away. A moment later, Calixta's door slammed shut.

Arrigo waited in front of Imelda's door. He held out a handkerchief, and Ulisse used it to wipe his face and neck. "Gods above," he muttered. He couldn't fault Calixta for being angry, or even for blaming Ulisse. Everyone responded to grief differently. But after Imelda's quiet sorrow and Venezia's stoic mourning, it had caught him off guard.

He didn't look at Venezia any significant way. Not before tonight, at least. Calixta was merely mad with grief.

Back to his original task. Ulisse combed through his hair. "Wait out here," he said to Arrigo.

"Should a king perform labor that a servant would?"

"I do all kinds of things a king shouldn't do."

Arrigo actually smiled, though it was as tight as his posture. Not because he was uncomfortable or he disliked Ulisse. Arrigo was simply that kind of man—as tightly wound as a line tethering a boat to the dock. "Yes you do, Your Majesty." He stepped to the side as Ulisse knocked.

Silence answered. Perhaps Imelda was already sleeping. But then came the sound of a soft tread across the floor, and a moment later Imelda opened the door. She pressed her hands to her mouth when she saw the wings—she didn't even seem to notice Ulisse.

She knelt and lifted a scrap of leather. "Grassie."

"It was the least I could do. So I did it." That was stupid. Gods, his interaction with Calixta had thrown him off. He rubbed his beard, focusing on the way his fingers pulled at the hair. It distracted him—somewhat—from his sudden and uncharacteristic awkwardness. "Shall I bring them in?"

She nodded emphatically, stepping out of the way as he dragged them through the door. She pointed at the corner behind her bed. "There. Please."

He could feel her watching as he took the wings, carrying them one by one to the appointed spot. When he turned around, her hands dropped from her cheeks, but the skin around her eyes was red from trying to scrub away her tears.

"I hope this brings you some comfort," he said. He tried to sound sincere, but after his rather fervent compliment to Venezia only minutes ago, his words echoed hollow in his chest.

Unexpectedly—most unexpectedly—she clung to his neck. Her tears dampened his doublet as he awkwardly wrapped his arms around her. He held his tender, heartbroken bride, but all he saw was Venezia's face in the flickering light of the basement torches.

Calixta was right—he shouldn't look at Venezia that way. And yet, he couldn't help it.

If he wasn't already headed for the three blazes of Fógo after this life, this would pave the way.

CHAPTER THIRTY-SEVEN

Clearly the slave trade paid well. That was Venezia's thought whenever she stood in Fia Pesaro's parlor, and today she held onto it tighter than normal. So many other things had happened that she didn't want to think about—or shouldn't. Like the night before when Ulisse told her she was beautiful. And the way her heart warmed to those words. The way it toppled even now as she recalled the memory.

Instead she focused on inspecting Fia's parlor. Murals filled the walls, scenes from their family's victorious history or some nonsense. Shantzese rugs covered the wood floors, thick and decorated with twining vines blooming with exotic flowers. It was difficult not to admire the rich colors, the way they shimmered when Venezia paced this way and that. Piles of pillows sat on each chair, and a massive portrait of Fia hung above the oversize fireplace. She wore a silver em-broidered dress with a ridiculous amount of corincanto—no doubt silk, which she didn't need—and strand upon strand of pearls sat on her ample chest. The woman decorated like new money, even though her family's nobility ran almost as far back as Venezia's.

Venezia stopped pacing. She was desperate. She had to admit it to herself. Fia had been on Venezia's side until the disaster of the state dinner. But Fia was still Venezia's best bet for an ally. She could sway others to Venezia's side, if Venezia set things right. The other Council members liked Fia more than they liked Venezia. Fia played by their rules. And there was nothing to suggest she'd earned her position by nepotism. Not that Venezia had gained hers that way, but those old men all suspected it.

Working with the head of a slave company was distasteful, to say the least. Slaves were an antiquated idea, born from barbarian years long gone. It was a pathetic sort of man or woman who had to own a person to make them work. That wasn't power; that was insecurity hiding behind riches. Lazaro was the perfect example of that fact.

But Fia was more than her family's trade. She was intelligent, cunning, and resourceful—the same traits Venezia valued in herself, though she used hers with different techniques. Venezia needed her. It galled her to admit she needed anyone—she'd seen what that had done to her with Lazaro—but unfortunately, Primo and Lazaro had backed her into a corner.

She had to get away from Lazaro. Anything to get away from him. She pressed a hand to the knife strapped to her thigh. She'd never let him hurt her again. She'd use him up and dump him in the lagoon.

Fia entered, wearing long, red wool. She fixed Venezia with a cold look, lifting her chin. "I know why you're here, and it's not going to work."

Damn that Lazaro. Damn him to the three blazes of Fógo and back. "My husband is nothing more than a slimy eel. I'd hoped he die by now, but he seems determined to live as long as possible just to spite me." That caught Fia off-guard. She paused, listening. Venezia gestured at a chair. "May I?"

"If you insist." Fia took a large wingback, flicking the pillows onto the floor as if they had cost mere trifles.

Venezia sat in the humblest chair, though no one would ever describe it as such. The back and arms were so padded it felt as if she'd sink into it permanently. "Over the last few weeks, I've become convinced he sabotaged me at the banquet. He knows we were allies, and he never drinks to such sloppiness. What are the odds he'd end up drunk and practically assault you on accident?"

"And why would he do that?"

"Because he doesn't want me to outshine him. He had a long run as Doxe, but he didn't do anything truly memorable. Meanwhile, I'd be the third female Doxe in Rialtano history. He doesn't like me for the same reason the ten other Council members don't: I'm not submissive. Yes, they let us serve on the Council, but they don't expect us to have our own opinions. Rialtano men want women to be feisty in one place, and that is not the Council chamber."

Fia pursed her lips as she considered this. The Monte temple bell gonged three o'clock outside.

"You hear their remarks as well as I do," Venezia said. "They insult our intellect and cunning regularly. I've never met a more condescending group than that lot in the Council chamber."

Fia chuckled. "You're right about that. But you're reckless."

"And if I were a man, they'd call me a renegade, a visionary." If things went her way, she *would* earn that title, now and throughout history. No way would she allow her legacy to waste away at the back of a dusty library, one name in a list of Rialtano Fleet Admirals. Venezia would shape the world as Doxe of the great Serenìsima Repùblica de Rialto. "You, Fia Pesaro, are not some timid, subservient girl either. You broke tradition by seizing control of your family business from three older brothers, none of them dolts. And under your influence, the Pesaro name has spread farther across the Muriseano than ever before. You know, as well as I, that we can't grow without risks. I don't want to work with anyone but the toughest, shrewdest politicians either."

Fia inclined her head at the compliment. Venezia was cozying up to her well, and she'd only just begun. Fia rang the bell. A woman arrived, bearing the red slave stitch on her left wrist. Fia commanded the woman to bring them wine, then settled into her chair, lacing her fingers on her lap.

"I am not my husband," Venezia said. "No one knows that better than you, the woman who ignored tradition and chose not to get married. We women stand on our own."

"And what will I get if I swing votes for you?"

"The wings my cousins invented." Venezia forced a smile. It hid the sorrow that clutched at her heart. Arturo. Poor, sweet, brilliant Arturo. Her mind flicked back to his final moments, when he smashed into the edge of the roof. Imelda had leapt for him. Venezia had frozen. Shameful. She'd never forgive herself for letting fear root her into place that day. Maybe she wouldn't have been able to save him, but maybe she would've succeeded. She'd never know.

It was also a shameful thing to turn around, so soon after his death, and use the very thing that killed him as bait. But she wanted to win too badly. She *needed* to, or she'd never be free of Lazaro.

It was another item in a long list of sins she'd have to account for before Giore on her judgment day.

Fia straightened, then covered her interest with a scoff. "They didn't seem to work that well."

Venezia raised an eyebrow. "Don't feign disinterest with me, siora. I know you want them. Everyone does. They will render the Bogasa Strait nearly worthless."

"Not for my trade."

"Not yet." Venezia leaned forward. "The first boat was not a war galley. It was a humble construction of wood and tar and pegs. Now we have ships with rams that can sink an enemy's boat to the bottom of the Muriseano."

"But your brother's marrying your cousin Imelda off to the greedy Eracleano king, yes? Seems her inventing days are coming to an end."

Another person with an ignorant opinion of Ulisse. Normally she'd rip a hole in Fia's fine wool dress for it, but she had to play nice. "I'll incentivize her to finish them after the wedding."

The slave brought the wine and left. The poor woman conducted herself professionally, but there was a stiffness in her movements that paid servants didn't possess.

Fia took a long drink. "I don't see how these wings benefit me if the Council has to pay for them."

"I'll pay for them myself, and pay to have a pair made just for you."

Fia tilted her head in appreciation.

Venezia ran her finger around the rim of her glass. "I have another asset. One my brother will not make use of. Do you remember Lieutenant Errari? He was at the the Zorzi celebration dinner."

"I remember you fawning all over him. How lucky he was to win." She arched an eyebrow.

"I fixed it," Venezia said. "I wasn't about to let him go."

Fia pursed her lips, but clearly she was amused. "Audacious."

"For good reason. He's unlike any other soldier I've met—he's stronger, faster, and most importantly, more motivated. And with my guidance, he'll become the best Lion we've ever had. Think of what we could accomplish with him. We can take over the Iliano Empire. And other lands—like Tedesk." Venezia resisted twisting her mouth. Tedesk's capital, Umbrug, was the most successful slave port in the known world.

Luckily, Venezia only needed to pretend to support Fia's industry until she became Doxe. Then Venezia would abolish it. She'd lose an ally in the process, but by then she would've acquired friends far more powerful than Fia Pesaro.

The mention of Tedesk, of course, truly piqued Fia's interest. She leaned forward greedily. "Lieutenant Errari is as good as you say?"

"Better."

"Well. May we both get what we want." She held up her glass.

Venezia lifted hers in agreement. "With me as Doxe."

"With you as Doxe."

Venezia took a long draught. The wine was excellent, but it didn't taste nearly as good as what she would drink to celebrate winning the Doxe seat. She could feel the crown on her head and the sash across her body. The look on Primo's face when she won would be the sweetest. Let her brother taste defeat for once. Let him know what it meant to be second. He thought he owned everyone and everything, but he didn't own Venezia.

No one did.

Chapter Thirty-Eight

Imelda sat at her spinning wheel, wool roving in hand. Her fingers started pre-drafting out of habit, and she set the wool down. She couldn't spin; she'd merely grown tired of sitting at her window and watching the world move on. What would she work on, anyway? Not the wings. Her pair leaned against the wall, while Arturo's sat in a jumbled pile in the corner next to the hearth. It broke her every time she looked at them, which was more than she deserved.

She threw the roving across the room as Venezia knocked and entered wearing a mourning blue dress and long gloves. She fixed Imelda with a firm look.

"I'm going to the temple to light candles for my miscarried children. You're coming with me."

"I'd rather not." The memories of the high priest pouring cold water over her head and her tears on Arturo's shroud were still too fresh.

"You should, whether you want to or not. You need to light a candle for Arturo. Besides, it's a beautiful day, and going outside will be good for you." She pulled Imelda to her feet and frowned as she appraised Imelda's appearance. "You're a mess."

It was true. Imelda wore her spinning dress, and her hair was in a haphazard braid with strands sticking out all over the place. Her eyes were probably puffy, and she hadn't washed her face since Arturo's death.

"You can't go to the temple like that. Let's get you dressed."

Venezia didn't call Editta. She pulled out Imelda's mourning blue dress and helped her change into it. Then she sat Imelda in front of her mirror, brushed her hair and re-braided it, then wound it around Imelda's crown. She knelt in front of Imelda and took her hands. "You'll learn to live with it. I know right now you don't want to, but it'll get easier. Some days you'll feel fine, even happy as you remember the time you shared with him, and some days will be awful. You can't hide in your room forever—but that doesn't mean you'll forget him or the pain. And that's fine. It's the way it should be."

They made their way outside. The sun shone in a cloudless sky, warming Imelda's cheeks. La Piaza del Leon felt empty after Carnevale nights. Politicians and merchants strode across the square, deep in conversation. Burly slaves bore nobles in seated litters, hurrying around children kicking a ball. Beggars sat on the steps to the temple, hands cupped for any offerings. The cart that had held Zitello's effigy had been removed, its spot now claimed by pigeons. The temple's white, green, and pale pink marble glistened in the sunlight, its five spires reaching toward the heavens as if in supplication. On the opposite side of the piaza, in front of Palàso Dogal, a matching marble Giatoro the Lion bowed in deference to the supreme wisdom and love of the gods. He bore the scar of his sacrifice—the lost eye—and his reward as well—his wings.

Venezia breathed deep. "I love this city, Imelda." Imelda glanced at her cousin, but the woman remained as indecipherable as ever. "You should finish the wings."

"I can't." Imelda took a shaky breath. "Not without Arturo. He was the genius, not me." Tears pricked at her eyes, and she blinked them away.

"You're smarter than you realize. Arturo would agree with me on that." She put her arm through Imelda's. "Let's go."

Venezia poured some coins in a beggar woman's hands then led the way inside the temple. Imelda blinked as her eyes adjusted to the dim light. Immediately the smell of incense encased her. Was this what Cielo was like—dark and smoky? It seemed that it should be full of light, like a warm spring day, with shining water and nesting birds on the rooftops. A few people sat in the pews, praying or gazing at the two altars. Ten at most, all of them nobles. Most islands had their own temples—modest things made of wood or brick with perhaps two stained-glass windows. The nobility of Riga and Monte had the privilege of worshiping in Rialto's most cherished building.

Imelda followed Venezia down the aisle to a table covered in candles. El Casteo de Giore provided candles with thick hemp corincanto wicks. Temples on less prosperous islands had one strand of hemp in their wicks. Those on the poorest islands could only dye their plain thread red to mimic corincanto. Venezia took two candles, giving one to Imelda.

"Didn't you have four miscarriages?" Imelda asked.

"Yes, carina, but you can only do one at a time." Venezia walked to Rea's altar on the left—Giore's right hand. Venezia knelt at Rea's altar, holding the candle aloft. "Mother Rea, I ask your blessing on my first unborn child. Bless her soul to feel our love. Amen."

Venezia stood and nudged Imelda, who knelt and lifted her candle. Rea's statue loomed above, looking down at Imelda with blank eyes. "Mother Rea, I ask your blessing on my brother Arturo. Bless his soul ..."

"To feel our love," Venezia prompted.

"To feel our love. Amen." Imelda's voice broke at the end.

They moved to Giore's statue. Under his intense gaze, they lit their candles. The flickering light made him seem to stretch to the heavens above. Imelda felt nothing in her Spirit Stitch, no warmth of wisdom or love from either god.

"Father Giore," Venezia said, "I ask your blessing on my first unborn child. Bless her soul to find your wisdom. Amen."

Imelda followed, with more help from Venezia. She left her candle with the dozens of others under his statue. Would these prayers reach the gods? If only she could pray for Anselmo, but these were for the deceased.

Whatever the gods' reason, they'd spared her and not Arturo. If only it had been the other way. Tears stung her eyes, and she blinked them away.

But Venezia was right—life proceeded without Arturo. She still wanted to be with Anselmo, would do anything to make it happen. Anselmo's presence was as strong as ever in her mind. He was northeast of her. If only she could feel a sense of his emotional or physical state. Or he hers—then he would know something was wrong. Whether that was better or worse, she couldn't decide.

"I wanted to tell you how Lieutenant Errari is doing," Venezia said as they returned to the front for Venezia to get a candle for her second miscarried child.

Imelda's heart jumped, and her breath caught. "I thought you weren't supposed to talk about it."

"I decided to make an exception." She paused, then sighed. "I know you love him."

Now Imelda's heart slipped. Had she been so obvious? How many people knew? "Of course I do." She forced her tone to be as light as possible. "He's my oldest friend."

After a moment, Venezia led Imelda to the side wing. It was even darker here, though colored light from the stained-glass windows cut through the shadows and bathed Venezia's face in red.

"Imelda." She cupped Imelda's chin. "There's no need to lie. How serious are your feelings?"

"We want to get married." The words were heavy on her tongue, yet once she spoke them she felt lighter. She'd carried this secret for so long. Only Anselmo and Arturo had known, and with Anselmo gone and Arturo dead, it had isolated her. But by telling Venezia, the only mother Imelda had ever known, it felt like an anchor had been lifted from Imelda's shoulders.

"You know this is a serious offense to the gods. You and Ulisse are betrothed."

"I loved Anselmo first. Shouldn't they be offended by Primo's lack of care for my happiness?"

As Venezia regarded Imelda, her face softened. "I think they are. I said I wanted to tell you how Anselmo is doing. He's had his struggles, but he's doing well now. It should only be a few more days until he emerges."

Imelda smiled at the good news, but then it slipped like a discarded scrap of silk to the floor. "But my wedding is so soon."

Venezia touched Imelda's arm and fixed her with a firm, yet kind look. "I was wrong before about marriage."

Imelda shook her head. "But you said—"

"I was lying, only trying to make you feel better. It's a huge gamble. A bad marriage can be dangerous. It can break you, and attitude will only get you so far."

Imelda's heart twisted. She walked to an arch and leaned against it. Nothing was as it seemed. Imelda had been blind her whole life.

Skirts rustled as Venezia walked over. "I'm miserable, Imelda. Lazaro is a terrible man, and an even worse husband."

"But you're so strong." Imelda turned around. Venezia's hands were folded at her waist. Her eyes seemed sad, but not for herself.

"I wish I could've gained my strength some other way." Her lips twisted bitterly. "I said love can grow, but I don't know anything about it."

It was so unfair. This life, this world. Unfair that Arturo had died. Unfair that Imelda couldn't marry Anselmo because of who his parents were. And unfair that Venezia had suffered for thirteen years.

"I want you to be happy, Imelda. Someone in this cursed family should be. I said Ulisse is a good man, and that is true. But I know him well enough to know you're not a good fit for him, nor he for you. You won't make each other happy."

The choir still sang, their gentle voices ascending to the ceiling and expanding to the fill the temple. But they couldn't soothe Imelda's troubled heart.

She shook her head. "There's nothing I can do. If Anselmo doesn't come out of the labyrinth in time, I have to marry Ulisse."

Venezia pulled Imelda into a tight hug. "You can do something. Save yourself, Imelda. No one else can. Not me. Not Anselmo. Finish the wings and save yourself."

Imelda nodded against Venezia's arm. Venezia gave her one more squeeze, then let her go. She cupped Imelda's cheek. "You are stronger than you realize. Now go."

Imelda rushed to the doors of the temple, then glanced back. Venezia stood with her gaze fixed on the gods as she touched her head then heart. With a deep breath, Imelda walked out into the blinding sunlight.

CHAPTER THIRTY-NINE

Imelda rushed to her room, only to find her wings missing. Arturo's were still jumbled in the corner, but her pair was nowhere to be found. She even checked the balcony, dropped to her knees to look under the bed, and tore her bed covers apart.

The wings were gone.

Someone had stolen them.

Her mind raced through the possibilities. Ulisse? Calixta? A member of the Council? They'd all been present at Arturo's flight and had rejoiced in his initial success. The wings were here this morning, and gone now. They had not disappeared in the night, whisked away by bandits while she slept. No, whoever took them had been able to march up here and carry them through the palàso's halls without anyone questioning them.

Or rather, have his guards carry the wings.

She ran through the living quarters to the state side of the palàso. Primo was in his office, and Beniamino let her in almost immediately. Primo sat at his desk, with his daughter, Cinzia, on his knee. She laughed as he put the laurel leaf crown on her head and it slipped down to her neck.

"Imelda!" Cinzia jumped off Primo's lap and ran over to hug Imelda.

"Where are the wings?" Desperation clawed at Imelda's voice. She couldn't control it.

Primo walked to the door and opened it. "Beniamino, can you take Cinzia to her mother please?"

"I want to stay." Cinzia ran over to cling to one of his legs.

Primo unwrapped her arms and kissed her head. "I'll see you at dinner, carina." He gave her hand to Beniamino, who closed the door.

Primo put his crown on its pedestal in the corner. He still wore mourning blue under his silver sash.

"Why?" Imelda grabbed her skirt with both fists. "Why, after everything you've put me through?"

Primo leaned against the corner of his oversize desk, kneading his temple as if Imelda was a knot of tension digging into his skull. "Imelda—"

"Don't use that tone with me."

"What's wrong with Ulisse? Hasn't he been kind to you?"

"Of course your greedy lackey has been kind to me." She resisted the urge to tug on her hair and took a deep breath. "I'm engaged to someone else."

Primo walked to the sideboard along the wall. Bottles and glasses covered its surface. "Engaged?" He took his time selecting a wine and pouring a glass. He didn't even bother offering one to Imelda—he knew she'd refuse. "I thought it was only a fling."

Imelda gawked. "You knew?"

"Of course I knew." His tone dripped with condescension. "You think you were keeping it a secret, flaunting him all over the city? You took him to Admiral Galbani's home. How could I not find out?"

"Does Ulisse know?"

"I don't think so." He sipped at his wine. "Do you know why Ulisse came earlier than expected? I sent for him when I saw you and Anselmo together at the lottery."

"Why didn't you say anything?"

"An Albizzi and a lowborn lieutenant about to enter the labyrinth? It wasn't going to last."

He took a long drink as Imelda sputtered. He couldn't have been more dismissive if he'd tried. They treated her like a little girl with nightmares, everyone telling her there was no reason to be afraid of the dark. They'd give her a biscotto and a pat on the head and tuck her under the blankets. No more. She balled her fists and marched up to him.

"It's not just a fling. We performed the Heart Stitch."

He leveled an annoyed look at her. He resembled Venezia so much when he did that. "You're bluffing."

Still he refused to believe her. She wanted to slap his haughty nose and cold, dark eyes. Instead, she pulled down the neck of her dress. His eyes snapped to it at once, the crimson lines dotted across her chest. His face darkened as he towered over her.

"You impetuous, foolish girl. Too long have I enabled your impulsivity, thinking it a charming quirk. That is a serious ritual, and it's blasphemous to do it lightly."

"I didn't do it lightly! I love him!"

"And what does that mean? You think he actually loves you? You are Imelda Albizzi, daughter of the greatest family in the republic, descendant of Italo Albizzi, the creator of the labyrinth. He was using you."

She swallowed. She would not back down. "I've known him since we were children. He wasn't using me. We're going to get married."

"Is that really the life you want—to be the wife of a soldier?"

"He'll be a Lion. A nobleman. He won't need to work, especially marrying me."

"I'll cut you off from family funds."

"But the wings—"

"You think the wings are best used to save you from marriage to a good man? Whoever you sold them to would only endanger the republic. That's why I had to take them. Venezia thinks they will help her start this war. And if the Iliani get them and decide to make us one of their territories again, we'll never survive. Not with flying soldiers raining black bane down on us."

"I'll run."

"To where? You know nothing about the world. And it's highly unlikely the soldiers will emerge from the labyrinth before your wedding. Even if Lieutenant Errari does, and you marry him, he will still work. Every soldier pledges a certain amount of time to serve. He'll be gone for years at a time, leaving you home with who knows how many children to care for, with who knows how little money to sustain you, and all the while you don't know whether he'll return or perish on the battlefield, or whether he's remaining faithful or visiting every brothel in town."

This time, she did slap him. She hadn't even thought about it, her hand had simply moved on its own. The sound bounced off the wood paneling behind him, and her palm stung. He stared at her in shock as his cheek turned red, then he grabbed her arms. It didn't hurt, but she couldn't break free even if she tried. Fear rooted her feet to the ground. She'd never seen such anger in his eyes before.

"I just want to see you well cared for," he said between clenched teeth.

"No, you want me to marry whoever benefits you most."

"I'm the head of this family and it's my responsibility to ensure our legacy. You *will* marry Ulisse."

"I won't—"

"You will, and I'll tell you why: if you marry Lieutenant Errari, I'll ensure he gets sent on the most dangerous missions, on every suicidal charge. He will fight on the front line until he dies. Do you understand me?"

He couldn't mean it. He wouldn't murder someone just because he didn't get his way. But then she really looked at him. Oh, he would. She could see it in his eyes, feel it in his grip on her arms.

"Why?" Her breath caught in her throat. "Why don't you want me to be happy?"

"Love isn't happiness." He pushed her away from him. He didn't retreat, though, and neither did she.

She glared up into his face. "I hope you burn in Fógo."

"You're not the first to feel that way about me." He returned to his desk and straightened his coat and sash. "Do the right thing, Imelda. Don't let your selfishness kill another person."

That came like a slap across her face. How dare he … and yet … he was right. She was selfish, and it had led Arturo to his death. It had broken his body from the crown of his head to the soles of his feet. The grating of his bones against each other haunted her at night.

"I'll let you keep Arturo's wings. Gods know why you want them, but if it gives you some comfort, you can have them."

It wasn't much, but it was something more than she'd had a moment ago … More than she deserved. Because she *was* selfish.

She wanted to marry Anselmo more than anything. And yet, if she truly cared for him, she had to let him go. And she had to break his heart to do it. If only she could see him one last time, stroke his cheek, and look into his blue eyes so he'd know why.

She loved Anselmo, and because of that, she'd marry Ulisse.

Chapter Forty

It was one thing for Anselmo to guess there was a second way to the island. It was a completely different thing to actually find it, if it existed at all. He spent the first day scouring the inner bowl of the labyrinth. It didn't take long to find the passage back into the swamp. He didn't dare go too far into the swamp, though, and cautiously searched the surrounding area. He found one dead end made of moving walls—clear from the absence of trees around them, though they didn't move. He climbed into a tree and watched for hours, but nothing happened.

He spent the night in the tree, dozing as best he could in a crook created by the trunk and two large branches. The mud fleas were back, and without his clothes to provide some protection, they were even worse.

The next morning a loud rumble woke him. He jumped to the ground, but it wasn't one of the walls near him. Maybe they needed to be triggered. He crept past the line of trees into the clearing, ready to jump away if the walls swung outward. Nothing happened. He continued forward until he was close enough to touch the stone. Cautiously, he put a hand on the wall and held his breath.

The wall remained still.

He made his way back to the path down to the lake, sloshing through the water and getting bitten every second by mud fleas. He reached the opening in the wall and looked down over the bowl. Scrub oaks covered most of his view. Had the others crossed the lake yet? He needed to get a better look somehow. The trees around him were tall, but he was too large for the branches at the top to support him.

He leaned against the wall. He hadn't eaten anything since the day before. Even with his corincanto, hunger weakened him. He'd gone hungry before, but not with such constant physical demands. He just needed to rest. He started to slide down the vine-covered wall then stopped. Vines. Vines covered the wall. He tugged on one and it held firm. He pulled harder, let his weight hang on it and it supported him.

Using the vines, he climbed to the top of the wall. He was about sixty meters from the swamp floor. He looked to the other side and froze. Right below him, vines grew down the wall and into a cave. It opened upward and had been hidden from the bottom of the lake bowl.

A hidden cave in the center of the labyrinth. He'd bet his life savings it led to the sword.

He used the vines to descend into the opening. The floor sloped downward out of the daylight and into the dark underground of the labyrinth. The fading light showed it curved before darkness swallowed it. He'd have to move slowly.

Anselmo started into the cave. The dusty ground was covered in strange footprints—undoubtedly belonging to the minotaurs. If the beasts frequented these passages, then the network must be extensive. Sure enough, within minutes the foul stench of animals hit him. He strained his ears for any sound, but there was only his breathing and soft tread. For hours Anselmo spiraled down into the darkness, then the path straightened and brightened.

The light was blue and shimmering, and there didn't seem to be any source of light—not torches or candles. Those would've given a yellow hue to the light. He looked up and backed into the wall.

Instead of rocks above, the ceiling was made of glass, revealing the lake. The moon floated in the sky, seeming to drift in the depths of the water. It was bright and fat, only a few nights away from full. Thankfully the moon was big. It would be impossible to see in here during a new moon or even a thin crescent. Gazing through water made him feel like he was looking down, but he could see the moon. It was disorienting. He held onto the wall to balance himself.

Tunnels under a lake made sense. But this glass-bottomed creation—it was astonishing. Italo Albizzi had truly been a genius, not only to devise this but to find a way to execute it.

The silhouette of a siren cut across the rippling moon. So deadly above, but here in this cave, with the soft, filtered light, it was peaceful. It was a beautiful, impossible sight. Imelda would've loved it.

It had been days since he'd thought of her. He'd feel guilty if he wasn't busy surviving. How was she doing? How soon was her wedding? Had she completed the wings? There was no way to find out while in the labyrinth. His only option was to get the sword and get out.

Grunts alerted him of approaching minotaurs. He ducked into the nearest hall and pressed himself against the wall. A pair of minotaurs rambled by. He held his breath as they passed—they might smell him and attack. If so, he should be able to fight two of them off, even bare-handed. But they didn't stop. The beasts passed. He counted to one hundred and continued on his way.

The path maintained a downward slope. Not as steep as before, but shouldn't he start moving upward at some point? Perhaps he'd gone the wrong way. He looked at the passages branching off this main one.

None of them angled up. This maze was worse than the swamp. He turned in a circle before deciding to keep his same direction.

After an hour, he reached a large cavern lit with torches around the perimeter of the room. Half of the cavern was pebble-strewn sand, like the beach above ground. The other half was a lake, its water as still as a dead body. On the far end of the lake sat a tiny island barely visible from where Anselmo stood. Vines hung above it. Anselmo's gaze followed them up to a high ledge jutting out from the side of the cave. Now he could see the need for the torches—the glass ceiling was gone. Anselmo was finally under the island.

The ledge was small, and a series of ascending ledges circled around the cavern to a hole in the ceiling. They looked close enough to jump between, but spaced far enough to make it precarious. And if you fell, water or ground would greet you the same and break your bones.

"It's about time you made it down here," a familiar voice said from behind.

Anselmo whirled around, unsheathing his sword. Ceso stood at the mouth of a small passage, a spear, helmet, and shirt in hand. Anselmo almost didn't recognize him—an old man with no context within the labyrinth. He wore his plain white shirt and brown wool pants as always. And he looked strangely comfortable standing in the heart of the labyrinth.

"Why are you here?" Anselmo stammered. "How did you get in?"

"As far as getting in, I have my ways. As for the why ..." Ceso tossed the shirt to Anselmo, then sat on a boulder, placing the helmet and spear in his lap. "I've been watching you, as I've watched all of my clients through the years, especially those who trained to become Lions."

Anselmo sheathed his sword and pulled it off. "You've watched me?"

Ceso snorted. "Not like that. I've been observing you, boy. With both my eyes and those of my sources—such as when you were in Zorzi." He untied a water skin from his belt and held it out. "Get an old man a drink?"

Anselmo took the skin, but eyed the lake warily.

Ceso waved his hand. "There's nothing in it. The trick of an underground passage up to the island was all they wanted."

Anselmo pulled his shirt on. It might not be a cuirass with leather pteruges attached, but it was better than being naked. He walked over to the lake, filled both of their containers, and gave Ceso his water skin. They both drank deeply. The water here was clean and crisp, a relief after the muddy swamp.

"How long have you been in the labyrinth?" Anselmo asked.

"I've been in and out since you entered. But we're not here to talk about me." Ceso grimaced and stood up. He ran his hand along the boulder, then sat when he'd apparently found a more suitable spot. "So your precious siora is betrothed to the king of Eraclea. There go your dreams of a happy future."

Anselmo walked back to the lake. He knelt and splashed water onto his face, taking his time to scrub his beard and comb through his hair. His gut reaction was to ask how Ceso knew, but it didn't matter. In fact, it had likely been noised about in most of the city—an Albizzi betrothed to the king with the sea silk. And since Ceso had been watching Anselmo, it would make all the more sense that he'd know.

Anselmo scooped water to his lips for one last drink. When he turned around, Ceso waited patiently.

"The Doxe will still elevate me when I leave the labyrinth," Anselmo said.

"And what will you do with that?"

"What do you mean?"

Ceso stalked over to Anselmo, spear still in hand. He left the helmet on the rock. "She might be married by then, and you have no backup plan. You can become a lazy nobleman once your time in the military is over. Find some industry to invest in and let your money work for you, then watch the galleys on El Canalasso and remember your days on them. Or you could use the opportunity to make something better of yourself. Something great."

"Not having to work sounds nice."

"Bullshit!" Ceso snorted. "You'd be miserable after a year, if not less. Not with the way your mother raised you. Think of what you can do as a Lion. You can rise through the ranks, yes, but you can carve your name into the tongues of generations to come. You, Anselmo Errari, are a sword, as fine as the one on that island above us. Life has honed you for far greater things than to spend slovenly days in a grand home. I can sharpen you further, into the deadliest weapon the world has ever witnessed. Glory and honor will be yours, beyond what any person has earned before. No one remembers noblemen. But no one would forget you."

"A god among men," Anselmo murmured, only half serious. He nodded at the spear. "Are you going to give that to me, or is it yours?"

Ceso jerked it away. "Act indifferent all you like, but I've gotten through to you after all these years. Of all my clients, you are the only one capable of it. They had your size and advantages from the corincanto. But none had your drive. You will never settle for anything but to be the best."

Ceso held out the spear, and Anselmo accepted it. He twisted it between his hands, felt the wood rub cross-grain against his skin—he could feel it even through the callouses he'd earned over the years. "I still think Imelda will succeed."

Ceso opened his mouth, closed it, hesitated. "With the wings?"

"How—"

"I have my sources, remember?" He tossed the helmet to Anselmo. "She might. But be prepared if she doesn't."

The old man wasn't going to give up on the idea. Anselmo wouldn't even consider it.

Anselmo stuck his spear into the ground and put his helmet on. "The sword's up there?"

"It is. But you can't get it on your own."

"Of course I can."

"No, you can't. You might be better than the other soldiers, but you need them. You should go apologize to that prince."

Anselmo laughed. "I'd rather figure out a way to get it myself."

Ceso threw his hands in the air. "You'll regret not taking my advice. At least go back to the surface and get your shield and cuirass."

"Why didn't you bring them?"

"I might be strong for my age, but I'm still an old man. Just walk along the inner wall. Eat something while you're up there. And hold back your strength."

"What's the point of my threads if I have to hold back?"

"Because you're being watched. No one watches anything other than their own backs on the battlefield, but in here it's completely different."

Ceso turned to go.

"Wait," Anselmo said. "You're not going to tell me how to get the sword?"

"If you're worthy, you'll figure it out." Ceso nodded. "See you on the outside."

CHAPTER FORTY-ONE

The Doxe's audience chamber reverberated with conversation as Venezia entered. Citizens of all classes filled the large, three-tiered room. Council members sat on the bottom, noblemen and upper merchants on the second level, and everyone else at the top. The tiled floor showed Rialto's crest, and at the top sat the Doxe's throne—mahogany with silver inlay and royal blue velvet cushioning. Above it was a map of the Muriseano Sea, and floor-to-ceiling windows flanked it.

Venezia walked to the opposition's side. Janus and Imelda were the only ones sitting there, with Janus's bodyguard standing beside him. Imelda held a folded piece of fabric in her lap that she kept looking at. Janus's man had a bag slung over his shoulder.

"Did you work on the wings?" she whispered to Imelda.

Imelda shook her head and looked away from Venezia. "They're too broken. I can't fix them."

What had happened to her resolve from before? Imelda's eyes flicked toward Primo, and she wiped at her cheeks. What had that damned man said to her?

Venezia looked at Janus. He nodded, then whispered to his bodyguard. After a moment, the bodyguard walked off.

Enrico Lando stood, and the room quieted. "Welcome, everyone, to our dogal election. Today is a momentous occasion because of the uniqueness of our situation: Fleet Admiral Dandolo has challenged her elder brother, Doxe Albizzi. It has been over a hundred years since the last time siblings pitted themselves against each other. That was Sior Ordelafo Michiel, who ran against his incumbent brother, Doxe Sabastiano Michiel. And, of course, Sabastiano won that election. You're seeing history made today."

Venezia gritted her teeth. The Council President was meant to stay neutral during the proceedings. Enrico was committing an egregious misstep. Venezia wouldn't let him get away with it once she was elected.

Enrico gestured to his right, where Primo sat. As incumbent, he was allowed to wear the sash and the crown, and he did, of course. "Doxe Albizzi will speak first, and then his younger sister, Fleet Admiral Dandolo, will have her turn. Your Serenity, the floor is yours."

The crowd applauded briefly as Primo stood. He resisted straightening his crown—quite a feat, no doubt—but he smoothed his sash. It shimmered in the light streaming in through the windows, a glowing reminder of the power he currently wielded. "Siori and siore of the noble class, citizens of the merchant, trade, and working classes, thank you for coming. I am honored that of everything you could be doing right now, you chose to attend this election. Without the power of the people, I wouldn't be standing here as the Doxe of La Serenìsima Repùblica de Rialto. Eight years ago, your representatives first gave me the sash and the crown, and again four years later. No matter what else I do in my life, this will be my proudest achievement. That you, the people, put your trust in me time and again."

He managed to actually seem humble. He must've practiced.

Primo clasped his hands behind his back and walked from side to side as he spoke. Not as if he were pacing, but to indicate he was including everyone in the conversation. "In the last eight years, Rialto has experienced steady growth. Our control of the salt trade has increased. We expanded the shipyard, creating more jobs, and its effects trickle down to the lowest islands. We bridged the gap between the government and the spinners guild, reducing their taxes. They have poured that money back into our economy by buying more fibers from our merchants. We've helped the priests repair and beautify neglected temples. Salterns have hired more workers. Shipbuilders have employed more craftsmen. Merchants have taken on new sailors for their larger fleets. All of this because of the policies we've enacted."

Without turning, he gestured toward the map of the Muriseano Sea above the Doxe's seat. "Outside the city, the republic flourishes. Under my rule, we gained the great city of Cinyras. Now both of i Occi de Zitello are our territories. When agitators in Zorzi tried to rebel, we promptly sent the armada to crush their revolt. I personally sailed there half a year ago to negotiate with the leaders of the insurrection. We have three territories, all as safe and prosperous as our city, and we control much of the Venetano peninsula. Frenza and Eraclea still owe their debts, and we have worked hard to ensure we stay on good terms with them.

"All of this I have accomplished in eight short years as the youngest Doxe ever elected. Think of what we could do in four, eight, even twelve more. We plan to eventually continue our westward expansion until we control the southern coast of the Muriseano from Zorzi to the eastern border of Shantze. We will continue to lower taxes for all classes as money pours in from our territories. Lastly, we're working with the Illustrious Empire of Ilios to secure lowered rates for our ships through the Bogasa Strait. The imperial family fully supports us. Imperial Princess Calixta stands with me today." Calixta inclined her head, her posture as sharp and square as Venezia's. Her robes were the most ostentatious ones yet, shimmering white silk covered in gold brocade that dripped power of every kind.

Primo clasped his hands behind his back once more. "My younger sister is going to try to sell her bid for the Doxe seat. She's a very convincing woman, and if I were you, I might be swayed. But once you know what I know, you'll change your mind. She is actively trying to start a war with the Iliano Empire. That conflict would doom thousands of our soldiers to horrible deaths. It might even bring bloodshed to our lagoon. Imagine Iliano black bane raining down on our city. Or don't, because the idea is far too terrifying to comprehend. There is growth, and there is insanity. I have only the best interests for Rialto. I think neither of myself nor what I stand to gain. I am honored to wear the sash and crown, symbols of our prosperity *and* peace. I am honored to be your Doxe, and will be honored to continue my reign. Thank you."

The room erupted into applause and whistles as Primo pressed a hand to his chest. So humble. He glanced at Venezia out of the corner of his eye, then returned to his seat.

Venezia stood. She may not have the sash and crown, but the many lines of rank on her shoulders spoke for themselves. Her boots echoed on the tile floor as she moved into the sunlight. The silver and bright blue stripes on her doublet sparkled as brightly as Primo's sash.

She looked around the room. At the Council members seated in front. At the nobles and merchants behind them, and the lower classes standing in the gallery. Many eyed her with suspicion, but their expressions would change by the end of her speech.

"Good morning, my fellow Rialtani. I'm glad you joined me today as I tell you about my plans for our great republic. Doxe Albizzi mentioned the war with Ilios I aspire to engage in. It's true. And I wasn't going to lie to you about it. Imagine the benefits we'd receive from such a conquest. Control of the Bogasa, which will reward us doubly. You won't have to pay fees to sail through the strait, and I will charge foreign ships to use it. You will no longer have to pay import taxes on your goods because they will come from within our vast republic. With the new money flowing in, I'll make massive city improvements. Any riches you are envisioning—triple them. I will accept nothing less for Rialto."

Primo hadn't looked at her directly during his speech, as if she weren't anything to worry about. He'd ignored her during their childhood, and he'd downplayed the threat of her candidacy the last few weeks. All to intimidate her. She turned to face him, to show it hadn't worked.

"Doxe Albizzi hurled the war at me like an accusation," she said. Primo kept his outward composure, though his mouth tightened almost imperceptibly. She ached to advance toward him, but didn't move. "He acts as if it were something to be afraid of." She turned back to the crowd, raising her chin and voice. "I am not afraid of war. I have faith in our military, while he clearly does not. Who knows better than I the might of our armada and the prowess of our Lions? I have trained them. They are truly the world's elite, and they fight for me. With them, I fear nothing from the Iliano Empire."

Venezia gestured toward Calixta. "Ilios is not our friend, no matter what Doxe Albizzi says or thinks. They sent their dazzling prince and princess as supposed allies, but in dark corners, they try to intimidate us with their deep coffers and threats of black bane. They embrace us with one arm and lighten our coin purses with the other. You will still pay the Bogasa fee, even with the Doxe's alliance. You will still pay import taxes on goods from the empire. Doxe Albizzi is not helping you. He's robbing you. And this isn't the first time.

"It's true that His Serenity negotiated with the rebels in Zorzi, but he hid one crucial detail: in exchange for their surrender, he had to significantly lower their taxes. We are receiving less money from our biggest territory because of His Serenity's failure to handle a revolt that should never have even happened. If I had been Doxe, I would've crushed the uprising before it could organize into real war."

She looked at the crowd, starting at the top with the lowest classes and working her way around the room. "All of you have felt the effects of this mistake. I've felt it as the Dandolo cotton and linen trade has paid higher import taxes. Wealth trickles down, but so does its lack." She reached the Council members, fixing them with a firm look. "You are rich, but you could be richer. You are great, but you could be greater. And Doxe Albizzi"—she pointed at Primo—"cannot lead you there. He is a politician. I have led men into battle. And make no mistake—this is a battle. One the current Doxe could never hope to win. You've seen His Serenity's record. He's spoken of steady growth, decreased taxes, international alliances as if these were things to be proud of. All of this is expected of a leader—Doxe Albizzi is a *competent* ruler. At best. But I will be a great ruler. I will settle for nothing less. You shouldn't either."

She sat as the crowd applauded. It didn't matter what the other nobles or the lowborns thought of the speeches. Speaking in public was simply to make the non-politicians feel important. All that mattered was how Venezia's words affected the Council members. And they all looked deep in thought.

Good thing they were the only ones who mattered. The common man—merchants and nobles included—feared change. The status quo was good enough, and they were happy to stay in line with it. It all came down to the Council. Which meant that—beyond Venezia's speech—it all came down to Fia. Had she been able to sway the five votes Venezia needed to beat Primo?

Imelda grabbed Venezia's hand. "You were amazing."

"Thank you, carina." Venezia turned to Janus. "What do you think, Sior Komnenos?"

Janus actually smiled. "You were very persuasive."

Enrico Lando stood and called for the Council members to head to the Council room. Venezia squeezed Imelda's fingers before following the others out the door. In the room, they took their seats. Beniamino stood in the middle, with Venezia and Primo to either side.

"Are there any sensitive questions or concerns the Council wish addressed?"

"What about your cousin's wings?" Orso Cancio called in his gritty, old voice. He was almost as disgusting as Lazaro. "The Council is impatient to get them. We have plans to use them in the summer trade season."

Primo, caught off guard, floundered.

Venezia stepped up. "I will deliver the final product when it is complete. And it will be finished in time."

She smiled at Primo as Enrico called for more questions, but none came. The Council was as hungry for the wings as Fia had indicated. This could only work in her favor, especially since Primo had misstepped so badly.

Enrico's secretary called them to the robing and voting rooms, one at a time. He called her name third. As she made her way to the doors, Venezia looked for Fia, seated across the chamber from her. Fia nodded. With a hum of anticipation in her gut, Venezia dressed in the black voting clothes. In the voting chamber, Primo, Enrico, and Primo's secretary waited. Today Primo wore the same black mask as everyone else, as he also voted in the dogal election. He stood inches taller than Venezia, while Enrico was shorter than her. She chose a spot on the wall opposite from them, faced it, and waited. The door opened and closed. Robes rustled and shoes tapped against the floor.

"Siori and siore, please turn around," Beniamino said. He wore the officiator's black robe and white mask. A page followed him, also wearing a black robe but no mask. She gave the ornate silver voting bowl with the draped black fabric to Beniamino.

Beniamino held up the bowl. "White is a vote for incumbent Doxe Primo Albizzi, and black is for Venezia Dandolo."

Venezia clutched her black rock until her knuckles ached.

"Due to the gravity of the vote," Beniamino continued, "you have as much time as you need to consider your choice. When you are ready to vote, hold out your stone in your fist, and I will retrieve it. Does everyone understand?" Thirteen heads nodded. "Begin."

Some people held theirs up right away. Primo was one of them. Beniamino began making the rounds. The only sounds in the room were the clatter of stones in the bowl and the crackle of the fire. Venezia counted to ten, then raised her arm. Beniamino reached her. She dropped her stone into the bowl, and he moved on. Several minutes passed as Beniamino collected the other votes. He and the page moved to the light of the fire and removed the cloth. They each counted twice, conferring in whispers. Venezia resisted the urge to fidget. Such a long, tedious way to vote. Changing it might actually be her first directive as Doxe.

Finally, Beniamino cleared his throat. "At a count of twelve to one, Primo Albizzi wins the election."

The other Council members applauded as Venezia's face flushed. So much for anonymity. And so much for allies. Which cloaked figure was Fia? Venezia would tear her to chum and throw her into the lagoon. She stalked into the robing room, tearing off the damned robe and mask as fast as she could. Then she went to the Council chamber. She pulled out her Fleet Admiral knife from her hip holster, and sat.

Fia came, just as Venezia knew she would. She may be a traitor, but she was no coward. She strutted in, large bosom held high and a haughty look on her face.

Venezia twirled the knife. "You lied."

Fia tossed a hand onto a curvy hip and shrugged. "I never *said* I would vote for you."

"Why?"

"I told you—your husband is a snake."

Venezia stabbed her knife into the arm of the chair and stood. "Didn't I agree with you? Didn't I say that's why we should work together as women?"

Fia's smile unfurled as slow and cruel as an enemy ship hoisting its flag. "You don't understand, Fleet Admiral. I already knew your husband was a snake long before the dinner. He knew you were going to run for Doxe, and he knew you'd try to ally with me. He paid me off. The bit at the dinner was an unpleasant surprise, I'll admit, but he's a nasty man."

Venezia took a step back—she couldn't help it. It was a sign of defeat, and Lazaro had won. This round, at least. But he didn't know that Fia was spilling it all, even more than the woman's breasts nearly spilling out of her low neckline. Venezia still had an advantage. She resisted the smile twisting inside her.

"When?" Fury laced itself through every sound of the simple word.

"While you were in Zorzi. When he bought that little plaything of his, he came to me personally." Fia had acted so nonchalant at her betrayal before, but now her voice shifted into something else—something Venezia hadn't seen coming. A tinge of sorrow wavered at the edge of her confession. Fia had lost a powerful ally in Venezia, and she knew it. She cleared her throat, straightened her back. "Paid me twice what she's worth after I agreed not to vote for you. I couldn't resist that kind of return on my investment."

Fia patted Venezia's shoulder. Venezia touched the side of her thigh, where her second knife was strapped against her skin. It would be easy, so easy, to slip her finers through the slit hidden in the folds of her skirt, snake the blade out, and stab Fia's hand. But it wasn't just Fia Venezia wished to injure.

"Don't look so offended," Fia continued. "You were outplayed. It's nothing personal." She made her way to the door, turning at the threshold. The long train of her dress coiled around her feet. "Get those wings to me. Who knows—I might be convinced to change my mind in the next four years. And don't worry, I didn't tell anyone about you fixing the lottery. I want Errari in the Lion ranks as much as you."

She left, leaving the door open behind her.

Janus entered and closed the door. "Are you ready for our meeting?"

"Bring him in." She always had contingency plans, because life always had nasty surprises.

Venezia pulled her knife out of the wood. Fia was wrong—it was personal.

Lazaro would find out just how personal it was.

Chapter Forty-Two

The air in the audience chamber buzzed as everyone waited for the election results. Imelda sat on the front row of the audience chairs, to the left of the Doxe—the opponent's side. Across the empty space from Imelda, Donatella attempted a reassuring smile for Imelda. Beside her sat Calixta, whose face was somber. Ulisse wasn't present. She looked around, but he was not in the room. Strange, since he was one of Primo's closest friends and most ardent supporters.

Imelda twisted the square of hemp-embroidered fabric in her grip. Anselmo's name was written across the top, red with her blood. Hopefully she wouldn't need to send it. She'd written the message before coming to the Doxe's audience chamber, and hadn't been able to leave it behind. Not that she was going to send it today, or tomorrow. She had to wait until he came out of the labyrinth so he wouldn't be too distracted to survive.

She gripped the fabric square as if to tear it apart. She'd had to write it. Primo had demanded it, but also Anselmo needed to hear Imelda's explanation in her own voice. The reminder helped her resist the temptation to rip the message. She'd told herself the same thing over and over as she'd cut her hand, dipped her quill in her blood, and wrote the letter that could crush him.

She tucked the hemp message into her pocket as the council president entered the audience chamber. Giore and Rea, please let Venezia have won. She'd stirred people up, and that couldn't be a bad thing. There was hope.

"Our Doxe for the next four years is once again Sior Primo Albizzi!" he announced.

People cheered and clapped. Imelda gripped her skirts. Four more years of Primo. Not that she'd be here, but just knowing he was in charge was bad enough.

Primo emerged from the door to the Council room, a grand smile on his face, and everyone crowded around him. They congratulated him, and men offered to buy him drinks. He greeted Donatella with a kiss.

Imelda stalked to the hall, then through the exterior doors to La Piaza del Leon. She sat on the steps, sending a flock of pigeons into the sky. Everything was going wrong. The last month held nothing but disappointment and heartbreak. Venezia's victory wouldn't have healed Imelda, but it would've been something. Venezia would've been so happy to win, and knowing her heart had just been broken brought Imelda to tears. Yes, Venezia wanted war. But surely the Council would've balked at that. Not that it mattered. Primo had gotten what he wanted yet again.

She watched people leave the building. Litters waited nearby, and the rich climbed into them. The poorer people walked away, but most of them smiled as they chatted animatedly. They were all so happy, all ignorant to Primo's sins. He'd fooled the republic, but those closest to him knew the truth. He cared about no one except himself.

Venezia was taking a long time. Imelda went back inside. Primo and the others—including Calixta, who kept glancing at Imelda—had moved down the hall, toward the exit, though congratulations still poured upon his head. Imelda walked to the Council room; the door was cracked open. She grasped the handle, but then she heard Janus mention her name. She paused.

"This man is as smart as you say he is?" Venezia asked.

"I was the high priest in Ilios before I joined Giore's Holy Order." The unfamiliar voice was gravelly and dark.

"For which you were exiled," Venezia said coolly.

"The point is," Janus said, "he can complete the wings. I'll keep him in Zorzi with me until he finishes them."

"The design is in these books?" the old man said.

"I'm sure it is. My cousin wrote in them constantly."

Imelda stifled a cry with her fist. Arturo's notebooks. Venezia had stolen them. Venezia—the one person left on her side—had betrayed Imelda. The only other woman left in the family, the one ally Imelda had always counted on. They both hated Primo. Shouldn't that be enough to bind them? But Venezia's hatred for Primo clearly outweighed any love she had for Imelda. If she even loved Imelda at all.

Janus grunted. "How much are the wings going to cost me now?"

"It all depends," the old man said. There was the soft sound of pages flipping. "Supplies, the time it takes to make them, how many people work on them. I'll give you an estimate after I look through these journals."

Imelda stumbled across the hall, catching herself on the windows overlooking the grand porch. She leaned her head against the glass as her breathing sped up.

Venezia had betrayed Imelda. She'd promised Imelda freedom, sealed it with the five kisses of promise, but it had all been a lie.

Imelda straightened. She forced herself to take a deep breath and hold it before exhaling slowly.

She turned around and took a step toward the Council room, then paused. Venezia was still in there, conspiring with those despicable men. How foolish Imelda had been.

She needed to walk in there and confront Venezia. She had to stand up for herself.

But how? How could she confront the woman who'd been like a mother to her? The woman who'd held her after Arturo died, the woman she'd trusted these last several days above anyone else?

Imelda steadied herself with a deep breath, smoothed her dress, and marched into the Council room. Venezia, Janus, and the old man—hunched and wearing a blood monk cloak with the hood covering his face—snapped their attention to her. Janus's guilty expression provided further evidence.

"You traitor." Imelda should've approached Venezia, but standing just inside the door was all she could manage. "I was coming to commiserate with you over your loss, but instead I heard you conspiring against me. You stole Arturo's journals. You stole my future!"

"I gave you the chance to finish them, Imelda. *You* denied yourself the opportunity to take control of your life, not me."

Imelda slammed the door against the wall. The sound reverberated in the room and down the hall. If anyone were out there still, they would probably hear that, as well as this confrontation. Good. Let them know what a snake Venezia was. "Why did I have to be born into this despicable family?"

"You're overreacting," Venezia said.

"How would you react if you learned your whole family was conspiring against you?"

Imelda walked away. Venezia didn't follow. She knew—knew she was guilty, knew Imelda wouldn't accept her apology.

Venezia was right about one thing. Imelda would have to save herself. She didn't need Venezia's money. And she'd ignore Primo's warnings. She'd fix Arturo's broken, battered wings and she'd fly away, leaving her contemptible cousins to their little games.

CHAPTER FORTY-THREE

Venezia stalked to the Senate building docks and tromped onto her góndola. Her gondolièr noticed her storm cloud expression, and refrained from speaking. It was clear how things had gone. Normally, riding on the water soothed her worries. The sun shone bright, but she didn't close her eyes to savor the warmth. She needed to confront Lazaro. Her head pounded. Her muscles ached. She'd run herself ragged the last several weeks. That was how she lived every month, but she felt it keenly at that moment.

Poor Imelda. The girl had been so upset. Venezia couldn't blame her. To learn Venezia, one of the few people she trusted, had betrayed her—it would wreck anyone. Venezia had created a rift she could never bridge, had wounded Imelda in a way that would never heal.

But perhaps it would be good for Imelda in the long run. She needed to be free of Primo, free even of Venezia. She needed to be on her own to figure out who she was. Yes, Venezia had crumbled Imelda, but the girl could rebuild. She would.

Venezia would miss her. No one would believe it, but it was true.

And what did the gods think of Venezia's betrayal? Had she damned herself to burn in Fógo for this? But she'd already done that to herself long ago. All the prayers and candles in the world wouldn't save her soul.

The góndolier tied the boat to her dock. Lazaro was up there, likely already aware of the the day's events. She stormed through the house to his study and slung the door open. He sat at his desk, writing a letter.

"I lost," she said.

"Of course you did." He finished his letter and returned the quill to its stand. "Did you actually think you'd win?"

"How could I win with my husband actively working against me?" Her headache grew, pounding behind her eyes. She should lie down. But she couldn't, not until she found out the truth. She leaned across the desk. "Fia told me you paid her off. You promised, Lazaro! You promised to help me become Doxe."

He stood, knocking his chair over, and planted his fists on the desk. "And you promised to be a loving and obedient wife. But five years ago you kicked me out of your bed, sleeping with knives under your pillow like some kind of crazy bitch. You were supposed to give me children, but your broken body couldn't manage it. You joined the military and lusted after power. I indulged you, but clearly that was a mistake. The less time you've spent at home, the less content with my companionship you've become. You're the one who drove me to other women. I was faithful until you refused me!"

"You did that to yourself." Every inch of her head throbbed and ached, but she couldn't leave now. "This loveless marriage is your own making. I could've been your greatest ally, but you chose to make me your enemy."

He slammed the table. "I've done nothing but adore you from the moment we met! If we are enemies, it's because your heart is as empty as your womb."

Of course he painted himself as the victim. His wife wouldn't love him after he raped her for years. Her knives begged to be used. He was strong, but she was fast. She could pull one out and slam it into his throat before he could—

Her brain flinched as the threat of a seizure hit. She stumbled back into the chair. Fifteen seconds. That's all she had.

Lazaro yelled something, but luckily her hearing was gone. Spittle flew from his mouth, landing on her face. She didn't wipe it away.

Her thoughts slowed.

Anxiety gripped her heart and twisted her stomach.

This forewarning was different than last time. She couldn't say how she knew—it was like trying to describe the difference between green and blue. Real terror pierced her. She was headed for a full convulsive fit.

Shock painted Lazaro's horrible, hateful face as he finally realized what was going on.

She blinked, and it seemed to last seconds. She was going to convulse—she needed to get on the floor.

Slowly, painfully slowly, she lowered herself to the rug.

This time, there was no balance act. The hurricane pushed her off the ship's rail, and she tumbled into the dark waters below.

⚬—✕—⚬

She awoke in her bed. Someone had opened her window and piled blankets on top of her. She sluggishly tried to push them off. Alessia was there in a moment, but Lazaro shoved his way over. His face twitched as they locked eyes. He waved for the maids to leave and sat on a chair beside her bed.

"You shook for half a minute, and you've been out for five." Anger sharpened his voice. He leaned close. "I'm glad you lost. The money I spent was worth it for you to finally know the disappointment I've experienced the last eight years."

She couldn't talk, and he knew that. He knew he held her a mute, captive audience for the next few minutes. He smiled, revealing those perfect teeth.

If only she could pull them out one by one.

"But you don't know the half of it," he said. "Twelve years ago I made an agreement. I wanted to find a second wife, and a lovely young woman had caught my attention. Her father had passed and her mother was bedridden, so I approached her older brother about marriage. He was young, but shrewd, and would not give up his sister without negotiations."

No. She wanted to tell him to be quiet, to stop him from talking so she wouldn't have to know. But a larger, louder part of her clamored for him to keep going. She needed the truth. It hurt, but she'd forge it into a weapon and use it to hurt others.

"He was young, shrewd, and, most importantly, ambitious. I knew that, but his request still caught me off guard: he wanted to be Doxe. Not only that, but he wished to be my successor, which would make him the youngest Doxe in history. Several Council members owed me favors, so it would be easy to ensure his election. I didn't like the idea of manipulating the vote, but I lusted after that girl—I lusted after you. So I agreed. All I had to do was convince you. I was unprepared for your own hunger for the sash and crown, but it made it easy to secure your hand."

For a moment she saw through his eyes as he must have seen himself. He'd been a widower of ten years looking toward a quiet—and lonely—retirement. He'd secured his political legacy, next he wanted to ensure his familial legacy. His first wife had been unable to provide him children, so he'd sought out a young bride. But Venezia had proven just as disappointing, suffering four miscarriages. Poor Lazaro. Everything was against him. The gods wouldn't give him children, and his wife wouldn't give him her body, so he bought slaves to satisfy his needs and endure his punishments. Poor poor Lazaro.

Laughter started low in her chest, barely audible. As it moved upward, it loosened the post-seizure paralysis, finally bubbling out. Lazaro stared in disgusted confusion as tears rolled down her cheeks.

"That's funny, is it?" he snarled. "Your brother sold you for a throne. You're no better than a common whore."

"My brother used me for his own gain? How surprising." It hurt far more than she would admit, but she'd deal with Primo and his betrayal another day.

"You're mad," he said.

She wiped her cheeks with sluggish hands as the laughter quieted. "That might be true. I didn't feel sane when I aborted my pregnancies."

He jerked to his feet. "Lies," he hissed.

Venezia's temporary mirth had faded. Her heart raged as she arched an eyebrow. The hot, metallic taste of blood sat on her tongue—she must've bitten her lip while convulsing.

"This is how deep my hatred for you goes, Lazaro. When I lost the first baby, I felt such immense relief that my child would be protected from your poison. But even more unexpectedly, watching you grieve the miscarriage was so satisfying, I denied you that joy three times after that. Three times I visited the apothecary and drank the tea. Three times I made myself bleed and lose the child my arms craved to hold. As painful as each one was, the relief of saving those children and the elation from cheating you outweighed it. Four times I watched you mourn, and I would do it four hundred times more if it meant hurting you again."

Lazaro's face went purple with rage, and for the moment he was frozen. What would he do when he recovered? He had never hit her, but she might have pushed him too far. Venezia was still too weak to counter it.

Alessia entered before he could raise a hand. "The doctor is here."

"Bring him in," Venezia said.

Lazaro whispered in her ear. "This isn't over."

She grabbed his shirt and kissed him. Before he jerked away, she bit his lip. They stared at each other with matching angry eyes and bloody lips.

"You're right," she said. "It won't end until you're burning in Fógo."

"I've loved you. All of these years, with everything you've put me through, my love never once faded."

"You have a terrible way of showing it."

He pulled himself free of her grasp as Alessia brought the doctor in.

"You reap what you sow, Lazaro," Venezia said as he turned to go. "You reap what you sow."

Chapter Forty-Four

It took nearly a full day to get back to the hot spring. Anselmo crept along the wall, lying low to stay out of sight of minotaurs and the men down in the valley. He spent the night on a mud mound by the hot spring, scratching and slapping at mud fleas. The steaming water of the hot spring was so tempting. The wall next to it had closed, but it would probably open if he got in and that wasn't a risk he was willing to take. He'd lived with mud fleas before. A few more days wouldn't kill him.

Though it might drive him mad.

In the morning he made his way back toward the tunnel entrance. He spied the others on the beach. They still hadn't used the boat to cross yet. Eleven men crouched in a circle, listening to Nikkoforos. Hadn't fourteen of them survived the sirens? Without Anselmo, that made thirteen, so it appeared they'd lost two men.

Anselmo arrived at the tunnel entrance by late afternoon. He sat to eat the last of his hard tack and inspect his target. The two towers stood in the middle of the sandy islet. The design was simple—identical towers, square, with arrow slits in the walls. But there was nothing connecting them that he could see.

Were there men in the castle? It seemed unlikely that the admirals would risk other men's lives just to further test the Lion candidates in the labyrinth. Then again, Ceso was somehow able to get in and out safely. Perhaps the military did too. Perhaps they used the same paths, and Ceso had discovered it somehow.

So there could be men in there. Unlikely, but possible. He had to be prepared.

The sky turned orange as the sun sank toward the eastern valley rim. A single, purple cloud floated in the sky—a hemp message, coming toward him. Were the generals changing their instructions? Anselmo didn't want to be caught on the wall when it hit, in case he lost his balance in the haze as he listened. He quickly climbed down to the floor of the lake valley just as the smoke enclosed his head, but it was not Fleet Admiral Dandolo he heard.

"Anselmo, my love." Imelda's voice rang in ears, but her tone was sad. He jerked backwards, falling against a tree as her message continued. *"I never wanted to write this letter, and I never thought I would. My wishes have not changed from our time together, but my cousin has forced my hand. The wings were a failure. Arturo is dead, and there is no hope left. I cannot marry you. I confronted Primo about our love, but he ignored it all. Without the money from the wings to free me from my family, I'm his pawn to use as he likes. I must marry King Contarini. I will be his wife by the time you get this, on my way to my new home in Eraclea. I know this news will break your heart, as mine has broken every day since Arturo's death. But please try to find happiness, Anselmo. Keep yourself safe. And remember that I will always love you."*

Anselmo stared at nothing as the smoke cleared. From somewhere in the labyrinth, a minotaur lowed, and several answered. Wind whistled down from the cliffs, much warmer than a week ago. Had it been that long? The days had melded together, feeling endless and and yet one long stretch at the same time. But it had to have been around six or seven days. And Imelda was married.

He looked at the island, where the sword waited for him. All so he could be with the woman he loved ... and now she was someone else's wife. And Arturo, his closest friend besides Imelda, was dead. They'd all fought the best way they knew how, but the Doxe had outsmarted them.

But had he really? What could he have done to force Imelda to marry that king? Threatened her life? There was no way. Family and duty were far too important to Primo. Anything else she could have ignored. But no, clearly that wasn't true. The Doxe had found something to leverage Imelda into marriage. It must've been something particularly cruel. Anselmo had tried to keep a neutral opinion about Doxe Albizzi's character, but this proved he was as bad as Imelda said.

Anselmo ripped his helmet off with a strangled growl. Only a week old, and yet it was as cloudy as his old one in the barracks. This gift from Ulisse, the king who stole Anselmo's love. Stole his very reason for living. But he was the Doxe's pawn as well.

Despite the anger and hatred for Doxe Albizzi, heartbreak outshone all else. Anselmo desperately loved Imelda. He'd loved her his whole life. He always would, until the day he died.

And Arturo, dead. The best man Anselmo had known. The gods had ripped him away, taken him to Cielo far earlier than he'd deserved.

Anselmo smashed the helmet into the sand beside him. A waste. A waste! Everything he'd done, all those years of training and working and breaking his back to become a noble, to marry Imelda—all of it for nothing. And all because of Doxe Albizzi.

What was the point of this now? Ceso was right—the gods did not exist. The priests said they valued love above all else, and yet they'd let Anselmo's love escape like water through open fingers. He grabbed the scrub tree behind him, uprooted it, and smashed it against the ground. He bashed it against the sand, over and over until the tree was nothing more than sticks. Sand and splinters sprayed his face. His entire life had led to this week in the labyrinth, and now he had no purpose.

Anselmo wiped his cheeks and found tears on them. It had been so long since he'd last cried—when his mother had died, eight years ago. He'd been fifteen, two years past getting his corincanto. She'd collapsed one day in the Albizzi kitchen. Anselmo carried her home and stayed by her bed as she lay unconscious for two days. Right at the end, she'd opened her eyes, grabbed his hand, and whispered, "Forgive me."

Imelda had come to check on him a short while later, and found him weeping beside his mother's dead body. She'd silently wrapped her arms around him and held him while he cried.

Anselmo's mother was the strongest person he knew. Betta Errari had given everything to him. He'd never asked how much six strands of corincanto had cost her, but he knew she'd saved and sacrificed for years. So he could have this chance, so he could become a Lion and carve his way through history and earn the right to nobility. He'd lost sight of that these last few weeks. He'd succumbed to Imelda's spell, and allowed himself to forget who'd made all of this possible. His success had been his mother's life work. Not her own prosperity. She'd cared only for him. She'd broken herself so Anselmo could reach heights of glory and honor no man had ever even dreamed of. He couldn't quit now just because he was lovesick. He'd get the sword, but he would do it alone, and he'd do it for his mother and no one else.

Anselmo tightened his armor and began climbing the vines to the the top of the wall.

He had a sword to claim.

CHAPTER FORTY-FIVE

Something rustled in the trees below Anselmo. He froze and looked down. A moment later, Rafael stepped out.

"What are you doing?" Rafael asked, eyeing Anselmo on the vines.

Anselmo scanned the surrounding area. Rafael seemed to be alone. But that didn't mean he was working on his own. Anselmo couldn't let him know about the tunnels, not without knowing if he was trustworthy or not.

He jumped down. "I've been scouting from the top of the wall."

"For another way to the castle?"

"I'm not looking for more minotaurs."

A smile flickered across Rafael's face before sobering again. "Where'd you get the gear?"

"I went back and got them." Anselmo's voice came out offended, which wasn't inaccurate. "What in the three blazes do you want, Rafael? Did the prince send you here to keep an eye on me?"

"Of course not." Now Rafael sounded offended. "I left them."

"And why would you abandon a whole troop of soldiers for one man?"

Rafael glanced behind him, then looked back to Anselmo and rolled his shoulders. "You're a survivor. The best I've ever seen."

Anselmo paused. "What do you mean?" The words came out slowly, as slowly as the suspicion leaving him.

"You knew about the mud fleas. You killed a minotaur single-handedly. You resisted a siren's lure. You became famous in Zorzi for your strength and bravery. And I have a feeling you've endured even more that I don't know about." There was something in his tone, his inflection maybe. Something unidentifiable, but it wasn't negative.

Then it hit Anselmo: it was admiration. He'd never heard that in his life, not from a highborn. Anselmo's fellow privates and lieutenants had seen his potential, but no rich man had ever looked beyond Anselmo's upbringing to give him any respect.

Rafael grinned. "Too bad you suck at following orders."

Anselmo snorted. "Only orders from idiots."

"Nikkos isn't an idiot. He's done better than I could've in these circumstances."

"Then why did you leave him?"

"Because I trust you more."

Rafael seemed earnest. And he'd been the only one of the Lion candidates to treat Anselmo decently from the start.

Anselmo nodded. "You can join me."

Rafael's posture eased. He jerked his chin at the wall. "That's the other way to the castle?"

"Yes. But first." Anselmo pointed his spear at Rafael. "We go back to get your gear. There's no reason for you to fight minotaurs while naked."

Anselmo held his spear in his mouth and started up the wall again. Instead of into the tunnel, he'd go the opposite direction, back to the hot spring once more.

But this time, he wasn't alone.

CHAPTER FORTY-SIX

Imelda hurried up the palàso stairs, holding a basket full of silk roving. She'd rushed to the nearest shop as soon as it opened and bought their entire inventory. She'd need it all to fix Arturo's wings. Even then, it might not be enough. But she had to try. She had to prove to everyone that she was capable, prove to them that they'd underestimated her all this time.

Once she got to her room, she locked the door and sat in front of Arturo's wings. They were a jumbled heap. Her wedding was only two days away. Could she do this in time? She would've bought silk corincanto, but the spinning guild shop had only had one skein—not nearly enough to mend these broken, battered things.

There was also the problem of the design. She needed to change it, but how? The pulley system was a mess, and she had no time to commission a new set. It hadn't worked that well anyway.

For a moment, she saw Arturo racing toward the palàso in the rain, saw the ropes tearing free of his grip, ripping out of the pulleys, falling to the streets below.

She squeezed her eyes shut and tried to banish any thought of the following moments, the last moments of his life. The sound his body made when he smashed against the palàso, the massive cracking of wood and bones. His scream cut off suddenly. His blood spraying her hands with every cough as she tried desperately to save his life.

She hugged herself tight and rocked back and forth. She could meet the same end if she managed to fix the wings. But it would be better than to live a life as Primo's pawn. She had no doubt he'd find ways to leverage his authority over her even once she was queen of Eraclea.

She couldn't give him that satisfaction. It was freedom or nothing.

But she'd only have that option if she finished the wings.

Imelda glanced northeast, where the labyrinth lay. Anselmo was alive. Surely she'd feel it if he died. Surely his weight in her thoughts would disappear. He must be exhausted, even more than she. He was facing dangerous beasts and moving walls that could crush a man. He was so strong, and she was trying her best.

She walked to her bedside table. She needed to hold the hemp message she'd written to him, as she had occasionally the last few days. It comforted her, somehow. To know she could destroy it if she succeeded. There was even peace in knowing she would send it if she failed and had to marry Ulisse. It would break Anselmo's heart, but it would give him closure. Give him the permission to move on and find love somewhere else, though in the deepest recesses of her heart she hoped he never would.

When she reached the table, it was empty. She'd put the message there before leaving for the shops. She flung open the drawer, then ransacked the wardrobe. As she began to tear her bed apart, Editta knocked and entered.

"I've come to help you dress for—what's wrong, mè siora?"

The bed held nothing. Imelda moved to the other side, crawling on her hands and knees to look under her plush chair by the fire. "I had a hemp letter on my nightstand. It was here when I woke up, but now it's gone. Have you seen it?"

Editta blanched. "I—I sent it. I thought you'd forgotten to, so I threw it in the fire this morning."

No. Oh gods, no. She jumped to her feet and stared the woman down. "I didn't tell you to do that. Why in Rea's holy name would you dare be so presumptuous?"

She somehow managed not to yell, but the woman's lips quivered. Editta had worked for the Albizzi family nearly her whole life. She would never commit such a mistake. She'd even moved to the palàso with Imelda. She'd loved Imelda's mother and had told Imelda stories about her as Imelda drifted to sleep. She'd never do anything to hurt Imelda.

Unless someone commanded her to.

Oh. Oh no. "Primo told you to, didn't he?" Editta cowered, but didn't answer. "Didn't he!"

"Yes, mè siora. I'm sorry to have betrayed you." Tears leaked from her eyes. "I couldn't refuse him—he's my employer. He's the Doxe and head of your family."

Imelda sighed. She took a handkerchief from her desk and gave it to the maid. "You were just following instructions." Editta stared at the handkerchief. "Take it. I promise I'm not angry." Not with the woman. Primo, however ...

She stormed along the hallway, intending to confront him. Almost to the stairs, she hesitated. She could guess what he might say—that she should've sent it days ago. If she told him why she was waiting—so Anselmo wouldn't be too distracted and risk death—he'd say something along the lines of anyone who got distracted by their personal life had no place in the Lions, or something equally stupid. They'd go nowhere, arguing in circles.

She'd always be his to control if she married Ulisse. If she somehow managed to stay, she'd belong to Venezia too. Why wouldn't they leave her alone? Why did they think they could pull the lines of her life and make her sail where they wanted?

She had to fly. She *had* to. But where would she go? She hadn't considered that yet. She'd focused so much on finishing the wings to be with Anselmo. What about the in-between? She didn't know how to navigate flying, and she didn't know how long the wings could keep her airborne. Even if she got to Zorzi, or Shantze, or any nearby city, she wouldn't know anyone there. She'd show up with a few hundred ducats, the ability to spin corincanto, and nothing else. She'd be as vulnerable as a seal pup.

Unless she went to the one foreign city where she knew people. She wound through the halls and knocked on Calixta's door. The princess bid her enter, and Imelda walked into a flurry of motion as Calixta's maids removed dresses from hangers and folded them into trunks.

"You're leaving already?" Imelda asked

Calixta handed a veil to her maid. "I just got word of a storm headed this direction. It's supposed to hit the night after your wedding, maybe the next morning. My ship's captain wants to be on the sea well before then. I won't be able to stay until Nikkos gets out. When he does emerge, Primo will send him on his most trusted ship." She paused. "I'll miss your wedding."

"I'm not—" Imelda began, then shut her mouth when she remembered the maids. "Can we talk alone?"

Calixta dismissed the women, then pulled Imelda over to sit on the bed. She wore the usual arrangement of jewels and fancy clothes, but her casual, even protective, posture altered her. She was still magical, far more than Imelda would ever be, even with her spinning gift, but she seemed more grounded. More relatable.

This must've been what Arturo saw in Calixta. And the woman had had the good sense to see Arturo for the treasure he was. Imelda had neglected checking on her, too wrapped up in her own mourning.

"How have you been?" Imelda asked.

"I'm ... coping." Calixta offered a sad smile. "Is this what you came to talk to me about?"

Once again Imelda pictured Arturo hurtling toward the palàso. Calixta had leapt for him the same moment Imelda had. Surely she'd cared about Arturo. Hopefully that meant she was someone Imelda could trust. Imelda had no one else.

"I can't marry Ulisse. And I want to come to Ilios and sell the wings to you."

Calixta put her hands up. "One moment, please. That's a lot to take in." She stood and started pacing. "You know I think you should marry Ulisse."

"Because it benefits your ally. But I'm in love with Anselmo." Imelda sighed. "You cared about Arturo, didn't you?"

"Very much."

"Then you understand why I have to try to be with Anselmo. Let me come to Ilios with you. I'll give your father the wing's design in exchange for my safety. When do you leave?"

"We're leaving tomorrow at midnight. I need to stay the extra day in case Nikkos makes it out." Calixta tapped her lip. "The wings are enticing, I have to admit it. And ... I don't blame you. Your cousins are terrible people. I know you love Venezia, but—"

"She betrayed me." The wound in Imelda's soul ached as if it were fresh. She wouldn't cry. She wouldn't cry. Gods, she had cried so much lately. She hardened her voice, fed her anger into it. "She stole Arturo's journals and gave them to some blood monk so he can finish the wings before me."

Calixta sucked her breath in. "We can't let that happen. I received word that Janus has already left." She resumed pacing. "We could hide you somehow, smuggle you to the ship."

Imelda shook her head. "The wedding eve party will last until at least midnight. If I don't show up, Primo will hunt me down."

"Indeed he will," Calixta murmured. She stopped pacing and snapped her fingers. "Finish the wings and fly to my ship. When we arrive in Ilios, my father will pay you for the wings. I won't let you give such precious belongings away for free."

Imelda sighed in relief. "Grassie. You're going to save my life."

"You're going to save your own life. Arturo believed in you, and I don't believe he trusted people lightly."

Imelda's heart clenched, and she smiled sadly. Calixta had seen Arturo for who he was in such a short time. She was right—he didn't trust people lightly. In fact, Calixta had been the last in a very short list of people who'd earned his confidence.

Her good mood faltered at the next step. "The problem is I'm out of ideas. Arturo had everything in his journals, and now those are gone."

"But he loved to read."

A smile grew on Imelda's face. "Yes, exactly. All of his books are at home. Do you ..." She pulled on a lock of hair. She could do this alone, or she could have a partner. Again. Not a replacement for Arturo—that would never exist—but another person to share in Imelda's success. "Do you want to come with me? There are so many books, I'll need help going through them all."

Calixta pulled Imelda to her feet. "I'd love to."

Twenty minutes later, they walked through the canal entrance to Cax' Albizzi. Imelda stopped suddenly as the sight of her home, dark from the curtains pulled tight, assaulted her. She instinctively gripped Calixta's hand.

"I haven't been here since before Arturo's death." She kept her voice low, as if the memories of the past could hear her. The ghosts of the people who frequented the halls—Mare, Pàre, Arturo, even Anselmo's mother. All gone, all dead. Her chest quivered. "It's the same. I feel like I could see everyone again right now."

Calixta squeezed Imelda's fingers. "Every good home is filled with good memories."

Imelda led the way to the staircase at the front of the house. The staircase wasn't as grand as the one at Palàso Dogal, but her feet recognized the cushion of the Shantzese stair runner, and her hands relished the feel of the railing's smooth grain.

"It smells like home," she said.

"What kind of smells?"

"I don't know. It smells like Arturo and Pàre, Renzo and Donte. And Anselmo." He'd spent time running around the house with Arturo and her when they were young. As a child, he'd smelled like the bread his mother baked in the morning. When they grew older, he'd come by to pick up his mother. Pàre pulled him into the parlor for a chat most days. He was always tired, having spent the day working at the salterns, and the scent of salt clung to his skin. Sometimes she could even see its remnants on his arms, where the sun had evaporated water and left behind the chalky residue.

They reached Arturo's room. The door gaped open. The inside was dark, of course, but light seeped in from the windows. The black curtains gave the shadows a blue tint. Arturo's room greeted her dressed in mourning blue.

Imelda walked to the bookcase as Calixta cracked open the nearest curtains.

"Imelda!"

Imelda rushed to Calixta, who held one of Arturo's notebooks. But when she opened it, it was empty—saved for future use. Except now it would remain empty. Arturo's loopy, messy script would never be scrawled onto a paper again.

Calixta put the notebook down. Together they approached Arturo's bookshelf. The bookcase reached far above their heads. All of the shelves were the same—full of volumes both thick and thin, tall and short, darkened with age. It was stuffed, books squeezed together that looked like they might explode outward if they were disturbed. All of the spines were cracked from age—and Arturo's frequent use hadn't helped. His death was so recent that no dust had yet settled on the closest shelves.

Calixta tilted her head to read the spines. "Where do we even begin?"

Imelda looked up. Arturo would've had a system, some way to demarcate the most important books. Then she noticed—every now and then, a book was turned around backwards, its pages facing out instead of the spine. When it came to his research and books, Arturo was meticulous. He had placed those books backward on purpose.

"Grab all the books that are backward," she told Calixta. The princess immediately started grabbing books. She tossed them to Imelda, who looked through the titles. "*A Treatise on Math, Wonders of the Natural World, The Gulf: Findings from a Life's Observation.* They all sound good. It's still too much."

Calixta dragged the desk chair to the bookcase and reached up to grab books off the top shelves. Imelda caught the books as Calixta dropped them into her arms.

"Careful, this one is really old." Calixta gently gave a book to Imelda. Its tattered cover was barely still attached. There was no title, not on the front or the spine. This was no professional book.

Imelda opened it, her hands shaking. *A Life Dedicated to Science by Italo Albizzi.* She flipped to the next page. Neat script covered the sheaf—which was to be expected—but what she hadn't anticipated was Arturo's loopy scrawl filling the margins.

"My ancestor's journal!"

"There are two more." Calixta grabbed the books then hopped down. Imelda sat right there, and Calixta knelt beside her. "Your ancestor?"

"The one who invented the labyrinth. These will have what we need. Let's hurry back."

They stood and left the room. Imelda hugged the first journal to her chest as they made their way down the stairs.

"Bless you, Arturo," she whispered as she hurried to the dock, leaving her home behind with all of its stolen memories.

Chapter Forty-Seven

Imelda paced in her room at the palàso. She'd retired from dinner early, under the pretense that she needed to go to bed so she'd have energy for the party the following night. Now she waited for Calixta to return with silk corincanto. After spending so much time at Cax' Albizzi, Imelda didn't have time to spin the silk roving she'd bought. Calixta had volunteered to personally find Imelda as much silk corincanto as she could. She'd been gone for hours—surely she should be back any minute.

Imelda studied Arturo's wings, still piled in the corner. After Primo stole her wings, she thought she'd have no way out. But Italo's journals were a treasure—full of brilliant information on everything from observations of animals around Rialto to ideas for new inventions.

Italo had been a genius, but a twisted one. Imelda shuddered. In addition to his expertise in corincanto, and several ramblings on religion and what makes a god, the journals contained drawings of dark designs. The worst depicted the most effective way to insert corincanto into a person's arteries and hide the knots so priests couldn't find the heretics. The drawings had been numerous and detailed. By then, she'd gotten what she needed, so she'd slammed the book shut, and hadn't looked at it since.

Someone knocked.

"It's me," Calixta said through the door.

Imelda opened the door to find Calixta and her guard both holding large baskets full of silk corincanto. There had to be at least two dozen skeins. Imelda took the basket from the guard, then pulled Calixta in and shut the door.

"Is this enough?" Calixta asked.

"If it's not, then the wings are beyond repair." Imelda set the basket on the floor and pulled Calixta into a tight hug. "You didn't have to go yourself. You could've sent more of your guards."

Calixta tucked a lock of hair behind Imelda's ear. "I needed to be more actively involved. Besides, no one says no to the imperial princess of Ilios."

"Where did you find all of this?"

"The spinning guild island."

Imelda knelt to inspect the corincanto. The quality was absolute perfection, smooth and tight. "Can you help me more? Or do you need to sleep?"

"This is much more important than sleep."

They pulled the wings into the center of the floor. They were a complete mess—this was going to take hours. Luckily, since Editta had already helped Imelda dress for bed, they wouldn't be interrupted. It would be a long night, but if it worked and Imelda freed herself, it would be worth it.

The fire crackled in the hearth, then burned down to embers as they worked. The temple bell rang the hours as the moon dragged itself across the windows toward its resting place in the eastern horizon. Piece by piece, they assembled the wings. They barely talked. It felt right, reverent somehow.

They made several mistakes and had to backtrack, but in the early hours of the morning, the frame was finally pieced together. Imelda's eyelids felt full of sand whenever she blinked. They ached from the dim light. Calixta's stomach grumbled. The candle burned low, so Imelda had to light another. She pulled herself to her feet to retrieve the silk and stumbled to the side. After this, she could rest. The day held no plans, so she could sleep as long as the sun roved the sky, if she wished.

Normally, it would be impossible to wrap the thread around the frame with the albatross skin still on. But there were enough tears in the leather that they were able to twine the silk around the wood every few centimeters. They wound at least twice at each spot, just to be safe. It would take a lot of corincanto; maybe as much as Calixta had bought. When Imelda reached the last bare patch of wood—and used the last of her thread—she inspected the spot where she'd started.

"Look." The wood was still broken, but when she peered close enough, she could see a fiber of wood branching the distance. "It's working." Thank Cielo above, it was working.

Calixta finished her final loop and made the sign of the gods. "Thank the holy mother and father."

"The albatross skin is a mess, and there are so many missing feathers." Imelda could hear fatigue weighing her voice down. "And I'll have to sew the harness back together using silk." More work, more time, more missed sleep.

"I'll send my guard to buy more feathers and corincanto. But for now, let's sleep."

Imelda stood and arched her back. "We need to move these." She couldn't leave them in the middle of her floor, not only because of the inconvenience, but also, she couldn't afford to risk Primo finding out what she was doing and stealing this pair. The temple bell rang four in the morning. Gods, she needed sleep. Her bed looked like Cielo itself. "Let's pull them under my bed."

Calixta crouched to help push the wings. Gently as they could while also still using enough strength to move the massive things, they maneuvered the wings under Imelda's bed one at a time. They had to pull the second one on top of the first to keep them hidden. Imelda had never worked so hard in her life. Her body ached more than she'd ever experienced. The thought of the exhaustion she was going to endure over the next twenty-four hours intimidated her. How could she get it all done? She wasn't strong enough. And yet, she had to be.

Imelda hugged Calixta. "Grassie tante. Grassie, grassie, grassie."

"Of course. Get some rest." After one last hug, the princess left.

Despite Imelda's fears and doubts, when she finally crawled into bed, she immediately fell asleep. Underneath her, the wings continued to knit themselves back together.

Chapter Forty-Eight

Venezia lowered the telescope to rub her tired eyes. Her body ached from her seizure the other day, and staring through the telescope all day made her head throb. She'd been standing in the sun on one of the labyrinth's watchtowers, the tallest at over twenty meters. Sending soldiers through the labyrinth was always exciting, but it took its toll on her. Once Janus's man finished Imelda's design, Venezia could watch from directly overhead. Only one of the many uses she'd find for the wings.

Anselmo ran along the innermost walls of the labyrinth, followed by Rafael Galbani. Anselmo'd had a few missteps figuring out how to work with the team, but having Rafael with him showed he'd figured some things out. And such strength and skill. It seemed impossible for someone to be so strong, and yet there he was. He'd have no problem getting out through packs of minotaurs. He would be a Lion within the next few days, and what a Lion he'd make. No one would stand in her way with him at her side. Wise she'd been to fix the lottery to draw his name. The risk was already paying off.

It was a shame Venezia hadn't been able to watch the labyrinth until now. Between Imelda's wedding preparations, Arturo's death, and the election, she'd had no time. Normally when there were soldiers in the labyrinth, she spent hours every day watching from the walls. Relying on the reports from Admiral Galbani and the vice admirals wasn't the same as seeing developments for herself.

Movement in Venezia's periphery caught her eye. She glanced over and bit down a growl. Her rat of a brother walked along the wall toward her, guards in tow. He wore his sash and crown. She ground her teeth. , just like her husband. Just like her father.

Primo's guards hung back as he approached Venezia.

She lifted the telescope to her eye. "Are you here to demote me?"

"Nonsense. You're the best choice for Fleet Admiral."

"Keep your enemies close," she murmured.

"We're not enemies, Venezia."

What a bold lie. She might've agreed with him a year ago—just because she wanted to take the sash and crown from him didn't make them enemies. His agreement with Lazaro, however, changed things. Enrico had spoken disparagingly to Venezia about pitting herself against her brother, but Primo had made the first move. Venezia's soul was soiled, but Primo's bore its own stains.

"How are they doing?" he asked.

Venezia offered the telescope.

He lifted it to his eyes. "I only see two men. How many are left?"

"Thirteen. Lazaro said he once had a group with no survivors." She jerked her chin at the labyrinth. "If they're smart, numbers won't matter. I have high expectations."

"Why?"

She cut her eyes at him. "I know how soldiers think. That's why you appointed me Fleet Admiral."

"Indeed." Primo handed the telescope back.

She tapped her nails on the telescope. "I wish we let more lieutenants in via lottery."

"Make a more convincing argument to the Council next time." Hubris tinted his voice. As if it was her fault the vote had gone awry. His face sobered. "I don't see Prince Nikkoforos."

"Admiral Galbani said he's alive and on the shores of the lake. They've been picking off the sirens."

"We need to get him out."

"That will compromise the test."

"He could die, Venezia. Then we'll have war—not in Ilios, but at our city. Even you don't want that."

"I've got Anselmo on it."

"That lowborn gutter slug Imelda's in love with? Are you a fool?"

"You were the reason no one from Rialto was willing to sponsor him. Did you threaten them all?"

"I simply told them he's a man not to be trusted." He scoffed. "And from what I hear, that's the case. He hasn't heeded the prince's leadership particularly well."

Primo saw everything in black and white, when the world was nothing but gray. She pocketed the telescope, and her hand fell to her side, next to her Fleet Admiral knife. She touched it lightly enough for no one to notice. "You're a fool to underestimate him."

"I underestimate no one."

She whipped out the blade and held it to Primo's throat. His crown toppled off his head. "Like you underestimated me when you sold me to Lazaro?"

Primo's guards rushed over, swords already drawn. Primo held a hand to stop them. "Lower your weapons, and go back to your station. I'm fine." He glanced at the sheath on her belt and made the connection. "That's the knife I gave you. It's too dull to do anything more than nick me."

"I sharpened it," she hissed. "I could kill you right now."

"You're too smart for that. You can't become Doxe if you're a murderer." He was infuriatingly calm. Because he was right.

The guards were still there, torn between obedience to their prime directive and Primo's command. Primo waved them back again, and they finally retreated, though they kept their swords out.

She lowered the knife. "Thirteen years, Primo. Thirteen years I've put up with that terrible man. I thought there was a purpose to enduring life with Lazaro, and I was right, but not in the way I'd hoped. Turns out I was helping *you*. I thought I was steering my own future, but it was yours all along."

"Surely it hasn't been so bad."

She fixed him with look. "Do you want to know how I discovered your betrayal? He told me. And, oh, how he enjoyed it, all while still claiming to love me." Did Venezia know love? Maybe once, long ago with Ulisse. What would she have been like if she'd married Ulisse? It was tempting to imagine a happy life, with children and the normal worries of marriage. She'd harbored such hope in her youth. But that part of her died on her wedding night.

Besides, if she had married Ulisse, she wouldn't be as strong as she was today. She'd be coddled and weak. Venezia would choose strength any day, no matter the cost.

"You don't need Lazaro." In addition to his crown, Primo's sash had fallen off. One of the guards picked the regalia up. Primo took his time dusting them off, putting them on, straightening them just right as he spoke. "You've accomplished so much, all with him and me both working against you. I'm impressed. Your speech at the election was especially powerful. Though you'd better keep yourself in check the next four years, or I *will* demote you."

Her hand with the knife fell to her side. She ... she didn't know what to think about that. It was like that moment in the Council chamber before the Janus vote. A moment of candid honesty, and a compliment at that. Why give her that? Was it a kindness or more manipulation? At that moment, she couldn't tell. She'd always thought of herself as more cunning than Primo, but he couldn't have been elected Doxe without sharp wits, let alone remain so for eight years. And the scheme with Lazaro had been his idea. Venezia had been the one underestimating Primo this whole time.

"Honestly, I'm surprised Lazaro's still alive." Primo smoothed the shoulders of his doublet. "Maybe he'll die soon, and you'll be free of him. I'm sorry it's been so terrible."

"No, you're not."

"If that's what you want to think." He nodded toward the center of the labyrinth. "Good job, as always. I'll see you at Imelda's wedding tomorrow morning." He adjusted his clothes once more then turned to go.

"I will be Doxe one day, Primo. I'll wear the sash and crown."

"I don't doubt that you will. But not until I've finished my run."

He walked to the nearest bridge and crossed over. Venezia sheathed her knife and turned back to the labyrinth. She pulled out the telescope and drummed her fingers on it. Primo was right—she didn't need Lazaro. She'd never needed him. He'd given her some guidance, here and there, but it had amounted to nothing. In fact, he'd only held her back.

That begged the question: if Lazaro was not an asset, why put up with him any longer?

CHAPTER FORTY-NINE

Anselmo and Rafael didn't have time to creep along the wall. They ran all night, reaching the hot spring by morning. They gathered Rafael's clothes and gear. There was still some hard tack, all of it covered by bugs. Anselmo's rumbling stomach didn't care. They wiped the bugs off the food, downed it, then climbed back onto the wall.

As they neared the tunnel entrance, Anselmo caught sight of the other group. They seemed to be making preparations to finally cross the lake. Some men inspected the boat, some watched the lake, some checked their swords and sheaths.

"They're not going to cross until evening," Rafael said.

"Why not?"

"That's when the sirens are least active."

They had time. But Anselmo increased his speed.

They reached the tunnel late in the afternoon. Anselmo dropped into the opening, followed by Rafael.

Rafael whistled softly. "You lucky son of a bitch."

"It took me days to find this," Anselmo snapped, then softened his tone. "But you're right, I was lucky." He couldn't deny it. The odds of him looking down at that exact spot to see the tunnels were too great.

But he wouldn't have been there to look if he hadn't already searched everywhere else.

They quickly crept through the tunnels. Twice they encountered minotaurs. The first time, they were able to avoid the beasts, three huge creatures with patches of silver fur on their backs. The second time, they ran straight into two younger ones. Anselmo and Rafael recovered from their surprise before the minotaurs. There was no time to assess. Anselmo thrust his sword into the beast's belly, then ripped up through its ribs. He whirled to help Rafael, but the man had already downed his beast with a stab through the heart. It moaned in pain before Rafael shoved his sword through its eye.

"That's going to attract more," Rafael said.

"Then we better pick up the pace."

Now they ran, swords out. It didn't take long until they heard roars of minotaurs echoing down the tunnels toward them. They ran faster. They reached the room under the lake, but there was no time to appreciate the impossible beauty. Rafael glanced up and his step stuttered. Anselmo grabbed Rafael's cuirass and dragged him back into action.

The minotaurs had almost reached them when they made it to the room under the island. They ran into the pond and swam for their life to the small island on the other side. Anselmo whirled around, sword up, as half a dozen minotaurs spilled out of the tunnel. They balked at the water, roaring in frustration.

"They can't swim." Rafael forced the words out between gulps of air.

"I guess we're both lucky today."

Rafael looked up. "Sword is up there?"

"I haven't gotten that far yet. But it's as likely as anywhere else."

"It's not like we have a choice anyway." Rafael sheathed his sword. "The ledges are just far enough apart that the jumps will be difficult. There might be some scrambling. We should leave our cuirasses here."

Anselmo glanced back to the minotaurs, then turned his gaze upward. Rafael was right. But who knew what waited for them above. Going up there without their cuirasses was an uncomfortable idea, but there was no other choice. They'd faced sirens while naked. This couldn't be worse.

Anselmo unbuckled the straps of his cuirass and pulled it off. "I'll go first." He stuck his spear in the sand, slung his shield across his back, then climbed the vines onto the first ledge. Across the lake, the minotaurs growled in frustration.

Anselmo misjudged the first jump, slamming chest first into the side of the second ledge. He grunted as pain from his broken ribs flared hot and sharp. But he was able to get a hold and pull himself up. With his cuirass on, he would've slid off. It was only a three meter drop from here, but farther up such a miscalculation would've proven deadly. Rafael hadn't been wrong when he'd suggested they leave their cuirasses behind.

On the third step, Rafael jumped before Anselmo could make the leap to the fourth. His hands tangled with Anselmo's feet, and Anselmo reeled. His arms swung, but he corrected and fell against the wall. Rafael stood and leaned on his knees.

"One person at a time," Anselmo gasped.

"Absolutely."

Anselmo looked up and counted how many ledges were left. Somewhere around fifty. And they'd only done three.

Jump by precarious jump, they climbed up the chamber.

Thirty ledges to go. The minotaurs' roars echoed off the walls, filling the air with their voices until it was almost palpable. Rafael made the sign of the gods before every leap.

Twenty ledges to go. Anselmo's palms grew sweaty, and he had to wipe them on his tunic before every jump. Rafael cursed every time he hit the stone edge.

Ten ledges to go. The sound of the minotaurs faded away. They must've grown bored and left. Anselmo's ribs felt made of fire. He'd be lucky if one didn't puncture his lungs.

Oh gods, let him be lucky. As lucky as he'd been to find the tunnel.

He glanced down. He could make out their cuirasses on the small island, and the pond surrounding them. Barely. Only by the glint of the torches off the brass and water surface.

Three ledges to go. Anselmo prepared himself to jump.

The sound of Rafael's body hitting the stone came from behind Anselmo, then Rafael's accompanying, "Shit. Shit shit shit!"

Anselmo whirled around. Rafael was slipping. Anselmo leapt over, almost overshooting the distance since he was jumping down instead of up this time. He tripped and fell onto his knees on Rafael's hand. Rafael yelled in pain, but his body kept slipping.

Anselmo grabbed Rafael's other arm before getting off Rafael's hand, but he couldn't get a good position for leverage.

"Grab my hand!" Anselmo said.

Rafael took Anselmo's wrist. Anselmo held onto the opposite edge of the ledge with his other hand. He braced one foot against the wall and dug the other into the dust on the stone best he could.

"Just let me go," Rafael said between clenched teeth. His forehead was covered in sweat. "Or we'll both fall."

"I've got you." Anselmo pulled. His foot slipped. He couldn't rely on that leg. With one arm and one leg, he edged back until he hit the end of the ledge. He continued leaning back, pulling with everything he had. Finally, Rafael's torso made it onto the stone, and he was able to swing a leg up. Anselmo helped him up, and they immediately rested against the wall, chests heaving.

"You could've gotten yourself killed." Rafael gulped at the air. Tears and sweat slid down his dust-covered face. "You're crazy."

Anselmo coughed a laugh and wiped his sweaty forehead on his sweaty arm. "Gotta be crazy to go into the labyrinth."

"I've never heard truer words."

They cleared the last ledges. When they emerged from the pit, they found themselves in what must be the main room of one of the towers. It was bigger than Anselmo had expected. They stood by the wooden exterior doors. Night had fallen, but lit torches lined the walls. The floor extended for several meters before dropping away. A long plank hung over the space, hanging by a rope on each end. Across the chasm stood a tall cliff. The ceiling was actually a stone staircase going from the second level up to a third.

They approached the plank. It was wider than it had seemed, more like a bridge. Anselmo looked down into the chasm. Small logs and hay covered the bottom, though still a fatal distance below. Some larger logs leaned vertically against the wall. He put his foot on the end of the wood plank and pressed down. Nothing happened, so he pushed harder. The opposite end lifted.

"One of us has to hold this end to lift it so the other can reach the taller ledge," Rafael said.

Anselmo looked Rafael up and down. He wasn't a small man, but he wasn't as big as Anselmo. He wouldn't be able to lift Anselmo up. Anselmo would have to stay behind.

"You have to be the one to continue." The words were like rocks in Anselmo's throat.

"Maybe you could jump."

"Not from an unstable surface. It's not worth the risk."

Rafael took a deep breath. "I'll give you the sword."

"No, if you're the one to retrieve it—"

"I'll give you the sword." Rafael's tone was certain, firm. Unyielding.

Rafael stepped onto the small bridge. The other end immediately lifted up, reaching the level of the other cliff. The plank also swung wildly, and Rafael dropped to all fours. From the chasm floor came the roar of a fire coming to life. Anselmo glanced over the edge. The fire was low, but gaining heat. It wouldn't take long until it climbed the logs against the walls high enough to reach the bridge. Anselmo would need to sit on the bridge the whole time Rafael was gone.

"Hold on." Anselmo slowly sat on the edge of the wood. It swung with his weight, but he widened his feet to stabilize it. He held the ropes. "Go."

The bridge shook and swayed as Rafael climbed. The room grew warm as the fire in the pit raged. Finally, the plank stopped moving.

"I made it." Rafael's voice echoed in the room, making him sound close and distant at the same time. "I'm going up the stairs." Then followed the sound of a sword unsheathing and footsteps on stone until it faded.

Anselmo prepared himself to wait.

It didn't take long before Rafael's feet were running down the stairs. "There's a doorway, and two ropes that look like they lift a bridge over to the second tower. We're stuck."

Damn it all, they'd need the others after all. If they made it.

Anselmo braced himself on the bridge. "Come back."

Rafael hustled back to Anselmo. "Hop off. I've got it."

Anselmo stood and turned. The fire had grown. If Rafael got off the bridge, it would catch fire.

"The others." Anselmo wiped sweat from his eyes. "Dusk, you said?"

"That was the plan."

"I'll check."

Anselmo stepped outside. The night was bright from the full moon. Halfway across the lake, he could see the boat. Men were shouting, and sirens were singing and crying. But the boat seemed to be moving, and no one seemed to be falling off.

The moon sat just above the rim of the valley, as bright and fat as it had ten years ago. The night he'd gotten his threads. All for this night, this opportunity, this life. *I know this news will break your heart, as mine has broken every day since Arturo's death,* Imelda had said. That barely touched on the pain that had hunted him the last few days. The week of Carnevale had been like a dream, sweet as honey, but it melted just as quickly. Only one week. Anselmo had been in here longer.

He breathed in the cold, early spring air. He'd spent his whole life driving himself to be the best. Ceso was right. His future was not in ruins. He would forge it into something new. It wouldn't be as sweet without Imelda, but he'd find purpose. Nobility. Just as his mother had wanted for him—but he'd use it as Ceso said, to become a legend. To have his name woven into the history of the world. It was a waste to wish for the soft life of a noble. Honor and glory would make him richer than even the Doxe.

Anselmo wanted more. So much more, and this time without Imelda.

He crouched in the sand, crossed his arms, and waited.

Chapter Fifty

The fire crackled as Imelda sewed the final stitch into the wings and lowered her needle. She'd finally finished mending the leather and replacing the feathers. The thread ran horizontally across the flight feathers from the albatrosses. She smoothed her hand down the length of the wings. They felt like silk.

Calixta sat on the bed, flipping through Italo's journals in an attempt to find a solution to the broken pulley system.

Imelda yawned, and her eyes threatened to close as she pulled herself onto her chair. Gods, she was tired. "Have you found anything yet?"

"Nothing beyond those disturbing drawings you told me about." Calixta shuddered and closed the volume she'd been reading. "I've got one last journal to look through."

Imelda yawned again and massaged her fingers. She'd woken up after only a few hours of sleep, just in time to sew the harness back together. Then she'd been whisked away to pre-wedding festivities all day, pampered by the women in her family. All save Venezia, who'd made the excuse of having to supervise the labyrinth. She knew Imelda didn't want her there.

Donatella had led the other women in the bridal duties. Imelda's skin had been buffed, and her hair washed then combed at least a hundred times. They'd planned her hairdo, and admired the dress, and massaged her tired body. That last part had been nice, especially on her sore hands and legs from sewing all night.

The women had chattered incessantly—about what, gods knew. Imelda hadn't had enough energy to pay attention. She'd been too distracted worrying whether she'd have enough time to repair the leather of the wings so she could escape tonight.

If she could escape. No, when. *When.*

Her vision spun, and she swayed in her chair. She put a hand on a wing, focusing on the feel of the feathers, the shaft in the center and the smooth vane to each side. She couldn't stop now.

La Canson would start any minute. Calixta's ship left at midnight. And if Imelda failed, in twelve hours she'd be on her bridal góndola, riding to the dogal barge for her wedding. The bustle of servants setting up the party on the street managed to get through her closed window. If she were going to discover anything and have time to act on it, she had to move now.

"I found something," Calixta said. She waved Imelda over and started reading out loud. "*'Hemp is as misunderstood as silk. Its primary function is not to deliver messages. Its power lies in connecting with the mind.'*"

Imelda sat beside her. "This has to be it."

Calixta nodded and continued. "*'If you wish to gain a connection with an object, simply use hemp. The actual act is frowned upon, since you have to sew it into your skin, so no one thinks to use it. We've become much too afraid of appearing heretical. I wanted the labyrinth walls to move, making it deadly even without the minotaurs. But how do you make stone move on its own? I couldn't connect my mind to the labyrinth—that is highly impractical. But I found a solution. Doxe Francolini was put off by my suggestion, though I was able to make him see the merits eventually. Emptying the jails meant the government spent less money sustaining criminal life. I'd get my labyrinth walls to move, he would get his minotaur pen, and the government would get richer. What did I do? Committed heresy. I stand by it.'"*

Imelda and Calixta looked at each other.

"This isn't going to be pleasant." Calixta took a deep breath. "'*I needed brains and skin, so we decapitated every prisoner.'*"

Calixta gasped, and Imelda covered her mouth.

Calixta swallowed, leaning closer to Imelda. "'*They're all sentenced to life,*'" she said in a near-whisper, "'*so I argue that this is a mercy. Better a quick death than unending days without sunlight or fresh air. I took their heads and ran hemp up their necks, through their brains, and out the eye sockets. Each labyrinth wall has at least two heads. These we covered with concrete. So you see, the walls are not stone—that is merely a decoration. At their core, they are concrete. And at their heart, the heads of dead men. Doxe Francolini said I was sick. I maintain that I am merely a scientist. I received no pleasure from this, only the pleasure of a successful experiment. My one regret is that I won't live forever to see how my labyrinth weathers the years. Perhaps Zitello will allow me an occasional glimpse from the three blazes of Fógo. If they indeed exist.*"

"Our Holy Mother and Father." Calixta slammed the book shut. "Imelda. You don't have to do this."

"But I do. There's no other way."

Still, Imelda couldn't ignore the nausea building in her stomach. Such blatant, despicable heresy—and condoned by the government. She would have to commit blasphemy if she were to save herself. Did she even have any hemp? She searched through her spinning basket, and found nothing. Then her bedside table. The same result. Finally, she took to her desk. There, in the bottom drawer, under drop spindles and skeins of corincanto, she found a small ball of hemp corincanto.

Did she have the courage to do it? Not from fear of the pain, but the flouting of Giore's commandments. This was no sacred act like the Heart Stitch. If she stitched hemp into her skin, she risked damning her soul beyond redemption. Italo may not have believed in the gods, but she did—and she feared suffering in the three blazes of Fógo under trickster Zitello's watch for eternity.

"Imelda, it's heresy," Calixta said.

"I don't believe our loving celestial parents want me to be miserable for the rest of my life."

Someone knocked on the door.

Imelda and Calixta looked at each other, then rushed to push the wings under the bed. Luckily, that morning Imelda had thought to put each wing on a blanket to make it easier to drag them back under her bed. They pulled the first one over, then pushed it as far under the bed as it could go.

"Who's there?" she asked, trying not to sound breathless.

"It's me," Primo said. "And I have a note from Calixta's captain that she's needed at the docks so they can set sail.'

"Calixta and I are saying goodbye. Give us a few minutes."

Calixta had already started pushing the other wing. Imelda helped her pull it on top of the first one.

"La Canson is about to start," Primo said.

"It can't start without me." She and Calixta struggled to get the wings all the way under the bed. Finally, Calixta dropped a blanket on the edge sticking out. Imelda shoved the books under her mattress, then opened the door.

Primo strode in then frowned as her took in her appearance. "Your hair isn't done. At least you're wearing something presentable. I'll fetch your maid. Your Imperial Highness, a góndola is waiting for you at the docks."

He walked out and called for Editta.

Calixta pulled Imelda into a tight hug. "I'll see you soon," she whispered.

"If I'm lucky," Imelda said just as quietly.

"You don't have to be lucky. You can do this. Arturo believed in you, and I do too." She kissed Imelda's cheek, squeezed her again, and left.

Imelda could hear her saying goodbye to Primo in the hallway as Editta entered.

The maid clucked her teeth. "This dress is hardly worthy of such an important event."

Primo walked back in. "There's no time for her to change. Everyone will soon be too drunk to notice anyway." He jerked his head in her direction. "Fix her hair at least." He folded his arms as Editta swept Imelda's hair over one shoulder and tied it with a ribbon.

Primo excused Editta.

"I don't want to go," Imelda said once they were alone.

"You don't have a choice. I won't have that tarnish on our family."

Always about appearances, this man. Imelda glared at him. "You're terrible."

"Because I care about our family?"

She jumped to her feet. "Because you care about nothing else! I know you made Editta send the message to Anselmo."

"You were supposed to send it days before."

"I didn't want to endanger his life! I can't imagine how much it distracted him. Is he even still alive?"

"You need to calm down."

"Don't tell me to calm down! I'm playing your stupid game, so you owe me this much: is he alive?"

Neither Primo's expression nor his posture changed. Imelda held her ground. "He is," he finally admitted in a tightly wound voice.

She slumped in relief. Anselmo was alive. He must hate her, but it didn't matter as long as he survived. And she'd find a way, somehow, to win him back. One day, when they were both free.

Primo walked over to her desk, which was littered with spinning supplies. He picked up a feather. "Planning on making another pair of wings? What, you think you'll fly away?" Outside, music began to play. A drum accompanied by a psaltery. He turned to her. "No more fooling around. Ulisse will start playing in a few minutes."

Once he did, they'd expect her to make an appearance. Outside, the music continued to build, a dulcimer and flute adding to the tune. But the melody was subdued, waiting for the main instrumentalist to join. Voices drifted up as the party grew.

"What are you holding?" Primo approached Imelda, then grunted in annoyance as he snatched the hemp corincanto from her.

No! Imelda lunged for him, but he held the ball of thread out of her reach.

"Give that back!"

"Who are you going to message? You think Lieutenant Errari will come to your rescue?"

He threw the hemp in the fire. It caught fire immediately, sending a cloud of purple smoke up the chimney.

"No!" Imelda fell to her knees. This was it. She had nothing left. That ball of hemp had been her final hope.

"Don't be so dramatic." Primo rummaged around in her wardrobe then tossed a pair of slippers at her. Imelda stared at the slippers and refused to cry in front of Primo. "Put them on!"

Ulisse began to play. Imelda shoved the slippers on. Primo took her by the arm and dragged her to the window, though she was still out of sight of the attendees on the street.

He opened the window. "She's shy," he called, and the people below laughed.

"I'll scream," she said quietly.

"Then Anselmo will die."

That's all he had to do—all he ever had to do. Threaten Anselmo's life, and she was a rope in his hands, to be used however he needed. Her body went slack, her arms drooping. He pulled her to the opening. "Now look happy," he whispered.

She gave a half-hearted smile and waved to the people below. No one would be able to tell the difference in the light from the street-lamps, not from this high. They all clapped and cheered, well on their way to drunkenness as Primo said. All the better—no one would remember if she didn't look thrilled once she joined them.

The street had been cordoned off and filled with attendees and tables of food. Dozens of people, people she'd known her whole life, here to celebrate a marriage she didn't want. They surrounded a group of musicians, with Ulisse seated at the front. The melody from his viol flew into the air, clear and haunting and beautiful. His eyes were closed as he pulled his bow across the strings, lost in the music. Soon the partygoers would demand something livelier, something to dance to, but for now, Ulisse's viol cried into the night.

Primo turned to Imelda. "Go to your betrothed, Imelda. You're getting married in the morning, and nothing will change that. It's time to stop dreaming."

CHAPTER FIFTY-ONE

Anselmo climbed the stone staircase with Nikkoforos, Rafael, and seven other soldiers. Three were left at the wooden plank bridge, more than happy to stay back where it was safe. It had taken the prince and the others more than an hour to reach the island, but they hadn't lost a single man crossing the lake. Impressive. They were equally impressed by Anselmo's discovery of the tunnels, and that he and Rafael had retrieved their clothing and gear.

"How many sirens did you kill?" Anselmo asked.

"Tonight? At least two dozen." Nikkoforos reached the top and surveyed the room. "Considerably more over the last few days."

The room was just as Rafael had described. A large opening across from the other tower and a long, nasty fall into a pit filled edge to edge with sharpened spikes. Two ropes hung on either side of the doorway, connected to some kind of pulley system.

Nikkoforos pulled one of the ropes. A short bridge swung out from the wall below the opening, then fell back. He nodded at one of the men. "Massimo, try the other." That rope lifted a bridge connected to the other tower. Together, the two bridges would cover the distance between the two towers.

"We're going to need two men on each rope, I think." Nikkoforos's gaze followed the lines of the rope-and-pulley system, then swung to Anselmo and the others. "Who wants to stay, and who wants to continue?"

"I'll stay," Massimo said quickly. Three other men volunteered as well. They took their places at the ropes and pulled, backing up until the bridges were fully raised.

Nikkoforos stepped to the edge of the bridge. "Hold fast." He ran across the bridge then turned around. "Pietro, you're next, then Reniero, Ciro, and Rafael. Anselmo you bring up the rear."

The men holding the rope grunted as the others ran across. Anselmo prepared to run.

"Wait!" one man called. He wrapped his hands in the rope. "He's huge, we need to be ready." All the men looped the rope around their hands and gripped tight. The first one nodded. "Go."

Anselmo ran across. The men cried out, and the first bridge slipped. Anselmo ran faster. The second bridge started tipping as soon as his foot hit it. His second step sent it falling faster. Anselmo jumped and landed half on the other side. Nikkoforos and Rafael helped him as the two bridges slammed against the walls.

"Rest, men," Nikkoforos called. "You'll need your strength when we come back."

Anselmo glanced down at the gap he narrowly avoided falling into. The pit between the two towers was so full of wooden spikes, there would've been no way to survive it.

When he turned around, he found himself in yet another large stone room. A set of four stairs sat on the far end, leading up to the next level. Rafael and the other three men stood in a line about a third of the way into the room. Anselmo and Nikkoforos joined them.

Somewhere in the distance, water roared as if from a waterfall.

"Where's the water?" Anselmo asked.

Nikkoforos looked around. "Probably the next obstacle. Let's focus on this first. Galbani, what have you found?"

Rafael pointed down. The floor seemed to be covered in raised stone tiles, about half a meter by half a meter. They were laid in a sixteen-by-sixteen grid reaching from one side of the room to the other, and from where Anselmo and the others stood all the way to the base of the stairs.

Rafael squatted to inspect the tiles. "Clearly we need to stand in a specific configuration. But how to figure it out?"

"And what they will do?" Nikkoforos said.

"Someone should step on the first one." Rafael stood and dusted his hands on his legs. "There's no other way to find out."

"I'll do it." Nikkoforos started to walk to the farthest left stone.

"Wait." Anselmo grabbed Nikkoforos's shoulder. He couldn't let the prince risk his life. Fleet Admiral Dandolo had made it very clear Anselmo had to keep him alive. "One of us should do it. You're the leader. No need to risk your life."

"I'm not doing it," one man said.

"You go, Errari."

Anselmo glanced at Rafael, who shrugged. "I agree with you but can't say I'm willing to volunteer."

Cowards. That was Anselmo's first thought. But he couldn't blame them. No one wanted to gamble with their lives.

"It's fine." Nikkoforos pulled free of Anselmo's hand. He stepped on the stone. A piece of the wall next to him, the same width as the stone but reaching to the ceiling, moved back.

"It's revealing a path," Anselmo said.

"All right then, we've figured out what happens when we get it right." Nikkoforos walked onto the next stone. The wall moved back into place.

A dart flew out of a hole in the right wall and landed in the prince's upper arm. He grunted in pain and quickly moved back a step. The portion of wall opened back up. "Rea cancaro." With a grimace, he pulled the dart out of his arm and dropped it. "And now we know what happens when we get it wrong."

Anselmo pulled his helmet off and scrubbed at his scalp. "How are we going to figure it out?"

"Give me a minute." Rafael's gaze was roving all over the room. "There are three gaps in the wall on the left, in line with the space between the stones. So there must be four portions of the wall. Four rows and columns of stones. We must reach a certain stone in each row. Ciro, get on the first stone in the second row."

Ciro took a step back. "No way in the three blazes."

"The first stone in each row is sure to be safe," Rafael said.

"I'm not risking it."

Anselmo shoved his helmet back on. "I'll do it." He walked onto the stone. Nothing happened. No wall movement, no dart. He pointed at the man named Ciro. "Take my place." Once Ciro stood on the stone, Anselmo stepped onto the third row's first stone. Again, nothing. A safe spot. "Pietro? You stand here." With Pietro on the stone, Anselmo stepped onto the final spot. Nothing happened again.

"Figured it out yet?" Anselmo asked Rafael.

Rafael started walking along the walls lining their portion of the room. "Give me a minute." He looked them up and down, felt along the stone. When he reached the last spot, he turned around, hands on his head, frustration on his face. "There's gotta be somethi—got it!" He pointed at the stairs. "There are four stairs. Four rows of squares.

And look at the riser on the first one. A single line carved into it. For one. The first stone."

"Three on the second," Nikkoforos said. "Two on the third. Two on the fourth."

Ciro shook his head. "I'm not going a step farther until we know that's right."

Anselmo stepped forward. The fourth portion of the wall moved back.

"Ciro, go to the third stone. Pietro, the second."

Pietro reached his spot first, sending the third portion of the wall back. Ciro walked to the third stone in his row, and the final section of wall moved. A narrow path now stretched from the front of the room to the stairs.

"Reniero? Rafael?" Nikkoforos said. Blood dripped down his arm from the wound on his arm. "You two okay with going ahead?"

"With all due respect, sir," Reniero said. "I'd rather stay behind."

"You should continue," Anselmo said to Nikkoforos. "Sir."

Nikkoforos stepped off his stone, and the first part of the wall slid back. He motioned to the Reniero to take his spot, and the wall opened again. "It's you and me, Rafael."

Anselmo's stomach clenched. Beyond those stairs, and whatever other tests lay beyond them, waited the sword. Anselmo would have to stay here while Nikkoforos or Rafael retrieved it. He'd have to watch them wield it for the rest of their time in the labyrinth. If the prince got the sword, he'd sail away with it as soon as they emerged from the labyrinth. If Rafael got the sword, he'd use it every day in front of Anselmo.

Anselmo didn't know which was worse. Both thoughts twisted him at his deepest level.

Rafael looked over to Anselmo. "Sir, I think Errari should have the opportunity to continue."

"Make him the bait," Ciro muttered.

"He deserves the chance to reach the sword." Rafael's voice was firm, full of Rafael's military upbringing.

"You're willing to forfeit this opportunity?" Nikkoforos asked.

"Without a doubt."

The prince gave a curt nod. "Take Errari's place."

Rafael reached Anselmo and gripped his shoulder. "I'd rather you have it than anyone else here," he said quietly. "No one wants it more than you. No one's endured more than you."

Anselmo nodded his thanks. He jogged across the stones and reached Nikkoforos, who waited at the base of the stairs. AT the top of those, there was another, much taller set of stairs in a U-shape from the first. Water rushed down a channel on the side of the stairs and dumped out of a hole in the wall out of the tower. Despite the channel, the steps were wet. Anselmo and Nikkoforos tread carefully as the roar of water echoed down the staircase.

They reached the top, a small room with water gushing out of a tunnel in the wall into a small pool, which drained into the channel down the stairs. There were no doors, and the only windows were arrow slits too narrow for a man to fit through. The only exits were the stairs and the tunnel.

Everything was wet. It didn't take long for Anselmo's arms, face, tunic, and legs to get covered in droplets. He wiped his eyes as he scanned the room for something, some kind of clue.

"Over there." Nikkoforos pointed at a horizontal, elongated hole in the wall to the right.

Anselmo didn't bother stepping around puddles as he walked over. His boots were already soaked.

The hole was pointed on one end, with a slightly larger blunt edge on the other. A large circle was cut into the wall around it. Nikkoforos ran his fingers along the edges of the hole, peered inside and paused to think.

"Does this shape look familiar?" he asked.

Anselmo inspected it again. Something about it tickled his memory, but he couldn't say what it was exactly.

Nikkoforos unsheathed his sword. "I think ..." He pushed the blade in. From deep in the wall, something clicked. They both looked at the tunnel, but the water didn't stop. Anselmo sighed.

"There's got to be something else." Nikkoforos tried pulling his sword out, but it was stuck in the wall. "You've got to be kidding me." He tried again, and again, clearly pulling harder each time, but the sword wouldn't budge.

"Try twisting it." Anselmo pointed at the circle around the sword.

The prince took the sword handle in both hands. Slowly, the stone circle spun until the sword blade was vertical.

The water in the tunnel slowed, then stopped.

Anselmo stepped to the base of the tunnel. At the top, the sword sat on a pedestal.

His heart leapt.

"It's up there." He couldn't keep the excitement out of his voice.

"Go. And hurry." Nikkoforos's teeth were clenched from the effort of holding the sword in place.

The climb up the tunnel took longer than Anselmo expected. The fit was tight, and water covered every surface. He slipped more than once, one time losing two meters of progress. But finally he pulled himself out of the confines of the tunnel and tumbled into water in the final room.

The room was small and simple. Another tunnel—this one closed but leaking water around the edges—sat on the other side. No windows on the walls, only torches. The only sound was the crackle of the torches and water dripping from the closed tunnel. The tunnel he had climbed up was half a meter off the ground. Water covered the ground, and the air sat damp on his skin. In the middle of the room, steps led to a tall pedestal that held the sword in a sleek leather sheath with silver accents on the tip.

Anselmo approached the pedestal, his feet sloshing through the water. The hilt of the sword was shaped like a lion's head with a sapphire embedded in the eye, as brilliant a blue as the coats of the Lions. The gem glittered in the torchlight.

Anselmo reached toward the sword. Was this real? Had he finally reached the end? His heart beat against his ribs like a war galley ramming into an enemy ship. Fire burned in his belly, and his ears rang. Everything faded from view as he gently picked up the sword.

It was his.

Finally.

The moment he'd worked toward his entire life.

The sword had a good weight to it. He unsheathed it and swung it. It was perfectly balanced as it cut through the air. He rubbed his thumb crosswise against the deadly blade. With the recurved shape and the hair-thin edge, this was a monster cleaver. No minotaurs would stand in his way, let alone human enemies. Anselmo would carve his way to history with this weapon.

He sheathed the sword then slung it over his body. It clunked next to his other sword, the one he'd thought so fine when Ulisse had given it to him only a week ago.

Ulisse. Imelda's new husband.

No, it didn't matter. It couldn't, not anymore. She was gone, and Anselmo had his consolation prize.

And what a consolation it was.

The sound of grinding stone filled the room. The center of the pedestal descended into a hole. Anselmo backed up and stepped onto something soft, something that hissed. He saw the snake too late. Black with green diamonds on its back, the jade mamba was already coiling to attack. Anselmo jumped away, but the mamba was quicker. It bit his heel, its long fangs piercing the soft leather of his boots, piercing the soft skin on his foot. The pain was sharp and exact, as strong as a knife. It didn't take long for the poison to burn through his veins.

First his bones shifted. He could feel them lose their symmetry, their density. His right hip joint made a sickening noise as his femur turned, and he fell into the water with a splash. His nose popped out of place. Anselmo groaned and held his face as the poison continued through his body. He tried to stand, but his muscles quivered. His stomach roiled. And worst of all, nothing healed itself. His body had lost all of its unique advantages.

The jade mamba had recoiled and seemed to be preparing itself for another strike. With an arm that weighed as heavy as an anchor, Anselmo unsheathed the sword and cut the snake's head off. Anselmo felt like he was moving through mud, but the sword sliced through the snake easily. Then the muscles in his arm failed him, and he collapsed onto the stone steps. His head hit the side of the pedestal, and everything went black.

Chapter Fifty-Two

The moon lazed above, bigger and brighter than normal. Its light danced across the surface of the highest Acqua Alta Imelda had seen in a decade, taunting her. Across the bridge, the tide spilled onto the next island. She'd been fine while on Centro and Riga, but once she stepped off this bridge, she'd have to wade through frigid water. It would get deeper with each island she crossed, until she reached Porto, where Calixta's ship might be waiting—if she were lucky. It was a gamble, but one she couldn't afford not to take. It was close to two in the morning. Perhaps Calixta had been able to convince the ship's captain to tarry a bit longer. Imelda's alpaca corincanto would help, but this much cold would completely overpower its effect on any submerged body parts. She wriggled her toes, anticipating the icy trek. All because of Primo.

But she wouldn't turn back. Anything was better than surrendering to Primo and marrying his lackey. She crossed the bridge and stepped down on the other side. The freezing water made her gasp as it soaked and filled her shoes. Her feet immediately began to ache. She'd have to hurry to avoid frostbite. If she could.

Four islands to traverse, with descending heights. The first only allowed enough water to cover her shoes. She held her dress up, but water splashed as she hurried. Frigid droplets flew onto her arms and face. She probably looked ridiculous, but at this gods-forsaken hour during Acqua Alta, the highest tide of the year, no one would see her. When she crossed onto the next island, the water rose to her shins. She started shivering; the alpaca corincanto was losing its effect on the rest of her body as well. She hitched her skirt up higher, then slung it over one arm. Her teeth chattered as she reached the third island and sunk past her knees. Her legs were frozen, but she'd started to sweat from the exertion. Her dress was heavy, and walking through the deep water made her labor more than she ever had. By the fourth island, she began to stumble. But she couldn't stop. There was no way she could go back. If ever there was a time to fly, this was it.

Finally the bridge to Porto came into view. Flickering streetlamps stood guard at either end of the marble bridge. This was the one meant for visiting dignitaries. At the base on the island she currently stood on, there was a góndola station with boats lined up, waiting for the morning's patrons. One man sat in an elevated hut at the servizio góndola, rubbing his hands in front of a small fire that flickered on the walls. Imelda slowed to pass silently by him. As silently as she could; it was impossible not to splash a bit, especially with the clumsiness of frozen feet.

She started up the bridge, and stopped. Two soldiers stood at the bottom. Deep in conversation, or else they would've heard her. She ducked down before they could spot her. Her gaze roved along the line of masts. None waved the red and gold flag of Ilios. Maybe they had docked further south. She crept along the canal, to the south bridge. Her legs trembled as she walked along the edge of the island. It would be wiser to go up a street so she could remain out of sight, but her muscles burned at the idea.

The southern bridge, plain and wide for hauling goods, was also guarded by two soldiers at its base. She climbed to the top of the bridge, staying low. Her body tingled as it rose from the icy water. Again, she searched the masts. Calixta's ship was not there. She looked out to sea. The full moon illuminated the lagoon. There was Calixta's ship, almost to the barrier islands. They'd gone, leaving her to her dreaded wedding and future.

She took a deep breath and walked back down the bridge. Tears burned in her eyes as she sank into the water, her dress pooling around her. There was nothing left. She could still swim to Porto, find some ship, any ship, to board. But her dress had doubled in weight from the water it had soaked up. She could strip down to her underclothes, but the cold had sunk into her brain. If she stepped into that canal, she'd succumb to her exhaustion and drown.

Her teeth chattered, and she shivered as the heat from her exertion left her. The sweat on her face mixed with the droplets that had splashed onto her cheeks. At least she'd tried. She hadn't let her ship sink without bailing it out with all she had.

She started back. Each island was higher, but the trek was harder. She crossed onto Riga, and finally the water was gone. Her slippers sloshed as she walked the empty streets. She dropped her skirt, and it dragged across the cobblestones, catching dirt and rocks. The hem would be black with mud by the time she returned to the palàso. Editta would cluck and fret over the ruined dress, but what did it matter? Imelda was marching to her future, marriage with Primo's ally and life without her wings, alone in a foreign city.

She walked to her home, Cax' Albizzi, and stared at the curtained windows. It had only been a month since Pàre had died. Her life had been completely ruined. She knelt there in the street, dress soaked to her waist, hair plastered on her face. She couldn't go back to the palàso. The sun would rise, her maids would come to ready her for the wedding, and she wouldn't be there. It wouldn't take long for Primo to find her, but staying here would be her last moment of defiance. It was all she had left.

She put a hand to her chest, over the Heart Stitch.

"I'm sorry, Anselmo," she whispered. This, more than anything, solidified her defeat. She'd never feel his arms around her. Never kiss his lips, look into his eyes, give herself to him again. It would haunt her for the rest of her life. No matter what the future held, she'd never remove the stitches. She'd never cut that tie to him. Ulisse would surely hate it, but he couldn't make her. It wasn't heresy, after all, just a glaring reminder of the price she'd paid to be his bride. With luck, he'd fall in love with her, even as she remained bonded to another man through life and into the eternities.

This was also her last chance to see her home. She walked in through a side door and up the servants' staircase. She longed to see the whole house, but didn't dare drag her muddy dress all over the fine rugs and clean wood floors. When she reached the second floor, she removed her slippers and held up her skirt. She went into her room, stripped her ruined dress off, and pulled on a nightgown.

Have I lost everything? Imelda looked around the room, at her ash-strewn hearth, at her desk littered with spinning supplies and skeins of corincanto, at her bed still mussed from her last night with Anselmo. She realized she was shivering, and pulled the bedspread off and wrapped herself in it. She trudged over to sit at her desk. Mindlessly, she picked at the contents then paused. Half a skein of spirit rose corincanto sat beside her basket of sewing supplies. The unused spirit rose from the heart stitch with Anselmo.

Imelda was bonded to Anselmo with spirit rose. She was bonded to the gods also, as all children were when they turned eight. Italo, in his journals, had spoken of bonding oneself to objects using hemp, but

Primo had taken her hemp. Now she had over a meter of spirit rose, which bonded as well as hemp.

Anselmo's presence disappeared from her mind, and she gasped. She clutched her heart as she sat upright. Had he died? What in Rea's holy name was happening? She held her breath, closed her eyes, and frantically searched her thoughts. The only sound was her breathing, quick and shallow. She refused to cry, refused to give up on him. *Anselmo*, she prayed. *Anselmo, you have to live.*

His presence flickered back into life, greatly weakened but unmistakably there. Whatever had happened, he was still alive.

She lifted the spirit-rose corincanto to her lips and kissed it.

Anselmo was still fighting. And so was Imelda.

CHAPTER FIFTY-THREE

"Anselmo! Are you okay?"

Nikkoforos's voice echoed up the tunnel. Anselmo forced his eyes open. They felt full of salt. His vision tilted and twisted. His ears rang. His head ached. He was lying on his back on the stairs, head floating in the water.

"Anselmo!"

"I'm fine." The words came out like a whispered croak. Anselmo took a drink from the water around him to clear his throat. "I'm fine." His voice wavered, but there was some strength in it.

"Look at you." It was Anselmo's mother's voice, her tone holding nothing but contempt. He turned around. She stood in front of the tunnel.

"How are you here?"

Her lip curled. "So weak."

"The snake …" He searched the water for his sword. "It's not my fault."

She rushed over and held a knife to his throat. Her body moved as if smoke, and yet he could feel the blade against his neck. "An enemy won't see fault! They only see weakness. Your weakness!"

He pulled himself to his feet, then stumbled back to his hands and knees and vomited. Water, bile, digested hard tack. There was nothing else in his stomach. He heaved again, his abdominals clenching, bitterness filling his throat.

The fire from the poison had made its way through his veins. Every centimeter of his body burned.

"Anselmo! I can't hold much longer!" Whose voice was that? A man. Familiar, and yet not.

Anselmo's mother circled him, arms behind her back. Her image flitted ahead a few steps, then back. Then there were two of her.

"I see the way you look at Imelda Albizzi," her two ghosts said. "She will never love you. Not as weak as you are. Strength is all that matters!" She came at him in a literal blur, flipping him onto his back before he could put his quivering arms up. For a moment, he was completely submerged. He choked on water, willing his hands to find the ground and push himself up.

His mother grabbed him by his tunic and pulled him up. She slapped his face. "You disgust me! Do better! Be better!" She continued to slap him over and over and over. He covered his head with his arms, but she jerked them away. He started to sob. It was awful when she got into these moods. How many times had he endured them? How many more would she put him through?

"I'm making you stronger!" Slap.

"You must have a better life than I did!" Slap.

"You'll be nothing like your father!" Slap.

"Anselmo!" The man's voice cut through his mother's image like a knife, and she disappeared.

Anselmo sat up. His mother appeared in front of the tunnel. Her face elongated and her body stretched until her head reached the ceiling high above. Then she snapped back to her normal shape. A snake's headless body floated beside him. Black with green diamonds on its back. A jade mamba. He recoiled from the serpent.

Wait. It was headless. It had bitten him.

His brain grew muddy as he tried to remember what had happened. He'd reached the sword. He'd grabbed it, and the snake had bitten him.

"This isn't real." He muttered the words, too afraid to look at his mother.

She appeared in his face and shook him. "Poverty is real! Hunger and cold are your reality until you make something of yourself."

"You're dead." He pushed her away. "You can't hurt me anymore."

"I'm making you strong. Everything I do is for your benefit. Everything I do is because I love you."

The plaintive tone of her voice made a sob clutch his throat. She'd meant it. Every time. And he'd believed her. She had made him strong. But had she needed to be so brutal? Like the nights she'd denied him dinner and made him sleep outside with only a thin blanket, so he could experience homelessness.

Would he be the same if she'd hadn't done those things?

Those questions didn't matter.

Strength was the only thing that mattered right now.

Above all else, he had to be strong. His mother hadn't been wrong about that.

He walked through her. The fire in his leg had taken over his torso, grown down his arms. His brain burned. His vision doubled and twisted. Every step was eternal agony. His mother followed him as he fell down the tunnel, assuring him over and over how much she loved him. She was crying now, begging for his understanding, begging for his forgiveness.

He tumbled into the room where Nikkoforos waited. The prince released his sword in the wall and rushed over to help him stand. Anselmo's whole body shook. He could barely stand.

"What happened? You've got two black eyes." Nikkoforos dragged Anselmo away from the tunnel as water began to trickle down it. "Who were you talking to up there?"

Anselmo wiped at his face. "I can't."

"Can't what?" Nikkoforos was solid, unlike Anselmo's mother, who still crying behind him. "What in the three blazes are you talking about?"

"Can't tell you." Every word was punctuated by a breath. His lungs were on fire. He was burning alive. "But I have to."

Anselmo's mother screamed. She split into two, four, eight bodies, continued splitting until her copies filled the room. Her scream bounced off the walls and inside Anselmo's head.

Anselmo squeezed his eyes shut. "A snake. A jade mamba. Bit me." Great, gulping breaths punctuated each statement. He could barely hear his own voice through his mother's shrieks.

Then his mother disappeared.

Nikkoforos went still. For a moment, there was only the sound of water pouring out of the tunnel. Then Anselmo noticed a distant roaring of beasts. Nikkoforos went to a window. "The lake shore is crawling with minotaurs. Looks like the lake has filled with sirens again." He stayed at the window, watching the scene outside. It felt like an eternity before he walked back to Anselmo. "You have threads."

"I do." Anselmo wavered. He was going to vomit again. He was going to pass out. No, he had to be strong. He had to beat this poison in his body.

"Anselmo." Nikkoforos gave Anselmo a shake. "Listen to me."

Anselmo's eyes rolled as the room spun.

Nikkoforos shook him again. "Look at me."

Anselmo put all of his strength into focusing on the prince.

"You can beat this. You're stronger than anyone I've ever known. But you're going to have to listen to me to survive."

Was Anselmo strong? Stronger than the venom making its way through his body, dismantling all of his advantages from his corincanto? Strong without his threads? Strong without his mother?

Moonlight poured through a window high above. The moon was huge—the largest Anselmo had seen in ten years. Since that night he endured one of the worst experiences a person could endure.

His mother appeared next to him, her fingers on his brow again, smoothing his hair off his sweaty skin. "This will make you strong." Her voice was sorrowful, but firm.

"You betrayed me," he said to her.

Everything in him revolted at the idea. When she died, they'd dumped her body off the shores of Sordo, with only one line of linen corincanto—all he'd been able to afford. But had Rea even taken her to Cielo? Or had she been damned, sunken to Fógo to endure eternal torment under Zitello's watch? At least Anselmo's torture had ended. She'd committed heresy to help him.

But no, she'd committed egregious sins long before that. Every time she slapped him in the name of love, every time she made him practice with bruised ribs and bleeding lips, every time she'd belittled him, she'd sinned.

"Everything I do is because I love you!" She raised her hand as if to hit him.

Her arm swung.

He caught her wrist.

"You tried to break me! That isn't love."

"Anselmo ..." Nikkoforos said, though he kept his distance.

But she hadn't broken Anselmo. He had already been strong, without her. He couldn't have endured her cruel parenting otherwise.

He planted his feet firmly on the stone. His muscles might not have wool strengthening them, but they were still strong. He'd trained his body for a decade, building endurance and strength to underlay the threads. His bones were dense from the weight of armor. And he could fight with open wounds. He'd endured a cut to the femoral artery and had survived.

That night, ten years ago, had strengthened him. By the threads, yes. But also the experience. In his boyish naivete ten years ago, he thought his threads would be the only cause of his strength. But his whole life had strengthened him. He'd honed his skills and weathered his mother's lessons and carried the weight of society's attempts to push him down.

His mother hadn't been the source of his strength. She'd been dead for eight years, and yet he'd only grown stronger without her. He'd worked at the saltern, served as fodder in the military, practiced for hours after the other soldiers went to bed. All to make him strong. Pain made him stronger. The venom burning in his veins didn't weaken him. It refined him.

"I love you!" Anselmo's mother appeared in front of him and screamed. But she didn't hit him. Not anymore.

"You don't know what love is." He took a step toward the stairs, and his knee buckled. He forced every quivering muscle in his body to hold. Then he took another step, his legs firm. He walked through her, and left her behind.

"That's the pain-in-the-ass Errari I know." Nikkoforos's eyes flicked to where Anselmo had been looking, but he didn't say anything about Anselmo talking to the air moments ago. "We have to hide the snake bite from everyone. No one else can find out."

Anselmo walked toward the stairs.

"Wait," Nikkoforos said. "I need a sword. Give me your old one."

Anselmo went to unsheathe his sword, then stopped. He removed the Lion sword sheath and flipped it around to offer it hilt-first to Nikkoforos. His knees threatened to buckle again, and his hand trembled.

The prince shook his head. "You deserve it."

"I'd be useless with it right now." Anselmo shoved the sheathed sword at Nikkoforos's chest. Everything in him demanded to pull it back, to rescind the offer, to sling it across his body and wield it through the labyrinth. He clenched his teeth. "You need the best weapon available to get us out of here, especially with me as dead weight."

Nikkoforos accepted the sword. He whistled as he swung it once. "This is as fine a blade as any I've ever held. Finer, even." He gripped Anselmo's shoulder. "I know what this means to you."

Anselmo's throat tightened as he swallowed the disappointment. "Let's get off of this Giore-forsaken island."

Chapter Fifty-Four

Venezia sat by her window all night, a letter in her hand. Alessia had delivered it around nine. It contained a simple message: *"He ate four quail breasts. She had one."* Four—what a greedy boy. But Venezia had accounted for Lazaro's glutton, and had bought eight. Eight poisoned quail breasts. The birds had been fed hemlock seeds prior to being butchered. Four breasts were lethal, but death would come slowly. It would take days for him to die. One week ago, she would've been fine killing him so passively, but learning about his scheme with Primo made Venezia crave something more active.

She'd bought his favorite meal and wine. Apparently he'd suspected the wine. He'd had Kari drink it first, and once she didn't die, he'd eaten with gusto. He knew Venezia was coming for him, but his suspicions hadn't saved him. He ate four breasts—*four!*—drank his wine, and slept with his slave.

Venezia had dined in her room, a simple meal of salumi and hard cheese, then waited. Alessia had delivered the message, received instructions to dispose of the extra poisoned quail, and gone to the kitchen to wait. Venezia would give her a hefty raise once the ordeal was over. Alessia had worked for the Dandolos since Venezia's wedding day. She'd watched the marriage evolve—or, rather, devolve—and had comforted Venezia often in the beginning. She would never tell—especially once she was thousands of ducats richer.

Venezia dozed off around midnight. She'd taken a nap before dinner, half out of preparation for her long night and half out of exhaustion from her convulsions the day before. Alessia woke her when the temple bell rang four in the morning. Surely the poison had taken effect by now. Venezia stretched tired, stiff muscles, grabbed two coils of rope, then went to Lazaro's room.

His fire had burned down to the embers. The glow was the only light in the room, but it was enough. Kari and Lazaro both slept in his oversize bed, Lazaro snoring loudly.

Alessia shook Kari. The girl woke, her eyes sluggish. She was obviously drugged. As Alessia pulled her to her feet, she noticed Venezia and the rope in her hands.

"Are you going to kill him?" the girl whispered.

"I am. And I'm framing it on you. Unless you want to rot in jail for the rest of your life, you'll go with Alessia right now."

"Let me help you."

Venezia apprised the girl. Kari was clearly trying to appear confident, with her shoulders held back and her hands in fists. But her posture kept slipping, goose bumps covered her nude body, bruises dotted her wrists and ankles, and her chin trembled. Venezia's gaze flicked to the tattoos on Kari's arm. She'd been no older than twelve when she received them. Only a girl.

"You're a fighter," Venezia said.

"I was training to be, once. I'd like to continue one day."

Venezia nodded. Why shouldn't Kari want Lazaro dead? She'd put up with his abuses for months now. Not as long as Venezia, but she deserved some catharsis.

"Fine. Help me tie him up, then go with Alessia."

"I want to watch."

"No." This was Venezia's moment, Venezia's victory. She'd let the girl help her, but she'd perform the deed alone. Just her and Lazaro, like those eight long years, though this time she'd be the conqueror and he the conquest.

Venezia gave Kari a coil of rope, then approached Lazaro. With so much of the poison, he'd be substantially weakened. But she could take no chances, in case the poison wasn't as potent as she anticipated. Kari tied his ankles to the foot board. He woke as Venezia looped the rope around his wrist, but in the dark, he couldn't tell who restrained him.

"It's about time you took some initiative, you dirty girl," he slurred.

Venezia checked the knots. Kari and Alessia left, closing the door behind them. Venezia climbed on top of Lazaro, straddling his hips.

He chuckled lecherously. "No blindfold?" He groaned and winced. "Maybe we should wait until morning. I feel awful."

"No blindfold for you tonight, Lazaro. I want you to see my face when I kill you."

He snapped to attention at Venezia's voice. She lit the candle on the nightstand, and Lazaro hissed as he pulled weakly at the ropes. He could barely move his limbs, so he jerked his head back and forth. Venezia held it still with one hand, and unsheathed her belt knife with the other.

His eyes cut to the other side of the bed. "What, you killed her first and now you're here to finish the job?"

"Kari's fine. She actually helped me tie you up. Isn't that funny, that the two women to share your bed in the last few months couldn't wait to kill you?" She leaned close, trailing a finger along his face. "I told you this wouldn't end until you were rotting in Fógo. I'm sick of waiting for you to die."

Lazaro's face flushed as he prepared for a verbal assault, but he started choking instead. Venezia rolled his head to the side, and he vomited on his arm.

"Look at the mighty Doxe Lazaro Dandolo." She wiped his mouth with a corner of his blanket then turned his face back to her. "Did you ever imagine your end would come at my hands?"

She considered her knife, watching the blade reflect the candle flame. "Recognize this? Primo gave it to me when he appointed me Fleet Admiral. It's technically ceremonial, but I have no use for ornaments so I sharpened it. Everything is a tool, even this pretty thing."

He somehow mustered the strength to spit on her face.

She wiped the vomit-flecked spit off and flicked it into his eyes. "The moment you snuck into my bed weeks ago, I started dreaming of your death. Poison was the obvious choice, but it's too passive. I *did* poison you, and you would eventually die from it. You ate far too much of that quail to survive for more than a week. But I crave violence." She pushed the knife against his throat. It nicked the skin, and a droplet of blood seeped out. "Starting in the military as vice admiral, I never did fight in battle. I've always wondered what it's like to kill a man. I've always wondered if I could actually do it."

He tried to pull his head free, but he'd grown far too weak.

She smiled. "The best part of hemlock is your mind will stay sharp the entire time. You'll suffer for as long as I make you. Now, how to do it? I'm tempted to remove your favorite toy first." She shifted her position so she could push the tip of her blade against his groin.

"Help!" Lazaro yelled.

Venezia slapped him. She leaned close, knife against his cheek. "No one's here. No one who cares about you, that is. Your wealth may pay their wages, but they've watched what you've done to me over the years. They're loyal to me. No one in this house will mourn your loss."

Tears dropped onto his face. She wiped at her eyes—they were hers. When had she began crying? She cut a path across his cheek. Blood seeped out, mixing with her tears. "You made me do this. You sealed your fate. Every time you forced your way into my bed and into my body, you brought your death ever closer."

Lazaro struggled again, but his strength was fading. Drool leaked out of his mouth. Pathetic. She was done toying with him. Her chest shuddered with a sob that threatened to break through. He deserved this justice, and she deserved to measure it out. She brought the blade to his eye. Her fingers didn't shake, and her resolve didn't crumble.

"I could've loved you," she said as the knife went in. His eye deflated. Lazaro jerked and screamed in pain as Venezia drove the blade in inch by inch. Blood and fluid oozed across his skin, into his hair, and onto her hand keeping his head still. "I wanted to. But you broke me. So I will destroy you."

Movement caught her eye. Kari watched from a crack in the door. Venezia didn't say anything, just turned back to her work. Lazaro's arms and legs jerked against their restraints. His other eye squeezed shut against the pain, tears seeping out. He gnashed his teeth and yelled, but she held his head firm. The knife sunk in several inches, and still he lived. She'd heard that could that happen, that a person could survive an injury like this. Venezia could continue to make him suffer, leave him there until he bled out or the poison took him, whichever came first. But she was tired of his existence. It was time to wipe Lazaro Dandolo from this life.

The blade hit the back of his skull. With a deft twist, she turned the blade, ripping wide the hole in his brain. Lazaro's body gave one last jerk, and went still.

Chapter Fifty-Five

Imelda rubbed her tired eyes. Even with wool corincanto in her nightgown, fatigue tugged at every inch of her body, every muscle and every joint. Immediately upon returning to the palàso, she'd pulled out her spirit rose corincanto and started sewing. She completed the first wing and stood, arching her back to ease the ache that permeated her bones. It didn't help.

The sky was lightening in the west when Editta arrived to help her dress. Donatella would undoubtedly arrive soon—after so much work, she wouldn't want to miss any of Imelda's preparations.

Editta paused when she saw the wings. "When did you fix these?"

"The last few days."

"You managed to hide them from me all this time? Pardon my impertinence, but that was clever. And they are beautiful." Editta smiled as she pulled the curtains open, and the room brightened. She moved Imelda's chair over to the second wing. "Mè siora, can I sew for you?"

"I have to do it myself."

Editta lifted her eyebrows. But as a maid, she couldn't say anything.

Imelda sat and retrieved her needle. With shaky hands, she threaded it with the remaining spirit rose. The corincanto looked like a vein hanging from the needle's eye.

A house bell rang in the distance. "I'll see what that is, mè siora."

"Open the balcony doors first," Imelda said.

Editta did as instructed then left. Rays from the rising sun spilled across the wings, illuminating them in golden hues. Even though the light was soft, the feathers looked sharp enough to cut her finger. Sharp enough to cut herself free from Primo's net. Sharp enough, perhaps, to cut the chains that bound Anselmo. She'd send him a message explaining everything, and they would be together.

Sewing the spirit rose wasn't easy—ideally, it would be done before the feathers. She lifted the feathers one by one and sewed the corincanto in one-handed. It needed to be in the leather directly as the movement would come from there. Italo's journal said the number of stitches was important, and for a proper connection between the mind and the object, she needed at least twenty on each side—fifteen in the object, and five in her skin. Imelda had enough thread for that many stitches, and no more. It felt divine, the way it worked out. Twenty was even an auspicious number—it was the number of days it took Giatoro and Ioanna to travel from Sacresta to the swamps where they founded Rialto.

Imelda's hope lifted with every stitch. They might not work—there was no telling until she tried—but she couldn't give up. She wouldn't.

Donatella entered, followed by Editta. Donatella *tsk*ed. "Why are you sewing? It's time to get dressed. Were you up all night?" She sighed and rubbed Imelda's back. "I didn't sleep much before my wedding either. That's why we put silk corincanto in our wedding dresses."

Imelda didn't look up. If she were well-rested, she could've sewn much faster. She moved painfully slowly, and her line was anything but straight. But the stitches were tight.

"Were these Art—" Donatella flinched. "Are they supposed to fly?"

"No." The lie came so easily. "And yes, they were Arturo's. I want to wear them with my wedding dress."

Donatella pursed her lips, no doubt thinking it macabre to wear the wings that killed Arturo. "They look beautiful. Now come on."

Imelda poked herself with the needle and sucked her breath in. Not the first time she'd done that. Blood seeped out of the prick and dripped onto a feather. Crimson seeped along the vane, down to the edge, making it look like a knife recently used. "The wedding isn't for an hour. It won't take that long to get dressed."

"But we have to do your hair, and you're not getting married without some kohl around your eyes and color on your lips and cheeks. Especially with how exhausted you look." Donatella paused. "Don't make me get Primo."

"Oh no, don't do that," Imelda said flatly.

Donatella left the room, returning with Primo minutes later. Imelda had fifteen stitches left. Her eyesight blurred.

"It's time to get ready," Primo said in his best Doxe voice.

"The wedding's not going to start without me."

Donatella made an exasperated sound.

"mè carina," Primo said softer to Donatella, "why don't you go get ready? I'll ensure Imelda gets her dress on, and she'll be waiting for you to do her hair when you get back."

It was a shame to annoy her cousin-in-law like this, especially when this was the last time Imelda would see her. Donatella had poured her heart into Imelda's wedding, and Imelda wouldn't even get to tell her how much she appreciated it. Not if she were going to fly away. If she *could* fly away ...

Donatella sighed, and Primo kissed her cheek. "You better have that dress on," she threatened at the door.

Imelda smiled. "I will. Promise."

Donatella disappeared. Imelda's smile did as well, replaced by a glare for Primo before she returned to her sewing.

"Siora Imelda looks hungry," Primo said to Editta. "Fetch her some breakfast." He moved closer to Imelda. He was already fully dressed—dark gray doublet, tailored black pants, freshly polished shoes. "How did this happen?" He waved at the mended wings.

"Magic." She poked her finger *again*. "Giore cancaro."

"Watch your language."

"Or what? You'll spank me like a naughty child?" Ten stitches left. She tried to urge her hands to work faster. but her fingers were clumsy from the lack of sleep. "Don't worry—they won't work. I just want to have a piece of Arturo with me at my wedding."

He rubbed his temple. "Fine. But hurry."

"Yes, Your Serenity." Eight stitches. She had to keep him talking. "Did you marry Donatella for political gain as well?"

"That's the way the world works, Imelda. We do what we can to benefit our families."

"So you lie to her every day and tell her you love her?"

"I do love her. She's given me two beautiful children, and has been a faithful companion for fourteen years. But you're right—I'm not in love with her." Imelda faltered and looked up. He stood over her, as if supervising her work. He looked tired.

"And then you'll marry your children off for more selfish reasons," she said.

"Selfish!" He paused, taking a deep breath to calm himself. "I found you the best man I know. I want you to be happy. I know you don't believe me, but it's true."

"If you wanted me to be happy, you wouldn't treat my life like one of your political games." Five stitches left. She found her last reserve of strength, and her work surged. "I don't believe anyone in this family. Even Venezia has shown her own traitorous heart." Primo reached for the wings, and Imelda jerked them away. "Don't you dare touch these. I won't have you soil my last memento of him."

The fatigue disappeared from his face, replaced with impatience as his jaw tensed and his eyes narrowed. "Then get your dress on."

"I don't want to marry that greedy king."

"Ulisse is anything but greedy! He takes care of his kingdom. In fact, he's incredibly humble to put up with ignorant opinions like your own."

"Humble! You're blind."

"And you're paranoid. You're as crazy as your mother."

How dare he. How dare he! She jumped to her feet. "If she was crazy, it's because you drove her to it!" she yelled in his face. "I know the stories. Of course I do. There she was, twin babies and two other sons besides, and you came to live with her and made her bail you out of all your trouble. You may not have pushed her into the canal, but your hand was in her death all the same!"

"And I've carried that guilt ever since!"

She took a step back as he scrubbed his face.

"You think I don't know what I did to her?" Primo said, voice hoarse. "Giulia was more of a mother to me than my own. She'd always provided a second home when I needed it. And when my father's hand became too heavy, when my dear mare wouldn't stop him, Giulia let me live with your family. She put up with my terrible choices and bad influence on your brothers, and loved me despite all that. I don't need you to tell me I killed her, because I face that knowledge every day."

"Then why did you move back home after her death?"

"I finally saw the consequences of my behavior. I returned to my relentless father and my bedridden mother and straightened up. And I wouldn't be Doxe today if I hadn't."

Relentless. Heavy-handed. Imelda gasped. "Your father hit you?" She couldn't imagine it. Giovanni was her father's brother, and true, they weren't similar men, but Pàre would've never hurt them. How could two siblings be so different?

A muscle in Primo's jaw tensed. "He always said weak men don't win the Doxe seat."

"But strong men marry off their cousins for political gain?"

"I will gain nothing from this marriage. Eraclea is already Rialto's ally, and Ulisse is my close friend. I mean it when I say I only chose him because he's a good man."

"And you expect me to believe you."

"I expect you to obey."

"That's your problem!" She gripped the needle, and it jabbed her palm. She grunted from the pain. "You're not my father or even my uncle! You're only my cousin, and you think I belong to you. You think everything belongs to you! I am not a commodity to be traded however you wish! Fine, let's say Ulisse's not greedy. But you are. Greedy for whatever power you can hoard. You're nothing but a loathsome tyrant."

"And you are a spoiled, ungrateful child!"

Imelda sat and finished the last stitch. Fifteen on this wing, Fifteen on the other, with a long tail of thread off each.

"Stop it with these already!" He made to grab them again.

She slapped his hand away, then stood to push his chest. It didn't move him, but it stopped him.

"I hate you." Her voice was cold and sharp. "More than I could ever express."

"I'm coming to feel the same way about you."

"Don't worry; soon I will be in the north and we can hate each other from afar."

Editta came in holding a tray a food. Primo composed himself, at least outwardly. But his movements contained a strained anger as he sat and intertwined his fingers together.

"Why put on the show?" Imelda said. "Editta knows how controlling you are. You did command her to send the message to Anselmo, after all."

"Put your gods-forsaken dress on, Imelda."

"Fine," she said. He didn't stand. "Are you staying?"

"Apparently that's the only way to ensure you'll actually do it," Primo said through clenched teeth.

Editta warily looked between the two of them before setting the tray of food on the desk and pulling the dress out of the wardrobe.

"Help me with these," Imelda said to the maid, tugging on the blanket that held one of the wings.

"Are you really going to wear those atrocities?" Primo demanded. "What will Ulisse think?"

"He's the one who brought them to me." She jerked on the blanket again. She'd been able to get them under the bed so many times the past few days, but she hadn't been this exhausted. Her arms held no strength. "You've asked everything of me. At least give me this."

Primo muttered, "Spoiled," as he waved his hand.

Imelda and Editta dragged the wings over to the screen. Imelda changed into her dress—with Editta's help, since it weighed at least four kilograms—and sighed. It was absolutely beautiful. The violet silk shimmered in the early morning light, and the red corincanto embroidery looped and twirled in elegant lines around the stitched pomegranates. Donatella had created a work of art, and Imelda was going to ruin it. She had no other choice.

Editta held out the wings' harness so Imelda could put them on. Imelda had modified the design to accommodate a dress. No straps between her legs, which meant the ones around her waist and arms were extra tight. Her breath was shallow as Editta stepped away. Imelda started tilting, and Editta helped her lean forward against the wall to counteract the massive weight on her back. Imelda took her needle and braced herself.

"Mè siora, what are you doing?" Editta whispered, her face aghast.

"It's spirit rose. So it's okay." Imelda tried to sound as confident as she'd felt that morning. "Please. It will make up for sending that hemp message."

Editta blanched. Imelda nearly flinched herself. Resorting to manipulation—she was almost as bad as Venezia.

Editta sucked her breath in and nodded.

"What?" Primo said.

Imelda held a finger to her lips.

Editta grimaced, but nodded. "She looks beautiful, Your Serenity."

Imelda's hand hovered over her chest. Having Anselmo sew corincanto into her skin was one thing. But to sew into her own chest would be different. There was no heady passion to fuel her, only desperation. She cut herself every time she spun, but a quick slice and continuous stitching were vastly different. Imelda threaded the needle with the spirit rose from the right wing, and plunged it into her skin beneath the dress's neckline. Pain flared in her chest, sharper than the Heart

Stitch had been. She had to bite her lip from crying out as tears pricked her eyes.

"Let me, mè siora," Editta whispered.

Imelda shook her head. Too long she'd let other people fight for her. This time, her victory would belong to no one but herself. She closed her eyes as she tied off the line and moved to the left wing. Each stitch was an offering to the gods and a penance for Arturo's death. He would've been a good husband for Calixta, a good father to their children. His death left a hole that could never be filled, not even by his and Imelda's great accomplishment.

She made quick work of the other set of stitches. Her lip was nearly bleeding from her teeth digging into it. As she tied off the last stitch, awareness of the wings flooded her. She could feel every inch, every feather that stirred when she moved. The wings had become a part of her. She released the wall, and her body balanced perfectly. The fatigue was gone, thanks to the extensive wool in the wings. Blood seeped from the stitches in her skin, but the stripes healed her. She'd become a new woman. Thread by thread, she'd made herself anew.

"Imelda!" Donatella called as she returned. "You better have that dress on."

Editta cleaned the blood off Imelda's chest with her own sleeve, her face full of remorse. "Good luck, mè siora," she whispered.

Imelda squeezed Editta's arm and moved out from behind the screen.

"Oh, Imelda!" Donatella grasped Imelda's hands. "They're incredible. Arturo would be proud."

"This is sick," Primo said.

"You're the twisted one."

Donatella came between them. "Not today! You two stop bickering for a few hours. I won't let you spoil this joyous occasion."

"I can, but I don't think Primo can manage. I'm no longer under his control." Imelda beamed. She couldn't stop herself. She'd succeeded, despite everyone underestimating her. It would've been far sweeter to have her brother with her. Arturo was supposed to give her away at her wedding—for the marriage she actually wanted. He still would, in a way. She could imagine him kissing her forehead. He'd smell of wine and hearth smoke. He'd tell her she was brilliant, that she had accomplished a great thing in the face of so much opposition. He'd watch her fly away without regret, only pride.

Primo finally lost his composure. "Editta, do her hair and be quick."

Imelda flapped the wings and grinned. Moving the wings felt as natural as walking—she never had to tell her feet to move, she just thought about walking and they did it. Same with the wings. They were linked to her as strongly as her hands and fingers, and would remain so as long as the spirit rose was sewn into her skin.

Imelda started for the open balcony door. "I said I'd put on the dress. I never said I'd do anything else."

Primo lunged for her. She blocked him with a wing. It hit him with an audible *thwap*, knocking him onto his back.

She ran outside and climbed onto the railing. Birds flew overhead, singing in the warm sun. With any luck, she'd join them soon.

"Imelda, no!" Donatella cried.

Primo grabbed her wrist, his grip tight enough to hurt. The wings beat against her back, trying to pull her free. Her feet slipped on the railing. Her free arm wheeled as she struggled for balance while trying to escape Primo's grip.

Finally she wrenched her arm out of his grasp and fell off the balcony. The wings automatically folded against her body for the descent. Donatella screamed. Imelda fell for a moment, hurtling toward the cobblestones below. *Fly!* she prayed. Not tentative, learning flight. There was no time for that. She was flying for her life. With a *whoosh*, the wings snapped open. They caught the air, and she swooped over the street.

Imelda turned her sights upward as the wings carried her into the sky, leaving Primo gaping below.

Chapter Fifty-Six

The rising sun on the western horizon was beautiful, of all the terrible things that could happen on Ulisse's wedding day. His head throbbed, and the growing light made his eyes ache as he stood on the balcony off his room. He'd drunk too much at the party last night. After playing, of course. Before that, he'd only had one glass of wine to relax him. Playing in front of friends was fine, an enjoyment really. Playing in front of strangers was not unpleasant ... but it was disquieting. It had gone well—everyone assured him he'd played beautifully, which was true—but then Imelda had joined the party. She'd put up a good face, but that was all it was—an appearance.

Ulisse walked inside, then back to the balcony. Back inside, to double-check himself in the mirror. His new black doublet looked sharp, his hair styled, his beard trim. A little stiffer than he liked, but up to Rialto standards. He appeared every part the eager groom, and the day was beautiful, and his bride was lovely, and it was all a waste because she was in love with another man.

Ulisse walked back out, then in. Out, then in.

"You're pacing, Your Majesty," Arrigo said. He was dressed in his usual attire, though today he also wore a ceremonial plumed helmet to mark the happy occasion.

"Am I a fool?"

"No, sir."

Ulisse put his hands on his hips. "If you were anyone else, I'd label you a sycophant right now."

"You know me better than that, sir."

"I should hope so, after twenty years of friendship."

"You mean service, sir."

"Not you too. Why is everyone so damned formal all the time?" Ulisse waved his hand in the air. "At any rate, despite what everyone says, I'm almost certain I am a fool. This one time."

Ulisse walked back out to the balcony. Venezia should be here any minute to take him downstairs to perform the mother-in-law traditions in front of even more strangers. Venezia, because Imelda's mother was dead. Because life had an even crueler sense of humor than he did.

Someone knocked on the door, and Arrigo opened it to reveal Venezia, of course. She held a basket filled with blood oranges, a skein of silk corincanto, and a pin cushion with sewing needles. Her maid stood behind her. Venezia wore a simple gray dress and appeared tired, but it didn't make her any less beautiful.

"I'm not good at sewing," she said after they kissed cheeks. She gestured out the door, then fell in beside him as they went through the halls.

"Just don't stab me," he said, "and you should be fine."

In the sitting room downstairs, a small crowd had gathered to watch the tradition. Faces Ulisse recognized after last night, but no names came to mind. Gods above, it would be so nice to return home after today. He might not like the people there any more than the ones here, but at least he could identify them.

A chair waited for him in the center of all these people he didn't really know, nor ever would.

"Where's Primo?" Ulisse asked.

Venezia unwound about a half-meter of silk from the skein, then cut it with the knife at her belt. "He was here, but Donatella fetched him a few minutes ago to tend to Imelda," she said quietly.

Her hands seemed to tremble, but it was so subtle Ulisse wasn't sure if they actually did. They were pink, as if she'd scrubbed them before coming. It took her a few tries to thread the needle, then she knelt beside him. Her fingers dipped inside his collar, grazing his skin as she pulled the fabric away from his neck. Then she began to sew the silk corincanto along the edge of the black cloth.

Despite her obvious fatigue, she'd scented her hair with . . . well, something amazing. Oh, wasn't this rich? At least the strangers and Venezia's maid kept their distance, thanks to Arrigo's glares. Ulisse would give that man a raise as soon as they returned home.

"You're the loveliest mother-in-law I've ever seen," he said.

Venezia snorted. "This is probably my one time to play this role. At the rate I'm going, that's one title I'll never have."

"If you had to choose between mother-in-law and Doxe, which would you prefer?"

Her eyes drifted away as she frowned. The needle embedded itself in his skin.

"Ow!" He slapped a hand to his neck and pulled it away to find blood on his fingers.

She sighed. "I told you I'm bad at this."

"Try not to maim the groom too much."

"Once this corincanto is in, it won't matter how many times I stab you."

"Silk won't help if you murder me."

She smiled, a small thing that didn't come easily. As if smiling were the most painful thing she could do right now. "If I wanted you dead, Arrigo wouldn't have time to save you."

Ulisse laughed. Arrigo didn't look so amused. "Lucky for me, we're 'old friends.'"

She turned his head straight. "Now stop moving or I'll nick you again."

She finished the sewing without further injury, then peeled an orange. This would be even better. At best, this tradition was merely awkward. He'd felt so odd the morning of his first wedding as Marina's mother fed him. For a sweet marriage, so the saying went, and to show the bride's family would always support the new couple.

But with Venezia kneeling in front of him, holding a spoon with slices of fruit to his lips, this tradition was torture. The orange burst as he chewed, but he barely registered the taste. He wanted nothing more than to kiss the fingertips that fed him. And do much more than that. Gods above, he couldn't stop himself from thinking of all the things he'd like to do right then. Some of them even involved the damned blood oranges.

Yes, this was sumptuous torment. He loved Venezia. The realization felt like a knife across his palm. Perhaps he'd never gotten over her. And here she knelt, performing the mother-in-law duties before he married her cousin. It was too late to back out now. He wouldn't do that to Imelda. She might not want to marry him, but surely she wouldn't appreciate the embarrassment of being jilted on the wedding barge.

Finally, *finally* the orange was all gone. Venezia rinsed her hands in a wash bowl as everyone congratulated him. Venezia paused, staring at her fingers in the water. Then she turned to him abruptly.

"I'll see you soon," she said. With farewell cheek kisses, she left, maid in tow.

Arrigo gave Ulisse a towel to wipe the blood off his neck.

"We really ought to stop that absurd tradition," Ulisse said quietly. "Remind me to officially abolish it when we return home."

The people moved toward the exterior doors. Maybe Ulisse should go for a walk. It was a beautiful day, after all. He was due at the palàso docks in a half hour; he had time to spare. Dawn grasped the white palàso with fingers of pink and orange. The water below, so far from the highest island in Rialto, was smooth as a baby's cheek. Góndole floated back and forth across El Canalasso, cutting soft wakes that waned as quickly as they appeared. The water was gray, but beginning to turn golden with the promise of day.

"I'm ready to go home, Arrigo. I'm craving a dive."

Harvesting sea silk had always calmed the swirl of ideas and thoughts in his mind. Swimming down to the rocks, cutting the plant that brought his city riches, staying as long as he could and then swimming up and up while his lungs begged for air … there was something primal in that, something that connected him to the hum of life. Sure, he could wear linen to breathe underwater, but where was the fun in that? As he swam, he forgot about politics, raising children, dealing with spoiled rich men and women demanding his service—all of those cares. For a few hours, it was only about the ebb and flow of the tide, the callouses on his hands from sailing, the fish and occasional shark swimming around him. His only concern was survival. It was a thing of beauty.

Ulisse breathed in the damp, salty air. He would be a good husband. A better one, this time around. He'd banish his feelings for Venezia and devote himself to Imelda. She would have no need to sail on the sea without him, as Marina had. They'd come to appreciate each other, and would live until their hair turned gray and their backs hunched with the weight of a full life. He'd see his son Berto crowned to rule as a just king, and would bounce grandbabies on his knee. That would be a good life. That would be enough.

A large cloud passed over the sun. But it moved too quickly, and the shade it cast too dark. The shadow, like a large bird, raced down the street. Ulisse looked up.

And nearly fell into the canal.

Clothed in her purple wedding dress, Ulisse's fiancée flew with wings turned golden by the morning sun. Imelda was headed north, toward the lagoon—and ultimately the gulf. Technically, Eraclea was that way also, at the tip of the peninsula. But she wasn't flying to his city; Ulisse was too smart to kid himself otherwise.

No, Imelda was flying to freedom. She was flying away from marriage with him.

He started laughing, right there on the waterfront. People stared at him, at the king laughing with his head thrown back. Some regarded him as if he were crazy, while others smiled as if they understood the joke. They didn't understand that he was laughing at himself, that the greatest joke of all was his rotten luck with love.

Chapter Fifty-Seven

Venezia went straight to Lazaro's room when she returned home. She had half an hour before she had to leave for the wedding barge, but she needed to see his body one last time.

She'd fallen asleep after he died, right on the bed. Then Alessia had woken her as late as possible, helping her clean and get dressed so she could go to the palàso for the mother-in-law duties. She hadn't had time to take in the scene.

Venezia walked into his room and sat on his bed. Lazaro's body was tangled in his blanket, ropes still around his ankles and wrists. Vomit covered his pillow next to his head. The smell of his excrement was thick; she could nearly taste the air. She expected him to sit up, or say something, or move in some way, despite the hole where his eye had been. The knife sat on the bed beside his head, soaking the bed sheets with even more blood. She felt the blade hitting the back of his skull, again and again.

Her body began to shiver. She held up her trembling hands. Venezia's hand never shook, unless she had a seizure. Never as she'd learned the knife, then the sword. Never when she'd practiced on dummies shaped like real people. Never when she'd ordered men to battle, ordering them to their deaths. And they hadn't shaken as she'd guided the knife through Lazaro's brain.

Venezia picked up the blade. This was what it was like to kill a man. No, not kill—murder. Killing happened on the battlefield, soldier versus soldier fighting for their lives. Venezia had tied an old man to his bed and deliberately ended his life. Her face had been in his as he had passed through fear and realization and pain. He'd been helpless, in a way. But so had Venezia on her wedding night, and every encounter after for eight years. He'd been in her face then, not caring about the fear he'd surely seen.

She'd murdered a man. And she would do it again given the choice.

Alessia opened the door, letting in a draft of fresh air. She gagged at the stench in the room.

"Mè siora." The maid put her hands on Venezia's shoulders and knelt in front of her. Her eyes flicked to Lazaro. With a shudder, she looked back to Venezia. "The ducal barge leaves for Siora Imelda's wedding in fifteen minutes. You must go."

"Yes." Venezia jerkily stood. Her voice felt hollow, as hollow as Lazaro's eye socket. "I ... tell them I knocked on his door, but when he didn't answer I left without him."

Them. The authorities, when Alessia summoned them. The Head of Police reported to Venezia. He'd believe her story. Kari would get the blame, and Venezia would finally be free.

She *was* free. She'd killed Lazaro. Alessia ushered her out of the room, and Venezia glanced at him. This was the last time she'd see his body not wrapped in mourning blue. He'd hurt her so many times, but he was nothing but an old man. He'd never hurt her again. The great Doxe Lazaro Dandolo, lying in his own shit, murdered by his wife.

She'd been unprepared for the shock of murder. She still held the knife, and her hands still trembled. Her bloody nightgown lay on the floor in front of her wardrobe. Alessia took the weapon, wrapped it in a towel, and set it by the washbowl. Kari waited by the fire, her pretty yellow hair gone. Alessia had cut it off, leaving less than an inch of fuzz. She'd colored it and the girl's eyebrows with kohl. An imperfect fix, but it should be enough to get Kari safely out of the city. Kari held a bag of money and wore one of Venezia's plain wool dresses.

The girl's slave stitch was stark against her pale skin, as stark as the blood on Lazaro's sheets.

"Alessia, wrap a ribbon around Kari's wrist then write a letter in Lazaro's name, releasing her. Be sure to put the family's official seal on it." Venezia folded her arms to stop the trembling. She fixed Kari with a look. "Find a maghiarzo to remove your slave stitch. Make sure you're across the Muriseano before you do, otherwise they'll discover the truth. Things will not end well for you if you don't heed my words."

The skin under Kari's eyes was dark, and she swayed softly as Alessia tied a ribbon on her arm. She was probably still under the influence of the hemlock.

"You took the tonic?" Venezia asked. An antidote for the poison, with bits of cotton corincanto to ensure complete recovery. Kari nodded. Alessia penned a letter and sealed it with wax, pressing the Dandolo family crest into it.

Venezia took the paper and gave it to Kari. "Now go, before it's too late."

"Mè siora." The girl fell to her knees. "I'm indebted to you."

"You owe me nothing, except your safe exit from the city. If you get caught, you'll put me in danger."

"Please." Kari clutched Venezia's skirt. "You saved me. My life is yours."

Damn Southerners and their pride. But something in the girl tugged at Venezia. She had a fighting spirit. It was buried—no doubt out of necessity to survive as a slave—but it was there, waiting for the right person to see it. Venezia had been that way. No one had noticed her backbone—she'd had to find it on her own. But what would Venezia have accomplished if someone had taken an interest in her? She could've been the youngest Doxe ever elected, instead of Primo.

"Come back in six months," she said. "Knock on the servants' entrance when the temple bell rings one in the morning. And either wear a wig or dye your hair."

Kari knelt and kissed Venezia's boots, her eyes shining. Alessia gave the girl a damp towel and escorted her out. Kari was an unexpected development, but she could prove useful. Venezia had plenty of eyes-and-ears, but one more could never hurt. And one that felt such loyalty? Kari could end up proving herself a treasure far beyond what Venezia imagined.

Venezia threw her nightgown into the fire. The bloody knife handle had smeared her fingers so they were red again. She washed her hands, until the red of scrubbing replaced the red of blood. She changed out of her dress and pulled on fresh underclothes that smelled of lavender. Wool corincanto embroidery adorned the hem. A wave of strength broke over her. She breathed deeply. With each routine movement, she woke up a little more. Rediscovered her fortitude. It had fled, exhausted from the emotional work of murdering her husband. Now her back straightened, and her chin lifted.

Alessia returned and laid out Venezia's favorite dress, made of black silk embroidered with silver. Then the maid went to the bowl of bloody water. Venezia intercepted her. This was the final step; she needed to complete it herself. She opened the window. The western sky shimmered with the early morning sun. She considered its beauty for a moment, then dumped Lazaro's blood into the canal far below. It landed with a splash, red mixing with the dark water. She'd imagined throwing his body to the murky depths.

This was, in a way, even better.

"You look ready to fall over, mè siora," Alessia said.

"The wool corincanto in my underclothes is holding me up." Venezia set the bowl back on her vanity. "I'll make it through the wedding."

"And then you'll rest?"

"And then I'll rest."

"Grassie, mè siora." Alessia smiled, though her expression held more sorrow than joy. Her gaze flicked upward, and she pointed at the sky. "Mè siora, look!"

Venezia followed Alessia's finger, then smiled. Imelda flew over the rooftops of the city. She'd succeeded. Bless that woman, she'd finished what Arturo started. Her wings were a work of art, softly feathered and moving as if part of her body. Her flight was a dance in the air.

Venezia's heavy limbs found their strength. It was a beautiful sight, though not the one she'd originally worked toward. But she could use this to her advantage. The last month had held so much disappointment. Losing the Janus vote. Losing the election. Losing Arturo. And yet, here was a glorious win. Her husband gone, and her cousin flying as sweet as the birds. Imelda was making history as she soared above the city.

Not only had Imelda invented the possible, but she'd freed herself from a loveless marriage. Ulisse wasn't Lazaro—thank Cielo above—but Imelda would not have been happy. Nor would Ulisse, in the long run. That man needed someone who recognized the gem that he was.

Venezia's heart swelled. She turned to Alessia with a smile. "There will be no wedding today."

With any luck, Fia would witness this flight. If not, her servants would, and she'd hear about it shortly. Imelda was flying north toward the gulf. Calixta had set sail during the night. Venezia would bet her title that her ship was Imelda's target.

The Council would be furious. They'd drooled over the wings ever since Arturo's disastrous flight. Seeing Imelda's success would only fan their greed, and watching her fly away from the city would fuel their anger. The Ilios connection made it all the better. It wouldn't be hard for Venezia to insinuate that Calixta had planned this all along. It would be easy, too easy, to convince them this wasn't Imelda's escape, but Ilios's theft. Those wings would help Venezia start a war more effectively than any blade. Primo had said that the sword wasn't the only tool and he'd been right—wings could be a tool as well.

With no wedding to attend, Venezia's schedule shifted. First, she had to frame her husband's murder on his sex slave.

And after that, she had a war to start.

Chapter Fifty-Eight

Anselmo, body full of fire, slowly, painfully, pulled himself out of the tunnel and onto the top of the innermost wall of the labyrinth. He squinted at the bright sunlight and reeled. Nikkoforos caught and steadied him.

"We're not out yet," the prince said. He wiped his sweaty face and looked out over the labyrinth.

When they'd reached the others, Nikkoforos had told them Anselmo got hit by a poisonous dart and sent them ahead through the tunnels. The lake had been full of sirens, and a host of minotaurs had waited on the shores of the lake. The tunnels hadn't been much better, churning with minotaurs. But the path the others created had allowed Nikkoforos to drag Anselmo through the underbelly of the labyrinth without having to fight off more than a dozen minotaurs. Anselmo had also fought, but with his burning muscles and double vision, he'd been barely more than a hindrance to the prince.

Still, they'd finally made it through, and apparently the night and much of the morning had passed. The sun was a quarter of the way through the sky, though a thin veil of clouds covered it. More gathered in the distance, dark and roiling with thunder.

The other soldiers were long gone. Hopefully they'd already made it to the gates.

"We can't stay up here for long," Anselmo said.

Nikkoforos nodded. "As soon as the lightning gets too close, we'll go down."

Anselmo looked across the labyrinth, trying to get his bearings. His vision split and joined, and stars danced everywhere he looked. "How far to the entrance?"

Nikkoforos held up a hand to shield his eyes from the sun as he scanned the area. He pointed to the left. "It's over there. If we can stick to the wall tops, it should only be a couple hours."

"If the storm doesn't close in too quickly."

"As long as that doesn't happen. Let's go." Nikkoforos started walking along the wall.

Anselmo grabbed his arm. "Nikkoforos, wait."

The prince turned slightly but said nothing.

"When we get out, will you—" Anselmo's throat seized. He swallowed bile. "What are you going to tell them?"

Nikkoforos grasped Anselmo's forearm in the Iliano greeting and put his other hand on Anselmo's shoulder. "I will die before I utter a word."

Anselmo's chest heaved. He pulled Nikkoforos in for a hug. This was a man truly worthy of his title.

"Anselmo." Nikkoforos stepped back and pointed at the sky. "Is that—?"

Anselmo looked up. A woman flew in the distance to the north, wearing huge wings of white and gray feathers. "Imelda," he breathed. But how? She was married, wasn't she? Had she seen him? Judging by her position, she'd flown over the labyrinth before they'd emerged from the tunnel. He tried to feel her in his mind, but it was churning too loudly, the fire too great. His heart burned brighter than before, from pain and now from hope.

Hope for more.

Nikkoforos clapped Anselmo's shoulder, a grin on his face. "Let's get you out of here, Errari. You've got to get those black eyes healed before you can see Siora Albizzi again."

Chapter Fifty-Nine

The last few days, Imelda had been too focused on completing the wings to think about what it would be like to actually fly. She'd imagined it so much in her younger years, but the last month's reality had filled her mind until there had been no room for fantasy. Ever since Primo had issued his ultimatum, the wings had become a tool, not a dream. They'd been nothing but spinning and stitching, corincanto and feathers.

But the results were breathtaking.

Arturo had tried to control the wings with his intellect and logic. But to fly was to use the heart. Intuition guided Imelda as she lost herself in sheer wonder. Clouds kissed her cheeks with dew. Cool wind sang in her ears. The currents in the air shifted around her, and the bird leather of the wings instinctively knew how to respond. There'd been no need to learn—the wings already knew, and they instructed her.

Imelda flew as one breathed.

The wings felt wondrous and new, and yet like they'd always been a part of her. In a way they had; she and Arturo had dreamt of them for so long. They'd always been there, furled deep within her.

She'd have to release the connection when she reached her destination. The thought was too sad to bear, so she pushed it off, and pushed higher into the sky.

The city was far below, but the people's shouts still reached her ears. She smiled at the look on Primo's face, his horror and indignation. Who else watched? Anselmo? Venezia? Ulisse?

Arturo? She knew, felt deep in her soul, that he could see her from Cielo.

Dark clouds gathered in the west, casting shadows that reached for the city. Calixta's ship sailed in open water, the only galley in the gulf. Its design was different from Rialtano ships, slightly altered dimensions, a horse figurehead carved at the front, gold accents rather silver. At the aft, her white dress like a beacon, waited Calixta.

Imelda glanced back toward the labyrinth. As she'd flown over it, Anselmo's presence had grown in her mind. He'd been close, so tantalizingly close. If only she could've landed and grabbed him, but the wings were meant to bear her weight and little else. She'd slowed her pace as she passed overhead and let the Heart Stitch guide her eyes. He'd been right below her, then behind her as she flew. The trees were too thick for her to see, but he was there. He was alive. And he would find her.

Imelda reached the ship, the wings flapping to slow her like a swan landing in the water. She stumbled onto the deck.

"You did it!" Calixta helped Imelda up and hugged her. "I knew you could!"

An older, bearded man bounded up and stared—presumably the ship's captain by the insignia on his chest. Imelda's hair was windblown and disheveled, but with all the silk corincanto in her dress it didn't matter. She could've been wearing a lobster shell and she would've looked amazing. She laughed and even hugged this stranger.

Anything might await her in their city, but it was better than what her home had to offer. She was finally free.

"I need to send a hemp message," she said.

The captain disappeared and returned minutes later with a hemp square, quill, ink, and a small, lit torch.

"Do you have a knife?" she asked.

He offered one, and she cut her palm. She barely flinched. She'd done this countless times in her life. Leaning on the ship's rail, she dipped the quill into her blood and wrote her message. The hemp square was small—she'd have to be brief. Hopefully it would be enough.

I'm not married. I finished the wings. I'm sailing to Ilios where I'll wait for you. I love you.

She spoke Anselmo's name into the square and held it in the flame. It caught fire immediately, brown fabric becoming orange flame becoming purple smoke. Once the hemp burned away, the smoke coalesced and drifted toward the labyrinth. Imelda clutched the rail as it sailed away. It didn't fly as a bird did—as she had—with swoops and updrafts. Instead it cut a straight path across the lagoon, taking the shortest distance to the island. To the man she loved. She would see him in Ilios. She could feel it in her bones, in her muscles, in the stitch across her heart that bound them together. Their destinies were intertwined irrevocably, now and forever.

The rowers propelled the galley back into motion. To Ilios, north by northeast. Wind caught the sails, the oars pulled back into the ship, and they sailed deeper into the gulf. Imelda turned away from the city, away from her past and toward her future.

Epilogue

The wind howled all afternoon, then stopped abruptly—the calm before the storm. Anselmo and Nikkoforos had been able to stay on the walls until the last hour, when the storm grew too close and the lightning too threatening. At this point, they'd reached the outermost corridor of the swamp. Anselmo's strength waned as they climbed down then slogged through the water, legs quivering with each step, but he was able to walk without Nikkoforos's support.

Imelda's voice echoed in his mind. She wasn't married. By the grace of the gods, somehow she wasn't married. She was free, and she was waiting for him. The venom in his legs burned, and cramps twisted his muscles, but her voice had given him the strength he needed. They were almost out of the labyrinth. He'd visit Ceso for anti-venom, wait a week, maybe two, then leave for Ilios.

He'd be a deserter. The idea made him sick. But there was no other way he could be with Imelda. She was the only thing that mattered—she had won their future together. It was almost too sweet to be true.

Finally, as night conquered day and the first raindrops hit their faces, the swamp ended. Anselmo stumbled onto the barren dirt incline. Nikkoforos helped him up. The inner gates closed behind them, and the outer gates swung open. Lit torches stood on either side, lighting the way out. With Anselmo's arm around Nikkoforos's shoulders, they walked out of the labyrinth.

Anselmo's strength finally gave out. He fell to his knees, bringing the prince down with him. Iliano soldiers rushed to pull Nikkoforos to his feet and help him to a small, ornate galley beached at the edge of the water. Doxe Albizzi followed them, issuing orders to his own guard to accompany the prince back to the city.

"Wait." Nikkoforos's voice was hoarse but no less authoritative. His men obeyed him, and he pulled the sword's sheath off. He held it to the Doxe. "For Errari."

"Your Imperial Highness," Doxe Albizzi said, "if you retrieved the sword, it's yours."

Nikkoforos shoved the blade into the Doxe's hands. "Lieutenant Errari is the rightful owner."

"Of course, Your Highness." Primo nodded at his guard. "Get him to a physician immediately."

"Your Highness," Anselmo said. The prince waited. Anselmo stood and saluted him, arm across his chest. "It was an honor to serve under you."

"And an honor to serve with you, Lieutenant." Nikkoforos waved and his retinue ushered him onto the galley, where they wrapped him in a cotton-corincanto blanket and shoved off for the city.

Anselmo walked to the platform where Fleet Admiral Dandolo and the other admirals waited. Today a canopy covered it to protect them from the rain, though the Doxe's black doublet looked soaked through as he climbed the stairs.

Rafael and six other soldiers stood in front of the platform. They looked as bad as Anselmo felt, covered in mud, red human blood, and black minotaur blood. Other than Rafael, the others were naked. No one had cotton-corincanto blankets. They shivered in the cold, early spring rain.

The soldiers approached the Doxe and gave weak salutes. Doxe Albizzi gestured for them to sit, and they practically collapsed onto the sand. Behind them, the chant of the prince's galley disappeared into the distance.

A guard saluted Doxe Albizzi. "That's all of the survivors, Your Serenity."

"Close the gates," the Doxe said.

The entrance to the labyrinth closed with a groan, like a dying minotaur.

Doxe Albizzi stood in the center of the platform. He always looked authoritarian, but something in his posture made him seem angry tonight. Imelda. Her escape would certainly put him in a foul mood. Perhaps he blamed Anselmo. But that was unlikely. Anselmo had been fighting for his life for the last several days. He couldn't have helped Imelda even if he knew how.

The Doxe cleared his throat. "Congratulations, soldiers. Eleven days ago, twenty-one of you entered. Only nine have exited. You were already considered among our top soldiers. Now you have proven yourselves as the elite. You have joined a world class of soldiers." He shifted slightly to look at Anselmo. "Lieutenant Errari."

Anselmo dragged himself to his feet and made himself take a step forward, though every muscle and bone burned in protest. "Yes, Your Serenity?"

"You are now a Lion, and therefore a member of the nobility."

"Thank you, Your Serenity." Anselmo bowed his head deeply as he fell back in with the group.

The Doxe's words felt barren in Anselmo's stomach—those words he'd longed to hear his entire life. The words his mother had sacrificed everything for. He wasn't going to be a Lion after all. In two days' time, he would abandon his and her life's work to be with Imelda.

"Each of you has proven your intelligence and skill," Doxe Albizzi continued. "You are, from this point on and forever more, Lions." Doxe Albizzi looked at the sword in his hands. The sapphire eyes in the lion's head sparkled in the wan light. "Fleet Admiral Dandolo? What do you propose we do about the Lion captain?"

Fleet Admiral Dandolo stepped up beside him and took the sword. While the Doxe seemed dour, she beamed.

Rafael pulled himself to his feet and saluted. "Fleet Admiral, may I speak?"

She nodded.

"Imperial Prince Nikkoforos giving the sword to Errari was not mere kindness." Rafael looked at the others. Finally he turned his attention to Anselmo. He didn't nod or give any indication of his thoughts—he didn't need to. "We believe Errari should be the captain, Fleet Admiral."

"You speak for the others?"

"I do. We would all follow his command."

"Then it is official. Lion Anselmo Errari, you are now a Lion captain, and these soldiers are under your command."

She offered the sword. Rafael nodded at Anselmo, his gaze lingering on Anselmo's twin black eyes. Would he and the others report Anselmo if he deserted? It was a hard thing to lose a fellow soldier, whatever the way.

Anselmo took the sword. Again its grip seemed made for his hand, and the sword felt like an extension of his arm. He'd have to leave it behind. He'd give it to Rafael—the man certainly deserved it.

Fleet Admiral Dandolo waited for them to sit, then lifted her chin as she regarded them. "You will each be given a pay raise and two weeks to recover from your ordeal. But don't get too comfortable." Her attention shifted to the lagoon behind them where the prince was being rowed back to the city. She smiled, tight and hungry. "Your first assignment will begin soon. Ilios has stolen something incredibly valuable from us, and we intend to get it back."

If you enjoyed *Feathers Sharp as Knives*, please consider leaving a review on Amazon or elsewhere!

Please subscribe to my newsletter by visiting my website, www.kristinaatkins.com. No spam, just periodic messages to say hi and update you about my writing.

(Like when Book 2 is coming!)

A Note on Language

I originally planned to create names and words that sounded Italian for this book. Then I discovered the Venetian language. Vèneto is a Romance language (not a dialect!) spoken by about two million people, most of whom live in the Veneto region of Italy. I couldn't write a book that is essentially a love letter to Venice without using its beautiful language.

Below is the comprehensive pronunciation guide (using English phonetics) for the most important Rialtano names, places, and words in *Feathers Sharp as Knives*.

People
Albizzi ahl-BEE-tzee
Imelda ee-MEHL-dah
Arturo ar-TOO-ro
Primo PREE-mo
Donatella do-nah-TEHL-ah
Cinzia CHEEN-zee-ah
Italo EE-tah-lo
Errari (author created based on Vèneto phonetics) ay-RRAH-ree
*double rs are rolled
Anselmo ahn-SEHL-mo
Betta BEHT-tah

Dandolo DAHN-do-lo

Venezia veh-NEH-zee-ah

Lazaro LAH-zah-ro

Contarini kon-tah-REE-nee

Ulisse OO-lee-say

Galbani gahl-BAH-nee

Rafael RAH-fah-ehl

Pesaro PAY-zah-ro

Fia FEE-ah

Lando LAHN-do

Enrico ehn-REE-ko

Ceso (author created based on Vèneto phonetics) CHAY-so

Giore (author created based on Vèneto phonetics) JO-ray

Zitello (author created based on Vèneto phonetics) zee-TEHL-lo

Rea (author created based on Vèneto phonetics) RAY-ah

Giatoro (author created based on Vèneto phonetics) jah-TO-ro

Ioanna ee-o-AHN-nah

Alessia ah-LEHS-see-ah

Editta eh-DEET-tah

Places

La Serenìsima Repùblica de Rialto LAH seh-reh-NEE-see-mah ray-POO-blee-kah DAY ree-AHL-to

Muriseano (author created based on Vèneto phonetics) moo-ree-say-AH-no

El Mar EHL MAHR

El Canalasso EHL kah-nah-LAHS-so

Fógo FO-go

Cielo chee-EHL-lo

Palàso Dogal pah-LAH-so DO-gahl

Monte (author created based on Vèneto phonetics) MON-tay

Riga (author created based on Vèneto phonetics) REE-gah

Centro CHEHN-tro

Sordo (author created based on Vèneto phonetics) SOR-do

Frenza (author created based on Vèneto phonetics) FREHN-zah

Venetano veh-neh-TAH-no

Eraclea (author created based on Vèneto phonetics) eh-rah-KLAY-ah

Sacresta (author created based on Vèneto phonetics) sah-CREH-stah

I Occi de Zitello EE O-chee DAY zee-TEHL-lo

Le Ixolè dei Ciclopi LAY ee-zo-LAY DAY chee-CLO-pee

El Pónte Grando EHL PON-tay GRAHN-do

Words

Doxe DO-zay

Corincanto (author created based on Vèneto phonetics) ko-reen-CAHN-to

Mè siora MAY see-O-rah

Mè sior MAY see-OR

Carnevale kar-nay-VAHL-ay

Pàre PAH-ray

Mare MAH-ray

Góndola GON-do-lah

Gondolièr gon-do-lee-EHR

Acqua Alta AH-kwah AHL-tah

mojer MO-zhehr

Grassie GRAH-see-ay

Caxa KAH-zah

Cax' KAZ

Caxe KAH-zay

Cancaro kahn-KAR-o

Carina kah-REE-nah

Piaza pee-AH-zah

Maghiarzo (author created based on Vèneto phonetics) mah-ghee-AR-zo

Ilios

While the people of Ilios speak a dialect of Vèneto, their names are mostly Greek. I chose this because when the ancient Sacrestano empire moved its capital to Ilios, they adopted names from the area, though the nobility continued to speak their own native language (Vèneto). (All exceptions I pulled from a list of Eastern Roman Empire emperors.)

Ilios EE-lee-os

Heraclius hehr-ah-KLEE-us

Nikkoforos nee-ko-FO-ros

Nikkos (author's variation of Niko) NEE-kos

Calixta cah-LIHX-tah

Komnenos KOM-neh-nos

Janus JAH-nuhs

With the exception of Chi Tu, all other place names are made up.

Trigger Warnings

sexual assault
references to pregnancy loss
domestic abuse

ACKNOWLEDGMENTS

Fourteen years after getting serious about my writing career, I'm finally writing my first acknowledgments.

Life can be a little crazy, y'all.

Since this is my first book, I'm going to thank everyone who helped me on my writing journey. So buckle in, because this is quite the list!

The first thanks go to you, dear reader. You took a chance on me and this book. I hate to be sappy, but you are a part of making my publishing dreams come true.

Next up, I want to thank my husband Kurt for, well, everything. You, sir, are a scholar and a gentleman. I'm one lucky woman to call you mine.

To my parents, Chris and Leslie Cooper, for teaching me to love books, magic, and people. To my siblings and siblings-in-law for being rad humans—Ryan and Mandi Cooper, Stephanie and Adam Crenshaw, Caroline and Skylar Hillebrant, and Collin and Raimee Cooper. Y'all have read my stories and cried with me at my failures and rejoiced with me on my successes. You've also put up with my antics, which is no small feat.

Thank you to my Sky fam for being ridiculously amazing and supportive people: Ara, Ashwin, Gabby, Gowri, Max, Paru, Ren, and Vivi.

Thank you to my writing community! To my writing partner, Celeste Tyler the lovely badass. You're brilliant, creative, powerful, and one hell of a cheerleader. To my old writing group, Amanda Lang, Brittany Peshek, and Jessi Wagner (rest in peace, dear Jessi). Y'all kicked my butt and made me do better. To David Boop, my first writing mentor, for introducing me to those fabulous ladies. To my Prose Before Bros ladies, Amanda Mills, Becca Lamoreaux, Bex May, Callie Hansen, Heather Chapman, Kelly Moore, Michelle Bulsiewicz, and Nicole Brouwer. Y'all rock. To my writing coach, Onyie Onyeabor, for helping me get out of my rut and back at the keyboard. And to every writer who's ever read my work and provided feedback: thank you. (There are far too many of you from the last fourteen years to name!)

I wouldn't be the writer I am today without my experience at Converse College's MFA program. Immense thanks to my professors Leslie Pietrzyk, Marlin Barton, and Robert Olmstead for teaching and guiding me. I still quote y'all.

Going way back to high school to thank Evelyn Hall, my sophomore year creative writing teacher. You saw something in me. Without that, I doubt this book would exist.

Now to everyone who helped bring *Feathers Sharp as Knives* into existence! To my beta readers Allison, Amanda, Amy, Anna, Caitlin, Camille, Celeste, Christina, Heather, Heidi, Jana, Jeanna, Julie, Kelsea, Kyle, Laura, Laurie, Rebecca, Ryan, Tanissia, and Whitney for your fantastic feedback. To my amazing editors Kristy Gilbert, Jolene Perry, and Kaylee Baldwin. Y'all saved me from myself. Thank you to Carlos Quevedo for the jaw-droppingly gorgeous cover art! It's unreal I have a cover so pretty. And to Kharis Courtney for the beautiful cover design that fits Carlos's work so well.

Thank you to Venice, Italy, for being the most amazing city on the planet. You were the spark that lit this flame.

Lastly and most importantly, I want to thank my Heavenly Mother, Heavenly Father, and Savior Jesus Christ for loving me, guiding me, and giving me this passion for writing.

About the Author

Kristina Atkins writes speculative fiction inspired by mythos from around the world, complex human relationships, and her own experiences living with mental illness. After earning her BA in Linguistics from Brigham Young University in 2008, she received her MFA in Creative Writing from Converse College in 2012. She lives in Denver, where she and her husband spend countless hours chasing their three young sons (and sometimes catching them!). *Feathers Sharp as Knives* is her first novel.

www.ingramcontent.com/pod-product-compliance
Lightning Source LLC
Chambersburg PA
CBHW061035310726
48969CB00004B/962